to chang ... ou made—or to choose a different career path, or to save someone's life—would you? Would you go back again if the future that resulted from this action was less to your liking than the original one? Would you be willing to journey back in history or into the future as a mere observer of events, and once there could you manage to resist the temptations of meddling? Would some small, thoughtless action have amazingly large repercussions? And would the stream of time prove capable of righting its flow back to the path it was intended to take, despite intervention by travelers out of time?

These are just some of the concepts explored in such original time twisters as:

"Jeff's Best Joke"—It started as just a standard archaeological dig in New Mexico, with some interesting finds and Jeff and Jim playing increasingly complex jokes at one another's work sites. But all of that changed when the stranger appeared. . . .

"In the Company of Heroes"—He was one of the wealthiest, most successful men in the world, but could even money and power help him reclaim the priceless treasure stolen from him in his childhood?

"Palimpsest Day"—What if there are moments that are outside of time and space, moments when everything can change, when you can be given a "second chance"? Would you—should you—take that chance?

PAST IMPERFECT

PAST
IMPERFECT

Edited by
Martin H. Greenberg
and Larry Segriff

DAW BOOKS, INC.
DONALD A. WOLLHEIM, FOUNDER
375 Hudson Street, New York, NY 10014

ELIZABETH R. WOLLHEIM
SHEILA E. GILBERT
PUBLISHERS
www.dawbooks.com

First Printing, October 2001
1 2 3 4 5 6 7 8 9

DAW TRADEMARK REGISTERED
U.S. PAT. OFF. AND FOREIGN COUNTRIES
—MARCA REGISTRADA
HECHO EN U.S.A.

PRINTED IN THE U.S.A.

CONTENTS

INTRODUCTION
by Larry Segriff

It's been fun watching science fiction grow up. A small caveat here: I don't go back to the early days of SF; I first started reading it seriously in the Seventies—the *Nineteen* Seventies—but I've seen an awful lot of change in the field in the past thirty years.

We started out as a literature of ideas. Reading the Golden Age of SF is like opening a veritable primer on the wonders of the universe: faster-than-light travel, bug-eyed monsters, ray guns . . . and time travel. Over time, though, the genre grew up and started paying more attention to style, characterization, and storytelling. This was, I think, a good thing for science fiction. We gained a richness of story, though we lost, I feel, something of the sense of wonder that had driven the genre from its birth.

Still, a funny thing happened while a part of the genre, at least, was exploring other elements of storytelling: science started catching up to fiction. Much of what was predicted by the early SF writers—submarines, spaceships, radio satellites, computers, lasers . . . the list goes on and on—has come true. Oh, we still don't have faster-than-light travel, and we haven't discovered any alien life-forms, but mankind has done many wondrous things that only a few years ago were considered pure fantasy. We've left the comfort of our little planet and looked down on the Earth from space; we've stood on the surface of the moon and planted a flag; we've even sent *Voyager* beyond the edges of our solar system; we've broken the atom and harnessed its power, both for good and for ill; we've cloned life and decoded the human genome.

And we've discovered a magical branch of science known

as quantum physics, which has, I think, forever torn down the thin veil that separated science fiction from fantasy.

My working definition of the difference between the two has always been that science fiction stories were built upon known laws of physics and strove never to break those laws; fantasy, of course, was free to violate as many laws as desired, as long as it did so in a rigorous and internally consistent fashion.

Quantum physics has changed all that.

Want to move an object with just your mind, or read someone else's thoughts? That, to me, would have been fantasy . . . until scientists found that two particles, physically unconnected and separated by vast differences, can influence each other. Change the spin of one particle, and the other will change its spin, too.

There's even a theory involving negative energy which allows for faster-than-light travel—and by that I mean true, practical, move a ship along the same course as a beam of light and have the ship get there first, faster-than-light travel. I mention this because up until recently science has assumed that you could effectively go faster than the speed of light by using a wormhole—but that's not really going faster than light. That's using a shortcut to get somewhere faster than light would if it took a longer route. To me, though, that's like taking several million miles of fiber optic cable, looping it and coiling it up so that the two ends were mere inches apart, and then racing a beam of light from one end to the other. The light would have to travel millions of miles of cable. All I'd have to do is take one small step for man . . . and yet I'd be able to say I went faster than light, just because I got there first.

Not really fair, if you ask me. But negative energy, at least according to some theorists, allows for true faster-than-light travel (okay, purists would find fault with this, because it still uses a manipulation of space-time, shortening or contracting space-time in front of the ship and stretching it out or expanding it behind the ship). But even this was considered impossible up until fairly recently.

And no discussion of quantum physics would be complete without a mention of Schrödinger's cat . . . without a doubt my favorite thought experiment. The experiment went like this: put a cat in a box. Hook up a Geiger counter to a radioactive isotope, so that there is a fifty/fifty chance that the Geiger counter will detect the decay of the isotope. If the Geiger counter does detect decay, kill the cat. If it doesn't, the cat lives for another experiment. Outside of proving that he was a dog lover and not a cat person, Schrödinger's question was, at the moment of the experiment, before the box is opened and the cat's status checked, is the cat alive or dead?

The answer was: both, and neither. Essentially, from the moment of the experiment until the box is opened, the cat is in a quantum state that encompasses all possible outcomes of the experiment. Further, Schrödinger showed that it was the act of opening the box—or, more accurately, it was the act of observation itself—that forced the quantum state to resolve itself into the final outcome, with a fifty/fifty chance that the cat was still alive.

What's even stranger, and more wondrous, is that Schrödinger's experiment has been shown to be true (and no, they didn't use cats in proving it). It's true, the act of observation itself resolves a quantum state.

Pretty cool, huh?

So why all this talk about quantum mechanics in a book about time travel? Because one of the other formerly impossible things that quantum physics allows is time travel. Oh, there are some limitations, some of which are pretty cool, too, like the fact that no time machine can travel back in time further than the moment of its own creation. And there is still a lot of discussion and disagreement. For example, some people point to the so-called "grandfather paradox"— you can't travel back in time and kill your own grandfather because then you wouldn't have been born so you could have gone back in time, and so on—as proof that time travel can't exist. Others say that quantum physics requires the creation of separate universes every time an action occurs, such as the decay of a neutron, for which there are different possible outcomes, and that time travel is only permitted across universes. Proponents of this theory believe that when you travel backward in time, you arrive in a parallel universe.

My point is that fifty years ago science said that time travel was impossible. Today science says that time travel may be theoretically possible, though extremely difficult, and only within certain limitations. The question is, what will science say about time travel fifty years from now?

Time travel. Like much of our science, it was once thought of as pure fiction. Like much of our SF, it was once thought of as pure fantasy. And if such things are possible, if particles can influence each other over distance, if cats can exist in quantum states until someone opens a box and looks inside, if time travel is possible, what other magical discoveries are waiting to be found?

Science fiction has grown up a lot over the years. Its stories are richer, its characters more complex. And now that science has caught up to much of its ideas, I suspect that our field will start pushing out again, testing the boundaries of fact and fiction, exploring the ideas that lie at the intersection of fact and fantasy, and giving science more ideas to prove right.

BLOOD TRAIL
by Kristine Kathryn Rusch

Kristine Kathryn Rusch is an award-winning fiction writer. Her novella *The Gallery of His Dreams* won the *Locus* Award for best short fiction. Her body of fiction work won her the John W. Campbell Award, given in 1991 in Europe. She has been nominated for several dozen fiction awards, and her short work has been reprinted in six *Year's Best* collections. She has published twenty novels under her own name. She has sold forty-one in total, including pseudonymous books. Her novels have been published in seven languages, and have spent several weeks on the *USA Today* Bestseller List and *The Wall Street Journal* Bestseller List. She has written a number of *Star Trek* novels with her husband, Dean Wesley Smith, including a book in this summer's crossover series called *New Earth*. She is the former editor of the prestigious *The Magazine of Fantasy and Science Fiction,* winning a Hugo for her work there. Before that, she and Dean Wesley Smith started and ran Pulphouse Publishing, a science fiction and mystery press in Eugene, Oregon. She lives and works on the Oregon coast.

The blood trail started at the front door. A light spray covered the wallpaper, so fine that it almost looked like part of the design. Then the spray became a spurt, and finally great arching lines of blood that had dropped down the walls into the baseboards.

Wheldon stepped inside the apartment, mourning the destruction of evidence. The crime scene was the entry itself. Even if he hadn't seen the body—facedown in the area where the foyer opened into the living room—he would have been able to tell from the blood that the crime had been committed here.

He could even guess, without examining the body itself, how the wounds occurred: a preliminary stab wound on the left side of the back, into some blood vessels but nothing major; other stab wounds lower, at least one somewhere vital; and the last in a major artery which caused death quite quickly.

The attack started when the victim arrived home and unlocked her apartment door. Her attacker followed her inside, stabbed her, pulled the door closed, and continued to stab until she was dead.

"Is there another way into this place?" he asked the patrolman outside the door.

"Nope." The patrolman was young, his face green. He'd been standing in the hall when Wheldon arrived, arms crossed, as if he were guarding the place. But Wheldon had seen enough rookies to recognize the reaction: the young man was trying to keep his lunch down and look official in the process.

"Who's been through?" Wheldon asked.

"The roommate—she's the one who called—my partner, me, the detectives, and the forensic guys."

Wheldon nodded. "Keep everyone else out until I give permission. And I don't want you guys to leave until we bag your shoes."

"Excuse me?" The patrolman looked at him with a mixture of shock and confusion.

"Your shoes," Wheldon said. "This is the fourth entryway stabbing I've worked on in the last two months. The problem with all of them is that critical evidence gets destroyed from the get-go. I'm making sure that won't happen this time."

"I gotta give you my shoes?"

"I'm afraid so, Officer," Wheldon said.

"But how'm I supposed to finish my shift?"

Wheldon shrugged. He walked farther inside, careful to avoid the spatter that had reached the floor. There was a smear near an end table, probably from a shoe. But the prints led into the living room and ended near the feet of the woman who had sat on the sofa, twisting her hands together.

The roommate, the one who'd called the police.

She was talking to one of the detectives, her head down, eyes averted. She was making a studied attempt not to look at the body sprawled near Wheldon on the scuffed hard-wood floor.

He studied her for a moment. She was thin, with a body style that would have been fashionable thirty years before, in the affluent '90s. He doubted her thinness had anything to do with diets and exercise. Judging from the apartment, she remained thin thanks to lack of cash.

Forensics was taking photographs using a handheld computer, two different digital cameras, and then the standard camera required by regulation. Scientific changes, which had brought so much to police work, were still hampered by regulations; good work was getting tossed out in court because it didn't meet guidelines set before the turn of the century. In the last twenty years, Wheldon's job had gotten harder, not easier.

"What're you doing here, Zack?" Amy Mannis approached him from the other side of the living room. She had her handheld out, and her white plastic gloves on. She looked official. "Dex and I drew this case."

"You get to assist," he said. "I'm overseeing you. I can tell you from the blood spatter alone that this one fits into a pattern."

Her lips thinned. "Why don't you wait until the preliminary report before you horn in on our case, Zack?"

"Because the last time I did that, the vital evidence was gone. You don't know what you're looking for."

"And you do?"

He glanced at the living room. The other detective and the roommate were watching the exchange. He lowered his voice so that they couldn't hear him.

"At first you thought robbery. But all that's missing are homemade DVDs and photographs of the victim, as well as some pieces of jewelry—anything with a gem or pearl on it."

Her expression didn't change. She obviously hadn't been here long enough to know what was missing. He'd only gotten the call half an hour ago, and the 911 report had come in half an hour before that.

"In the roommate's bedroom—not the victim's—you'll

find the bed turned down and a Godiva truffle in its original box sitting on the pillow. That room will be neat as a pin even if it hadn't been left that way."

Amy started. She had seen that.

"The jewelry will be missing from the roommate's room. The victim's room will be untouched."

"Son of a bitch." Amy shook her head. She knew that he would take charge. He'd worked with her before. She hated playing the subordinate. "I don't suppose I have a choice."

His smile was thin. "I don't suppose you do."

The victim was Rhonda Schlaffler, a forty-five-year-old book editor who worked just off Times Square. Divorced five years before, no alimony, no children, living off her salary which barely covered essentials, and saving for an apartment of her own.

Her roommate was thirty-four-year-old Trisha Newman who managed a Greek restaurant off Times Square. Newman, who'd never been married, had a spotty employment history, and a tendency to quit jobs in the heat of anger. She was also extremely competent, so when she did find work, she was promoted rapidly.

The women had met when Newman advertised for a roommate through one of the apartment services. They'd lived together for five years, but never socialized. Newman didn't even characterize them as friends. Still, she'd been upset and terrified—upset at her roommate's death, terrified at the staged scene aimed at her.

The body confirmed what Wheldon had already guessed. The first wound, somewhat shallow, in the back beneath the rib cage, catching some blood vessels. Two more wounds, also in the back, near the spinal cord, and the fatal wound in the neck, severing the carotid artery.

The only surprise was matching rips in the collars of victim's coat and shirt, caused by a hand gripping them too tightly and pulling, straining the material until it tore. Either the victim had made a near-successful bid to elude her attacker or her knees had buckled and he had to use her coat to hold her up while he finished the job. Judging by the blood spatter, she had nearly gotten away.

Wheldon had come to all of those conclusions by late evening of the first day. His greatest gift as an investigator was his ability to place himself at the crime scene—to see things that others missed.

It was also his greatest curse. His mind was always filled with what-ifs and would-have-beens. After thirty years of tough cases, he had become quiet and morose. His friends wouldn't let him drink with them anymore, and he'd stopped dating ten years before.

The job was everything, and everything, for the moment, focused on Rhonda Schlaffler.

Her last few seconds must have seemed like hours.

He doubted she'd noticed her attacker following her, although he might have joined her in the elevator, making her uncomfortable. Or maybe not. Maybe she had been the kind of woman who closed into herself in an elevator, ignoring the people around her. In either case, she had gotten off the elevator on her floor, pulled her keys out of her purse, and unlocked both deadbolts on her door.

She'd pushed the door open before noticing him behind her, but there was no way to tell whether or not she had gone inside voluntarily. Perhaps he had shoved her forward, perhaps he had just followed her—the evidence was inconclusive about that. What it was conclusive about was that the attack started just inside the door. He had to still be standing in the hall when he stabbed her the first time.

Unfortunately, the building's security system was as primitive as its locks. An old-fashioned buzzer system on the front door instead of a doorman, security cameras set up in the 1970s and not maintained since, and a super who was away from his apartment more than he was inside it. New York had too many buildings like this, and the killer knew it. He seemed to know a lot about his victims and their roommates, and he used that knowledge to achieve his ends, whatever they might be.

That was what Wheldon couldn't figure out. He couldn't tell from the evidence whether he was trying to find a serial killer, defined as someone who killed randomly and indiscriminately within a certain physical or personality type, or a series killer, defined as someone who killed for a select period of time to fulfill some kind of pattern only he saw.

After the second murder, Wheldon had ruled out murder for hire. Neither victim had been wealthy enough, nor had they had enough enemies to justify the expense.

In fact, he had found only a handful of things in common between all four cases: the manner of death, the victim's gender, the neighborhood, the presence of a female roommate, the Godiva truffles and the turned-down bed, and the stolen DVDs and jewelry.

Everything else was different. The victims' ages ranged from twenty-four to fifty-three; their incomes ranged from $20,000 a year to $80,000; and their marital status ranged from divorced with children to permanently single. None of them worked in the same place or even the same neighborhood, none of them frequented the same shops or restaurants, and none of them had the same friends. They even used different online services.

The murders weren't quite random, but they were random enough to give him fits. After the second killing, he'd entered the information in the FBI's National Database of Unsolved Crimes. He'd thought the Godiva trick unique enough to bring a hit from another state, should such a thing exist. But after the third killing, he'd given up hope. He'd found nothing else like it in his search of unsolved crimes nationwide.

He'd also found nothing when he searched for murders connected to chocolates. His investigation of the Godiva boxes didn't help either—they were all from different batches which had been on the market all over the country on the day of the murders, and hundreds of them were sold in New York City alone—with most of the purchasers paying cash.

Even though he entered information from the fourth murder into the database, he had no illusions this time. He knew he would have to catch this killer on his own.

And he knew he would probably have to wait until the killer struck again.

Wheldon had already moved the Schlaffler case off his desk when the Suits came to visit. In the two weeks since Schlaffler's death, Wheldon had overseen four other difficult homicide investigations and helped solve three of them. The fourth would be wrapped within the week.

Solving difficult cases was his specialty, which was why the Godiva cases really bothered him. Still, he hadn't thought about them in two days when he arrived at his office to find two women in cheap black suits waiting for him.

They looked official. He figured they were either Internal Affairs, coming to see him about some of the cops he'd overseen, or the Feds, wanting to argue jurisdiction on something he hadn't even heard of yet.

He wasn't surprised when they flashed their shiny Bureau badges at him and asked him to shut the door. He did, after he ran their badge numbers through his hand-held, and saw photos that matched the faces before him. The women smiled as he did that, one of them commenting that she liked his caution.

He'd learned, over the years, that caution made him a good cop.

"Agents Ambersson and Kingsbury," he said as he sank into his chair. "Your identification checks out, but doesn't tell me what unit you're in."

"That's right," said Ambersson. She was younger than he was by at least twenty years, a bright-eyed thirty-something who still had the patina of a true believer. "Our status is on a need-to-know."

"And our superiors believe you need to know," said Kingsbury. She was closer to his age, with a deep rich voice, and a world-weary manner. He got the sense that she tolerated her partner, but didn't entire approve of her.

Wheldon folded his hands, leaned back, and waited. They clearly wanted something from him, and they would take their own sweet time to get there.

"We understand you've been investigating a series of murders in the West Eighties," said Kingsbury.

"That's right."

"We're particularly interested in the last murder. Rhonda Schlaffler."

Despite himself, he felt a surge of hope. At last a breakthrough. Maybe Schlaffler had a secret double life. Maybe she had been under FBI surveillance for political actions in her college years. Maybe she had been a Person of Interest in another crime.

"According to the information you entered in our

database," Ambersson said, "you can pinpoint the time of death to a fifteen-minute window, is that correct?"

He frowned, somehow not expecting them to pick up on that detail. "Yes."

"You came to this conclusion how?"

"Her workplace uses an electronic ID system. Her employee identification number ran through the exit machine at 6:05 p.m. She walked with a friend to the subway and took the train home. It arrived at her stop at 6:32 that night. The stop was a two-minute walk from her apartment. Even if she stopped somewhere, like a deli, she had to have arrived before 6:50."

"Because?" Kingsbury asked.

"Because her neighbor received a visitor at 6:50—his ex-wife. He didn't get along with the wife, and didn't want her inside the apartment, so he talked with her, more like argued with her, in the hallway for the next half hour. He watched Schlaffler's roommate unlock her apartment door, enter, and heard the screams. We figure Schlaffler arrived home at the earliest at 6:35 and died before 6:50, since there was no other way out of the apartment."

"Not even a fire escape?" Ambersson asked.

"A point of contention between Schlaffler and her landlord. There had been a fire escape out the bathroom window, but the iron had rusted through and fallen away from the building. Anyone trying to exit that way would have had a three-story drop before hitting another fire escape landing, which probably wouldn't have supported the perp's weight."

"I trust you checked this," Ambersson said.

Wheldon was beginning to get impatient. He wasn't used to being quizzed on his cases. "Of course. We looked for fibers, blood, hair, asked residents about strangers or anything out of the ordinary, even checked with the two homeless guys who slept in the alley, and we turned up nothing."

"Excellent," said Ambersson.

"Excellent?" Wheldon asked. Whatever response he had expected, it was not that one.

She wasn't paying attention to him. Instead, she was looking at her partner and smiling as if they'd caught the killer without Wheldon's help. "Sounds good to me."

Kingsbury shrugged. "I'd like something tighter, but this'll have to do."

"What are you talking about?" Wheldon asked.

The agents turned toward him. The look of expectation was still on Ambersson's face. Kingsbury's expression hadn't changed at all.

"For the past three days," Kingsbury said, "we have conducted an investigation of you."

"Me?" Wheldon frowned. "For what?"

"A high-level security clearance. If you sign the forms we've brought with us, you will receive a six-month clearance, subject to renewal and review. We have brought documents with us for you to sign. Anything you learn because of your security clearance will remained classified. You can't speak of it to anyone. Ever. Is that clear?"

"No," Wheldon said. "I haven't requested security clearance, and I really don't want one. I have no desire to work for the FBI, and I don't appreciate being investigated."

He said that last a bit breathlessly. It was, he realized as he spoke the words, the real reason he was irritated. He was the one who conducted the investigations. He wasn't the person who was investigated. He'd worked his entire career at being a clean cop, despite all sorts of temptation. He didn't appreciate having that spotless record examined now.

"It's just a matter of routine," Ambersson said.

"For you, maybe. Not for me."

Kingsbury held up her hand. It was a small gesture, meant to silence her partner, not Wheldon.

"You want to find this killer, don't you?" she asked Wheldon.

"Of course."

"Well, we have the means to do so. We can do it with or without you, but you know the most about these cases. It's better to have the primary detective involved."

"How can you help me?" he asked.

"In order to answer that question, you have to accept the security clearance."

He stared at her for a moment. She stared back. Ambersson shifted in her chair like a child caught on the sidelines of an adult fight. Kingsbury continued to wait.

He was actually considering it. This particular killer

frustrated him. The brazenness of the murders, the suggestion of making things right for the roommates, the personal nature of the thefts, disturbed him more than he wanted to admit.

Besides, the FBI had already conducted their investigation of him. Nothing he could do could change that.

He sighed. "If I accept your damn clearance, I'm not going to have to do anything else, am I?"

"Like what?" Ambersson asked.

"Like join the FBI?"

Ambersson started to answer, but Kingsbury held up her hand again.

"Of course you won't." Kingsbury shot an irritated glance at her partner. Wheldon's sense that the two of them were a marriage of convenience rose again. "You've got it only for this case. That's why the clearance is limited."

"What do I tell my superiors?"

"Nothing," Kingsbury said. "We've already briefed them and told them we need you to catch this killer. They've approved your time away."

He glanced at the cases on his in-house computer. He closed 85 percent of the cases he was involved in—the best closure record in the precinct and, in some years, the best record in the entire department. Six months was a long time to concentrate on one case. The others would sit until they got cold.

Finally he shook his head. "I can't afford the time away."

"It may only be for a few hours, Detective." Kingsbury's irritation had turned on him.

"You've gotten me a six-month clearance."

She nodded. "They don't give three-day high-level security clearances."

"So I'll be back here within a few days?"

"Probably."

"And if not, a week? A month? Six months?"

Ambersson smiled at him. "I wouldn't worry about the time, sir."

The "sir" surprised him. It seemed involuntary, an acknowledgement of their age difference. It also seemed a bit condescending, as if his advanced years had made him a doddering fool.

"I have to worry about the time," he said. "It's what we lack around here."

Ambersson's smile grew. "Then accept our clearance, and we'll make sure you have more of it than you could ever imagine."

Kingsbury's cheeks flushed—not with shame, he realized, but with a sudden anger. He got a sense that Ambersson would get a tongue-lashing once he was out of earshot.

"Can you guarantee me we'll catch this killer?" he asked Kingsbury.

"Can you guarantee me that everything you told me about the case is accurate?" she asked.

He nodded.

"Then I guarantee you, we'll catch the killer."

He took a deep breath. He was almost as curious about how an FBI agent could guarantee that a murderer would get caught as he was about who this killer actually was.

"All right," he said. "Hand me the documents. I'll take your clearance. But I'm leaving if we haven't made any progress in a few days."

"Don't worry," Ambersson said as she tapped her handheld. On his desk screen, a series of documents appeared, the signature line blinking. "You'll be pleasantly surprised at the kind of progress we can make."

He'd been to the New York branch office of the FBI dozens of times, but had never been allowed anywhere except the public areas. For the first time, they let him keep his gun and handcuffs. The two agents took him to a documents room where he got his security badge and some temporary identification.

Then they led him through a labyrinthian series of corridors, each gray and lit with fluorescent bulbs that dated from the previous century. They went down several flights of stairs, until they reached what had once clearly been a parking garage.

The concrete beams remained and, in some places, so did the oil-stained concrete floor. Parts of it were covered in carpet, but the deeper the women took him into the building, the more of the old parking garage became evident. The walls that had been added seemed both old and temporary. Some of them appeared to be made of fraying particle board. Others were no better than the cubicle dividers popular when he was just starting out.

So when the women opened a double-locked steel door at the very bottom level of the former parking garage, he entered with trepidation, expecting even rattier furnishings than he had seen at the upper levels.

Instead, he found himself in a stainless steel room, filled with modern lighting and wall-to-wall computer access. The floor was covered with carpet so thick that he couldn't hear his own footsteps. The furniture was comfortable, and the area was warm and inviting in a medicinal sort of way.

People looking both busy and productive, hurried along their way. Many of them smiled as they passed him. Most of them were as young as Ambersson. Some seemed even younger. He and Kingsbury were the oldest people in the room.

"Welcome to the Temporal Offices of the FBI," Ambersson said, her tone smug.

"Excuse me?" He glanced at her.

She put a hand under his arm and led him forward. Kingsbury followed. She was the only person in the area who did not look happy. If anything, it seemed like she had swallowed something that tasted bad.

Ambersson led him to a wall covered with glass. Just inside the wall sat people hovered over digital consoles. Beyond them was another room. Only he couldn't quite see that room clearly. He felt as if he were looking at it through a layer of water. Something—the room in front of the glass, the second level of glass beyond, or the room itself—altered his perspective.

He felt like he should remove his glasses and clean them, only he didn't wear glasses any longer. He'd gotten laser surgery fifteen years ago and hadn't had a problem with his vision since.

Until now.

He looked at the women in the hallway. They seemed the same. Something about the room, though. Something about it made him very uncomfortable.

"What's this?" he asked, trying not to let his discomfort show.

"The Temporal Chamber," Ambersson said, that note of pride and awe still in her voice.

"We have ourselves a time machine," Kingsbury said dryly.

"What?" He glanced around. "That's not possible."

"It's very possible," Ambersson said. "We've just gotten the technology, but it's existed in experimental form for three years. We—"

"How come I haven't heard about it?"

Ambersson shook her head slightly and tapped his security badge. "Top secret, remember?"

"That's not what I meant," he said. "A discovery of this important should have leaked. The scientific journals, if nothing else—"

"Parts of it have," said Kingsbury. "You just weren't able to put the pieces together."

"Me? Or the world?"

"The world," she said. "When it became clear that time travel was even a remote possibility, the government bought a lot of scientists. Those who didn't play got discredited."

"Those who did lost their chance for recognition."

"In exchange for unlimited funding and the chance to work in a brand new universe." Ambersson smiled at him. "And they succeeded."

"Giving miracle technology to the FBI?" He felt as if his entire world had turned around.

"Various branches of government are using it. The Congress, in a closed session, decided to allow each government agency the chance to use this technology—subject to certain guidelines, of course."

"Of course," he muttered, feeling cold. He didn't like the idea of the federal government having secret control of time. "How does this work?"

"Complete temporal revisitation is possible," Ambersson said. "Interference is strictly forbidden, of course. But observation is allowed. And that's what we're going to do with your help."

The case. He'd forgotten about the case. "Why's interference illegal?"

"Because they don't know what it does," Kingsbury said quietly.

Ambersson shushed her, but Wheldon turned his back on the younger agent. "What do you mean?" he asked Kingsbury.

"They haven't studied this enough. It's new technology.

We might change the current timeline or we might be creating alternate universes. No one knows, and no one knows how to test it." Kingsbury didn't approve. He could see it in her eyes.

"That's not entirely true," Ambersson said. "Tests are continuing—"

"So why are you involved?" Wheldon asked Kingsbury, ignoring Ambersson.

"My theory is that it's better to have too much information than not enough. These younger agents, they see only the possibilities. Not the dangers."

"We know the dangers," Ambersson said. "That's why we insist on full clearance—"

"So why me?" Wheldon asked.

"We've been dealing with old cases, solved cases," Kingsbury said, "ones where we knew the timelines to the letter—or at least we thought we did. At the moment, we're limited in how far back we can go in time. Our system is still quite primitive, and we can only go back with certainty about five years. They tell us that will change in the near future, and then we can begin unraveling history's mysteries."

Her voice got even drier. She found all of this objectionable in a way he didn't yet understand.

"This case isn't old," he said.

"Precisely." Ambersson moved so that she was beside Kingsbury. Her eyes were bright with anticipation. "We have just gotten permission to look at unsolved cases in which the timeline is clear. We have strict rules. We couldn't pick a single case. We had to pick something ongoing that would have a positive impact if solved. You have a serial killer. We can identify him and stop him."

"I don't see how." He didn't like her certainty that the Godiva killer was a serial killer. He didn't like assumptions at all. "We can't prevent him from murdering Schlaffler. All we can do is watch. He's not going to scream out his name as he does so, and we already know he left no fingerprints. If I understand you correctly, we can't call the police to arrest him as he comes out of the building, and we can't pluck a hair from his head to get a DNA sample."

"We can follow him home," Ambersson said.

"To what end?" Wheldon felt his own frustration growing. "I don't know how many things are done in the Temporal Unit of the FBI, but in the rest of this country, you need to build a solid case based on evidence—evidence that will hold up in court. You bring me a machine I can't talk about, send me into the past to observe something I never could have seen on my own, and expect me to somehow magically prevent this slob from killing again. I think I'm better off doing this the old-fashioned way."

He pushed past both the women and started for the door.

"Grand juries can hear Temporal cases," Ambersson said. "Testimony is secret and the records can be sealed. You will be able to get an injunction on your eyewitness testimony alone."

He stopped, intrigued despite himself. "Then what? Once the case goes to regular court, your little secret will be all over the news."

Ambersson shook her head. "We picked your case very carefully, Detective. New York is one of the few states without a sunshine law. We can have the case tried behind closed doors and the record sealed."

"Sounds like you have it all figured out," he said. "What do you need me for?"

"It's not our case," said Kingsbury. "Not our jurisdiction."

"And it's not hard to make it your case. We clearly have a multiple killer here," he said. "All you have to do is request jurisdiction and you'll get it."

Kingsbury's smile was thin. "We're with the Temporal Unit, Detective. We don't solve cases. We're trying to see if this new technology has a place in the FBI. For this to have FBI jurisdiction, we need to place other agents on this case."

"So?" he said.

"We prefer not to."

"Why? Because I'm easier to control?"

Ambersson bit her lower lip, but Kingsbury shook her head. "Sunshine laws," she said. "We take on this case within the FBI, and there's a chance that we'll end up in Federal court. We're not ready to do that—in fact, we don't dare risk having this technology revealed just yet—and at the moment, we're the only division who has to use the technology in court."

He stared at them. He didn't want to think about the implications of what she had just said. Wheldon's head spun. "I suppose there are no laws governing the use of the time travel."

"Only natural laws," Kingsbury said. "Which we don't entirely understand."

He didn't want to know that. He wanted to be blissfully ignorant of all the possibilities which had just opened before him. But he couldn't ignore those possibilities in the future. Knowledge was irreversible. And he wasn't the sort of man who forgot anything he learned.

"We need you, Detective," Ambersson said.

Wheldon looked at Kingsbury. Now he was beginning to understand why her expression was permanently sour.

"It's a tool," she said.

"So was the atomic bomb," he said.

She nodded. "There's still a killer out there, someone smart enough to attack swiftly and leave a little forensic evidence of his presence. This might be your best chance to stop him."

It might be his only chance, but she was too polite to say that.

"All right," he said. "I've been taking you on faith. Why don't you show me how this cosmic delusion of yours really works."

Five hours of meetings later, he was ready to go. Kingsbury would accompany him. She was along to oversee the entire case and to make certain he acted within regulations.

They tried to give him a crash course in both time travel and in the rules the Temporal Office had established. Time travel, they had discovered, only worked backward. No one seemed to be able to go forward, which one of the techs took as proof that predestination did not exist.

Another tech explained to Wheldon that so far, they had seen no evidence that the Butterfly Theory was an actual fact. The Butterfly Theory, they'd had to explain to him, was that a change in the smallest, least consequential thing—such as stepping on a butterfly—could change the course of history.

However, they didn't want to take any chances. Everything was planned to the exact detail, at least so far as they could know it. The technology was too new to tamper with. Perhaps taking a taxi meant for someone else might have no cosmic effect, but what happened if that taxi, which was supposed to end up in Queens, ended up in Washington Heights? And what happened if the driver, on the way back to midtown, got stabbed by a passenger he picked up near the George Washington Bridge? Would that be sufficient to change the timeline for the rest of the world?

No one knew. And no one wanted to risk it.

There were other time travel theories that had yet to be fully tested as well. The theory of alternate universes. Some believed that each new action taken in a past timeline opened up a new universe rather than changing the past. But there was no concrete evidence on this yet either. Some travelers believed that small things were different upon their return to their timelines. Others said nothing had changed.

And then there was the thing the techs all feared the most: that a man might meet himself in the past. Some believed that would cause instant death to the person involved. Others thought it would be a curiosity and nothing more; still others believed that such a meeting would wipe out, not only the man involved, but also everything around him. It might even, one tech said in a hushed tone, cause a rupture in the space-time continuum that couldn't be resolved.

Wheldon didn't like any of this. It made him wish, even more than he had wished before, that he hadn't been called in to play in this experimental project.

But he kept thinking about Schlaffler, the way she had died, how another woman, while he dithered here, might be dying in just the same way.

So he memorized and listened, and thought about the way that crimes happened and laws were made, about the way that men like him were always behind events and never in front of them, about how his job was to pick up pieces, not repair them.

But ultimately, he was a rules and regulations man, and he did his best to understand everything the techs had told him. He would do the best job he could within the parameters they set, and he would live with the consequences, just like he always did.

The actual room was ice-cold as if it were a poorly functioning refrigeration unit. The cold had pockets and he thought he felt several different breezes coming from different directions, sources unknown.

He'd needed no special preparation, no special training. They had a copy of his latest physical on their desk, and their doctor double-checked his blood pressure and his heart rate, finding nothing out of the ordinary.

The room was large and dark, and it magnified noise in the way that a lake did on a calm, moonless night. Kingsbury helped him toward a small platform, then she clung to his arm as if she were the one traveling for the first time.

He could see the technicians who had been teaching him about this new science. They sat on the other side of the leaded glass window, preparing their calculations to send him and Kingsbury into the near-past. The techs had a wavy undefined quality, as if Wheldon were watching them through fog. He felt as if part of himself had already been displaced, sent to a future he would never completely understand.

A wave of nostalgia ran through him—not for the past, but for his naïveté. He wished he had never picked up the report on Schlaffler, never met Kingsbury or Ambersson, never crossed the threshold into this cold, shifting room. But he had, and nothing could change that.

He was trapped in this place forever.

"Here we go," Kingsbury said, tightening her grip.

And a feeling, not unlike the heady, dizzy sensation he got when he dropped off to sleep after a long and exhausting day, ran through him. The placement of the breezes seemed to move, too—he felt as he were going from cold spot to warm spot to cold spot without changing his position.

He couldn't see anything except windows before him—leaded, black-tinted, they didn't seem to change. He could no longer see the people behind them, however, and he found that unnerving.

The entire experience was unnerving. He hadn't moved at all, and yet he knew he was somewhere—somewhen—else.

"Here we are." Kingsbury sounded breathless, as relieved as he felt.

"How do we know we're in the right time?" he asked.

She glanced at him, her face pale and dotted with beads of sweat. Obviously this mode of travel wasn't one a person got used to. She pointed over his head. He turned.

A clock, with the time and date in large digital numbers, was attached to the wall over his head. He hadn't noticed it before, but then when he had entered the room, he hadn't looked.

The clock, with its date two weeks in the past, made him feel even more disoriented. Part of him believed, however, that they were playing some sort of trick on him—see how the stupid detective would react in a darkened room, after being told he was a rat in a maze.

"Let's go," Kingsbury said.

"What about the techs?" he asked.

"We're not to talk to them. They don't know what's going on."

"But they've seen us."

"Perhaps," she said. "It's the only real risk we're supposed to take."

She continued to hold his arm, using it to pull him out of the room. The bright lights and clean lines of the hallway made him woozy. He stopped, put a hand on the cool concrete wall and took a deep breath.

"Nauseous?" she asked.

He hadn't been nauseous since he was a rookie, but this feeling was close. "Dizzy."

"It's normal. It'll pass." She stood, no longer touching him, not even patting his back. She just waited.

"Don't we have a timeline?" he asked.

"This is built in." Her voice was flat. She continued to wait.

It took a moment for him to accept the solidity of his surroundings. As the wooziness passed, he realized he hadn't been in this hallway before. He wondered if it were specifically designed for travelers coming from the future so that they wouldn't run into the busy young agents who populated the Temporal Offices.

"All right," he said.

Kingsbury let out a sigh, revealing her impatience for the very first time. Then she led him down the hallway to the stairwell.

It smelled damp and old, the concrete flaking. He could hear cars honking above him, shouts on the street, the sounds of New York on an average day. Yet he couldn't remember what kind of day it had been—rainy, sunny, cold, or warm. He could remember Schlaffler's apartment and the body, sprawled on the hard wood, but he couldn't remember the weather or what he'd had for lunch or what kind of casual conversations he'd had.

Was his life that unimportant that he couldn't recall it two weeks later? Had he allowed his work to so consume him that it was the only thing that mattered to him, the only thing he remembered?

Kingsbury pushed open a steel door, and stepped outside. Thin sunlight came through the canyons between the buildings. The air had a slight chill.

The street sounds seemed louder here, yet less real, as if the pale light diminished them somehow. Or maybe it was his knowledge that this day was two weeks dead, a mere shadow of its former self, only a memory—yet one they could walk through.

"Come on," Kingsbury said. She waited for a break in traffic, then hurried across the street.

Wheldon followed, being just as careful, the instructions he had received sticking with him. Anything—a fender bender, a missed appointment—had potential significance. He had to be cautious of his every move.

Kingsbury waited for him on the corner, near the subway stop. He joined her, and they went down the stairs together. The air smelled of exhaust, and he could hear the rumble of the trains. Everything felt real. Only those first few moments in this time period had reminded him that he was from a not-so-distant future, and what he had felt in those moments might have been caused by his imagination, by what he believed might happen.

Kingsbury paid their way in with tokens, then led him to the right train. She glanced at her watch. "Now we have to be precise."

"Why now?" he asked.

"Some of our guys were here before, making sure we have a nearly empty car."

Kingsbury glanced at her watch. People joined them on the platform as the first train arrived, but she didn't let him enter it. They stood with a handful of others, waiting for a different train.

The others were long gone by the time the second train arrived. She counted five cars from the wall, then stepped inside. He stood beside her and was about to sit down when she stopped him.

"We'll stand," she said.

Five others entered around them and took the available chairs. But, as she had predicted, the car was nearly empty when the train pulled out.

According to Kingsbury's watch, they were almost two hours early. He had no idea what they would do in the intervening time. As the train clacked down the tracks, he tried to remember where his other self—his younger self as the FBI called it—was at this moment.

When the call had come in, he had just come back from dinner—a knish from a stand across the way. He remembered that not because the meal was particularly good, but because it had formed a lump in his stomach when he saw Schlaffler's body, one that stayed with him all night, and made him swear off knishes for the next two weeks.

Before that, he had been writing the final report on a rape/homicide in Central Park, and before that, he'd been overseeing a lineup in an incredible brutal murder of a bodega clerk.

His younger self had to be witnessing the line-up, completely oblivious to his future, happening simultaneously.

Kingsbury clung to the overhead bar and stared at the windows, even though all that was visible through them was darkness. She seemed to be the only one in the Temporal Office who had an inkling about the kind of power the government now had. Or perhaps she was the only one who was disturbed by it.

Wheldon was glad she was traveling with him and not Ambersson.

The train was slowing down.

"This is our stop," Kingsbury said.

He braced himself, paying attention, suddenly, to the

people around him. He had no real idea who he was looking for, who the perp was. He guessed—because the statis-
tics were on his side—that the perp was a man, but he
wasn't certain of that. Anyone on this train could be the
killer. Anyone with enough anger and a willingness to use
a knife.

The train stopped and the doors opened. Wheldon followed Kingsbury onto the platform. The enclosed smell of
oil, grease, and exhaust seemed even more intense here.
People swirled around him, intent on finding the exits.

"Now what?" he asked. They were still early.

"We wait." She led him to a metal bench, and they sat.
She took out her handheld and tried to be inconspicuous.
He watched people, as he usually did when he was waiting
for something.

The subways hadn't changed during his entire life nor
had the people who rode them. All income levels, all atti-
tudes. Only the fashions shifted and the items that people
carried. When he'd been a boy, there had been newspapers
and books and magazines under people's arms. Now everyone had their handhelds. Newsstands were long gone, replaced by food and beverage vendors selling anything
prepackaged, from chips and candy bars to cola and iced
coffee.

He'd never really thought about the past and the present
before, how they flowed into each other, merged and mingled and became something else, something that differed
from day to day.

Occasionally, Kingsbury would look up from her handheld to inspect the platform as if it had somehow changed,
and then went back to her absorption. Her screen, shaded
so that no one looking over her shoulder could read it,
hadn't shifted since she sat down. He knew her study of
the machine was all an act.

At 6:32, just like he'd had in his report, Schlaffler's train
stopped. Kingsbury didn't even look up. Only Wheldon
watched the passengers disembark.

The train had been crowded, people packed together so
tightly that they stumbled out of the exit instead of stepping
easily. It took him a moment to see Schlaffler. She was
wearing the same clothes she died in—the tweed jacket
with matching skirt and sensible shoes—but the colors were

different, lighter, prettier, without the deep dark stains caused by her blood.

Her hair was falling out of its neat bun and her shoulders slumped as she moved forward—showing either exhaustion or depression, he couldn't tell which from this distance. No one seemed to be following her, but he couldn't be certain of that.

He tapped Kingsbury slightly, and they both stood. To anyone watching, it would seem as if they were getting ready for their train or they were meeting someone. Kingsbury slipped her handheld in her pocket and took his arm, turning her face toward his as if they were having a conversation. He put his hand over hers in a manner that would look protective, and then followed Schlaffler toward the exit.

She stopped at the food stand. Her hand hovered over the chocolate bars, then she shook her head and walked on. The movement made the knot in his stomach return. The man who was going to kill her was carrying chocolate, but he wouldn't give it to her.

He would give it to her roommate.

Wheldon wanted to warn her, to turn her away from her home, but he had been cautioned against that. It might not do any good—the perp might kill her elsewhere—or it might succeed, and then he would have altered the past in an unacceptable manner.

His shoulders tightened. Never before had he had this kind of advance knowledge and it made him nervous. Even when he conducted stings, he had the belief—the hope—that the potential victims would get out alive.

He shuddered. He was watching a dead woman walk.

Kingsbury's grip tightened on his arm. She gazed up at him, her expression intense. Wheldon nodded once—he understood the rules—and then he concentrated on Schlaffler.

They followed her at a discreet distance, always able to keep her in sight. No one else seemed to be behind her. She took the stairs out of the subway slowly, as if each one were a burden. Her head was down, her hair covering her face.

Depression, he thought again. Or intense sadness. Maybe even loneliness. He could feel it radiating off her, part of her body language, the listless way she moved.

At the top of the stairs, she bumped into a young man. His face flushed, and Wheldon could feel Kingsbury stiffen beside him. The young man cursed at Schlaffler, then continued down the stairs. He jumped the turnstile, and disappeared on the platform.

Kingsbury did not relax.

They reached the top of the stairs. Schlaffler was standing in front of a sidewalk flower vendor, staring at the hothouse roses. She leaned toward one, sniffed, and shook her head.

"They had more of a smell when I was a child," she said to the vendor. Her voice was deep and rich. It startled Wheldon. He'd imagined her to have a voice as listless as her body language.

"You gonna buy one, lady, or not?" the vendor asked.

She leaned back as if the vendor's harshness startled her, then shook her head, a small apologetic smile on her face. Then she continued to walk toward her building, head down, shoulders hunched even more.

"Damn," Kingsbury whispered.

Wheldon glanced at her.

She shrugged. "I didn't need to see this."

He understood. A lot of the work he did forced him to reconstruct a victim's life. But he had never seen a victim walk before, interact with the world around her, or breathe.

Schlaffler was letting herself into the building now.

"What time is it?" he asked Kingsbury.

"Six-thirty-six," she said. "You're good."

He nodded, not feeling as if he'd accomplished anything. No one was following Schlaffler except them. No one seemed to be watching her except them. A chill ran down his spine. What had he missed?

The door was swinging shut. He bounded up the stairs and caught it just before it closed, holding it open for Kingsbury. As they stepped into the building's foyer, the elevator doors closed across from them. They'd missed the opportunity to ride with Schlaffler.

He cursed and ran for the stairs. Kingsbury followed. They took the steps two at a time, hurrying up several flights. If he pushed, Wheldon knew he would arrive before the elevator did. It was nearly a hundred years old and very slow.

He shoved the door open on the sixth floor. The hallway was empty, the elevator's doors closed.

Schlaffler hadn't arrived yet.

Kingsbury stepped out beside him. "We need a good spot to watch."

"Already picked out." Wheldon moved her toward the corner where the hallway turned, and they leaned against the wall, arms around each other, as if they were waiting for a friend to come home and let them in.

They weren't visible from the elevator or Schlaffler's apartment unless someone was looking for them. But their view of her apartment door was clear.

The elevator opened and Schlaffler got out, adjusting her purse strap as if she were trying to pull the purse closer to her body. She looked even more uncomfortable than she had outside.

Wheldon tensed. He couldn't see what had upset her, and he didn't dare move closer.

Schlaffler made her way to her apartment. No one was behind her.

"What is this?" Kingsbury whispered.

Then, just as the elevator doors closed, a hand slid between them and grasped the left door. The doors held for a moment, then slipped open. A man peeled himself off the elevator's side wall and hurried into the hallway.

He fit the profile: slender, white, rather plain. But he was younger than Wheldon expected, and his eyes were cold. His hands were stuffed in the pocket of his coat, and Wheldon thought he could see the shape of a box and a knife.

Wheldon's heartbeat increased. He had to clamp his lips together to keep from shouting a warning.

Schlaffler stood in front of her door, fumbling with the locks. She'd managed the lower deadbolt, but the upper was giving her trouble.

The perp walked down the hall, his shoes not making a sound. He slipped behind her as she turned the second lock.

Kingsbury's fingers bit into Wheldon's arm. He could feel how nervous she was.

Schlaffler shoved her door open, and the perp was on her, one hand over her mouth, the other slipping the knife into her back. She made a single, startled cry, muffled by his hand, and then disappeared into the apartment.

Wheldon cursed and ran forward, Kingsbury clutching at him. He reached the apartment as the perp pulled the knife out for the second time.

Wheldon grabbed the man, yanked him off Schlaffler, and tossed him into the hallway. The man hit the wall and slid down it.

Kingsbury was shouting at Wheldon to stop when a woman pulled open a door, and Wheldon yelled at her to call 911.

The perp got to his feet. Wheldon turned, unable to reach him. The perp started to run, but Wheldon tripped him. The perp went sprawling, the knife skittering from his hand. Wheldon pulled out his gun and aimed it at the back of the perp's head.

"Move and I'll shoot, you piece of shit," he said.

Kingsbury came up beside him. She was shaking. "What are you doing? You have to let him go."

"It's too late," he said.

The perp moved. Wheldon shoved the gun against his skull.

"Make sure Schlaffler is okay, and make sure someone called 911."

"No," Kingsbury said. "We've already made a mess of this."

"And I'll make a worse mess if you don't help me out."

Another door opened. Wheldon couldn't see the person behind it.

"It's all right," he said to the person who opened the door. "We're cops. Call 911."

The perp's hand was inching forward, toward the knife. Wheldon knelt, shoving his knee into the perp's back. Something made a cracking noise. He hoped it was the perp's spine.

"They're on the way!" a man's voice yelled.

The elevator doors opened again. A woman stood inside, clutching her hands together. When she saw the people on the floor, she leaned back in the elevator, and let the doors close.

The ex-wife. Apparently, she had arrived a little later than the neighbor had initially claimed.

Kingsbury bent over the perp and shoved at him with her foot. "Who are you, asshole?"

The perp closed his eyes. She shoved at him harder.

"Answer me."

The perp squirmed beneath Wheldon. So much for the broken back. "I'd answer her, buddy."

The perp inched his hand forward. In a minute, he would reach the knife.

Wheldon shoved the gun harder against the perp's head. Kingsbury kicked the knife farther down the hall, and then she stomped on the perp's hand. "You gonna talk to me?"

He squinched his eyes tightly closed, and then his mouth for good measure.

"Asshole," she said again and moved out of Wheldon's line of sight. After a moment, he heard her crooning, telling someone she'd be all right. A deep rich voice, filled with pain, answered, and Wheldon's shoulders relaxed. Schlaffler was alive, then. He hadn't taken this risk in vain.

His knee was getting sore and his shoulder ached from the pressure of pushing the gun against the perp's head. It seemed to take forever before he heard sirens below, and knew that his relief had arrived.

The paramedics came up first, taking the stairs. Wheldon waved them toward Schlaffler, and they disappeared into the apartment.

Then the elevator doors opened. The roommate had arrived. It must have been 7:20.

She looked terrified. Someone told her to remain at that end of the hall. Her gaze kept going to the open apartment door.

Finally the cops arrived. They cuffed the perp, then covered him as Wheldon moved away. He flashed his badge at them, but Kingsbury covered for him, telling them she was FBI and this was a planned sting.

She told them to book the perp and she'd meet them at the precinct. She waited until they took the perp down the stairs before pulling Wheldon aside.

"You made one hell of a mess of this," she whispered. "We've got to figure out what to do now and how to make sure this guy gets charged with a crime. The problem is that there's two of me and two of you in this timeline and things are about to get very confusing."

"No, they aren't," he said. "Your younger self is going to take care of this."

"How?" she said. "She doesn't even know about you or this case."

He nodded. "Give me something of yours, something she'll recognize. I'll go to her and explain. She's with the Temporal Unit. She'll understand."

"No, she won't." Her voice was calm. "I never thought I'd break the rules. She won't believe you."

"Really?" he asked. "You never thought of this? Never wondered how hard it would be to just observe?"

She looked away. "No."

He didn't believe her. "Then why did I hear your footsteps behind me when I ran to stop the murder?"

She didn't say anything, and that surprised him. He expected her to lie, to say she was trying to stop him. But she could have stopped him easily. She had ahold of his arm when the attack began. She could have held him back.

Instead, he had felt her fingers slipping away, maybe even felt a slight nudge from her body, propelling him forward, making him act in her stead.

Maybe that was why she had picked him. Not because this was his case, but because she could trust him to break the rules. She had studied him, after all. She had gotten him the clearance. She knew how much he cared about the victims after they died. Did she think he'd stop caring just because they were alive?

And then his eyes narrowed. Of course she hadn't. She knew him. They all knew him.

"You set me up," he said.

Kingsbury raised her gaze to his.

"What the hell is going on?" he said.

She shrugged, looking remarkably calm, considering what had just happened. "You didn't understand the mission. You acted without thinking, saving the woman. And I couldn't stop you, so now we have to deal with the consequences."

"What?" he breathed. He had never misunderstood a mission in his life.

"Fortunately, you'll be fine. We brought you in from outside, and we'll never make that mistake again." Then she grinned. "At least, that's what we would have told the folks who administer the new technology if they knew what you'd done."

"What?" he asked.

"At least," Kingsbury said, "we now know what happens when someone takes an action in the past. I'll be able to brief the entire unit when we get back. Unofficially, of course."

People stood in the hallway, watching them, staring at the open apartment door. A couple of cops surrounded the roommate, interviewing her.

His shock was turning into anger. "You risked my life."

"Not really," she said. "We figured one of two things would happen. Either you would push him out of the way and we'd both vanish, going back to a brand new present with no knowledge of what we had done, or we'd be standing here, discussing how we changed things."

"You used me."

"Yeah."

"Why the hell couldn't you have done this yourself?"

Her smile was guileless. "It's against regulations. They'd have taken the technology away from us if things hadn't gone as we'd planned. We would have had to blame you. But we were lucky. As it stands right now, they'll never know. Only you and I know what we did. Schlaffler's still dead in our lifetime. We saw a few things, but we didn't get the perp's name. And that's all that happened."

He looked down the hall at the open apartment door. He'd thrown the perp against the wall. He'd felt the man's back beneath his knee. He'd heard Schlaffler speak after the attack.

"I did all this for nothing?" he asked.

Kingsbury shook her head. "She's fine in this timeline. We have him. You probably saved several lives, not just hers. The problem is that we didn't get his name. We don't know who this guy is. Once we get back to our own time-line, we're screwed."

"Maybe," he said softly.

She frowned at him. "What?"

He stared at the scene. In his mind's eye, he could still see the perp, peeling himself off the side wall. The hand, catching the doors as they split apart, the fingers grabbing the edge.

He said. "We can make a case."

"Against whom?"

He smiled. He was already imagining it. The prints removed from the elevator door, the sketch artist drawing the perp's face, the legwork—going to various Godiva stores in New York, canvassing the neighbors.

Because Wheldon had seen enough to know this perp had staked out the building. The perp knew what time Schlaffler got home. He probably knew when the roommate arrived. Wheldon would wager the perp knew everything about both women.

Only he hadn't been interested in Schlaffler. He'd been targeting the roommate, planning to free her from the person who weighed her down. That was why he cleaned up the room, added the chocolates, made the place more inviting.

Wheldon could catch this guy easily now, using old-fashioned police methods, building an old-fashioned case that would stick.

"You gonna tell me how we'll have a case?" Kingsbury said.

"I'll tell you after I send your younger self to the precinct," he said. "I want a little more time to think about this."

The roommate as wiping tears away from her eyes. The cops were still talking with her. The neighbors had inched closer, watching everything.

Kingsbury hadn't moved. She was looking at the apartment door, too.

"I wonder why she was so sad," Kingsbury said softly.

It took him a moment to realize that she meant Schlaffler. From Schlaffler's perspective, her day had gotten even worse—arriving home to be stabbed by a crazy man waiting in an elevator.

She would never know how close she came to being another statistic, how the fine spray of blood on her apartment wall would have become a spurt that dripped rivers into the baseboard if Wheldon hadn't been there.

She would never know that in another universe, she had died.

Wheldon had saved a life.

He had never done that before, at least, not directly. By

pulling the perp off her, he had saved a number of lives—not just in this new universe, but in his as well. Because Kingsbury had brought him back here, Wheldon would be able to make sure this perp would never kill again.

And that pleased him. Even though he was annoyed at being used, he didn't mind that the blood trail had led him here, to this moment.

To this odd, but somehow satisfying, point in time.

THINGS I DIDN'T KNOW
MY FATHER KNEW

by Peter Crowther

> If there is an afterlife, let it be a small town
> gentle as this spot at just this instant.
> —Dana Gioia, *In Cheever Country*

Peter Crowther is the editor or co-editor of sixteen anthologies
and the co-author (with James Lovegrove) of *Escardy Gap*.
Since the early 1990s, he has sold almost 100 short stories
and poems to a wide variety of magazines and anthologies on
on both sides of the Atlantic. The first collection of these stories—*The Longest Single Note*—appeared in 1999 while *Lone-
some Roads*, the second, won last year's British Fantasy
Award. *Cold Comforts*, containing 18 of his crime and mystery
stories, appeared earlier this year on CD-ROM and *Conun-
drums To Guess*, his fourth collection, is scheduled for publication in 2002. September 2001 saw the publication of *Darkness,
Darkness*, the first installment in his multi-book SF/Horror cycle
Forever Twilight, and he recently adapted his story "Eater" for
British television. He lives in Harrogate, England with his wife
and two sons where, in addition to writing and editing, he runs
his small press imprint PS Publishing.

Something was different.

Bennett Differing opened his eyes and listened, and
tried to pinpoint what was wrong. Then he realized. He
couldn't hear his wife's breathing.

He shuffled over, pulling the bedclothes with him, and
stared at the empty space beside him on the bed. Shelley
wasn't there. He looked across at the clock and frowned.
It was too early for her to get up. She always stayed in bed
until he was out of the shower. Why would she be getting
up at this time?

Then he remembered. She was meeting her sister, going to the mall for their annual shop-till-you-drop spree.

As if on cue, Shelley's voice rang out. "Honey?"

"Yeah, I'm up," Bennett shouted to the ceiling.

"Well, I'm on my way. Lisa gets in at 8:15."

Bennett nodded to the empty room. Around a yawn, he said, "Have fun."

"Will do," she shouted.

"Take care."

He could hear her feet on the polished wooden floor of the hallway downstairs, going first one way and then another—Shelley suddenly remembering things like car keys, house keys, purse.

"Will do," she shouted. "It's a lovely morning."

Bennett flopped back onto the bed. "Good." The word came out as a mutter wrapped up in another yawn.

"What?"

"I said, *good.* I'm thrilled for you."

The feet downstairs clumped back into the kitchen. "I'll be home around eight. Lisa's getting her bus at seven."

"Okay."

The sound of feet stopped, and then he heard them coming quickly up the stairs. "Can't go without giving you a kiss," Shelley said as she ran into the bedroom. Now that the door had been opened, he could hear the radio downstairs.

She leaned across him and kissed him on the forehead, making a smacking sound. He knew she had made a lipstick mark, could see the mischievous glint in her eyes as she surveyed her work with a satisfied smile.

She ruffled his hair lovingly. "What are you going to be doing today?"

Bennett shrugged, yawned and turned his face away from her. He could taste the staleness of sleep still in his mouth.

"Oh, this and that."

"Words!" Shelley snapped at him, jabbing a finger in his stomach. "Make sure you do your words before you deal with e-mails." She smiled and rubbed his stomach—another sign of affection. "Will you be okay?" The question came complete with inflection and frown.

"Sure," Bennett said. "I'll be fine. I'll get lots done."

"Promise?"

"Promise." He raised his clenched fist to his head and tapped two fingers against his temple. "Scouts' honor, ma'am. I'll do my words."

She stood up and picked up her watch from the table by her side of the bed. Strapping it onto her wrist, she said, "Well, have a good day. There's a sandwich in the refrigerator."

"Great."

She stopped at the bedroom door and scrunched herself up excitedly. "You know," she said, rubbing her hands together, ". . . you can smell it."

Bennett shuffled up and rested his head on his hand. "Smell what?"

Shelley frowned. "Christmas, of course." She straightened her sweater where she had rucked it out of her skirt. "You can smell it everywhere: the cold . . . and the presents, egg nog, warm biscuits. The skies are clear and the air is crisp . . ." Bennett half-imagined he could hear sleighbells, and his wife nodded as though in response to his thoughts. "And I think we're going to have some snow," she added with a devilish smile—she knew Bennett hated snow.

Bennett groaned. "Oh, goody."

She waved a hand at him. "You know, you're turning into Scrooge."

He flopped his head onto the pillow. "Bah, humbug!"

Shelley smiled. "Okay, I'm on my way. See you tonight."

"Yeah, see you," he said to the slowly closing door.

It seemed like no time at all before the front door slammed and he heard the Buick's engine fire into life. Then three soft pips on the horn as Shelley pulled out of the driveway.

Suddenly the house was quiet, the only sound that of the car moving off along the street. Then, around the silence, drifting through it like a boat across a still lake, the sound of the radio gave a sense of life, albeit muffled.

Bennett could hear a funky jingle and the weatherman distantly telling anyone in Forest Plains who was bothering to listen at this time in the morning just what the weather was doing. Rain coming in from the west, heat coming in from the east . . . all elemental life was there: winds, twisters, cold fronts circling, warm fronts sneaking up for the kill, maybe even a tremor or two.

"Maybe even snow!" he said to the pillow.

But there *was* something else, too. Even *he* could smell it. Smell it in the air. *Was* it Christmas? Did Christmas *have* a smell . . . a smell all of its own, not just the associated things that society had tacked onto it?

Bennett sat up in bed and looked at the clock. It was a little before seven, two minutes to his alarm ringing, the clock dancing side to side like on the cartoon shows, demanding attention like a family pet, craving a human touch to let it know its job was done for another night. He leaned over and hit the switch.

The clock seemed to settle on its curlicued haunches, and Bennett half imagined it pouting because he had robbed it of its daily chore.

He yawned, scratched places that itched, and threw back the sheets.

It was cool. Cool but not cold.

Bennett slid his legs out of bed and rested his feet on the floor. It was part of the getting-up process, a kind of air lock sandwiched between sleep and wakefulness. The first ritual of the day.

He sniffed a bear-sized sniff and drew in everything and anything.

Somewhere in that sniff, alongside the fresh coffee and toasted bread smells that Shelley had left behind in the kitchen and which were now threading their way through the house, were the smells of his bedroom and his clothes, the wood grains and varnish of the furniture, the oily odors imbued by the machines that had stitched the mosaic linen of the curtains and stamped the twists and whorls on the bedside lampshades; old smells, new smells. Unknown smells. Smells from near and faraway . . . smells of other people, other places, other times.

And small-town smells. Plenty of those . . . so different from the smells of the city, New York City, where Bennett had worked as an insurance adjuster for twenty years before turning to writing full-time and hiding himself and Shelley away in Forest Plains . . . a town as close to all the picket-fenced and town-squared small towns as could possibly exist outside the pages of an old well-thumbed

Post, particularly in these dog days of the second millennium.

He sniffed again and glanced at the window.

Outside, over the street, gulls were circling. On the wires running across the posts that stood sentrylike alongside the grassy lawns, the neighborhood regulars—sparrows, chaffinches and thrushes—were perched . . . like hick locals lazing on a front porch watching an invasion of bike riders crazy-wheeling and whooping around the square.

Bennett frowned and got to his feet, finding new places to scratch as he staggered to the window. Now he could see what was happening.

"Huh!" was all he could think of to say. Someone had taken the world while he had been dragging himself from his bed. Someone had stolen everything that was familiar and had covered it with gauze. But this was a moving gauze, a diaphanous graveyard mist that, even as he watched, was drifting along Sycamore Street, swirling around the tree trunks, twisting itself like ribbons through the leafless branches, washing up the sidewalks to the polished lawns and onward, stealthily, reaching, conquering and owning, pausing every now and again to check out a crumpled brown leaf before moving on.

He leaned on the sill and yawned again.

It was the mist he could smell. He wondered why Shelley hadn't mentioned it. He'd have told her to take special care. In fact, if he had known it was this bad—because it *was* getting bad . . . thickening by the second, it seemed—he'd have driven her over to the train station at Walton Flats. And anyway, hadn't she said that the skies were clear? He looked both ways along the street. Maybe it *had* been clear when she looked out, but that must have been some time ago.

Bennett frowned. Well, whatever it *had* been . . . it was foggy now.

Now the mist was pooling all around, settling itself onto the trees and the pavement, resting on the sidewalks and the dew-covered lawns, investigating the promise of warmth offered by his partly-open window.

The mist had a clean, sharp smell, snaking across the sill and around him into the room, sliding beneath the bed and inside the louvered wardrobe doors, checking out the threads, evaluating the labels. Evaluating *him*.

Bennett watched it.

Soon it would make its way out of the bedroom door and onto the landing. It would find the spare bedroom— *nothing here, boys . . . let's move on*— and then the stairs leading down to the kitchen and the tinny radio sounds.

Bennett stretched and threw the window wide.

A boy appeared out of the mist, dodging the tendrils that grasped for but never quite caught hold of his bicycle wheels. The boy was standing on the pedals, pumping like mad, a cowlick pasted down on his forehead, a brown leather sack across his chest filled with news and stories, comments, cartoons and quotes. The boy reached into his sack, pulled out a rolled-up paper, and made to throw, his arm pulled back like a Major League pitcher. As the paper left his hand, spinning through the milky air, he caught sight of Bennett and smiled.

"Hey, Mist' Diff'ring!" the boy yelled, a *Just Dennis* kind of boy, his voice sounding echoey and artificial in the silent, mist-shrouded street.

Forest Plains was full of boys just like this one, all towheads, patched denims, and checked shirts. But many of them didn't have names, at least not names that Bennett knew. They were just boys, boys who whispered giggling and mysterious behind your back when you bought something—*any*-thing—in the drugstore; boys who viewed any structure as merely something else to climb; boys who propped up the summertime street corners, drinking in the life and the sounds and the energy; boys with secret names . . . names like "Ace" and "Skugs."

He'd heard two of them talking in the drugstore just day before yesterday, the one of them calling over to the other—*Hey Skugs, get a load of that, will ya!*—holding up a comic book, his eyes glaring proudly as though he were responsible for the book and the story and the artwork. And the second boy had dutifully sidled up the aisle to his friend, and equally dutifully exclaimed *Wow!* as he was shown a couple of interior pages. *Wow! Neato!*

Bennett had wanted to interrupt, stop the boys in the middle of their comic-book explorations, and ask *What kind of a name do you have to wind up with Skugs?* But he knew it wouldn't make sense. It would be Charles or James—which would only explain "Chuck" or "Jim"—and the surname would probably be Daniels or Henderson, both equally unhelpful. And that would have meant him having to ask, *So why "Skugs"*? And then the boys would have looked at each other, shrugged, dumped the comic book back on the rack, and run out of the store giggling. Bennett suddenly felt that *he* wanted to be standing out in an early-morning street, alone with an invading mist, hair plastered onto his forehead, Schwinn between his legs and his old leather *Grit* sack around his shoulder, drinking in the sights and smells and sounds of a life still new . . . still filled with so many possibilities; suddenly wanted a secret name of his own . . . one that made no sense at all and that would make adults frown and shake their heads as he ran off laughing into the life that lay ahead.

He wondered what the secret name was for the boy in the street and, for a second, considered asking him. But then he thought better of it. At least he knew this kid's *real* name: it was Will Cerf.

Bennett waved. "Hey, Will. Looks a little misty out there," he shouted as the paper hit the screen door below him, its *thud* sounding like a pistol crack.

"Fog," the boy retorted, his face serious, brow furrowed.

Fog. Such an evocative word when spoken by a voice and a mind still alive to things not so easily explained by the meteorological charts on the morning news programs.

The boy stopped the bike and straddled it, one foot on the curb, and waved an arm back in the direction he'd just ridden. "Coming in thick and fast," he said, sounding for all the world like a towheaded Paul Revere thumbing back over his shoulder at the advancing British troops. For a second or so, Bennett glanced in the direction indicated and felt a small gnawing mixture of apprehension and wonder.

"Down by the scrapyard," Will Cerf added. "Cold, too," he almost concluded. "And damp." The boy rubbed his arms to confirm his report.

Bennett nodded absently and looked back along the street.

Already the first fingers of fog had consolidated, holding tight onto picket fence and garage handle, wrapping themselves across fender and grill, posting sentries beside tree trunks and fall-pipes, settling down alongside discarded or forgotten toys lying dew-covered on the leaf-stained lawns.

"Gotta go," Will Cerf said, a hint of sagacious regret in his voice.

"Me, too," Bennett said. "You take care now."

The boy already had his head down, was already reaching into that voluminous bag of news and views, his feet pumping down on those pedals, the tires *shhhh*ing along the pavement. "Will do," came the reply as another airborne newspaper flew through the mist, gossamer fingers prodding and poking it as it passed by. "You, too," he added over his shoulder.

And then, as if by magic, Will Cerf disappeared into the whiteness banked across the street in front of Jack and Jenny Coppertone's house. The whiteness accepted him— *greedily,* Bennett thought . . . immediately wishing he hadn't used that word—and stretched over to Audrey Chermola's Dodge, checking out the JESUS SAVES sticker on the back fender before swirling around the rain barrel out in front of her garage, climbing up the pipe and over the flat roof to the backyard beyond.

Bennett pulled the window closed.

Outside, visibility was worsening.

Now the power lines and their silent bird population had gone. Even the posts were indistinct, like they were only possible *ideas* for posts . . . hastily sketched suggestions for where they might be placed. The Hells Angels gulls had gone, too. He leaned forward and looked up into the air to see if he could see any shapes negotiating the milky currents, but the sky appeared to be deserted.

Deserted and white.

As he watched, a milky swirl of that whiteness rushed at the glass of the window making him pull back with a start . . . it was as though the mist had momentarily sensed him watching it, like a shark suddenly becoming aware of the presence of the caged underwater cameraman and his deep-sixed recording lens. Then the cushion of mist moved off, lumbering, up and over the house . . . out of sight. Bennett craned forward and tried to look up after it . . . to see what it was doing now.

Just for a second, he considered running to the spare

bedroom, where Shelley always kept a window wide to air the room . . .

But then his bladder reminded him it needed emptying. He turned away from the window and padded out to the bathroom.

Taking a pee, Bennett was suddenly pleased that Shelley wasn't downstairs. Pleased that she hadn't heard the newspaper hit the screen door because then she would open it, bring the paper inside into the warmth.

And that would mean she would let the fog inside.

He *hmph*ed and shook his head, flushed the toilet.

Downstairs, on the radio, The Mamas and Papas were complaining that all the leaves were brown. Bennett knew how they felt: roll on, summer!

He closed the bathroom door and stepped into the warmth of the shower, feeling it revitalize his skin.

Through the steamed-up glass of the shower stall, Bennett could see the whiteness pressing against the bathroom window. Like it was watching him. Lathering his hair, he tried to recall whether he had heard the radio anchorman mention the fog.

After the shower, Bennett shaved.

The man staring back at him looked familiar but older. The intense light above the mirror seemed to accentuate the pores and creases, picked out the wattled fold of skin beneath his chin . . . a fold that, no matter how hard he tried and how hard he stretched back his head, stoically refused to flatten out. That same light also highlighted the shine of head through what used to be thick hair, the final few stalks now looking like a platoon of soldiers abandoned by their comrades. If he were still able to have a secret name now, it would be Baldy or Tubby or maybe even Turkeyneck. As he shaved, he tried to think of what names he *did* have as a boy: he was sure he used to have one, and that it had annoyed him for a time, but he could only think of Ben.

He pulled on the same things he'd been wearing last night. Despite the fact he had two closets literally brimming with shirts and sweaters, jogging pants and old denims that were too threadbare to wear outside the confines of the house, Bennett considered the wearing of yesterday's clothing as something of a treat . . . and something naughty, something he could get away with the way he used to get away with it as a kid.

There were so few things an adult could get away with.

Feeling better, more refreshed, he opened the bathroom door and stepped out onto the landing. As he neared the staircase, he could hear thick static growling downstairs, and—just for a second—he almost shouted out his wife's name as a question, even though he knew she was long gone to the mall.

He padded downstairs slower than usual, checking the layout over the rim of the handrail as the next floor came into view.

In the kitchen everything was neat. Shelley had left out the cutting board, a jar of marmalade, and a new loaf out of the freezer. The coffee smelled good. But first things first: he had to attend to the radio. Bennett leaned on the counter and pushed a couple of the preset buttons to zone in on another station . . . anything to relieve that static. But each time he hit a button, it was the same . . . Didn't even falter, just kept on crackling and hissing and . . .

whispering

something else. He leaned closer, put his ear against the speaker, and listened. Was there a station there? Could he hear someone talking, talking quietly . . . *very* quietly indeed? Maybe that was it: maybe it was the volume. He twizzled the dial on the side, but the static just got louder.

Bennett stepped back and looked at the radio, frowning. He had been sure he could hear something behind the static, but now it was gone. He switched it off. He'd watch TV.

After flicking the set forward and backward through all the available channels, Bennett gave up. Static, static everywhere. Static and voices, soft faraway whispering voices . . . saying things—he was sure they were there and they were saying things, but he just couldn't get them to register. He tossed the remote onto the sofa and sat for a few minutes in the silence.

Coffee. That was what he needed. That would make things right.

He strolled back into the kitchen, poured a cup, and walked across the hall into his office.

The cumulative smell of books and words met him as it always did, welcomed him back for another day.

He powered up the old Aptiva, heard it click once—the single bell-tone it always made—and then watched the screen go fuzzy.

"Huh? What the hell's going on here?" he asked the room.

The millions of words and sentences tucked up in the double-stacked shelves of books and magazines shuffled amongst themselves but, clearly unable to come up with a good response, remained silent.

Bennett placed his coffee on his mouse mat and shuffled the mouse. Nothing. The computer wouldn't even boot up. He pressed the volume button on the CD-ROM speakers and heard the static invade his office.

Along with the faraway whispering voices.

He flipped the Rolodex until he got the number for the maintenance people and pressed the hands-free key on the fax/telephone at the side of his desk. This time he knew there were voices in that white haze of crackle coming from the fax machine . . . and the voices sounded like they were chuckling.

Forgetting the coffee, he went out into the lounge and picked up the handset of the house line.

It was the sound of the sea and the wind, the hiss of the tallest trees bending to the elements, the hum of the Earth spinning. All this and nothing more. Nothing more except for the unmistakable sound of someone—some*thing*—calling his name . . . calling it as though in a dream.

Now the panic really set in. It had already been lit and its flames fanned without him even seeing the first sparks, but when Bennett walked quickly to the front door, opened it, and stepped out onto the stoop, the fire became a conflagration in his stomach.

The fog was everywhere, thick and solid, unmoving and ungiving, leaving no single discernible landmark of the street he and Shelley lived on. It was an alien landscape—no, not so much a landscape as a canvas . . . a blank canvas sitting on an old easel in a musty loft somewhere in the Twilight Zone, and Bennett was the only dab of color to be found on it.

And he felt even he was fading fast.

He stared toward the drive at the side of the house and was pleased to see that he could make out the fence running between his property and Jerry and Amy Sondheim's. He didn't know whether to be relieved or dismayed by the fact that Shelley had the car. Then he decided he was relieved: if the car *had* been there, he would have gone to it, slid into his familiar position behind the wheel, and driven off.

Driven off where? a soft voice asked quietly in the back of his head.

Bennett nodded. He couldn't have driven anywhere in this. Nobody could drive anywhere in this. Christ, what the hell *was* it?

He stared into the whiteness, trying to see if there was just the tiniest hint of movement. There was none. The fog looked like a painted surface, as though the entire planet was sinking into a sea of mist, submerging itself forever, removing all traces of recognizability. No radio or TV, no telephones . . . not even any Internet! Was this the way it was all going to end? The whole planet being cut off from itself as though nothing existed? As though nothing had *ever* existed?

It was right then—as Bennett was looking first to the left along Sycamore Street to where it intersected with Masham Lane, trying to imagine the old bench Charley Sputterenk erected in memory of his wife, Hazel, and then to the right, down toward Main Street, trying to see if he could hear the distant sound of moving traffic—that he heard something moving in the fog.

He snapped his head back to face front and stared, stared hard. But he couldn't see anything . . . except now the mist seemed to be swirling a little, right in front of his face . . . as though something was pushing it toward him. Something coming toward him and displacing it . . .

"Hello?" His voice sounded weak and querulous and he hated himself for it. Hated himself but was unable to do anything about it. The mist continued to swirl, and Bennett's eyes started to ache with the effort.

"Somebody out there? Need any help?"

This time he had tried to make his tone initially mock-serious—*Jesus Christ, is this some weather or what?*—and then helpful . . . a fog-bound Samaritan calling to a lost and weary traveler.

The sound came again—a hesitant shuffle of shoes on

sidewalk, perhaps?—and was accompanied by what sounded
to be a cough or a low, throaty rumble.

Bennett took a step back, reaching his hand behind until
it touched the reassuring surface of the door jamb, and felt
something under his foot. Quickly glancing down, he saw the
folded newspaper. There was something sticking out of it, a
gaudily-colored handbill protruding from the printed pages.

He bent down and scooped up the paper and its contents
and then backed fully into the house, allowing the screen
door to slam and pushing the house door closed without
turning around, and securing the deadbolts top and bottom
before turning the key.

There had been no sound out there, no sound at all. And
there should have been. Even if the fog had shrouded the
entire county—though it was far more likely that it had
merely entrapped Forest Plains, and possibly only a couple
of the town's many streets—he should have been able to
stand on his own doorstep and hear something . . . a siren,
a voice, a car engine, someone's dog howling at the sudden
claustrophobic curtain that had dropped down.

But it was silent out there.

More silent than he could ever have imagined.

And he should have been able to see *some*thing . . .
anything at all: a glimpse of windowpane across the street,
the muted and silhouetted outlines of roof gable or drain-
pipe, the indistinct shape of a parked car whose owner was
either unable or unwilling to brave the murk.

But there was nothing to see at all through the whiteness.

The thought came to him.

. . . *somehow I don't think we're in Kansas anymore,
Toto.*

That it wasn't Sycamore Street at all. And it wasn't Forest Plains. And the mall where Shelley was shopping-till-
she-dropped with her sister, Lisa, was a world away.

He went to the window at the side of the door and
looked out into the street. It was the same as before. He
could see his own drive and his own lawn run down to the
sidewalk, and he could see the vague outline of the road . . .
but nothing more.

The handbill slipped out of the newspaper and fluttered
to the floor at his feet just as he thought for a moment that
he could see a shape forming out in the whiteness, but

nothing appeared . . . though the mist now seemed to be swirling thickly in the middle of the street.

Bennett lifted the handbill and stared at it.

It was just a regular-sized insert, like any of the ones that dropped out of Bennett's *Men's Journal* or Shelley's *Vanity Fair* . . . ablaze with color and just three lines of curlicued fonts, serifed letters, and ubiquitous exclamation marks, all of the text bold, some of it italicized.

It read.

Congratulations to **Bennett Differing***!*

in huge letters in the very center of the sheet, with Bennett's name appearing to have been typed into place on a line. Below that, the handbill announced

You have won a visit from your Father!

with the words appearing in slightly smaller lettering, employing the best sideshow-barker's spiel, and in a typesetting nightmare of a mixture of small caps, dropped first letters and the typed-in words "Your Father." And then:

Have a Good Time!

And that was that.

Bennett turned the sheet over to see if there was anything on the back, but there was only a pattern of swirling lines, like the ones printed for security on foreign currency.

Won? How could he have won anything when he didn't recall even entering any competitions? And his father? John Differing had been dead some twenty-seven years. Maybe it was some kind of gag. Maybe everyone on the street—maybe even everyone in Forest Plains—was receiving a similar handbill in their newspaper. Bennett wished he could ask young Will Cerf to look in the other papers he was delivering to check out that particular theory.

Outside, a *haurrrnk!* sounded . . . like a ship's horn.

Bennett looked up at the window and saw a shape forming out of the thick swirls of mist in the middle of the street. Someone was walking toward the house . . . walking slowly, even awkwardly. Someone had been hurt.

With the handbill still clutched in his hand, Bennett rushed to the door and started to release the deadbolts. But then he stopped.

Who was this person? Maybe it was some kind of wierdo, some transient brought in with the fog . . . like the guys that howl at a full moon. And here was Bennett busily opening the door to let him inside.

He pushed the top bolt home again and moved back to the window.

The shape was now fully emerged from the mist: it was a man, a man in a dark suit, no topcoat—*no topcoat!* and in this weather!—and wearing a hat. Bennett immediately assumed an age for the man—he had to be older than seventy, maybe even eighty, to be wearing a hat. Hardly anyone he knew wore hats these days, at least around Forest Plains.

The figure stopped for a moment and moved its head from side to side like he was checking out the houses. The man had to have 20/20 vision no matter how old he was: when Bennett was last outside he wasn't able to see across the street let alone distinguish one house from another.

When the man started moving again, Bennett thought there was something familiar about him. Maybe he'd come out of Jack Coppertone's house across the street . . . it wasn't Jack himself—too old, though Bennett still couldn't see the man's face—but it could be Jenny's father. Bennett rubbed the glass and remembered that the mist was outside the window, not inside. But, no, it couldn't be Jenny's father—he was a short man, and fat. Whereas the man walking across the street was tall and slim, moving with a soldier's gait, straight-backed and confident . . . despite the fact that he had just had to stop and check which house he was heading for. Whatever, and whoever the man was, Bennett didn't think he posed a problem . . . and he *could* be in difficulty. Lost at the very least. And it would be good to speak with somebody.

He moved back to the door, released the last bolt, and pulled it open.

The man's shoes on the black surface of the street made a *click-clack* sound. The mist swirling around his arms and legs looked like an oriental dancer's veils, clinging one second and voluminous the next . . . and brought with it now the unmistakable sound of distant voices muttering and whispering. Then his face appeared, frowning and unsure, one eye narrowed in an effort to make some sense of the house and the man standing before him, the shadow of the hat brim moving up and down on his forehead as he strode forward.

He looked wary, this fog-brought stranger from afar. As well he might.

The house, Bennett knew, he had never seen before.

And when the traveller had last seen the man standing before him in this alien street, that man had been little more than a boy.

The whispering voices echoed the word "boy" in Bennett's head like circling gulls warning of bad weather out on the coast.

He successfully fought off the urge to cut and run back into the house . . . to throw the deadbolts across—how appropriate that word suddenly seemed: deadbolts—to bar the stranger's way . . . to erase the errant foolishness of what he was thinking, of the silly *déjà vu* sense he had seen the man before. But he was just a man, this stranger to Forest Plains . . . a man lost and alone, maybe with a broken-down Olds or Chevy a couple of blocks away near the intersection with Main Street, a trusted and faithful retainer that he cleaned and polished every Sunday but which now languished with a busted muffler or some other vehicular intestine trailing down on the road.

The traveller stopped and looked at Bennett, just twenty or thirty feet between them, the man out on the sidewalk and Bennett standing in the open doorway of his home, screen door leaning against him, the fresh and welcoming lights spilling out onto the mist which held their shine on its back and shifted it around like St. Elmo's Fire.

"Hey," Bennett said softly.

The man shifted his head to one side, looked to the left and then to the right. Then nodded.

Bennett crumpled the handbill into a ball and thrust it into his pants pocket. "Quite a morning."

"Quite a morning," came the response.

It was as though someone had pumped air or water or some kind of helium gas into Bennett's head. There were things in there—sleeping things, memory things that lay dormant and dust covered like old furniture in a forgotten home that you suddenly and unexpectedly went back to one magical day . . . things awoken by three simple and unexciting words delivered in a familiar voice and a familiar drawl the accuracy of which he thought he had misplaced— or, more realistically, had filed away and ignored.

These things grew to full height and shape and revealed themselves as remembered incidents . . . and the incidents brought remembered voices and remembered words: these were real memories . . . not the cloying waves of rose-colored-eyepiece nostalgia that he got watching a rerun of a favorite childhood TV show or hearing a snatch of a one-time favorite song. He saw this man—many versions of him, each older or younger than the one before—playing ball, laughing, talking . . . saw him asleep.

"You lost?"

The man looked around for a few seconds and then looked back at Bennett. "I guess so. Where am I?"

"This is Forest Plains."

"Where's that?"

Bennett shrugged and tried to stop his knees shaking. "It's just a town. Where are you heading?"

"I'm going—" The man paused and closed his eyes. When he opened them, he smiled at Bennett. "Home," he said. "I'm going home."

Bennett nodded. "You want to come in for a while? Have a cup of coffee?" He had never heard of a ghost that came in for coffee, but what the hell . . . *all* of this was crazy, so anything was possible. He glanced along the street and saw that the mist seemed to be thinning out, the first vague shapes and outlines of the houses opposite taking hesitant form.

The man followed Bennett's stare, and when he turned back, there was a wistful smile on his mouth. "Can't stay too long," he said.

"No," Bennett agreed. He nodded to the fog. "Bad day."

The man turned around but didn't comment. Then he said, "You ever think it's like some kind of vehicle? Like a massive ocean liner?"

"What? The fog?"

The man nodded, gave a little flick of his shoulders, and stared back into the mist. "Like some huge machine," he said, "drifting along soundlessly and then—" he snapped his fingers, "—suddenly pulling into a port or a station, somewhere we've not seen for a long time . . . sometimes for so long it's like . . . like we've never seen it at all. And it reveals something that you weren't expecting . . . weren't expecting simply because you don't know how far you've traveled." He turned back. "How far not just in distance but in time."

"In time?" Bennett said, glancing out at the swirling mist. "Like a time machine," he said.

The man smiled, the intensity suddenly falling away. "Yeah, like a time machine. Or something like that."

Bennett stepped aside and ushered the man into the house.

The man who looked for all the world like John Differing removed his hat and held it by the brim with both hands at his waist. Looking around the kitchen, he said, "Nice place."

Bennett closed the door and stood alongside the man, noting with an inexplicable sadness that he seemed to be around four or five inches shorter than he remembered. He followed the man's stare and drank in the microwave oven, the polished electric burner plates, the chest freezer over by the back door, the small TV set on the breakfast counter. What would these things look like to someone who had not been around since 1972?

"*We* like it," Bennett responded simply. "So, coffee?"

The man shrugged as Bennett walked across the kitchen to the sink. "Whatever you're making."

"Coffee's fresh. Shelley—my wife—she made it. It might have gotten a little strong, sitting. I'll just boil some water."

"Uh-huh. She here?"

"Shelley? No, she's out. Shopping. Christmas shopping. With her sister. Does it every year." Placing the kettle on its electric base, Bennett pulled a chair from the table. "You want to sit down?"

The man shook his head. "No, I don't think I can stay that long. Don't want to get too settled."

"Right."

The man placed his hat on the table and straightened his shoulders. "Mind if I look around?"

"No, no . . . go right ahead. Coffee'll be ready in a couple of minutes."

He watched the man walk off along the hallway and tried to think of all the things he wanted to ask him. Things like, what was it like . . . where he was now? Things like, did he know who he was . . . and that he was dead? Did he even know that Bennett was—

"This your office?" The voice drifted along the hallway and broke Bennett's train of thought.

"Yes." The kettle clicked off and Bennett poured water into the electric coffee jug.

"You work from home?" The voice had moved back into the hallway.

"Yeah. I gave up my day job about five years ago. I write full-time now." He went to the refrigerator and got a carton of milk.

Pouring steaming coffee into a couple of mugs, Bennett wondered what the hell he was doing. The fog and the fact that it had cut him off from civilization had messed up his head. A stupid handbill—he felt in his pocket to make sure it was still there . . . make sure he hadn't imagined it— some half-baked ramblings about the fog maybe being a time machine that the dead used to travel back and forth, and the appearance of a man who looked a little like his father had freaked him out. Looked like his father! What the hell was that? He hadn't even *seen* his father for twenty-seven years.

He shook his head and added milk to the mugs. The fact was he had invited some guy into the house, for crissakes. Shelley would go apeshit when she found out. *If* he told her, of course. Putting the milk back in the refrigerator, he suddenly thought that maybe Shelley *would* find out . . . when she got home and found her husband lying in the kitchen with a knife in his—

"What kind of stuff do you write?" the man asked, standing right behind him in the kitchen.

"Shit!" He spun around and banged into the refrigerator door.

"Pardon me?"

"You startled me."

"Sorry."

"That's okay. I'm sorry for—"

"Didn't mean to do that."

"Really, it's okay." He closed the refrigerator door and

took a deep breath. "Guess I must be a little nervous." He waved a hand at the window. "The fog."

The man walked across to the counter by the sink and nodded to the window. "Looks like it's clearing up." He reached a hand out toward the two mugs and said, "Either?"

Nodding, Bennett said, "Yeah, neither of them have sugar, though. There's a bowl over to your—"

"I don't take it." He picked up one of the mugs and, closing his eyes, took a sip. "Mmm, now that's good. You don't know how good coffee tastes until you haven't had it for a while."

The man continued to sip at his coffee, eyes downcast, as though studying the swirling brown liquid.

Bennett considered just coming right out with it there and then, confronting this familiar man with the belief that he was Bennett's very own father. But the more he watched him, the more Bennett wondered whether he was just imagining things . . . even worse, whether he was in some way trying to bring his father back. After all, who ever heard of a handbill that advertised returning dead relatives? He might just be putting two and two together and getting five.

On the other hand, maybe it *was* his father. It could well be that there were forces or powers at large in the universe that made such things possible. Maybe Rod Serling had had it right after all. Maybe the dead did use mist as a means of getting around—so many movies had already figured that one out . . . and maybe they did travel in time.

Bennett took a sip of his coffee and thought of something he had often pondered: if a chair falls over in an empty house miles from anywhere, does it make a sound? Natural laws dictate that it must, but there were plenty of instances of natural law seemingly not figured out. The thing was—the thing with the chair in the deserted house—there was no way of proving or disproving it . . . because the only way to prove it was to have someone present at the falling over, which destroyed one of the criteria for the experiment. So maybe whatever one *wanted* to believe could hold true.

The same applied to the man in Bennett's kitchen. So long as Bennett didn't actually come right out and ask him and risk the wrong response

John Differing? No, name's Bill Patterson, live over to Dawson Corner, got a flooded Packard couple blocks down the street, and a wife in it—Ellie's her name—busting to get home soon as this fog's cleared up.

it was safe to assume the man was Bennett's father. And the plain fact was there were so many things that supported such a belief. Things like . . .

"My father drank his coffee that way, sipping," Bennett said, pushing the encroaching silence back into the corners of the room where it didn't pose a threat.

The man looked up at Bennett and smiled. "Yeah?"

Bennett nodded. "Looked a lot like you, too."

"That right?"

Bennett took a deep breath. "He died more than twenty-seven years ago. He was fifty-eight." He took another sip and said, "How old are *you?* If you don't mind my—"

"Don't mind at all. I'm fifty-eight myself."

"Huh," Bennett said, shaking his head. "Quite a coincidence."

"Looks like it's a day for them," the man said as he lowered his cup down. "My boy—my *son*—he always wanted to be a writer."

"Yeah?"

"Yeah. I must say, I never had much faith in that. Seemed like a waste of time to me." He lifted the cup again. "But a man can be wrong. Could be he made a go of it." His mouth broke into a soft smile. "Could even be he'll get real successful a little ways down the track."

Bennett wanted to ask if the man ever *saw* his son these days, but that would have been breaking the rules of the game . . . just as it would have been courting disaster. The response could be *Sure, saw Jack just last week and he's doing fine.* And Bennett didn't want that response. But the more they talked, the more sure he became.

They talked of the man's past and of the friends he used to have.

They talked of places he had lived and things he had done.

And in amongst all the talk, all the people and all the places and all the things, there were people and places and things that rang large bells in Bennett's mind—so many coincidences—but there were also several people and places and things that didn't mean anything at all. Things Bennett had never known about his father. But he still refrained from asking anything that might place the man in some kind of cosmic glitch . . . or that might provoke an answer that would break the spell.

In turn, Bennett told the man things about his father . . . things that not only was he sure his father had never known but also that he himself hadn't known. Not *really* known . . . not known in that surface area of day-to-day consciousness that we can access whenever we want.

And each time Bennett said something, the man nodded slowly, a soft smile playing on his lips, and he would say, "Is that right?" or "You don't say," or, more than once, "You make him sound like quite a man."

"He was. Quite a man."

For a second, the man looked like he was about to say something, the edge of his tongue peeking between those gently smiling lips

thank you

but he seemed to think better of it and whatever it had been was consigned to silence.

Bennett placed his mug on the counter and pulled the handbill from his pocket. "You believe in ghosts?" he asked.

"Ghosts?"

"Mm hmm." He moved across to the man and showed him the handbill. "Got this today, in the newspaper. Ever hear of anything like that?"

The man shook his head. "Can't say that I have, no."

"You think such a thing is possible?"

The man shrugged. "They do say anything's possible. Maybe ghosts see everything in one hit . . . the then, the now, and the to come. Maybe time doesn't mean anything at all to them. Could be they just hop right on board of their fog time machine and go wherever or whenever they've a mind."

Bennett looked again at the handbill, his eyes tracing those curly letters. "But why would they want to come back . . . ghosts, I mean?"

"Maybe because they forget what things were like? Forget the folks they left behind? They say the living forget the dead after a while: well, maybe it works both ways."

He shrugged again, looked down into his coffee. "Who knows."

Was the man nervous? Bennett frowned. Maybe he was breaking some kind of celestial rule by moving the conversation to a point where the man would have no choice but to corroborate Bennett's belief . . . and maybe that would mean—

He thrust the handbill back into his pocket, and the man looked immediately relieved, if still a little apprehensive.

"Yeah, well," Bennett said in a dismissive tone, "what are ghosts but memories?"

The man nodded. "Right. Memories. I like that. And what is heaven but a small town . . . a small town like this one. A small town that's just a little ways up or down the track."

Now it was Bennett's turn to nod. "You know," Bennett went on, "we used to play a game, back when I was a kid, where we used to say which sense we would keep if we were forced to give up all but one of the senses, and why.

"Kids would say, 'hearing' and they'd say 'because I couldn't listen to my records', or they'd say 'sight,' 'because I couldn't read my comic books or watch TV or go to the movies.' "

"And what did you say?"

Bennett smiled. This was a story he'd told his father on more than one occasion. "I used to say I wouldn't give up my memory, because without my memory nothing that had ever happened to me would mean anything. Everything I am—forget the skin and flesh and bone, forget the muscles and the sinews and the arteries—*every*thing I am is memories."

The man smiled. "You ever stop to think that maybe you're a ghost?"

Bennet laughed. "Did *you*?"

And the man joined in on the laughter.

Bennett suddenly realized he could see the house across the street quite clearly. Could see the front door opening . . . could see the unmistakable outline of Jenny Coppertone stepping out onto the front step, staring up into the sky. Then she turned around and went back into the house.

Bennett heard the muted sound of a door slamming.

The fog's hold on the world was weakening.

He looked across at the man standing in front of the sink, saw him frowning at the mug of coffee, shuffling his arms around like he was having difficulty with it. Maybe it was too hot for him . . . but hadn't he been drinking it all this time?

Outside, a car went by slowly, its lights playing on the mist.

Then the *haurrrnk!* blasted again, the same sound he'd heard before . . . but different in tone now. This time it sounded more like a warning.

The man dropped the mug and Bennett watched it bounce once, coffee spraying across the floor and the table legs and the chairs.

Bennett watched it roll to a stop—amazingly unbroken—before he looked up. The man was looking across at him, his face looking a little pale . . . and a little sad.

"I couldn't . . . I couldn't keep a hold of it," he said.

"You have to go," Bennett said. He knew it deep in his heart . . . deep in that place where he knew everything there *was* to know.

"Yes, I have to go."

"I'll see you off—"

The man held up his hand. "No," he snapped. And then, "No, I'm sure you've got things to do . . . things to be getting on with."

"Memories to build," Bennett added.

"Right, memories to build." He moved forward from the counter, unsteadily at first, watching his feet move one in front of the other as though he was walking a tightrope. Bennett made to give him a hand, but the man pulled away. "Can't do that," he said.

They stood looking at each other for what seemed like a long time, Bennett desperately wanting to take that one step forward—that one step that would carry him twenty-seven years—and wrap his arms around his father, bury his face in his father's neck and smell his old familiar smells, smells whose aroma he couldn't recall . . . how desperately he wanted to give new life to old memories. But he knew he could not.

As he reached the door, the man stopped for a second and turned around. "You know, my son, when he was a kid, he had a nickname."

Bennett smiled. "Yeah? What was it?"

"Bubber."

"Bubber?" *Oh, my God . . . Bubber . . it was Bubber because I—*

"He had a stutter—nothing too bad, but it was there—and his name was . . . his name began with a B."

Bennett could feel his eyes misting up.

"Kids can be cruel, can't they?"

It was all he could do to nod.

The door closed, the screen door slammed a ricochet *rat-a-tat* and Bennett was alone again . . . more alone than he had ever felt in his life. "Take care," he said to the empty kitchen.

And you, a voice said somewhere inside his head.

He waited a full minute before he went to the door and opened it, stepped out into the fresh December air, and walked to the sidewalk.

The fog had gone, and the watery winter sun was struggling through the overhead early-morning haze.

Cars were moving up and down, people were walking on the sidewalks, but there was no sign of the man.

"Hey, Bennett!"

Bennett gave a wave to Jack Coppertone as he pulled the handbill from his pants pocket. It was now a flyer for The Science Fiction Book Club; maybe that was what it had always been. As he folded it carefully, thinking back to that final sight of his visitor pulling open the door, he suddenly turned and ran back to the house.

On the table, right where the man had placed it, was a hat.

Bennett walked carefully across the kitchen, heart beating so hard he thought it was going to burst through his chest and his shirt, and reached for it, closing his eyes, expecting to connect with just more empty air.

But his fingers touched material.

And he lifted it, not daring to open his eyes . . . he was breaking rules here, of that he was sure . . . but maybe, just maybe, if only one or maybe two senses were working, he could pull it off. He lifted the hat up and buried his face inside the brim.

What are ghosts but memories? he heard himself saying from just a few minutes earlier. And there they were . . . memories. The only question was, were they from the past or the future?

Almost as soon as he had breathed in, the fragrance dissipated until there was only the smell of soap and the feel of Bennett's hands cradling his face. But deep inside his head, the memories were still there, smelling fresh as blue bonnets in the spring air.

Haurrrnnnnnnnnk!

Outside the window it had started to snow.

For Percival Crowther (1913–1972)
. . . and all other fathers, wherever they may be.

JEFF'S BEST JOKE
by Jane Lindskold

Jane Lindskold is a full-time writer and a sometime archaeological volunteer. She is the author of over forty short stories and numerous novels, among them *Changer* and *Legends Walking*. Current projects include a new fantasy series, the first volume of which, *Through Wolf's Eyes*, is due for release in 2001. With regard to this story, the author would like to note that any resemblance between the characters and any archaeologists of her acquaintance should be regarded as wholly complimentary.

The onyx frog didn't start it, but it certainly continued it, and, in a sense, it ended it.

At least the frog was there at the end, both witness and testimony to a decision that would reshape history. The onyx frog didn't do any deciding. That was left to two archaeologists.

Jeff and Jim were colleagues, but more importantly, they were friends. Superficially, they couldn't have been more different, but they were alike where it counted. Maybe this similarity of spirit was why Jeff was the only person—other than Jim's immediate family—to get away with calling him Jimmy.

Jeff was tall and rangy, clean-shaven, and fair—the perfect cowboy type. No one who met him was surprised to learn he'd ridden rodeo in his youth. Jeff wrote cowboy poetry, too, rhymed verse that often held a note of poignancy underneath the broad humor. He'd married young and in his mid-forties already had a daughter married and a son in high school. A devout Christian, he volunteered with elder hostels and at church events. Talkative and easygoing, he was the more approachable of the two.

Where Jeff evoked the cowboy, Jim more resembled the mountain man. His long reddish-brown hair grew well past his collar, his thick beard covered jaw as well as chin—though it stopped short of descending in a Santa Claus cascade across his chest. He was a big man, though not overly tall, with broad shoulders and short legs. In his mid-forties, Jim had surprised those who'd cast him as a confirmed bachelor by venturing into marriage for the first time. He collected coins, made arrowheads, and enjoyed target shooting. Gruff and taciturn from a shyness that didn't seem to fit with his outer appearance, he sometimes intimidated people who didn't know him well.

Two more different friends would be hard to find, that is if you didn't know they shared a passion. Both were archaeologists—not merely by profession, but by avocation. The differences in their physical appearance were canceled by the invisible but irrevocable marks of their calling.

When they walked, their eyes inadvertently scanned the ground for the tiny flakes of stone, sherds of pottery, scraps of bone that might mark the presence of past inhabitants. When they did look toward the horizon, it was to note the variations in the rise and fall of the land that might indicate a buried structure.

Both had worked in New Mexico for so long that they no longer saw any feature, any structure, merely for what it was. They saw it for what it had been. Their minds were filled with fact, anecdote, and history regarding some three centuries of Spanish occupation, fanned out through the various indigenous traditions, and supported it all on prehistory.

In a sense, every day they walked through time.

Jim and Jeff were both field archaeologists. Neither could have traded hands-on contact with the material of their studies for a teaching post at some university than they could have walked with their gazes fixed on some distant horizon. Their advanced degrees were tools like their trowels and wheelbarrows, their writings—and both had written volumes—the means of recording and sharing their discoveries.

At the time when the onyx frog entered their lives, both Jim and Jeff were employed by the same museum. Their primary focus was archaeological clearance—that is, removing and recording items of archaeological interest so that when the area was destroyed (usually to build a road, but sometimes for a structure) information about those who had lived there before would still be available.

Their current project, of which they were co-directors managing a crew of a dozen or so, was along a rural road outside of Taos, New Mexico. The site—which rested along a bluff overlooking pastures on one side, lightly populated residential areas on the other—had proven incredibly productive. They'd found several pit houses and so many surface structures that when they packed up at night the ground looked as if it had sprouted tarps the way a damp forest floor might sprout mushrooms.

The crew had been in the field for months by then. They'd started in a winter so cold that everyone bundled into layers that could be stripped off as the day progressed, then resumed when the sun began to set and the thin air at some seven thousand feet relinquished the day's heat too quickly. They'd progressed through a spring that brought winds that drove sand and grit into the pores of their skin, and continued into a summer so hot that the younger members of the crew—optimistically trading healthy skin for suntans—worked in shorts and the briefest of tops.

Jim's chestnut-brown hair was bleached to straw blond where it extended below the faded red baseball cap he had worn for so many years that the strap in the back was secured with staples and the museum logo on front was almost unreadable. Jeff—who was lucky in that Taos was his hometown and so he wasn't separated from family and domestic comforts—was limping from a knee too long abused by extremes of heat and cold and the demands of hard labor.

Given the general exhaustion of the crew, it really wasn't surprising when the practical jokes started. At first they were little things—a person's favorite shovel or trowel disappearing then mysteriously reappearing right where it should be, a goofy face drawn in the dirt where it would greet someone pulling back a tarp.

Then the tricks started getting more clever and, while no one in the crew was unimaginative, Jim and Jeff proved themselves true tricksters. Jeff first hid the onyx frog in a wheelbarrow that Jim was using. As Jim was tossing the dirt up from six feet or so deep in a pit house, he had no idea the frog was there until he was screening and found the anomalous thing—clearly of modern Mexican manufacture—amid materials that should have dated no later than the year 1,000 AD.

Jeff couldn't hide his mischievous grin and so wasn't completely surprised when the frog showed up amid the potsherds in his own grid. After that the frog went the rounds several more times before vanishing completely. By then, however, the tricks had become more complex.

One weekend when most of the crew had dispersed to their various homes, Jeff drove out to the site. Carefully, so as not to disturb in the least the stratigraphy of the midden Jim was then digging, he slid a 1950s license plate into the packed trash and dirt. Jim's profanities when he discovered the plate—and momentarily thought all his conclusions to that moment had become as much trash as what he'd been so laboriously removing—were eloquent.

Jeff laughed loudly, one up in their unscored competition.

Jim got even, though, taking advantage of Jeff's absence one afternoon to salt Jeff's current grid with a perfectly elegant arrowhead of Jim's own manufacture. Some might think this unprofessional—after all, a modern arrowhead might well be mistaken for a prehistoric one. Indeed, so Jeff thought, crowing as the arrowhead appeared in its three or more inches of perfection amid the less noble remains of pots and broken tools.

That is, so Jeff thought until he held the arrowhead up for closer inspection and saw the sunlight shining through the bottle glass from which Jim had made it. Obsidian—which is, after all, just another form of glass—is never so clear and flawless. Moreover, Jim's broad grin, merry and wicked, gave him away.

It was about time for the frog to reappear when the visitor arrived at the site.

Visitors were not unheard of. Indeed, hardly a day passed that someone didn't stop. Most merely wanted directions—most commonly to the Millicent Rogers Museum. Many, however, learning that these were archaeologists at work, stayed to tour the site and ask questions.

Public outreach was part of museum policy, so someone was detailed as tour guide. At first, Jim and Jeff as co-directors had taken most of the tours, but by now everyone on the crew could do the spiel, so someone who needed a break from dirt and buckets, shovels and screens, would take the visitors around.

Jeff and Jim didn't mind sharing the limelight at all. Directing the project provided enough distractions from the actual work of digging that they didn't need another.

This visitor, however, wasn't about to be fobbed off on an eager assistant. Arriving at the site—and oddly enough no one saw him come—he marched up to a young woman who was pushing a wheelbarrow full of dirt over to the screens and announced in ringing tones:

"Take me to your leader."

Cranks were also not unheard of at the site. Only a week or so before, the crew had been visited by a gentle vagrant who announced that he was King William, a prophet come to help the modern world. Would-be Native Americans, often college students bedecked in beads and leather, or former hippies with visionary histories they'd spent decades refining, showed up. As long as they weren't rude or interested in damaging the site, they got the tour just like anyone else.

Less pleasant were the occasional enthusiasts who arrived to harangue the archaeologists for their disrespect in invading "sacred ground." These weren't dissuaded from their passion by the fact that several members of the crew were local Indians, quite interested in being part of the uncovering of their own history.

At first, Jim and Jeff thought this visitor was going to be one of these disapproving ones. He crossed his arms across his chest and stared at them through narrowed eyes of an indeterminant shade. He was slightly shorter than Jim but stringy in build, with hair that grew weedily past his earlobes, mingling gray with what might once have been light brown. He was conventionally clad in khakis and a polo shirt.

"So what do you have here?" the visitor asked, his voice nasal and aggressive.

"A prehistoric site," Jeff replied, his tones mild and measured, the same one he used for elder hostel tours, "probably dating to some nine hundred to a thousand years ago. We've found the remains of several pit houses—one of which may have been a kiva or sacred house . . ."

"Like a temple?" the visitor interrupted, something in his inflection letting on that he knew—or thought he knew—the answer and was testing them.

"More like a restricted club," Jeff said, "used for ceremonial retreats or meetings, perhaps for educational purposes. Similar structures are still used today by the local Pueblos."

Jim, seeing the situation well in hand, had returned to his digging. He was deep in a pit house now, removing careful shovelfuls of dirt and tossing them without even looking up into the wheelbarrow. They landed with steady precision, but Jeff, who knew Jim well, knew that his co-director was still attending to the conversation and knew from this that Jim, too, had sensed that this visitor was something out of the ordinary.

Jeff continued his well-practiced spiel.

"In addition to the pit houses, we've found a good number of surface structures."

He gestured to indicate the closest. Unlike the pit houses which, having been dug into the ground were comparatively well-preserved, these had melted back to nothing much more than an adobe wall a foot or so high.

The visitor sniffed.

"They don't look like much. Were the walls much higher originally?"

Again, there was that note of challenge in the visitor's voice, and Jim set aside his shovel and mounted the ladder to the surface. He made as if checking the dirt in the wheelbarrow for something, but in reality he was putting himself at Jeff's disposal.

"Probably so, and the adobe foundation was augmented by wood and brush—rather like a ramada with low walls," Jeff replied equably, glancing over at Jim with the slightest of shrugs.

"Nothing in this part of the southwest," Jeff went on, "is as physically impressive as the stone ruins at Chaco Canyon up in northern New Mexico or the cliff dwellings at Mesa Verde in Colorado. Folks are often disappointed. They figure the prehistoric people always did things on that grand scale. Fact is, they didn't, any more than folks today build everything on the scale of Saint Francis Cathedral or the Santa Fe Opera House.

"Usually," Jeff concluded, "what we find are more like little towns, a gathering of a few dwellings, maybe lived in by an extended family."

The visitor sniffed, approvingly this time. Apparently, they'd passed some test.

"So these people were Anasazi?"

The term—deprived from a Navajo word sometimes translated as "ancient enemies" or, more politely, "ancient ones"—was falling out of fashion with the archaeological community, but Jeff was far too polite to correct a visitor.

"That's right," he agreed. "They were pretty widely spread throughout New Mexico and into Colorado and Arizona."

"And then," the visitor said, his voice thrilling, "they just disappeared. Where do you think they went?"

Jim turned from his wheelbarrow, the restless motion of the potsherd he turned between thumb and forefinger the only indication of his annoyance.

"They didn't go anywhere," Jim replied bluntly before Jeff could frame a more tactful reply. "They're still here— just down the road at Taos Pueblo."

He gestured with a toss of his head to where two Indians were digging a surface feature.

"Verne and Russ, they're probably directly related to the people who lived here. Their own oral traditions support the physical evidence."

The visitor showed neither the vague disappointment nor the curiosity expressed by most of those who received this explanation. All he did was sniff.

Emerging from her pit house, Susie, a senior assistant with a sense for the passage of real time that both the co-directors lacked, called the lunch break. Her expression as she led the general exodus toward the trucks made quite clear that she—along with the rest of those in earshot—had been following the conversation and that she was hoping the break would cause their increasingly annoying visitor to depart.

The visitor, however, didn't take the hint, remaining in place even after Jim had brought his and Jeff's lunches from the truck. Seating himself on an upturned five-gallon bucket, the visitor stated with what he clearly thought was sophisticated blandness:

"What would you say if I told you that some of the Anasazi didn't just move to Taos Pueblo?"

Jim and Jeff exchanged glances, then Jeff replied diplomatically:

"Well, there is evidence that they didn't all go precisely there. What Jimmy meant was that the ones who lived here at this site probably were ancestral to the current residents of Taos Pueblo."

The visitor wasn't to be distracted. He wiggled impatiently on his seat and lowered his voice into the confidential range.

"I don't mean just these and just here. I mean the Anasazi at large. I mean an answer to the mystery of why ruins like those at Chaco Canyon were abandoned so suddenly that food was left in larders, grinding stones with corn in their troughs, sandals right where the people might have stepped out of them."

Jim made one last grab for common sense.

"There is some indication," he said, "that Chaco may have been less a residential center—like our modern cities—than a ceremonial center. If that was the case, then the items left behind may have simply been left on the assumption that the people would return in due course for the next appropriate event. However, drought conditions—for which there is ample evidence in the dendrochronological records—probably led to the abandonment of those centers. There simply wouldn't have been enough water for a large gathering."

Jim paused, slightly breathless, his enthusiasm for his subject having banished his usual taciturnity.

The visitor shook his head, dismissing this theory as of no consequence in the matter he wanted to discuss.

"That may be true, in part," he said mysteriously, leaning in toward them. "Certainly the part about the drought is undebatable."

"Glad that something is," Jim muttered into his sandwich.

Jeff hid a grin in a swallow of soda.

The visitor continued on:

"I know, I *know*," he repeated, as if emphasis could substitute for fact, "that at least some of the Anasazi vanished through time, transported by aliens who had need of them."

Jim and Jeff traded glances that said as clearly as words, "Well, this fellow beats King William as our most memorable visitor."

"Need?" Jim said a bit faintly, picking one point out of a string of improbables.

"That's right," the visitor replied matter-of-factly. "The aliens were related to the Grays who crashed near Roswell in 1949. Indeed, those Grays were what you might call advance scouts for the time travel element. As you certainly understand, time travel is a difficult business."

Jim and Jeff said nothing, though Jeff glanced at his watch. Lunch break still had twenty minutes to run. Now firmly up on his hobby horse, the visitor rushed on without waiting for a response.

"However, the Roswell incident is only peripheral to what happened to the Anasazi. When drought threatened the extinction of a large portion of an intelligent and creative people, the Grays—as I will continue to call the aliens, though you of course understand that this is just shorthand . . ."

He stared at the two archaeologists until Jeff managed a polite, "Of course."

"The Grays," the visitor went on, "decided that this provided them with a solution for a labor difficulty. They offered sanctuary to a portion of the Anasazi and that offer was taken up.

"They didn't," the visitor continued as if one of his auditors had offered an objection, "restrict such offers only to the Anasazi, of course. Traces of the alien presence can be found worldwide. Cave paintings showing figures with elongated bodies and oversized heads. Haloed figures—clearly meant to be depictions of spacesuits or force-shields. Repeated spiral motifs indicative of journeys, and, most tellingly perhaps, the Hopi 'Man in the Maze' are all evidence that the aliens and their time travel techniques were widely known."

Jim couldn't resist.

"Time?" he asked. "Not space?"

The visitor snorted so vigorously that several locks of his weedy gray hair fluttered around his face.

"Time, not space!" he repeated indignantly. "Sir! Surely even you are aware of the common principle in physics that time and space are merely aspects of the same thing! It's all in how you look at it. We perceive our journey through space in a limited fashion, usually when we voluntarily perform some act of locomotion."

He waggled a finger like an indignant grammar school teacher.

"However, even when we perceive ourselves as unmoving—for example at this moment when we sit here on these remarkably uncomfortable buckets—we are moving through space, carried by the motion of the planet on whose surface we dwell. The planet itself is not limited in its motion to its orbit around the sun. The sun itself moves as part of the complex orbit of the galaxy around its center, and the galaxy moves about the heart of the universe!"

His voice had risen from its conspiratorial murmur to resemble an evangelist enthralling the congregation. Jeff tried to break into his narration.

"You're making me dizzy," he said with a laugh, "and speaking of time . . ."

The visitor gave no sign that he had heard other than dropping back into a near whisper.

"And motion through time is no more complicated than motion through space. Decades ago modern physicists deduced the role of gravity and relative motion in effecting the passage of time. Practical experiments involving clocks and jet airplanes confirmed what the formulas had predicted. Time is not an absolute. Time will pass differently in a moving vehicle than in a stationary—that is perceptually stationary—object. Time even passes differently at the top of a high building than at its base."

He grinned with what he clearly thought was wry humor.

"If only those youth-worshiping socialites thought, they'd realize that living in a penthouse is the worst thing they could do. There isn't a *fountain* of youth. If anything, youth would be found a cellar—for time passes more slowly in the basements of the world than in its elevated penthouses."

Jim and Jeff stared at each other, aghast, wondering how to respond—and how to get rid of this madman. Susie's voice, calling out from where the crew had been gathered by the trucks, gave welcome interruption.

"Break's over, guys. And if you're done with your tour, Sonja and I have some questions about what we've come up against."

Jim rose stiffly and picked up the small cooler in which he carried his lunch.

"Excuse us, sir," he said to the visitor, "but no matter what physics says about time, ours is up."

The visitor also rose, his expression peevish.

"But I haven't finished telling you about the Anasazi. It's very important. I've taken considerable risk . . ."

Jim gave an apologetic smile and nod, then strode off to where Susie waited. Jeff paused.

"I'm sure it's important," he said, able to summon his usual courtesy because he knew Jim was going to call him over any moment, "but the fact is our job isn't to worry about the present location of the Anasazi, it is to deal with their past."

The visitor frowned, then brightened.

"I understand," he began, "If I . . ."

Jim's bellow, slightly faked to ears that knew it, interrupted.

"Jeffrey! If you could come over here, Susie has something I can't figure out. Looks like a frog . . ."

Jeff swallowed a laugh and turned to reply.

"Coming, Jimmy. Be right there."

He turned back to the visitor, but the weedy little man was gone. Jeff shrugged and hurried over to where the onyx frog had indeed made a reappearance.

Later that afternoon, he dismissed a passing thought that not only hadn't he seen the visitor leave, he hadn't heard a car drive off either.

After the visitor departed, things went on with only two remarkable changes. One was that the practical jokes progressed to involve complex relocations of Jim's favorite trowel—a five-inch Marshalltown whose steel blade had been worn down to a mere three and a half inches by constant, loving use. These jokes often incorporated the entire crew coordinating with the speed and accuracy of a professional ballet so that the trowel crossed the site to its new hiding place in a matter of minutes. It got so Jim stopped looking for the trowel at all, trusting it would turn up when and where he least expected.

The second change was a certain thoughtful silence on Jeff's part. He'd always been the talkative one, the one who could be counted on for the joke or anecdote that would lighten a dull afternoon. Now he fell into long, inexplicable silences. When Jim asked him if anything was wrong, Jeff just shook his head and grinned.

"Been thinking about time travel and the Anasazi," he said with a grin. "The Man in the Maze, Gray Aliens, wormholes, string theory, and all of that."

Jim started to laugh, then frowned.

"You have, haven't you?" he said. "That fellow didn't mention string theory or wormholes."

"Must have heard about them on television," Jeff said in a dismissive tone. Then he paused, "Wouldn't it be something, Jimmy, if there was a science to time travel? Think of what we could learn if we could go back through time. No more guessing whether that rock was a ritual object or an ax—or both. So many questions could be answered."

Jim nodded.

"It might be nice," he admitted. "Of course, we'd be unemployed."

Jeff grinned. "Would we be? Seems to me there might be a whole new type of work for archaeologists as tour guides to the past."

Jim might have forgotten the conversation entirely except that a few days later, Verne, another of the crew's Taos residents, mentioned having seen Jeff in a local restaurant deep in conversation with a man who looked remarkably like the one who'd been at the site.

"They didn't see me," Verne said. "They were kind of leaning over the center of the table and the weird little guy was drawing pictures all over a sheet of paper. Lots of lines and stuff, with arrows at the tips, and spirals. Jeff was nodding, and the guy was talking up a storm. I was going over to say hi, but when I saw who Jeff was with, I cut out."

Jim was still trying to figure out if he had any business asking Jeff about this—Verne could have been wrong after all, and it would be rather embarrassing to discover that Jeff had been planning something with the head of his church and that all Verne had seen was electrical diagrams or something—when the onyx frog made its final appearance.

It hadn't been the best of weeks for Jim. First of all, his trowel was missing again, and this time it showed no signs of reappearing.

Then, early Monday morning he'd found a body buried beneath the floor of the pit house he'd been excavating. Jim didn't really like bodies—not for themselves, but because of the fuss they caused. There were special reports to file, visits from the police who had to confirm—though in this case such confirmation was pretty routine, given that the body had been under about eight feet of dirt and covered by a layer of baked adobe—that the body wasn't a modern murder victim. And then, of course, there was the slow process of the excavation itself.

Jim had found the lower part of the body first. Further digging showed that it had been buried in a flexed position— knees drawn up toward chest. That was good evidence that this was a deliberate, ritual burial, perhaps of an important person, maybe just of someone who'd dropped dead during construction.

As he dug, Jim discussed the possibilities with Susie, who, as an osteologist, was assisting. Everyone offered their theories, of course—all but Jeff who was strangely uncommunicative. He was clearly interested, though, dropping by several times every day to take photographs of everything—even the floor while it was still mostly intact over the body.

Because of the possibility that grave goods would have been buried with the body, Jim and Susie worked carefully around the edges first. One of Jim's self-depreciating jokes was that the only time he'd found an intact pot it had been with a shovel, and he was determined that the same thing wasn't going to happen this time. Often grave goods were buried near the body's hands, cradled, as it were, in the curve of the flexed body.

They saved that section for last, a sense of muted excitement infecting the entire crew. It had already been a promising burial. Susie had removed an entire heishi bead earring from near the skull. A few turquoise beads scattered in the dirt suggested that the corpse had been someone either wealthy or very respected—and the two were not usually thought of as separate in prehistoric cultures.

Jeff kept coming over, camera in hand, nearly every hour on the hour. Susie teased that if she'd known how many pictures he was going to take, she would have had her hair done. Jeff smiled, but there was something odd about his bearing, a sense of alertness and anticipation bordering on agitation.

Shortly after lunch break, the dental pick Jim was using tapped against something hard and seemingly metallic. The sensation sent warning signals to his trained sense of touch—that something here was not precisely unfamiliar, but most certainly unexpected.

"Found your pot?" Susie said, looking up at the cessation of his steady movement.

"Found something," Jim replied tersely. He reached for a brush. Contrary to popular opinion, lots of archeology is done with shovels and even backhoes. Still, there remain times when only delicate brush work will do.

By the wordless communication common in groups of people who have worked together for a long while, news spread that Jim had found something new. Crew members recalled that they were permitted a break every hour and drifted over. Jim didn't seem to notice, not even when Jeff's camera clicked and flashed nearby.

There was quite an audience when Jim uttered a single, expressive explicative.

"Shit!"

He moved more rapidly now, the brush pushing away dirt in impatient little motions. Something glinted metallically. Light glinted off a polished surface.

Jim bellowed again.

"Jeffrey!"

He rocked back on his heels, staring down, exposing his discovery to the equally astonished gaze of his crew.

"Jeffrey!"

Jeff, who had descended into the pit house as soon as the rumors started to spread, hunkered down, disregarding his bad knee.

"Right here, Jimmy."

Jim glared at him, pointed down with the tip of his dental pick.

"How the hell did my trowel and that damned frog get in here?"

Jeff looked down. There, still coated with traces of adobe so hard that it looked as if it had been baked over it, were Jim's beloved three-and-a-half-inch Marshalltown trowel and the now ubiquitous onyx frog.

Jeff looked at Jim.

"I put them there, Jimmy."

Mutters of surprise and astonishment, followed by a few loud, nervous laughs greeted this announcement. Jim didn't laugh, though, and seeing the fierce expression on his face the crew members simultaneously recalled that breaks didn't last forever. Susie made herself scarce.

When the two co-directors were alone down in the pit house, Jim looked his friend squarely in the eyes.

"There's no way you could have put them there—not like you did, say, the license plate. There's no way. The body wasn't buried that deeply. I didn't break the floor over that section until this morning. You want to tell me something?"

Jeff took a deep breath and flipped over a bucket for a chair. More slowly, Jim also took a seat.

"I did put them there, Jimmy," Jeff began. "Remember that little man who was out here a couple weeks back?"

"How could I forget him? Mr. Time and Space are the same thing."

"He came to see me a day or so later, came by my house," Jeff continued. "He said that something I'd said about our job not being where the Anasazi went, but who they were had given him an idea how to get through my stubbornness. I'm going to cut a long story short . . ."

Jim forced a smile. "That'll be a first."

"Really, you don't want to hear about all the stuff he told me. He repeated himself a lot—went into long harangues. Still, he started to convince me. I think what did it was when he asked me how, if I was really a scientist and really interested in learning about the past, then how could I turn down a tool like this?

"That question really bothered me. After all, if the only

thing that was keeping us from a major breakthrough was fear of seeming stupid, well, then I wasn't the scientist I wanted to be. I let him convince me to give it a try. He said he could take me back in time to when these pit houses were being constructed and asked me to pick one in particular. I chose yours because I haven't had anything to do with the excavation."

Jim nodded. "Controlled experiment."

"That's right. He took me back. I'm not going to go into how except that it had something to do with a device that's planted out in space near Jupiter where the planet's mass masks the distortion of the space/time continuum."

Jeff looked at him as if waiting for laughter, for scorn. Jim looked his friend squarely the eyes, then down at his battered old trowel and the onyx frog half-buried in the adobe.

"Go on, Jeffrey."

"We went. We came out here. He had some type of disguise. I didn't understand it. Tell the truth, I didn't even try."

Jeff shook his head in wonder.

"It was amazing. This bluff was here, but stripped like a new construction site. The air was amazingly clear and smelled mostly of dust and juniper sap from the peeled posts and the bark, and of wood smoke, too, and sweat . . . There were dogs running around with naked kids—it was spring, I think, just like now.

"A bunch of men were taking a look around the finished pit house—no roof, yet, just the pit. They were pretty pleased with themselves, like you'd expect given all the work they'd done. Then a wailing started off in the distance, down by the creek at the base of the bluff . . ."

Jim frowned. "There's no creek."

"There was then," Jeff insisted. "One of the reasons they built here, I think."

"Right. We can check that, soil samples, maybe coring," Jim stopped himself. "Sorry."

Jeff grinned.

"Hey, I thought you were going to be hauling me off as crazy. You can talk all you want."

"No. Go on. The crew's going to get curious pretty soon."

Jeff nodded.

"The wailing was a burial party—that fellow right there by our feet. He was an important old guy, forties maybe from the look of him. He'd died during the construction and his family wanted him buried close to home.

"They set him in a place prepared below the level of the floor. Everyone gave him gifts—mostly flowers, but you'll find a pot right below the trowel, nice Santa Fe black on white."

"Thanks."

"My guide took me down as part of the general procession. Nobody paid us much mind. I'd brought the frog and the trowel—had them in my coat pockets. I'd planned all along on planting something and I wanted something that the whole crew would know and that wouldn't deteriorate over time. Without letting my guide know—I hadn't asked permission you see—I slipped them down there. The flowers hid them, and I figured the old guy wouldn't mind a few more gifts."

"Sure, that trowel might come in handy in the supernatural realms," Jim replied. "I sure find it handy in the here and now."

"And then I came back. I've been sweating all week while you've dug, waiting for you to get there. Man, it seemed like you were working around the stuff on purpose! Anyhow, now I have pictures of the whole process, from solid floor through today. Proof that time travel is possible."

Jim studied him, thought of what that kind of proof would mean to the world—and what it would mean to their immediate lives.

"People are going to think us as loony as we did that visitor," he said at last. "Are you sure you want to come out with this? We can cover it up—not the body, what you did—I can tell people you salted the burial last night, that I had thought the adobe seemed more broken than it should. Only Susie's going to really be sure it wasn't and she wasn't actually digging that part. We can convince her. We've got a reputation for elaborate practical jokes."

"My best one ever," Jeff agreed. "Yeah, it would work. But do we want to cover it up? Time travel is real, as real as your trowel and that darned frog."

Jim frowned. "Did you ever find out what that fellow is after?"

"Coyote." Jeff grinned. "That's what he told me to call him, though he made it clear it's an alias. Coyote told me that he wants to shake things up. He thinks that current science is moving too slowly to avert disaster. He figures that meddling is the way to avoid some unnamed but terrible destruction. He's a maverick, working on his own. That's why he was so edgy and cranky."

"Why'd he pick us?" Jim asked. "Why not a president or something?"

"Ever tried to get an appointment with the president?" Jeff replied. "Anyhow, he said he'd read our book—the one on migration patterns through the Rio Grande Valley. Thought we'd be interested, tantalized."

Jim shook his head. "We haven't written that book."

"Yet."

"Shit!"

"Yeah. That's kind of how I felt."

Jim rose slowly to his feet.

"Where're you going, Jimmy?"

Jim ran a hand through his beard.

"Call the crew. We've got a lot to tell them. I figure if we can't convince them, then this Coyote has more work to do. Maybe I'll make him take me to the building of the pyramids at Giza."

Jeff grinned and, pulling off his cowboy hat, wiped his forehead against his sleeve.

"You're with me, then? Great! I've been sweating this." He sighed. "Maybe I'll sleep tonight."

Climbing the ladder from the pit house, Jim hollered over the edge for the crew to join them. Then, looking down at Jeff, he said, "Sure I'm with you, but there's one thing I wish you hadn't done."

"Oh?"

"I wish you hadn't used my trowel. It was my favorite, and somehow," Jim shook his head thoughtfully, "somehow I think it's just become an artifact and I'm not going to get it back."

IN THE COMPANY OF HEROES
by Diane Duane

Diane Duane has now been writing professionally for twenty years. Besides creating her own universes, such as the Young Wizards and Middle Kingdoms worlds, she has also worked extensively in other creators' territories—counting among these her forays into animation (everything from *Scooby-Doo* to *Gargoyles*), comics (*Batman* in animation, and *Spider-Man* in prose), and, of course, *Star Trek*, in comics, novels, and on the screen. She lives with her husband Peter Morwood in a quiet corner of County Wicklow in Ireland, pursuing galactic domination in a leisurely way, with the assistance of three cats, four computers, and six hundred or so cookbooks.

Robert Willingden was rich, famous, and powerful. But the riches were the wrong kind, the fame bothered him, and the power wasn't the sort he wanted. The power he did want, he'd lost when he was ten, when his childhood had been stolen. *And now,* he thought, *at last, at last, I'm going to get both of them back.*

He'd had been holding onto that thought with all his might since he got the e-mail a week ago, the one which, after the headers, had contained only one word: "Ready." Since then, his staff at corporate HQ had been wondering what was the matter with him—though none of them would have dared say as much to his face, not even his personal assistant Chei Hou.

He smiled at the thought of what Chei must be doing right now. Probably she was maintaining her usual outer appearance of stereotypical serenity, while underneath cajoling, threatening, or blackmailing everyone within range to find out how he'd managed to disappear. Doubtless, she was finding it more difficult than she'd expected. But Rob had always suspected that there might eventually come a time when, for reasons of business or pleasure, he would need to get away completely undetected. For that purpose, years back, he'd spent some months assembling the set of documents that until the night before last had lived untroubled in his office safe.

Lawyer Ron had helped him with this part. Lawyer Ron was a Southern-born American attorney now based in Liechtenstein, that ultimate haven for private dealings in this increasingly disclosure-friendly world. Ron's business and the Web site which reflected it were ostensibly to do with specialist investment banking, which was how he and Rob had originally met, in the days when CortCorp was still a relatively small and hungry wireless-technologies firm, with only a thousand employees scattered across high-tech havens in California, Indonesia, and Ireland. But once you had proceeded to a position of trust with Lawyer Ron— meaning that he knew where a few of *your* skeletons were hidden—then that soft drawl over the phone might tell you about various special services which Lawyer Ron did not advertise on his Web site. Some of his investors were eager to establish residencies or identities in countries other than their present ones. Some of his clients he helped in this way, some he left to their own devices—for Ron was a surprisingly ethical man for someone through whose hands so much money passed, and he had no truck with crooks trying to ditch the law, or dictators trying to flee their fleeced countries with billions that belonged to someone else. Once he was certain of your reasons, Ron could help you . . . for a price, and always with the utmost discretion.

That was how Rob came to have the set of "extra" passports—Ron would have frowned at the term "forged." "I always obtain my materials at source," he'd said to Rob over the phone long ago, in the offended tone of an artist whose integrity had been called into question. The passports bore Rob's face, but someone else's name, and they referred to an involved backstory which Rob had been required to memorize—a whole invented history of parents, places, jobs held, a whole false life completely supported by documentation planted in a hundred places. Rob had paid high for this at the time—or had thought he had. By his present standards, the price was now peanuts, and worth every penny, at the moment when he most desperately needed to go somewhere and not be noticed.

Normally he could have gone quite openly. Normally the excuse would have been, "I'm going to visit my money." It would have been true. Since the GSM-using countries had started hardwiring Rob's "Henchman" data exchange protocol into every cell phone they manufactured, Cort-Corp had grown to twenty times the size it had been ten years ago, and had millions of francs' worth of sheltered investments in Switzerland and Liechtenstein. Rob dropped in fairly frequently to see his European regional managers, to make sure that things were running smoothly. But this trip, the unavoidable public ruckus that attended his arrival anywhere would have made it impossible to do what he was going there for.

So, this trip, he'd laid a false trail. He'd sent his second-string Learjet and his executive staff to Eleuthera, telling them that he wanted to take a week off in the sun, but he had a few last-minute things to tidy up before he left. The first-string jet, the Longhorn Lear, he had ordered unhangared and out to its "ready" stand on the civil-aeronautics side of Sea-Tac. And there it would sit for a good while yet, because Rob had called a cab to meet him several blocks from HQ, slipped out of the building through one of the two blind spots he had designed into his own security, caught first the cab and then a train to San Francisco, and at nine the next evening was on a Swissair flight to Zürich.

To keep his cover as complete as possible, he'd flown coach . . . not that it was such a hardship, just this once. It was almost a treat, in some ways. Instead of being surrounded by the kind of people who usually hemmed him round—employees with important papers for him to sign, or nonemployees who desperately wanted his attention and support for one project or another—now his world was bounded by seats full of businessmen who carried their own briefcases, and vacationers in sweats, and mothers with fidgeting children. When the flight attendants dimmed the lights about fifteen minutes after takeoff, Rob relaxed almost completely. No one had recognized him so far, since the back of economy class was not a place that most people would expect Robert Willingden to be. In the darkness, with his seat light turned off, a blanket tucked up around him, and an eyeshade on, no one was now going to recognize him at all. He was a little nervous about how his documents would be treated at Zürich . . . but there was no point in worrying about that now. He put the thought aside.

Besides, he had been sent a good omen. When Rob came back from using the lavatory before he settled in, walking slowly behind the drinks cart that the flight attendants were trundling up the aisle, in the seat directly behind him, spotlit by his seat light against the darkness, he saw a small blond boy. Other kids in the plane might be squirming and screeching and trying to scheme their way out of their seat belts, but this one was completely oblivious to being strapped in. He was buried deep in the first of a pile of about twenty comic books.

Rob smiled as he settled back into his seat and pulled the blanket up around him. As he started to put his eyeshades on, though, he stiffened in shock for just a second. Past him, in the wake of the flight attendants, lit just faintly by the blue-green light of the little LED movie screens hanging down every three rows, a shadowy figure went softly by, carrying what looked like a box.

Rob blinked, and then saw the shape better in the light coming from between the curtains that separated the first-class galley from the rest of the plane. A male flight attendant had passed him, carrying a couple of small flats of soft-drink cans, stacked one on top of the other. *Not a thief. Not something stolen . . . something of mine.*

Nonetheless, Rob swallowed, nervous. Now the omens had fallen both ways. There was no telling what might happen.

Rob put his eyeshade on and did his best to sleep.

All this had begun when his favorite clock got broken—the nineteenth-century Thomas crystal regulator mantelpiece clock that he wouldn't trust even his personal staff with. Rob had been going to Zürich anyway, to visit Trudi, his trusts-and-portfolio manager at Bank Julius Baer. It had suddenly occurred to Rob while he was packing that if there was anything you should be able to do in Switzerland,

it was get a broken clock fixed. He had Chei make a few
calls, and when he had the name of what was supposed to
be the best clock repair place in the city—"Zeit Zone Zürich" it was called—Rob had padded and boxed up the
Thomas himself, and strapped it himself into the other
lounge seat in the main cabin of the number-one Lear.
Once Rob was finished with his business in the cold, lovely
Beaux-Arts building on Paradeplatz, the limo took him
about fifteen minutes' drive out into the suburbs, to a ten-
foot-wide shopfront at the end of a line of stores that
seemed about as close as the Swiss could get to a strip mall.
Considering the place's reputation, Rod had been expecting
something ornate, in an eighteenth-century housing, like one
of the high-powered watch and jewelry stores on Bahnhof-
strasse. Here, though, was a mirrored plate glass window, and
beside it, a couple of steps up to an aluminum-and-glass
door: nothing more.

Rob had pushed the door open, stepped in, glanced
around, and found that there was nowhere in particular to
go. He was hemmed in by a waist-height table directly in
front of him, and a chest-height counter directly to the right
of him. Behind the counter a worktable was butted up
against the front window and the light gray side wall. On
a high stool behind the workbench sat a young blond guy
with a jeweler's loupe in his eye, carving delicately with a
scalpel at some tiny piece of metal held in vise-forceps
under a magnifying lamp. Sitting in front of the other,
lower table-counter was an ancient lady in equally ancient
furs, and she and a shop assistant in jeans and a T-shirt
were examining a watch of such chaste and severe plainness
that Rob thought it was probably more expensive than any
mere Rolex, with or without a few carats' worth of
diamonds.

No one had given him more than a glance when he came
in. It was as if they were completely used to giant bullet-
proof Mercedes limos pulling up outside and emitting the
presidents of multinational corporations. Maybe they were.
But at this point in his life, Ron wasn't used to this kind
of treatment. His face was just too well known. All the
same, he wasn't going to make a big thing of it. He stood
there quietly, waiting.

At last the guy who had been working at the bench on

that microscopic piece of metal paused in his work and stood up, turning to Rob. *"Kann Ich hilfen Sie?"*

Rob's German was not great: it didn't have to be. He had translators for that. For a moment he considered calling his chauffeur in, then put the idea aside. "Uh, *entschuldigen Sie mir bitte, Ich spreche kein Deutsch.* Does anybody here speak English?"

The man behind the counter and the lady in the furs both looked briefly at Rob as if he'd just arrived from Mars. Then they went back to their conversation about the watch. *"Ein moment, bitte,"* said the man to whom Rob had been speaking, and went through a door in the back wall of the shop, a few feet away.

That was when Uli Siegler came out from the back of the shop. Rob had had an image of the owner of this place as some bewhiskered ancient with wrinkled eyes and careful hands. On first sight, the man in his mid-twenties, in a white polo shirt and faded blue jeans, had come as a surprise. The gray eyes were not wrinkled, but thoughtful, behind little oval spectacles, in a smooth face that looked oddly like that of William Tell on the five-franc coin— sharing the long straight nose and high forehead, but with a buzz cut above it all that might have puzzled Tell. The man's hands were as careful as Rob had expected, though, as he reached out to take the box containing the Thomas from Rob.

"A very beautiful timepiece," he had said without any other preamble, putting the box down on the counter and taking out the clock. "American. Eighteen . . . ninety? Yes. And very sensitive to vibration, I am afraid. Was it bumped or dropped before it stopped working?"

"Uh, yes. Not very hard. Someone fell against it at a party."

Uli made a *tch, tch* sound under his breath as he removed the lead-crystal dome over the Thomas. "Fortunate that the crystal was not broken, since it is original. Mmm, yes, I see. The escape wheel broke a tooth when it fell over. Those were always a weakness in the Thomases built in 1890: he got a bad batch of brass that year, the wheels machined then did not last long. . . . And the entrance pallet, you see this sharp bit here that rocks back and forth to let the escape wheel move?—see how that is bent. Mmm, both must be replaced. Perhaps also the crutch pin: I will test it."

"How long will this take?" Rob said.

"Is the need urgent?" Uli said.

"No, not really."

Uli thought. "One week, then. If you will leave me an address, I can ship it to you."

"Not *this* clock," Rob said, maybe too forcefully.

Uli smiled at that. "I see you are attached to it. This is good. Will you be over here for that long?"

"Until the Monday after next."

"Then here is my card. If you call at the end of a week, I will have the clock ready for you."

Rob left the shop wondering just why it was "good" that he was attached to the Thomas. Well, it had been his grandfather's, the only memento he had of that cranky, kindly, good old man, many years dead now. He was determined to take good care of it.

As the limo had brought him back into town, he caught himself humming a song:

Oh, my grandfather's clock
was too large for the shelf . . .

Rob raised his eyebrows at the old memory. *I guess I should have a bigger shelf made for it if I'm going to leave it out in a public area of the house,* he thought. *And one a little more out of the way. I don't want it to be wrecked. . . . And looking a little more closely into the security for that room might be smart, too. As bad as having the clock get broken would be seeing it get stolen . . .*

. . . like some other things . . .

The memory had dropped down around him as suddenly as night at the equator. Dripping darkness, cold air, the acrid scent of wet, scorched oak: and a shape dodging away hurriedly through the hole the firemen had hacked in the roof the night before. A man, all in dark clothes, carrying away a box . . .

Rob had put the memory forcibly aside as he stepped in the door of his hotel, the Schweizerhof, considering instead where he might go that evening. He caught the slightly annoyed glance of one of his security people at the busy main street outside the hotel, and did his best to hide his grin as he went inside. Most of his staff couldn't understand why their boss disdained the two high-priced hotels by the lake, theoretically much better ones than this. Rob knew, though, that his security people suspected the real reason. While staying at the Baur au Lac or the Dolder Grand, it was impossible for Rob to slip out undetected late at night and do the thing his staff despaired of—go for a good long walk by himself in city streets, without a bodyguard. His chief of security had been going nuts about this kind of thing ever since the attack at the economic forum in Brussels by the Societé des Anarchistes de Tartes, when a protester who didn't like CortCorp's company's investment policies had rushed out of the crowd and hit Rob square in the face with a very passable short-crust pie shell full of chocolate *crème patissiere*. For a few weeks Rob had behaved himself while his staff calmed down . . . but nothing his people could say was going to get Rob to change his habits this late in his life. If his number came up, piped onto a pie or scratched on a bullet, so be it. Meanwhile, late at night in the city streets was still where Rob came up with some of his best ideas; and in that way, after mornings of meetings and afternoons of negotiations, he amused himself for some days.

On his second Saturday morning in the city, Rob woke up to find a message on his hotel room's voice mail: Uli's voice, saying, "I will be done with the clock this afternoon: I will bring it to the hotel at six." Rob's return call to the shop just rang and rang. *Maybe he's working on it at home or something* . . . But then Rob wondered how Uli had known which hotel to call. *Maybe he saw something in the papers.* That was almost certainly it. Rob couldn't go much of anywhere without the press noticing, whether or not he was on company business and attended by the usual complement of press releases.

At six o'clock Uli turned up almost exactly as Rob had seen him the other day, the only difference a dark suede jacket thrown over the polo shirt in a nod to the Schweizerhof's unspoken dress code. He sat down across from Rob in the hotel's pompous, chilly, little first floor caviar-and-champagne bar, and took the lid off the wooden box he had set on the table. From the cotton-wool padding inside it, Uli brought out the Thomas, set it down, lifted the dome, and gave one globe of the downhanging "pawnshop" pendulum a push. The pendulum immediately began to rotate, and the clock, set for six, began to chime.

Rob smiled at it, then looked up again. It was a shock to see Uli looking at him. Somehow, irrationally, he had expected to see his grandfather—had expected to hear him saying, "I want you to have this . . ."

But that had been more than twenty years ago, before Rob's company took off . . . in what now often seemed like a previous life. Rob swallowed. "Can I get you something to drink?"

They sat there talking casually for a long while amid the white marble walls and the polished tables, and every now and then one or another of Rob's dark-suited security staff peered in the door from the lobby and went away, reassured. The conversation went in every possible direction, and Rob couldn't remember much of it. It couldn't have been the fault of the wine: he didn't have that much. He did, though, remember Uli glancing up from his second glass of a Dôle red as blood, and saying, "I have been working with time for a long while. But you know this also: otherwise you would not have come to me."

The phrasing struck Rob as odd . . . and obscurely it frightened him. Many people who thought there was no end to his riches had tried to sell Rob the impossible over the past decade. He had seen more than his share of perpetual motion machines, and had been invited to bankroll several different kinds of attempted cold fusion. Rob thought he'd developed a good early-warning system for the ridiculous, and could get up in the middle of the most formal meetings and vanish when it presented itself. Yet now he sat right where he was while Uli talked. He could never remember afterward just how the conversation got from that point to his realization that Uli claimed to be doing repairs, not merely on clocks, but on time itself.

"Or I assist them in being made," Uli said. "The client merely enables me to enable him to do the work. This is nothing new. There is something you wish to repair."

It was not a question.

Plainly this conversation was going to surpass even Rob's usual definition of odd. A little breath of cold passed over the back of his neck. A draft. *And it's freezing in here, with all this marble.* But he didn't succeed in convincing himself. *Who is this guy?* Rob thought.

But then—and maybe this time it was the wine, a little— he thought, *Why should it matter? My people are within call. And if he tries selling the story to the* National Enquirer *or something, I'll just buy the pub rights from them—*

Rob went ahead and told Uli about the theft, and all the while the fear grew in him that Uli would find it foolish, and laugh. But that gray-eyed gaze rested gravely on him, unsurprised, all the while he told the story; and when Rob ran down at last, Uli merely nodded and said, "I think you must attempt this repair."

Rob could now only try to hide his embarrassment by scoffing. "Oh, yeah, sure. Let's just go back in time and put it all right."

" 'Right' can look many different ways," Uli said, not rising even slightly to the bait. "But all your life since then, it seems, has been a rage against that night, when the thief came and stole from you what you valued most in the world. It is not that much good has not come of your actions since—but the good seems to have come to everyone else but you. You will not, what is the phrase in English, accept delivery on it."

"You're going to tell me I have to 'just let it go,' " Rob said, scathing.

"No. I am going to tell you that you must catch it first," Uli said. "What you do with it after that is your business. But I can put you where you can make the attempt to stop the theft. If you succeed, you can then stop walking the streets of city after city at night, looking for what you desire, and finding everything else instead. Not, as I say, that you have not done good. But it would make more sense to do it on purpose, rather than by accident."

Rob turned his empty wineglass around and around on the round marble table, and said nothing.

"It is irresponsible," Uli said, "to leave things broken when they can be repaired."

That was almost exactly Rob's grandfather's voice: stern, uncompromising. A shiver went down Rob's back. Finally he looked up. "What's this going to cost?" he said.

"A great deal. But not more than you can afford, and

not so much that your company directors will try to have you committed. This is about a repair, not further damage."

Rob sat quiet for a few moments more, while Uli drank what was left of his wine. "Payment first, I suppose," Rob said, trying to hang onto some shred of at least sarcasm, if not control.

"Not at all. Payment afterward, when the repair has been tested."

This sounded completely unlike any scam Rob had ever been involved in. All of those had required up-front investments with lots of zeroes before the decimal point. And it was very hard to look at those gray eyes and find even the shadow of deceit in them.

"What if it doesn't take?"

Uli didn't say a word. But the look he gave Rob said, *Coward! Stop stalling!*

Rob wanted to call for another glass of wine, and temporize . . . but the challenge in those eyes was hard to bear. Ever since his company really took off, he had been lauded everywhere as a risk-taker, a daring man. He had always known this was less true than it sounded. Now here was someone who was waiting for Rob to prove the lie.

". . . So what do I do?" Rob said.

Uli straightened up, his expression going more neutral. "Wait," he said. "The preparation takes some time. I will e-mail you. You should give me an address that is private to you, that others won't see."

Rob reached into his pocket, pulled out a business card, felt inside his jacket for a pen, and on the back of the card scribbled down one of the five most wanted private e-mail addresses in the world. Uli took the card, read the back of it, slipped it into his wallet and got up. "I will bill you for the clock," he said, "after you have taken it home and had a chance to let it run a while in place. I think, though, that you should move it to a place of more safety: somewhere your ex-wife cannot bump into it 'by mistake.'"

While Rob was still trying to think what to say to that, Uli reached down to the clock, adjusted its minute hand two minutes further along, and replaced the crystal dome over it, while the pendulum serenely spun on its axis. "Good night," he said, and went out the door that led onto the street.

Rob sat there looking at the clock until it chimed six-thirty.

How did he know?

Shortly he glanced up and saw the waiter standing near him, curious, watching the golden gleam of the pendulum under the bright lights. Rob ordered another glass of the Fendant, and drank it slowly. Then he put the clock back in its box, took it upstairs to his suite, and the next morning, went home to wait.

And now the waiting was over. After fourteen hours of intermittent sleep and nervousness, Rob took off the eye-shades, made one more visit to the lavatory to put himself in order, and got off the plane, walking down what seemed endlessly long plate glass-walled corridors, all full of a slanting golden afternoon, to Swiss passport control. "Business or pleasure?" said the uniformed man in the glass booth as Rob handed him his passport.

"Pleasure," Rob said, as the control officer peered at the picture. "I'm going to Luzern."

The control officer gave Rob a weary *aren't-you-all?* look, stamped the passport, and handed it back. "Enjoy your stay."

And that was all. *Thank you, Lawyer Ron,* Rob thought, and went to reclaim his baggage. Ten minutes later he was on a train from the airport's underground train station to the center of the city. Fifteen minutes later he stepped out under the echoing, overarching roof of the Hauptbahnhof.

Rob paused only briefly there, stopping outside the station's main newsstand to study the tabloid-headline easels that stood outside it, while diners next door at the "sidewalk café" tables gazed at him incuriously and without recognition. The newspaper *Blick* would certainly have plastered the disappearance of the world's tenth richest man all over its front page, but at present its Helvetica-Bold headlines were only shouting about some crooked financier in a money-laundering scandal. *So nothing's made it to the media yet,* Rob thought. That would have been Chei's doing. It would have offended her sense of order to have the world find out that he'd vanished before the company could find some way to cover for his disappearance. Naturally she was sensitive to what such news could do to the company's stock price; her own several hundred thousand shares made certain of that.

Satisfied, Rob went to the bank of phones over by the escalators that led down to the locker level and the shopping center below that. He found a one-franc piece, deposited it, and dialed the number that by now he knew by heart.

"Hallo?"

"I'm here," Rob said.

"Good. Go get some sleep. Come and meet me tomorrow at six. You have the directions?"

"Yes."

"Good. Tomorrow, then." And Uli hung up.

Rob went out to the tram plaza next to the station, found the Number Four tram, and rode it for about a mile to where the River Limmat has only one more bridge to pass under before it pours itself all swan-laden into the lake. There he made his way up a narrow cobbled alley to one of the little hotels that serves the Old Town, checked in, showered, and lay down on the bed, just for a little while, to stretch the kinks out of his muscles. . . .

Their house had been one of the oldest ones in town, built in the late eighteen hundreds and then added to again and again, over the following decades and generations, until it went straggling off in five different directions. The core of it had been a solid, stone-built edifice of two storeys, with the shop and back kitchen downstairs and the bedrooms upstairs. As the business had grown, the shop had been enlarged out toward the back, an extension had been built out to one side, a huge storage shed erected down at the bottom of the garden: and these were added to in their turn. By 1920, Willingden Feed and Grain was the biggest grocery operation in the small city that had grown up around it. By 1960, it was beginning to head toward decline, threatened by the supermarkets going up elsewhere in the county. But there was still a lot to do in the shop, and as soon as he got old enough, Robby had been given various jobs to do—cleaning the meat slicer, polishing the tremendous brass cash register, sweeping up in the shop, bringing up slabs of the home-cured bacon from the cold cellar. For these services he was given two dollars a week, on Friday afternoon, when the rest of the staff got paid. And when the staff went home with their pay packets, Robby ran straight down the street to Mr. Garibaldi's newsstand and bought comics.

Comics were genuinely the only thing that he and his parents disagreed about. In every other way, Robby's parents gave him nearly everything a child could want. But to them, fantasy was suspect. Dreams were something pleasant but useless that you did while you were asleep, and the characters in the comics were to them emphatically "just made-up silliness."

Of course Robby knew the comic-book heroes were made up, dreams of a special kind. He wasn't stupid. But they were the only dreams he had in color, and he treasured them. The bold terrible fire of explosions, the brilliant costumes like bright flags cracking across an otherwise gray sky—the flash of the silver underlining to Captain Thunder's cape, as he rode the lightning crackling around him to destroy Emperor Fulgor's evil plans one more time; his courtesy and tenderness to the beautiful Minna Whelan, who loved him but could never be trusted with the secret of his identity, or with his love, because the terrible Gift of the jealous Lightning God might destroy her—to Robby, all these things somehow made life seem worth living. It seemed to him that everything worthwhile about people— courage, certainty, truth, knowledge, honor, the right use of power—was to be found in the comics. The newspaper, that banner of reality, seemed to have nothing but bad news in it, robbery, accidents, court cases, death. Life was desperately dull in Robby's little town, and he was only ten years old, and would be stuck there for a long time yet before he could go hunting truth and honor on his own terms. For the time being, right now, he needed heroes . . .

. . . and then they were taken from him.

Robby's mother called Robby's comics a waste of money, and actually discussed with his father whether they should stop giving him an allowance at all, if he was going to spend it on "that junk, it's going to rot his mind, he won't be able to tell the difference between reality and fantasy . . ." Robby already knew the difference all too well: reality was overhearing conversations like that one, and peering around the corner of the dining room door to see his father, his back turned, nodding slowly. Robby took the hint and "vanished" his complete collection of *Captain Thunder* up to a box up in the attic, carefully lined with a cut-up garbage bag to keep out any moisture from possible leaks, with the comics all lined up inside it, in order, each in perfect condition in its own glassine bag. He already knew what every kid eventually discovers—that adults have so much on their minds that if you stop showing them one specific thing that bothers them, the odds are good that they'll forget all about it in a matter of days. His mother, also, had given him the hint he needed after he got a bad mark on a math test. "This wouldn't happen if you weren't spending all your time on those trashy comics; don't let me catch you reading them any more, or I'll burn them!" Robby immediately made sure she would be unable to catch him reading them, by no longer doing so anywhere except in bed, under the covers, after he knew his mother was asleep—he would set his alarm on its softest setting and wake up at three a.m. There he would read, again and again, the single comic he brought down from the attic box once a week when his mom and dad were both busy downstairs in the shop, and afterward hid in the floor space under a loose board beneath his bed. To cover himself, Robby made sure the last thing his mother saw at night was him reading a math textbook, and whenever she chanced to notice how tired he looked in the morning, she would say approvingly to his father, "Look how hard your son has been studying . . . !"

And then, just as things seemed to be settling down, the attic caught fire.

Or part of it did. It had started as a chimney fire, started by something truly idiotic: his father throwing a pizza carton onto the dining-room fireplace. It burned too hot in a chimney that hadn't been swept in a long time, and set the built-up soot on fire. By the time the fire department got there, the chimney fire had actually gone out . . . but the heat of the scorching brick had set alight the old dried-out roof joists nearby, and the roof over the extension of the house was already burning merrily, the tar under the shingles melting and dripping down from the roof. To put the fire out before it got at the rest of the house, the firemen had to chop a hole in the main attic roof and go into the side attic that way. Everything in the extension, from roof to cellar, was drenched. The whole neighborhood was standing around, wondering at the damage, by the time the firemen left.

The main part of the house was undamaged. But now Robby found himself staring at his bedroom ceiling in the darkness. He'd lain awake for a long time, thinking about how lucky he was that the comics hadn't been hurt. But they were still up there. At least it wasn't going to rain tonight. He'd thought of moving them, but that would have made his mother start asking him questions—and in the present atmosphere of soot, dripping water, and frayed tempers, Robby hadn't wanted to start anything he'd regret later.

The trouble was . . . he heard something. Now he realized what had awakened him. There was someone up there.

It came to him instantly what was happening, and Robby slipped out of bed, threw on a bathrobe, opened his door silently, and went down the hall to the attic stairs. The whole town had been out there, today. Someone had seen the hole in the roof. Someone had sneaked over the back gate into the service yard and found the ladder, where it always stood by the feed shed, and right now someone was upstairs, going through their attic, seeing what he could steal. . . .

Robby crept up the stairs, avoided the one that creaked, opened the attic door, closed it behind him, and stood still, letting his eyes get used to the dark. Starlight and a blue-green light reflected from the sodium-vapor streetlights out behind the back gate showed him a silhouetted form: a man, moving, a man with a box in his hands. Robby's comics box . . .

"What are you doing?" Robby whispered, furious. "Put it down!"

The man froze just for a second, looked at him, his expression impossible to read in the dark. Then he was gone, down the ladder.

Robby rushed to the hole, yelled after him, "Stop! Thief! Mom, Dad, there's somebody up here, there's a thief!" But by the time the house was roused, it was too late. The man had vanished into the darkness. "What did he take?" Robby's father had asked, and when Robby wailed, "My comics!" his mother had said, "Is that all? What a relief that's all he had time for. But why would anyone do that? It's not like they're worth anything."

"A collector," Robby said, already beginning to drown in grief. "*Captain Thunder* Number One is worth fifty dollars now."

His mother looked over at the burned, dripping roof joists. "Oh, don't be silly. There are much more valuable things up here."

"It's downstairs he had his eye on, more likely," Robby's father said. "Probably he was going to try to get down into the shop from the inside, and break into the cash register or the safe. Instead, when you startled him, he just grabbed the first thing he could lay hands on and ran off." He gripped Robby's shoulder. "Good job, son. We'll get that roof fixed first thing in the morning."

They went back to their beds, and sent Robby back to his own. But there was no more sleep for him that night, and no more joy, ever. They were blind to the dreams that had been in the box, blind to the joy that those dreams had brought him . . . and now the dreams were gone.

For a week's worth of mourning he tried to tell his mom or his dad how he was hurting . . . but they couldn't understand. *You'll get over it, you'll feel better in a while, it's nothing important* . . . was all he heard. After a while, when Robby bought new comics and found they didn't make him happy any more, because he was afraid they, too, might get stolen, he started to wonder if his folks were right. Eventually, a few months later, with a final sob of the soul, he gave up, and walled the pain away in the back of his mind, along with the old joy he had felt in the company of heroes. There his childhood ended. Rob turned all his attention to the kind of dreaming that seemed to please his dad and mom—the kind that showed him how to build practical, useful things. Over time he and his work became very useful indeed, to millions of people. His dad had died very well pleased with him. So had his grandfather, who had given him the clock. *You were always good at taking care of things,* the old man had said a few weeks before he died. *You'll take care of this*—Robby hadn't contradicted him, briefly remembering the one thing that had really mattered to him, the thing he hadn't been able to protect. Now, though, he stood again in the attic, looking at the place in the shadows where the box had been, a long time ago, and he thought: *If I can just beat the thief there . . .*

. . . I can save the box.

Uli was there, too, looking at him, gray-eyed, business-like, but with that hint of edge about the eyes like steel, sharpened. He said, *But you know this also: otherwise you would not have come to me again.*

This is a repair I think you must make.

It is irresponsible to leave something broken when it can be fixed—

Rob woke up with a sudden terrible shock, one of those falling-out-of-bed sensations that leaves you with your heart racing as you stare at the ceiling. Diffuse, warm sunlight lit the white-walled hotel room and glanced off the Miro print over the head of the bed: afternoon light. *I dozed off for a few moments,* he thought. But when he looked at his watch, he saw that the calendar had clicked over one. It was tomorrow.

—and I'm going to be late if I don't get going!

He showered and dressed and caught the Number Four tram back up to the Hauptbahnhof, pausing only long enough to look at the easels in front of the newsstand again. Today the headlines were shouting about the licensing of a new brothel in the city, but there was nothing about the disappearance of Robert Willingden. Rob grinned and went out into the April morning again, back to the tram stand, where he caught the Number Twelve tram to the suburbs.

About twenty minutes later, the tram slid humming to a stop in front of the neighborhood's post office. Rob got out and walked east to the curve in the road, bore right around it past the Co-op grocery store, where an orange-coated employee was bringing in the metal racks that displayed plants and potting soil outside during the day, and made his way two doors down to Uli's shop.

Uli met him at the door, let him in, locked the door behind him and turned the front-of-shop lights off. From the back room, cool light spilled through the door. "This way," Uli said.

Beyond that door lay a prosaic, linoleum-floored, gray-

walled, windowless workshop lit by a pair of downhanging
fluorescent tubes. Plain pinewood workbenches, each with
its own magnifying lamp and all perfectly tidy, were lined
up all around the walls. The one nearest the door had a
PC and monitor sitting on it, the monitor showing what
looked like a display from some spreadsheet software, possibly the shop's accounts. The other workbenches all had
delicate tools hung on pegboards up above them, and
clocks of every kind sat on the work surfaces, the shelves,
or, in the case of the various grandfather and grandmother
clocks, on the floor, awaiting repair.

*My grandfather's clock was too tall for the shelf . . . so it
stood ninety years on the floor . . .* sang a child's nervous
voice in Rob's head. He tried to ignore it as he looked at
the other clocks hanging on the walls, ones that seemed to
be working fine—case clocks, antique civic clocks, and a
giant version of the beautiful black-and-white Bauhaus SBB
railway clock with the "hovering" red-dot second hand that
pushed the minute hand over on reaching the 12: next to
that, also black and white, an over-jeweled Felix-the-Cat
clock with eyeballs that glanced from left to right and back
again in time with the pendulum tail: clocks with simple and
ornate faces above every kind of pendulum imaginable—
disks, mostly, though near the door Rob saw one with a
silver crescent moon at the pendulum's end. And, back in
the shadows between two wall-mounted cupboards, with a
pair of massive pinecone weights dangling below it, hung a
mahogany-and-ebony cuckoo clock covered with more
carved scrollwork, antlers, acanthus leaves, and other beau-
tifully graven garbage than Rob had ever seen in his life.

"First one of those I've seen here," Rob said, as Uli went
over to one of the desks and rolled what looked like a
gray steel typist's chair away from it toward the middle of
the room.

Uli grunted. "German," he said, and went to the other
side of the room to pull a red metal toolchest on wheels
over beside the chair. "I would not have it here, but unfortunately the tourists expect them."

"I thought they all came from here," Rob said.

Uli gave him an ironic look. "Given the choice to either
make cuckoo clocks or Rolexes," he said, "which would
you make? Those things come from the Black Forest . . .

and meanwhile, Orson Welles has a lot to answer for. Sit down."

Rob sat down while Uli pulled the top drawer of the chest open, revealing a number of white paper packages about two inches square. Rob suddenly realized that what he had mistaken for a toolchest was actually a medical crash cart, and besides the white paper packages, that top drawer was packed with soft foam cut out to hold numerous syringes and vials. Rob looked nervously at these as Uli picked up one of the paper packages and peeled it open, revealing a round self-stick electrode pad with a trailing wire. Rob found that he had begun to shiver. He hoped Uli would think it was anticipation. "You said you were going to tell me how this works . . ."

"Ach, there I would come up against the language barrier," Uli said as he parted Rob's hair toward the back and touched the electrode into place: Rob felt a brief sting of cold from the lubricant on the pad. "You of all people should know how it is. Talk tech to the nontechnical, it just muddies the waters." Uli peeled another electrode and chose another spot, put the contact in place. "The mind knows the time. The heart knows the place. Everything else is engineering."

"Oh, come on. That's just too New Age and fuzzy. There must be more to going back in time than just using the mind and the heart."

"Hold still. The spatial dislocation is handled by limbic and subcortical keleological transit processes," Uli said, putting another electrode in place at the base of Rob's skull. "Does that sound better to you? And if it does, why? All instrumentality or intervention useful to humans in this world can at base be classified in one of three ways: as science, magic, or chicken soup. There is no special virtue in science when one of the others will do as well. To prefer it all the time is snobbery. Though, in this case, it is valid enough: you think the mind and the body are two different things? Where one goes, the other must follow, assuming there are no unresolved issues to interfere. But anyway, it is not back in time you go," Uli said. "It's forward."

Rob's eyes widened. "Uh, listen, Uli . . ."

"It is the same thing," Uli said, unconcerned, as he fastened on the last electrode. "You cannot change the way the river flows. Time can only go forward: it is no good as time otherwise. You will just go all the way around, until you come out behind the originating time instead of in front of it. Is this a problem for you?"

Rob blinked. "It seems a long way out of the way, I guess."

"The only way to get where you are going," Uli said, "*cannot* be out of your way. By definition." He checked the last connection. "Ready?"

Rob looked around him, carefully, so as not to dislodge the wires. "Is that all?"

Uli consented to smile just a little. "You want flashing lights? Machines that make big impressive noises like overheating engines when they run? Unfortunately, I must disappoint you." He went over to the PC on its desk by the wall, checked it, tapped briefly at its keyboard, did something with its mouse, clicked a couple of times, and then walked carefully once right around Rob, checking the big blind free-standing cabinets.

"It's a car battery in there, right?" Rob said, looking at the metal toolchest. "And tomorrow morning there's going to be a big headline in *Blick: Billionaire Victim of Homebrew Electroshock Treatment.*"

"Too many words for *Blick*. Still . . . 'homebrew,'" Uli said. "I wonder how they will translate that into German? Probably they will just say 'homebrew.' We usually find other languages' neologisms cooler than our own." He looked at Rob, and his expression said *tch, tch.* "You are a very reasonable man," Uli said. "The problem is, now you must go where reason will not take you. That, you must let go."

The tone had turned just briefly stern again, showing that glint of steel at the edge. Rob swallowed, feeling a sudden resonance in his mind, in his bones, between this moment and some other. Everything abruptly went uncertain. "I've done this before, haven't I?" he said.

Uli simply looked at him. *Why did he seem so unsurprised by what I told him?* Rob wondered. *How did he—*

Otherwise you would not have come to me again, memory said.

Rob blinked. *Again . . . ?*

But a second later, the world steadied itself once more.

Just déjà vu, Rob thought. *I've had it a hundred times before . . .*

Just never in a situation like this.

I think . . .

Uli crumpled up the electrode-peelings and put them in a small garbage can by one of the workbenches, then picked up a dishtowel and came back to Rob, standing in front of him. "Now the final warning," Uli said, coming around in front of Rob again and wiping the electrode-lubricant off his hands. "I told you this before, but no one believes me until we get to this point. So I tell you again. The past is amber: a solid. The odds that you will be able to change anything, to free anything from the amber and bring it back, are a million to one. If that is the point of your travel, I must remind you of this now."

Rob frowned. *We'll see about that,* he thought. "I'm going anyway."

"Of course you are. Everyone does." Uli shrugged. "So, go well. And now, think about where and why you go." He turned. "When you get back, would you like a coffee?"

"Uh, yes, thank you."

Uli went out and shut the door behind him. Rob waited for a shock, a buzz . . . but nothing happened. Finally, because doing anything else would force him to admit to himself that he'd been had, Rob sat back in the typing chair, closed his eyes, and thought about why he was going.

The where took no time at all. The first thing he noticed was the faint clean scent that he hadn't smelled in thirty years. Rob opened his eyes in the dark and looked around him. He was standing in the back yard, down by the gigantic quince bush that had always threatened to take over the whole area around the back gate where the store's trucks parked. It was in flower, the peach-colored blossoms now bluish-pale in the starlight and the light of the mercury vapor streetlight beyond the high chain-link gate. Up at the top of the slight rise on which they stood, the house and store loomed dark. Everything was silence.

Except for a slight rustling in the bushes near where the ladder hung against the feed-shed wall.

Aha, Rob thought, and smiled grimly in the darkness, his fists balling at the sound. He stepped toward it, stopped.

"You have till the count of three," he said, "to get your sorry ass out of here before I call the cops. One—"

Nothing.

"Two—" Rob paused. "Buddy, you don't know about Sergeant McCallister down at the precinct, do you? He really likes taking suspects into that back room, and—"

A man's shape all in dark clothes erupted out of the bushes, running helter-skelter for the gate. He swarmed up it, over it, dropped to the far side, and ran.

Rob stood there waiting for the sound of footsteps to vanish down the back alley. Then he turned, looking at the house. There was a growing tumult in his head that he was having trouble understanding, but one thought came clear through it: *I just want to see them. Just want to know they're still there.*

Silently Rob unhooked the ladder from the side of the feed shed and went up the hill with it, past the parked trucks, up the old stone stairs to the house. Very quietly he extended the ladder, and went up it carefully: a fall here would be bad.

The hole in the roof gaped before him. Rob braced himself carefully against the shingles there, stepped in.

Darkness. But he was used to being in here in the dark . . . and he knew, better than anything, the exact location of the thing he had come for.

The box was there, on the floor, behind a pile of other boxes. Rob knelt down in front of it, reached out to it, eased the top flap open. The special smell of the glassine envelopes floated up to him. He reached out in the dim light coming through the hole in the roof and reached out to touch the edge of *Captain Thunder* Number One.

Something hit him from behind, knocked him flat.

Rob went face down on the plywood covering the rafters, only a few feet from where the flooring stopped entirely and he would have gone straight down through his own bedroom ceiling. A second later someone was pummeling his back, his neck, the back of his head. "You bastard!" a small voice whispered in fury. "Leave them alone! Leave my comics alone! They're all I have!"

Rob rolled sideways, away from where the rafters went bare, back toward the piled-up trunks and boxes in the dark. The small violent attacker fell off his back, scrambled to its hands and knees at the same time Rob did, stared him in the face.

It was Robby. *Was I really that skinny?* Rob thought. *Did I really think that buzz-cut looked good on me?* But the small figure in striped pajamas and bathrobe was glaring at him in utter rage, and questions of how he'd looked when he was ten now withered in the glare.

"I dreamed this happening, just a little while ago," the boy whispered. "I kept waking up and falling asleep again all night, and I dreamed it different ways. Once the other guy just went out with them. I yelled, but he got away. This time the other guy ran away, and you came in instead. But you just want to steal them, too, and I won't be able to stop you, and it's going to be the same! It's always going to be the same! Why did you make it this way?!" Robby was crying now, but in no way did it take the edge off his rage. *"What kind of bastard keeps trying to steal some kid's comic books?"*

Rob started to answer. "You've got it all wrong," Rob whispered. "That wasn't me! I came here to—" *Steal them before the other guy did?* he thought. *Boy, he's not going to like the sound of that—*

And then Rob fell silent as, in memory, this scene in which he stood represented itself to him another way, in memory . . . as if he was seeing it all happen from a slightly different angle. That dark shape escaping out the hole in the roof, with the box under his arm—this time Robby saw a profile. It had been a stranger's face to Robby then.

But it was not strange to Rob now, for he saw it every morning in the mirror.

He reeled. *I did steal them first . . . at least once.*

Why didn't I remember this before? Because I hadn't made it happen yet?

Or maybe now I have . . . and my memory is of the world I made. And the me *I made . . .*

"Oh, my God," Rob said softly as he knelt there, and he hid his face in his hands. He had very little time. It would only take a few minutes for his dad and mom to hear what was happening, and get up here.

What will I do . . . ?

How many times have I been in this moment?

Lots, probably. I have enough money to do it again and again.

But how many times have I screwed it up?

He would have thought that once you'd repaired time, you shouldn't have been able to remember how it had been broken. But apparently if you stood at the right spot, you could. Memories were tangling and writhing in Rob's head like a nest of snakes, images and realities jostling one another, trying to push one another out of place. Here, at the nexus moment, they were all accessible. *Unresolved issues,* Uli had said. . . .

But these are what I came for. What I'm going to be paying millions of dollars to reach. I don't want to just see them. I want to take them back with me. I want to save them. That's what all this is about.

He rubbed his eyes, let his hands fall. "Robby, listen to me," Rob said. "Let me have them. I can take them where they'll always be safe."

"What's the use of them being safe if I can't have them?" Robby said, anguished.

"But you will have them. I'm you."

"You're not me *now!* And I don't care about having them when I'm old! I care about having them now! I *need* them now!" His voice choked up. "I dreamed you, too. I don't want to be the me I'm going to be if I have to lose these! *I don't want to be you!*"

Rob fell silent, unable to think of anything to say to that. Except, eventually:

Neither do I.

That's what all this is about.

Downstairs, Rob's parents' bedroom door creaked. His and Robby's heads both turned.

Do it now, said a voice in the back of his mind. *Take them. Run. It'll be what happened. And* Captain Thunder *will be safe with you.*

Rob stared at the box.

What kind of bastard steals comic books from a kid? said another voice.

Rob put his hands on the box again, one on either side. He had never felt anything as utterly as he now felt this plain smooth cardboard against his skin. Inside the box, all the color, all the joy, a whole childhood lost, seemed to boil and seethe like a cartoned volcano.

If you don't take them now . . . you won't *be you,* said one of the voices in his head. *Beware . . .*

Footsteps started to come up the stairs. Rob's eyes met Robby's.

Rob tried to swallow the lump in his throat, failed. "Captain Thunder," Rob said with difficulty. "would never steal. Not even from Emperor Fulgor."

Very slowly, Robby's eyes began to shine with something besides repressed tears.

Rob got hurriedly to his feet, blinking. He made his way to the hole in the roof, stepped out of it, found the first step of the ladder. He heard the attic door open. Rob went down the ladder too fast, blinking hard, unable to see where he was going in the dark. *It wasn't supposed to go this way,* he thought, as he misstepped, and fell—

The crash shook every bone in him. Rob sat up too suddenly, and immediately felt woozy. There were work-benches all around him, and pegboards on the walls: and the noise hadn't been him falling after all—just the sound of something in the workshop blowing up.

"Come on, now," Uli's voice said. "Sit up. That is right. Here is your coffee."

Bleary, Rob reached out and took the plain white ceramic coffee mug. The stuff in it was brewed stronger than he usually liked it, but it was also half milk: he drank it down greedily. When Rob finished, he looked around and saw Uli kneeling by the red metal crash cart, poking at its innards with a resigned expression and making that *tch, tch* sound again. "Oh, my," Uli said, "that was the equivocator."

"Will it take long to fix?"

"The time machine will be working again by last week," Uli said, standing up, "if I can get the parts." He smiled that seldom smile at Rob again. "See, now, who says the Swiss have no sense of humor."

It didn't seem to be a question. "So," Uli said. "It is as I told you, yes? Bringing things back . . . is usually impossible."

Rob looked for somewhere to put the mug. Uli took it

from him, and they both noticed the way his hands were shaking. "Yes," Rob said. "Physical things, anyway."

Uli looked at him thoughtfully, and nodded. "Yes. Meantime, the tram back to the Hauptbahnhof will be along in a few minutes. So: are you satisfied?"

Rob wasn't sure what to answer. Yet he felt better than he had for a long time before he left: more cheerful— somehow more whole. *Why? I didn't get what I came for.*

But he had gotten something else instead. "Yes," he said.

"We will see," Uli said. "I will bill you for the repair after you return home and have some time to see whether it is complete. Meanwhile, I suggest you contact your staff tonight. Your company is about to announce that they have mislaid you, and if that happens, the stock price will suffer, which will in turn impair both my fee and your ability to pay it."

Rob drank the coffee for a few moments, thinking, then stood up. "Why do you need to charge a fee at all?" he said. "With this technology, you could be richer than I am."

Uli sniffed, an amused sound. "I do not need the fee," he said. "But if you did not pay what the trip was worth to you, you would get no result. Now hurry: the tram comes in two minutes."

He walked Rob toward the door. One last glance Rob got of the workshop as they left it—a closer look at the unusual clock hanging on the wall near the doorway, the one with the pendulum like a crescent moon. As Rob went by it, he saw he had been wrong about the crescent shape. It was not a moon. It was a scythe, the inner edge glinting with the gray of sharpened steel.

At the door on the street, Rob paused. "Are you for real?" he said. "Is this place for real? Or will you just vanish when I go?"

Uli made that amused sniff again. "Without me, there is no reality," he said. "But meanwhile, one must make a living. You will not need me in this mode again. But if one of your clocks breaks—" He shook Rob's hand. *"Auf wiedersehen."*

Rob went around the corner to catch the tram.

Half an hour later he called his office from the Hauptbahnhof, and spent some time sweet-talking Chei into forgiving him. The next morning, the second-string Lear was sitting in a civil-aviation slot at Kloten, and Chei met him at its door with his proper passport and a pile of paperwork. By that evening they were home, back at HQ: and when the ruckus had settled down and everyone left him alone at last, Rob went to the safe to put away his bogus passport.

The click of the safe's opening sounded odd, muted. As the door swung open, he saw why.

It was almost completely full of stacked glassine envelopes.

His hands trembling, Rob reached in to the top of the left-hand stack and drew the envelope out. Inside it was a dramatic splash of gray and silver against a sky full of clouds and lightning, and a heroic face, smiling, half-hidden under the silver helmet: *Captain Thunder*, Issue One.

Rob sat down shakily at his desk, slipped the comic out of the envelope and laid it carefully on the blotter. He read it, cover to cover, as twilight settled down outside the floor-to-ceiling windows. The old, old joy came up from the page to meet him, as if it had never been gone.

But now it *had* never been gone. . . .

Trembling, Rob turned the last page over, and the single piece of white notepaper lay revealed between the last page of small ads and the back cover. The printing at the top of the page said *WILLINGDEN FEED AND GRAIN:* at the bottom, it said *Call HArmon 180.* And between these, someone had written, *Thanks for everything.*

Carefully Rob closed Issue One and pushed it aside. Then he put his head down in his hands and cried for what he'd lost that he'd suddenly got back again—

—not the comics.

DOING TIME
by Robin Wayne Bailey

Robin Wayne Bailey is the author of a dozen novels, including the *Brothers of the Dragon* series, *Shadowdance,* and the new Fafhrd and the Grey Mouser novel *Swords Against the Shadowland.* His short fiction has appeared in numerous science fiction and fantasy anthologies and magazines, including *Guardsmen of Tomorrow, Far Frontiers,* and *Spell Fantastic.* An avid book collector and old-time radio enthusiast, he lives in Kansas City, Missouri.

M*y name is Samuel Enderby. I am the Director and Chief Researcher of the Enderby Institute for Temporal Studies. I am a Chrononaut. And I am a murderer.*

I'll never forget that sun, how I stared in awful horror at it as it floated, red and swollen, on the watery horizon of that too-blue sea—a sea that shouldn't have been there. The sky was just as strange, an unnatural cobalt color that stabbed my eyes with its wrongness. That weird light affected everything. Even the sandy beach glimmered with an intense, incorrect whiteness.

The beach. As far as I could see, it was unmarred by driftwood or stone, shell or seaweed, any sign of life. Only the strong, warm wind had left any ripple in the sand, and closer to the water, the straining roll of a weary surf stirred a few loose grains.

How my fingers trembled and fumbled as I unstrapped myself from my seat and rose to stand. I had been holding my breath unconsciously, but now, half-afraid, I filled my lungs. The air was thin; it tasted of salt, clean, yet strange. I turned slowly, gripping the back of the chair for balance, because—I admit it—my legs felt weak from fear and uncertainty. A stark line of cliffs, a massive escarpment really, seemed to mark the coastal boundary. I scanned the jagged, razor-sharp summits for long moments seeking movement, a tree swaying in the breeze, perhaps, or a bird. Nothing but a devastating stillness. I returned my attention to the beach, running my gaze up and down its length. Then, finally, once more I turned toward the sea.

No blade of grass, no weed. No bird winging in the sky. And that surf—oh, it moved, but it was the twitch and rattle of a dead thing whose nerves had not yet admitted its own demise.

I had to tear my gaze from it before despair overcame me. A console of controls made a semicircular arch around my chair, and I tried to still my trembling as I bent over the banks of my newly designed quantum computers and monitors. The displays were still flashing their warnings, but the familiarity of the keyboards under my fingers and the technology in which I felt such pride calmed me. This was only a problem. Problems always had solutions.

Blinking in that hurtful light, I went to work. It didn't take long to determine what had happened, although the *why* proved more elusive. I settled back in my seat to face an inescapable conclusion. I had overshot my mark. A number glared back at me from the primary display, astonishing in its magnitude, judgmentally cold in its significance. No reason to panic, I told myself. Still, I found it hard to swallow, and despite the harsh heat of that giant sun, a chill ran up my spine.

I stared again at that sun, raising a hand toward it, measuring its painful glow through spread fingers with a squinting gaze.

I had programmed a jump of one thousand years—four times as far as any of my previous jumps. Perhaps the success of those earlier excursions had gone to my head; no doubt some would find it ironic that, despite my obsession with time, patience had never been one of my virtues. But I saw no reason to yield to the advice of my colleagues and financial backers and proceed at a more cautious pace. In my arrogance, I had expected to find the walls of the Enderby Institute still rising around me, and if not the institute, then surely its successor or some similar agency

charged with the continuing advancement of my research.
I even dared to imagine a university named after me, maybe
even a city rising out of the isolated Nevada desert.

Those fantasies taunted me now as I continued to stare
at the number on the display

Ten million years.

Something had gone wrong, and—I couldn't help it—I
shivered. Still, I detached a palm-sized keypad from the
console, rose to my feet again, and strode across the smooth
metal deck of my time platform. I hesitated for some reason I couldn't fathom. I'd never considered myself an emo-
tional man, but I felt at the core of my being, not just out
of time, but out of place, an alien on my own planet.

Or whatever was left of my own planet.

Finally, steeling myself, I stepped down onto the sand.
When I'd gone ten paces, I turned and looked back. My
footprints seemed like cuts and slashes on a pristine canvas,
a violation. And my beautiful platform, a sleek disk of steel
and plastic science with its six inwardly curling pylons of
probing instrumentality, looked to me now like nothing so
much as a dead bug on its back.

I struggled to dismiss such thoughts and tapped out a
code on the keypad, locking the jump-controls. I tapped
out a second code. In response, various devices within the
pylons went to work analyzing air quality, monitoring radiation levels, meteorological phenomena, and more. My time
platform was as sophisticated a planetary probe as any ever
launched into space, only the world it was designed to study
was the world of the past and the future.

As my machine got to work, I resolved to do the same.
I had my own observations and discoveries to make, my
own questions to answer. What had happened to my world,
to my Earth?

Slipping the keypad into a pocket, I headed northward
up the beach with my long black shadow at my right side
for company. I kept glancing at the sun, watching it sink
lower and lower into the sea, knowing that night was coming. Still, I walked. When the stars began to appear one by
one, I began to feel an oppressive sadness that deepened
with every step. The stars that I had called by name in my
own time were unrecognizable to me now, and the constel-
lations I had known since childhood were no more.

Perhaps it was the heat or the thinness of the air, but I couldn't think rationally. I strove for a scientist's detachment, but that eluded me. I felt as if I was in a nightmare. I was thirsty, but had no water. No food, either, though I was not hungry at all. I should have returned to the platform, but the deadness of the darkening landscape had a mesmerizing quality.

When my legs at last grew tired from trudging through the sand, I stopped to rest. The waves that dappled the sea's surface were weak, small things. I noted the timid encroachment of the water as the sun went down. What had happened to the tide?

The answer came shortly when a faint light began to shine in the eastern heavens above the escarpment. My spirits lifted somewhat as I anticipated the moon, the unchanging and familiar moon. I knew that orb well, knew its mares and mountains by name. I knew that cratered face like the face of an old friend, and I desperately longed for a friend now. How could I explain to anyone the loneliness I felt, sure that I was the only human being, indeed, the only living thing, on—even now it is hard to say—a dead Earth.

I turned my back to the horrid discoloration that marked the sun's westward setting and sat down in the soft sand to await the rising of the moon.

Then, though it unmanned me, I began to weep.

It was not the moon that rose above the cliffs, but a milky ring of shattered fragments and dust. The moon— my moon!—was gone. What remained hung like a stark mockery in the sky. I cried, and wondered if my sanity was slipping away.

I wanted nothing more than to return to my platform and try to make my way home. *Home.* That word had never held such power before. I didn't know what accident or mistake had brought me to this dismal future, but I wanted, needed, to be quit of it, to forget it entirely if I could.

Yet, if I didn't know how I got here, could I get home?

In near-darkness, I started back down the beach. I didn't know how far I'd walked, but it didn't matter. With the keypad, I could always locate the platform. I put one foot in front of the other, shuffling through my own oncoming footprints without even my shadow for company now.

In this state of mind I walked for maybe an hour without ever lifting my head. There were wonders to see, had I not been blind to them. That ring that was once the moon had a beauty, as did that soft, quiet sea, and never had a night sky been so resplendently bejeweled. Yet I was filled with grief and mourning for a past and for things I couldn't even guess at.

An unexpected rush of wind caused me to stop in midstride, and finally I looked up. The air crackled with energy, and down the beach the night seemed to waver as if with heat-shimmer. Every hair on my body stood suddenly on end, and my heart hammered. I knew this phenomenon! There was no way it could be happening, yet it was!

When that patch of wavering blackness exploded, I threw up my hands and jerked my gaze away from the impossible spectrum of light that burst forth, and when the light subsided, and I dared to look . . .

Despite the energy signature, there wasn't another time platform, after all.

There was only a man. Whoever he was, he seemed totally disoriented. His bald head rolled back on his shoulders as his knees buckled. Without even putting up his hands to catch himself, he fell forward on the sand and lay still.

I ran toward him and threw myself down at his side. He gave a little moan as I touched his arm. Not dead, then! As gently as I could manage, I rolled him over and felt for a pulse at his throat. It was quite strong, suggesting that the cause of his collapse wasn't life threatening. He moaned again. His eyes fluttered, and he shot out a hand and caught my wrist. "Who—who are you?" His voice was a harsh whisper of fear. The words were English, though I couldn't place his accent.

I tried to calm him. "My name is Enderby," I answered. "Samuel Enderby. Your turn now. Who are you, my friend, and more importantly, how did you get here?"

He released my wrist and sat up slowly. For the first time, I took note of the nondescript gray coverall he wore and the eight-digit number printed above his left breast pocket. His stubbled face and the inch-long scar at the left corner of his mouth only emphasized a generally rough appearance. "Prisoner 31463577," he answered automatically as he rubbed a thumb and forefinger over his eyes. Then, he gave me a hard look. "Sanders," he added sharply. "Name's Sanders."

Prisoner? Surely, I was still having some nightmare.

"As for how I got here, asshole, same as you, I guess." He scooped up a handful of sand and tossed it into the air at nothing in particular, then sneered. "Drop-kicked through the goalposts of eternity by the Nevada State Correctional System. The long, long, long walk. Don't do the crime, if you can't do the time." He looked around as he sagged back on one elbow. "But, man, I never thought it would be like that. I feel like I've been turned inside out." He held up a hand and wiggled his fingers. "Everything's still tingly."

He wasn't a large man. Rather short, actually, though of stocky build. I suspected the ill-fitting coverall concealed a lot of muscle. I should have left him lying there while he was still weak, but a dreadful curiosity compelled me to stay. Like myself, Sanders was obviously a time-jumper, though maybe not a willing one. And the Nevada connection we shared couldn't have been coincidence.

"You got any food or water?" he asked, sitting up again. Then his gaze narrowed, and he pointed. "Say, they let you keep a wristwatch!" He jumped to his feet and kicked a cloud of sand. "Shit, man, they didn't let me keep anything! They took everything away but this rag I'm wearing before they launched my ass!"

The numbing effects of his journey had clearly worn off. I had a thousand questions I wanted to ask: what year he came from, how he got here without a platform, why he'd been sentenced to this extreme form of banishment. So many more! I did no more than glance at the wristwatch that had sparked his agitation as I rose to my feet.

And Sanders jumped me. His fist hammered my jaw, and I hit the sand hard. When I struggled to get up, he slammed a foot into my ribs. He straddled me then, pummeled me with three hard punches, maybe more, and I blacked out.

I awoke with sand in my mouth and pain in every part of my body. My watch was gone, of course, and so was Sanders. I rose unsteadily to my feet and trudged down to the sea to wash my face. The water was cool and cleansing.

But suddenly, I straightened. My watch wasn't the only thing missing. I patted my pockets frantically.

The keypad!

Half running, half-stumbling, ignoring the growing heat and the strangely bright light of the rising sun, I made my way down the beach. Two sets of footprints guided me now, my own and Sanders'. I cursed and prayed at the same time.

Only a circular depression in the sand marked the place where my time platform had rested. Sanders' footprints trailed straight by the spot and continued southward. I doubted if he'd even seen the machine. I'd programmed a safety feature into my platform, and if any commands or numbers were punched into the keypad that were not predetermined codes known only to me, the machine jumped three seconds into the future and remained there until recalled by the correct sequence.

It was easy to imagine that a man like Sanders, having stolen the keypad from my pocket, had punched any number of keys in a vain effort to determine its purpose. And unable to understand its functions, he had nevertheless kept it.

I had no choice but to follow him. I cursed myself again. I was a scientist, not an adventurer. How ill-prepared I was for this accidental expedition. No food, no water—and I was horribly thirsty—but worse yet, I was weaponless.

Sanders proved a cunning rat, and like all rats, he had a sixth sense about traps and mazes. His footprints turned suddenly inward away from the sea and toward the escarpment. He'd found something that had eluded me—a way off the beach and up to the summit. It was a fissure, a split in the rock itself that angled steeply up behind the facade just wide enough for a bold man to climb. In different light it would have been practically invisible. As it was, the way was full of shadows, and the surprising smoothness of the stone promised treacherous footing. Nevertheless, I attacked the climb with a vengeful determination.

By the time I reached the top, I was panting and drenched with sweat. I sank to my knees on the rocky soil to rest, peeled off my shirt, and tied it around my waist. My lips were raw and swollen, my throat parched. I tried to remember when I had last taken a drink of water, then barked a short, self-pitying laugh at the answer—ten million years ago! I knew I couldn't go much longer.

I struggled to my feet. That keypad was my only hope.

Though I had achieved the cliff summit, the ground continued to slope upward at a gentler angle. I wasn't a tracker, and without the beach's soft sand I saw no clear footprints, but I guessed that Sanders would have gone straight up that incline, following the path of least resistance.

At the top of this gentler slope, I stopped again. My breath caught in my chest. I raised a hand to shield my gaze from the harsh sun, which was approaching zenith and stared wide-eyed with disbelief, hope, even a certain gratitude. I've never been a religious man, but I gave thanks to God.

I was not hallucinating, and it was no mirage I saw. Below me sprawled a shallow valley, and though the grass that waved in the wind was brown and withered, still it was grass. Here and there, a few gnarly trees clawed and twisted their way up from the earth.

But there was more! From my vantage, I gazed upon a collection of thatched huts, and moving among those crude dwellings—no sight was ever more welcome!—men. I ran headlong down the rocky hill, slipping and sliding in the loose stone and dust, screaming and waving my arms for attention. Faces turned my way; hands rose to block the sunlight and shield squinting gazes. No one moved, though.

And when the first blades of crisp grass pushed up from the soil under my shoes, I also stopped as if paralyzed in mid-step. They were rough-looking, most of them bearded with long hair, though a few were bald. Their clothes were tattered rags if they wore clothes at all. The majority of them appeared gaunt, thinly malnourished. Still, they were many, and I was one.

As I stood there, halfway down the hill on the edge of that unlikely Eden, I realized that they were like Sanders, convicts and prisoners from their own times, sent—launched, as Sanders had put it—on a one-way journey to a prison without bars or barb-wired boundaries, without guards or wardens.

I recoiled at the elegant cruelty of it.

Yet, if I felt sympathy for these men, it was dampened

by the next logical realization. What kind of criminals would warrant such punishment? Only the worst, of course—murderers and killers, the hardened and habitual felons, the sociopaths deemed beyond rehabilitation. Men like Sanders, who might have killed me for a wristwatch.

I swallowed. I was not a violent man. In my entire life I had never struck another person in anger. I had never thought of myself as a coward, but neither had I ever really tested my courage. It was a wholly new and unfamiliar fear I felt now as I stood looking at those creatures. It was the fear a sheep felt surrounded by wolves.

But I was no sheep. A sheep might have run away. I didn't have that option. I was half mad with thirst, and they had to have water. At a more cautious pace, I entered their compound, doing my best to hide my trepidation behind a glower as wary and dangerous as theirs.

There had been perhaps ten men moving about when I had first started down into their midst, but more had emerged from the huts, alerted by the others, twenty, then thirty or so. I saw no women among them, nor children. Only men. I distrusted the silence with which they greeted me, but neither did I speak.

As I approached the center of their ring of huts, another figure emerged from the farthest hut. He was a wild-looking creature, whose face was half-hidden behind a gray beard, and but for a white scrap of cloth tied around his loins, he was naked. His rangy strength was quite apparent, as were the numerous moles and skin cancers that marked his shoulders.

He regarded me with a cool, blue-eyed authority, and I knew at once that he led this band. I drew my own sun-burned shoulders back and lifted my head as he came toward me. There was almost a look of amusement in those eyes, and I thought again of wolves and sheep.

I tried to introduce myself, but when I opened my mouth, all that came out was a rasping croak. A wave of dizzying weakness overcame me suddenly. My legs turned rubbery, and I sank to my knees. The world spun.

He leaned down, gripped my chin in a not-ungentle fashion, and raised my head. For what seemed like long moments, his gaze bored into me. "Carry him inside," I heard him say.

I was seized by my arms and legs and borne across the compound to his hut and there deposited on a pallet inside. I blushed and burned with shame at the indignity of it, but there was little I could do. My strength had completely left me. Someone even supported my head when a wooden ladle of cool water was held to my lips.

I sipped, determined not to make a greedy fool of myself, and managed finally to rise up onto one elbow. "I'm not usually so helpless," I said when I found my voice again. My throat still felt raw and painful, and I sipped some more. "The heat . . ."

"The thin air is worse," my host interrupted. He squatted down on his haunches on the opposite side of the hut and dismissed the men who had carried me with a gesture. "Deprived of sufficient oxygen, your body tires more quickly. It gets to all of us at first. Most of us adjust."

I started to tell him I had no intention of remaining long enough to adjust, but then thought better of it. I felt his gaze on me, but it held no malice. I relaxed a little and sipped more water. He waited silently until I finally finished the ladle. I couldn't help examining it before I passed it back to him. I turned it over, ran a finger along the smoothly polished wood. "Carved from a single piece," I commented. "Nice work."

"We're lucky to have a wood-worker in our camp," he said, as he took the ladle and dropped it into a wooden bucket. "We put a premium on men with useful skills."

I rubbed a hand over the back of my skull. My head ached furiously, from the sun and the heat, I assumed, and the exertion. "There was another man who should have come this way before me," I said. I described Sanders. "He took something from me. I have to find him."

"We don't tolerate thieves among us," he answered quietly. "We can't afford the trouble they cause. But no one else has come this way today."

"Then I'll be going. Thank you for . . ." But my legs folded before I got to my feet. My host caught me, and eased me back onto the pallet.

"Rest." It was an order. He was a man used to giving orders. "The afternoon sun is hotter than hell itself." He looked at me with frank appraisal. "You wouldn't get very far." Then he added, "I doubt your friend will either. I'll send someone to take care of your cuts." He paused at the entrance and gave me another of those strangely penetrating stares, as if he were evaluating or judging me, then he left.

I lay back on the pallet. It was soft enough for a woven mat of grasses and leaves, and I soon fell asleep. I dreamed of the keypad and of Sanders beating me, of his fists crashing down at my face. I dreamed of pain and woke flailing at the air.

"Ease! Ease!" Gentle hands lightly but firmly caught my arms. The dream-image of Sanders' face faded away, and another came into focus. The naked black man that leaned over me slowly smiled as I stopped struggling. "I express sorrow," he said, his accent and manner of speech even stranger than Sanders'. He held up a small clay pot containing a pungent-smelling salve. "I should have brought wakefulness before offering healing. No intention to startle or bring fear."

I touched a spot above my left eyebrow where Sanders' fists had made the deepest cut and found some of the sticky salve there. "That stings!" I grumbled. I took the small pot and sniffed it, wrinkling my nose at the aroma. "What the hell is it?"

He shrugged as he took the pot back. With the tip of his finger, he applied another dollop to the corner of my mouth, and I tried not to wince. "It is what heals," he answered simply. "No botanist among us. One doctor long ago with . . ." he hesitated, as if searching for the right words, ". . . herbal skill. He went to cancers shortly when I came."

My face was apparently a mess. So were my knees and hands and elbows. With deft care, he treated cuts and scrapes I hadn't even been aware of. The stinging lasted only moments before giving way to a pleasant numbness. "Do you have a name?" I asked as he worked.

"Call me Ishmael," he answered. "The Boss give me that name. He said it was because I came from the sea." He inclined his head and grinned. "It is some joke," he continued. "I don't understand it."

"It's from a book," I told him, "called *Moby-Dick*. It's a nineteenth century work. . . ." I stopped suddenly. Ishmael had placed a tiny clay lid on his pot of medicine and set it aside. He seemed suddenly interested in my shirt, which was still tied around my waist, and he ran a palm over one of the sleeves.

I allowed him to examine the fabric. "Ishmael," I said, "what century are you from?"

He inclined his head again thoughtfully, and I had the abrupt impression that he was interpreting my question into another language. "Twenty-seventh century is mine," he answered at last.

My host interrupted us, ducking low as he came through the hut's entrance. He was sweaty and streaked with dirt as if he'd been at some hard work. "How is our guest, Ishmael?" he asked. "Awake, I see."

The black man retrieved his pot and prepared to leave. "Samendy was very tender, very harmed." He looked back at me and made a crisp nod. "He will heal to make many more questions."

When my host and I were alone again, I sat up. I rubbed my neck. In truth, though, I hurt in just about every part of my body. "I assume you're the one he calls 'the Boss.' "

He rolled his eyes. "Not my idea," he answered. "We give each other names here and keep the one that sticks. Our old identities, the times and places we each came from, they don't mean anything here. We don't talk about them much." It was a subtle caution, and he changed the subject immediately. "Do you feel up to a walk, and maybe a bath? It's only a dip in a lukewarm spring."

"I should be leaving," I told him. "I've got to find Sanders."

"You'll need something to eat," he replied. "Food is being prepared now. Please, walk with me."

He possessed a strange mixture of intensity and charm that made him a hard man to resist. I began to see how he had risen to lead this unlikely tribe of exiles and criminals from many times. I really wanted to be after my keypad, but the promise of food proved as strong as any physical chain or bond, and when he held out his hand, an oddly personal gesture I thought, I nevertheless let him help me to my feet.

He introduced me to his followers as he showed me the compound. They all called him, "Boss," or "the Boss." The wood-carver, whose name was Queequeg, shook my hand

and grinned shyly. Starbuck was their stonecutter, and he took pride in showing me the assortment of flint-flaked knives and crude axes they used for tools. Ahab was their cook; he wasn't one-legged, but he was quite lame from a broken leg that hadn't healed well.

"You must be quite enamored of Melville," I said to my host. "It's nice to know at least one classic has survived the ages when so little else has."

He didn't answer, but led me to the outskirts of the compound to show me a large wooden trough and the narrow clay pipe system that carried water from farther up in the valley. "I designed the piping myself," he said proudly. "I showed them how to work the clay, and they did the work. It breaks regularly and requires constant patching, but when resources are scarce, one makes do."

We followed the piping northward up the valley. The worst of the afternoon heat was past as the sun had slipped beyond the western slope. I untied my shirtsleeves and slipped the garment on, letting it hang open and loose. He watched me with an unfathomable look in his eye. I thought perhaps he wanted the shirt for himself, but he didn't ask.

The piping led us to a natural spring that bubbled up from a rocky outcropping. I appreciated how cleverly my host had designed his system, letting gravity transport the water farther down into the deepest heart of the valley. I had wondered as we walked why he hadn't established the compound closer to the spring's source. Now, looking back, I understood how the valley walls, themselves shadowed and shielded the compound from that huge, cruel sun, allowing direct exposure for only a few hours each day.

A shallow pool had formed around the spring. My host untied the dirty white rag he wore around his waist, cast it down beside the pool, and submerged himself. I undressed more slowly, folding my filthy trousers with needless care, placing my shirt beside them, then removing my boots and underclothes. He scrutinized me as I stripped; I slid into the water without meeting his gaze.

"I can't remember when I last saw so many clothes on a single man," he said. There was a quiet mirth in his voice.

"Most of us arrive with a coverall and shoes, or perhaps trousers and a shirt. But those wear out quickly."

"I'm appalled at what's been done to you," I snapped, surprised by my own sudden intensity. "A marvelous tool for research has been abused and twisted to a vicious purpose."

His eyes narrowed sharply. I shrank back to the edge of the pool and turned away, knowing I'd made some mistake, but uncertain of what it was. Yet my flash of anger hadn't abated. It infuriated me that my technology, my monumental work, had been perverted into this pathetic excuse for penal reform. I turned back again and forced myself to look at his skin cancers, at the undeniable signs of malnutrition that even "the Boss" couldn't disguise.

How could I explain the overwhelming rage I felt? Whatever the crimes of these men, surely this was no just punishment. Those blue eyes that peered at me from under wet ropes of gray hair, from a face lined and weathered and reddened, why didn't they accuse me? Why didn't they judge and condemn me? How could he not see my guilt?

We laved and washed ourselves in silence, then he took his scrap of a loincloth and washed that, too. Following his lead, I washed my own shirt. When we spread our clothes on the rocks to dry, I settled back once again to relax in the water while he seated himself on a stone with only his feet in the pool.

He studied me from his perch. "You're a man of thought and intelligence, Samuel Enderby," he said softly. "I don't get much chance to talk with someone like you. Most criminals are disappointingly dull, or worse, stupid."

I remembered that Ishmael had spoken a broken form of my name. "How do you know who I am?" I asked. Perhaps I should have felt some alarm that he did, but I didn't.

A smile split his gray-bearded face, and he looked askance, as if embarrassed. "You mumble in your sleep. Ishmael and I overheard."

I leaned forward to brace my elbows on my knees, and he mistook me. Holding up a hand, he reassured, "No, no—no secrets I promise you, my friend. Only your name, and Sanders, and some cries as if you were being beaten in your dreams."

"I was," I admitted. He'd called me friend. I didn't quite know how to react to that. "I've never experienced such a beating before."

"And you never will again," he responded, his gaze turning hard. "It only takes one beating like that to make you tough, to turn you hard. It leaves you with a kind of madness, a determination to kill the next son of a bitch who ever tries."

For the first time I saw in those eyes and on his face, in the way he clenched his fists on his thighs, the look of the killer, and for the first time, I feared him. Yet, at the same time, I felt an iron in my belly that hadn't been there before, an almost reflexive instinct that told me he was right. He might have attacked me right then, and he might have beaten me savagely—but he wouldn't have found it so easy as Sanders had.

He relaxed and leaned back, changing the subject as he rolled his gaze up toward the rose-tinted sky. "I remember people." He said it so quietly that I wondered if it was to me he spoke or to himself. "Crowds of people. Masses of humanity." He closed his eyes.

I spoke with the same softness, watching him, because he fascinated me. "Do you ever wonder where they all went? What became of mankind?"

He shrugged and stirred the water with a toe. Then he looked up again and waved a hand in a broad gesture. "Out there, perhaps. When I have any hopeful moments at all, I hope out there. I dream of them sometimes, scattered among the stars, thriving."

He licked his lips and drew a breath that betrayed his weariness. I looked at his cancers again and thought he didn't have long to live. "Or maybe we're all that's left," he continued. "There's evidence that a massive solar flare brushed the Earth a million years or more ago. Some of the upper strata are fused. The seas are empty, as if all life had been boiled out of them. And there's the moon." He grinned suddenly. "Or rather, there isn't the moon anymore. What a cosmic joke it would be if, by being projected so far into the future, we are all that survives. The gods would be laughing."

"You were a man of science," I observed, wishing I had some name to call him by, because I could not quite manage *boss,* "and a philosopher, as well."

He rose from the pool, startling in his naked, emaciated glory. "I was someone else," he answered. "I can't even remember who." He turned and snatched up his loincloth. "I don't want to remember."

I got out of the pool, too, and though my clothes were still damp, I pulled them on to keep from looking at him. "Why are there no women in your camp?" I asked as I tied my shoelaces.

The question astounded him. He threw back his head, braced hands on his hips and laughed heartily until my cheeks burned with embarrassment. "You don't get ice water in hell, Samuel!" He laughed again and started down the hill, tying his wrap in place as he went.

Some inner voice warned me to run away, to make an immediate escape for my own good while his back was turned, yet I hurried after him. We strode into the compound side by side without speaking another word, and I could tell in the faces that turned toward us, the lean and wasted faces, that I'd been accepted into their ranks. I rebelled at the idea, even as I wondered what name I might be given, or if I would be given another name at all.

Night was falling, and a smoky fire had been built at the center of the compound using tightly bound bundles of grass for fuel. Ahab commanded several men, who labored over clay pots and nursed the flames. The air smelled rich with surprising flavors, and my mouth watered.

The Boss touched my shoulder and steered me toward a hut that was larger than the others. I marveled to find a long, low wooden table inside, and a dozen men already seated cross-legged on the grass-matted floor around it. The plates and cups, though all of the same clay color, were ornate with etchings and markings. I was directed to a place at the center along one side of the arrangement.

Two men whose names were unknown to me rose to speak in whispers to the Boss. I was distracted as still another man moved around the room ladling water into the cups, but from the corner of my eye, I glimpsed one of the two passing a grass-woven bag into my host's hands. He nodded and came to sit beside me while the two took other seats around the table.

Ahab appeared through the entrance bearing a large flat bowl, which he placed on the nearest end of the table. It was quickly passed around the table, each man dipping into it with his hands and depositing a measure on his plate. Following the custom, I plunged my fingers into the warm, sticky mixture, an orange-colored substance that reminded me of a dish called *manioc* I'd once tasted. It smelled like sweet potatoes, and I assumed it was made from some root.

I devoured it.

Ahab delivered another bowl. This one contained a cold, washed vegetable that looked like radishes, but possessed a citruslike flavor. I looked around the hut, noting the more leisurely pace the others took with their food. "What about the rest of your camp?" I whispered to my host. "I thought I counted more than thirty when I arrived?"

He leaned closer as he licked his fingers, and I felt his hand on my back. "They're being fed, don't worry. But the hut can only hold so many, and most of these are the Seniors—those who've been here longest."

Ahab entered the hut again. On each hand he balanced a large, round platter piled high and steaming. The sweet aroma nearly made me faint as one of the platters was placed between the Boss and myself.

"Meat!" I exclaimed. The other platter passed from hand to hand. The Boss helped himself to a thick slice from our platter, and I did the same. It was so hot it burned my fingers, and I blew on it before popping a strip into my mouth. I chewed quickly, swallowed, and took another bite. "I thought there weren't any animals left," I said between mouthfuls. "This is delicious!"

"Direct your thanks to them," the Boss said, pointing to the two men who had intercepted him earlier. "Grampus and Rachel. They brought you a present, by the way." He reached into the grass-woven bag on the floor beside him and placed my wristwatch on the table. I stared at it, dumbfounded.

"They also brought this back." He held up the keypad that controlled my time platform. "But I think I'll keep it for now. I haven't had a toy to play with in a long while."

I tried to snatch it. "That's mine! I need it!" His face darkened, and a look of warning came into his eyes as he put the keypad back in the bag and thrust it under his leg. "I told you once, Samuel, I can't abide thieves."

I returned his stare, stunned. He wasn't going to let me

go. I picked up my watch, looked at the still-ticking sweep hand without really seeing it, set the watch down again. What could I do? My heart hammered in my chest. I tried to calm myself, to think.

I picked up another strip of meat, trying not to look at anyone, trying to slow my excited breathing, and I put it in my mouth.

I looked at the watch again.

My hand brushed the platter as I reached for my cup of water.

Then, an uncontrollable shivering seized me. I dropped the cup, spilling the contents. "Oh, God!" I cried, leaping up. "Oh, my God!"

The Boss tried to catch my hand, but I hit him in the face as hard as I could and leaped over his sprawling form. Someone tried to block my way I knocked them across the table.

I was outside. Beside the fire, Ahab looked up sharply. A score of others were gathered around him, chewing and eating. I ran from them, ran past the last hut and up the hill past the spring and pool, and farther still. I ran until I fell from exhaustion. Then I rolled over and vomited.

Later, under the cold light of the stars and that ghastly pale ring, I crept back, pausing only long enough by the pool to find a sharp-edged rock. A few men still sat around the dying fire, but they were easy to avoid. I was as much a wolf now as they.

For a long time I listened at the rear wall of the Boss' hut, hearing nothing. On hands and knees, I crawled silently around to the entrance and inside. It was dark, and I could barely see him where he slept naked on the same grass pallet where I had earlier lain.

I didn't give him a chance to wake and raise an alarm. I slammed the pointed stone into his throat, leaned on it, pushed it deep. He emitted one soft sigh, and nothing more.

With bloody hands, I searched the hut for my keypad, my ticket home and back to sanity. There was no trace of the grass bag. I found it, instead, wrapped in the white loincloth he'd set aside. Clutching it to my chest, I sneaked out again, made my way out of the valley, back to the escarpment, and in the dawning light, back down to the beach. There, I sat down in the sand at the edge of the water, and as I unwrapped the cloth from around the keypad, something caught my eye

A faded label still attached to that scrap of white cloth. A label that matched the shirt I was wearing. I think I screamed. I don't remember.

My name is Samuel Enderby. I am the Director and Chief Researcher of the Enderby Institute for Temporal Studies. I am a Chrononaut. And I am a murderer.

I think also that I am quite insane. I try to forget and I cannot, not in sleep, not in alcohol. So I look for meaning, and I can't find that, not in prayer, nor in this volume of Melville upon which I have become quite fixated. I try to forget, but I cannot, and I think that I must go back, because I know who I am now.

I am Leviathan, and I churn the boiling seas.

Only those salt waters at the end of the world will ever wash the taste of Sanders out of my mouth.

PALIMPSEST DAY
by Gary A. Braunbeck

Gary A. Braunbeck is the author of the acclaimed collection *Things Left Behind,* as well as the collections *Escaping Purgatory* (in collaboration with Alan M. Clark) and the CD-ROM *Sorties, Cathexes, and Personal Effects.* His first solo novel, *The Indifference of Heaven,* was recently released, as was his Dark Matter novel, *In Hollow Houses.* He lives in Dayton, Ohio and has, to date, sold nearly two hundred short stories. His fiction, to quote *Publishers Weekly,* ". . . stirs the mind as it chills the marrow."

1. Teach Your Children

Toward the end of her life my mother developed a fervent belief in reincarnation. During our last conversation in the hospital (in which she confessed something that stunned me), she asked about the state of my life, nodded her head in sympathy when I told her I was having trouble dealing with my sister's care and had briefly considered putting her in a group home, and then said the single most amazing thing that she'd ever said to me: "You know what you need to do, hon? You need to walk out of here today and live your life as if you were already living it for the second time and as if you had acted the first time as wrongly as you are about to act now."

I remember the way the sheets formed a perfect outline of her cancer-ravaged body. I imagined that the mattress had adapted itself into the shape of her underside. Then an odd image crossed my mind: Mom's body had been taken away, but the sheets still held the impression of Mom-front, while the bed had the shape of Mom-back, and in between was this space cast in her form where sheets and bed thought she still existed.

It wasn't until later—weeks after her funeral, she and my father side by side in Cedar Hill Cemetery—that the full weight of her words hit me. She was trying to tell me that it was possible for a person to turn the present into the past, and that the past may yet be changed and amended. Each moment of which life consists is itself dying as it's being experienced, and will never recur (or, at least, it's not *supposed* to)—but it's that very transitoriness that challenges us to make the best possible use of each moment. *Live your life as if you were already living for the second time and as if you had acted the first time as wrongly as you are about to act now.*

Those words, and their unspoken subtext that second chances exist simultaneously within *first* ones, were my mother's last and greatest gift to me, a blessing to live without fear of further regrets.

Then Laura came back into my life and I discovered they were a warning, as well.

Electrons would have to be 10^{22} times more massive for the electric and gravitational pull between two of them to be equal. To produce such a heavy particle would take 10^{19} gigaelectron volts (GeV) or energy, a quantity known as Planck energy. Coupled with this is the Planck length, a tiny 10^{-35} meter. Quantum physicists now believe, with the advent of such miracles as the Large Hadron Collider, it might very well be possible to circumvent Heisenberg's Uncertainty Principle and measure spacetime's most staggeringly small quantities without *collapsing the wave/particle duality. Using Planck time—10^{-45} of a second—it's theoretically possible to measure a spacetime quantity as small as 1.62×10^{-33}. The trick is to make sure it goes smoothly, because at that size, space and time come apart.*

Lately, I've been thinking about this. A lot.

If something were to happen during that period of measurement, then something else, and if the two events were separated by only 10^{-45} of a second, then, when the measuring is over, it would be impossible to tell which came first, space or time.

So what would happen then? And how would we know?

*   *   *

2. Lucky In the Morning/Roll With the Changes

There was a time when Ayds (spelled with a "y") was a popular and surprisingly tasty dietetic candy that came in plastic bags containing individually-wrapped pieces. You could easily find it on store shelves right alongside Sweathog coffee mugs, *The Wit and Wisdom of Archie Bunker,* Kiss comic books, and *Chico and the Man* lunch boxes. The manufacturer stopped making it when the Center for Disease Control concluded that the so-called "gay flu" was a much more virulent and less discriminating strain of virus than was first suspected, because AIDS (definitely *not* spelled with a "y") was spreading beyond the partners of the nameless "Mr. X" and into the general population. The bags that were still on store shelves were slowly and quietly recalled, and by the end of July 1982, it was nowhere to be found.

On the morning when all of this shifted into a higher gear—some twenty-plus years after Ayds had ceased being manufactured—I awoke to find three pounds of it in my refrigerator.

It happened like this:

The previous night I was awakened by Blair bumping around in the hallway. My sister tends to get up at least once every night to use the bathroom, but there's a catch: She likes to lie in bed and wait until the last possible moment before making a beeline for the john, just to see if she'll make it in time. She enjoys the hell out of it . . . probably because she's not the one who has to deal with the various paraphernalia when she loses her little game.

Because she'd lately started bumping into things, I put a small night light in the hall which I turn on before going to bed. I heard her stumbling around and starting to cry, so I cleared my throat and called out, "Wait for your eyes to adjust to the light, honey."

When there was no further noise, I took it to mean she'd found her way all right, and went back to sleep.

I woke up around 8:30 a.m., got dressed, and was starting downstairs when my foot caught on something at the edge of the landing and I almost fell.

There used to be a section of old carpeting at the top of the stairs that had come loose and was sticking up just enough that you could easily slide your foot right under it if you weren't paying attention, lose your balance, and fall face-first down the stairs.

I had removed the carpeting from the house about a year ago, after both Blair and myself had experienced one near-miss too many. (The house was now polished hardwood floors top to bottom, courtesy of Yours Truly's efforts.) I looked down at my feet and saw absolutely nothing that could have tripped me, but I swear it felt as if I'd caught my foot in that old piece of carpeting.

"Sharp as ever, aren't you, Danny?" I whispered to myself. I went downstairs, made a pot of coffee, then went outside to retrieve the paper.

I was just turning to go back inside when a voice shouted, "Looks like your paint job ain't holding up so good!"

I turned and saw our neighbor from across the street, Mr. Finney, working in his garden. I waved to him as he rose from his rhododendrons and started walking over. I met him at the curb, and we shook hands.

"What's wrong with the paint job?" I asked. I had painted the house about a year ago with an all-weather brand that cost more than I could probably afford, but I'd figured it was better to shell out the cash once and not have to worry about it again for several years.

"Take a look," he said, and pointed.

Running from the eaves of the house to nearly the floor of the front porch was a streak of white paint. Mr. Finney accompanied me as I went for a closer look. Last year, when I'd spent the better part of a week painting the house myself, Mr. Finney—a seventy-eight-year-old widower who likes to keep himself occupied with gardening and neighborhood gossip—had loaned me his extension ladder to save me the cost of renting one. Then he'd spent several hours each afternoon sitting on his porch watching me work, always offering a cold glass of lemonade when I'd finished for the day.

"That's a damn shame," he said. "I mean, after you did all that work."

The streak was about the width of a standard seven-inch paint brush, and formed a nice straight line down the front of the house.

"How long's it been this way?" he asked.

"I don't know. I mean, it sure as hell wasn't this way

yesterday. I'd've noticed something like this when I came home."

"You sure about that?"

"Yes. Look at it!"

Finney shook his head. "Maybe we got ourselves some practical jokers running around the neighborhood."

"I don't think so." I pointed up toward the eaves. "They would've needed a ladder to get up there, and if they did this in the middle of the night, I would have heard them. My bedroom window's right there." I stepped forward and looked at it more closely.

It looked like hell. It was too thick in places, cracked, and several chunks of it had fallen off to reveal the old wood underneath.

"Huh," I muttered to myself.

"See something?"

I reached out and scraped some of the paint into my hand. It flaked off easily, almost turning to dust instantly.

"This is the *old* paint," I said.

"But I thought you scraped everything before you started to—"

"I did. My hands were sore for a month." I looked up to the eaves, then followed the streak all the way back down. "I was particularly sure to get all the paint here on the porch—and I mean *all* of it. You know, so the front of the house'd look good when visitors showed up. Dad always used to say that you could get a little sloppy with the sides and back if you had to, but make damn sure the front looks good."

"Sounds like your dad. I sure miss seeing him and your mom around."

"That makes two of us."

"But at least they ain't suffering no more. They're in a better place."

"I know." Truth was, I *didn't* know. Twelve years of Catholic school had left me a devout Agnostic, and many nights when I thought of my parents, I so *wanted* to believe there was something more after this life, but I just . . . couldn't.

I sighed and slipped the paper under my arm. "Looks like I'm gonna have to trouble you for a ladder loan again."

"You know where it is. Come get it any time. I can even

whip up a pitcher of lemonade. The recipe's Ethel's, you know. Lord, that woman could whip up some tasty treats!"

"I know. I remember the birthday cakes she used to make for me when I was a kid. She'd always cover it with foil, leave in front of the door, then ring the bell and hurry away before I saw it was her."

"That was my wife—Ethel Finney, the Birthday Cake Fairy."

"She never copped to it with me, you know."

He smiled. "I know. She liked doing stuff like that." A wistful shadow crossed his face for a moment, then was gone. "Get whatever you need from my garage, then we'll have some lemonade."

"Thank you." Now it was my turn to shake my head. "I'm *positive* I scraped all the paint off before applying the new coats. And why would someone do something like this in the first place? As practical jokes go, it's kind of lame—not to mention rude."

"Takes all sorts to make a world, I guess."

We exchanged a few more trivial pleasantries, shook hands again, and he started back to his garden. I was just opening the door when he called my name again and came up to the front steps.

"Don't tell me you saw another spot like this one?" I said.

"No, no, it ain't that at all. Something just occurred to me. Back about fourteen, fifteen years ago when your dad was still alive, he wanted to paint this house 'cause he couldn't stand the way the white always showed every bit of dirt?"

". . . yeah . . . ?"

"Well, I was out here one morning when he come out, and there was . . ." He stopped himself, then waved it away. "Never mind. You'd think I was getting senile."

"No, I wouldn't. I wish I had half as sharp a memory as yours." Which was true. Mom always used to say that Mr. Finney was the man to ask if there was something about the history of this neighborhood that you'd forgotten.

"Well," he said, "your dad come out here one morning and waved hello to me—I was workin' in the garden—and then he did the same thing you did, he got his paper and turned around, and there was a streak of paint—" he pointed to the front porch, "—right in that same spot. Eaves to porch, just like this one. He cussed up a storm and we went to take a look and found out the paint was still wet." He stood staring for a moment—not at me or the house or the streak, but into the depths of a past that was probably more alive to him than the world he was stuck in now—and suddenly blanched.

Thinking he might be having a heart attack or something, I went down and put a hand on his arm. "You okay?"

"Yeah, yeah," he said, snapping from his reverie. "It's just that . . . I remember your dad cussing about the damn kids that'd done it, painting a streak of 'workman's gray' down the front of the house." He gave a short laugh. "This is gonna sound nuts, but I'd almost swear to you that streak of paint your dad found was the exact same color as the house is now."

"I don't remember him asking me to help him clean it," I said.

"That's just it," said Mr. Finney. "He didn't have to clean it. We found it around eight-thirty in the morning, and it was gone when we looked again around ten."

"Gone?"

"Uh-huh." He looked at his watch, then at me.

"Guess you think I'm weird, huh?"

I knew what he was getting at. "We'll see at ten," I replied. "Meet you by the curb?"

"I'll be there."

I always used to wonder where, precisely, the soul is located. If the soul is to be found in space, then where *the hell is it? Physicists think of time and space as a sort of four-dimensional sheet with the possibilities of other disconnected sheets. Could the soul reside in between the layers? On the other hand, space-time could be envisioned as enfolded by, or embedded in, a higher-dimensional space, much as a two-dimensional surface or sheet is embedded in three-dimensional space. So why couldn't the soul inhabit a location in this higher-dimensional space which is still, geometrically speaking, close to our own physical spacetime, but not actually in it?*

If that's the case, then could it be that that "smallest, un-

seen" quantity—the 1.62×10^{-33} at which space and time come apart—is actually the location where the soul physically goes to roost after death?

3. One Foot In History/The Weight

Back in the house, I laughed softly to myself. There were a hundred explanations for what had happened—both with Dad and with me—but if Mr. Finney was trying to turn his morning into a short romp through *The Twilight Zone,* who was I to ruin his fun?

I poured myself another cup of coffee and went to the refrigerator for an orange.

I opened the door and discovered the bags of Ayds setting on the top shelf.

I was still staring at them when my sister Blair came up behind me, pointed at the bags, and said, "Mommy."

"Huh?"

She looked at me as if I were some sort of dim-witted puppy. *"Mommy's candy."*

"Oh. Thanks for clearing that—"

Then it hit me. When I was teenager and Blair was barely two (she was a late-in-life baby), our mother went through a phase where, for some reason, she decided she needed to lose weight. Despite that the woman probably weighed 120 pounds soaking wet, she started buying and gobbling Ayds by the bagful, so no matter what, there were always several bags of it—say three pounds' worth—in our fridge, same shelf, same spot.

I stared at the bags and whispered, ". . . Jesus . . ."

I inherited our parents' house (along with the care of my sister) after Mom's death. I've replaced most of the appliances in the kitchen, except for the refrigerator. It's the same one my parents bough right after they were married, and soon will celebrate its fiftieth year of operation. The damn thing's a wonder; it has never, *ever* broken down.

I pulled out one of the bags just to look at it. I was holding something that, to the best of my knowledge, had ceased to exist when I was fifteen. Blair stomped her foot and put her hands on her hips, her lower lip jutting out in a pout that would look right at home on a three-year-old's face. "Thas' Mommy's candy," she said. "Gonna get it if you eat any."

Blair has Downs' Syndrome. She's creeping up on thirty but has the mental capacity and verbal skills of a five-year-old. The doctors were certain that she wouldn't live through her teen years, but she's beaten the odds. Hell, she'll probably live to bury me. She lives with me because I promised Mom and Dad that I would not put her into any sort of home . . . and because of a certain piece of advice Mom gave me at the end of her life.

I don't keep Blair closed off from the rest of the world; she attends a sheltered workshop five days a week where they teach her basic social and personal skills—what they refer to as "habilitation training"—and she has many friends. Hers is as fine a life as I can provide for her on what little is left from my parents' insurance (after final medical bills and burial expenses) and what I make as day manager and co-owner of Cedar Hill's largest and most successful used bookstore. Believe me when I tell you that "successful" is a bit of a euphemism when applied here, but the store's got a sufficiently large enough clientele and a good enough reputation that business is steady. Steady enough. Thank God the house is paid for.

Blair came over and yanked the bag from my hand, tearing it open and scattering dozens of wrapped pieces all over the kitchen floor. She stepped back, dropped the mangled remains of the bag, and gasped. "Oh . . . lookee what you made me do."

"*I* didn't make you do anything," I snapped, with a bit too much irritation under the surface. "You did this all by yourself. If you wanted to see it, I would have given it to you, but you didn't ask. *Did you?*"

She glared at me, hands fisting at her sides. She chewed on her lower lip, took a deep breath, and then spit on the floor. *"Pancakes!"* she growled.

Caring for Blair takes up nearly all of my non-work and -sleeping time. Most days she's well-behaved, but she has these episodes, usually lasting two or three days at a time once they start, where she hates the world as well as everyone and everything in it. I've often wondered if these "spells" (as Dad used to call them) are triggered by some complex realization somewhere in her mind that she's different from a lot of people, and this realization makes her angry and hateful. And *hateful* is definitely the word for it.

I pointed to the candy and the spit. "I'm not cleaning that up."

"Don't care."

"I think you should apologize for what you said."

"No."

"*Blair. . . .*" The warning in my voice was clear.

She glowered at me for a few seconds longer, then stomped over to the kitchen counter, picked up the sugar canister, and dumped its contents on top of the spit and candy. Then she slammed the canister down so hard it bounced a foot into the air and came back down with half of it dented in.

"Stop it," I said.

Her response was to spit again—this time at me.

Like I said: hateful.

She was hating me, hating that it was Saturday and there was no workshop to attend, hating that I never let her go anywhere alone, not even to the little market at the end of the street, and most of all hating that I would make her clean up this mess. So she spit on the floor and growled her version of "Fuck you!" at me. (Blair has her own special meanings for several words: *Pancakes* is *Fuck You, Mama-Frog*—one word, two caps—is *My Period Has Started, Sakteboard* is *Time To Watch Television,* and *Kahoutek*—one she learned from me during my brief but infamous Astronomy Craze of 1974—is what she says instead of *Gesundheit.* That one gets weird looks and big laughs from people every time.)

I grabbed the broom from its place beside the pantry and held it out. Blair stomped her feet and released one of her patented tantrum screams, then wrenched the broom from my hand and did a Babe Ruth with it right upside my head, snapping the handle in half, bloodying my nose, and leaving most of the bristles stuck in my hair, beard, and face.

I reached up and wiped away some of the blood, then sat on the floor looking up at her. Blair has a very powerful swing, and an even worse right cross. I've been on the receiving end of both more times than I care to remember.

"Do you feel better now?"

"Pancakes! Pancakes! PANCAKES!"

I shook my head and continued to sit there, too tired to get mad about it. In a little while she'd start feeling really awful about what she'd done, come to me all hugs and apologies, and things would go on as they had before until she had another "spell" later tonight, or tomorrow. This was always the pattern. For the next seventy-two hours, life would be a miserable proposition.

There followed several moments of silence. Blair would either blow up again, go to her room to listen to records or the radio, or scribble on one of her dozens of sketch pads. (Blair loves to draw and waterpaint.)

I waited, hoping it would go no further than this—which was mild in comparison to some of her fits. She once broke my nose with a punch when I forgot to pick up microwave popcorn for our Friday Night Movie. (Blair has broken my nose twice.) Another time she came out of the bathroom and threw a *very* used, very bloody tampon right in my face. I never did find out what that had been about.

One of the things I hate about myself is those times— usually post-fit—when I think about how much easier my life would be if: A) Blair were living in a group home, or B) If she'd never been born.

I know—that second one is unforgivable. But it's there, and eventually I'd have to deal with it. Just not now, not *then,* not that morning.

I reached up and pulled the paper towel roll from a nearby counter and used about a thousand sheets to wipe away the blood from my nose and hands—some of the bristles had managed to scrape my fingers enough to draw blood.

I finished, then sat back against the wall and—my nostrils stuffed full of torn paper towel—leaned my head back and swallowed.

I was surprised to feel tears in my eyes. I quickly wiped them away before they spilled down my face. Christ, what was the point sometimes? I'd had such *dreams* in this house, in this kitchen, when I was growing up: I was going to be an astronaut (a ruptured spleen at age six had killed that one), then I was going to be a rock 'n' roll star (had to hock my guitars and amplifier when I was fifteen to help out with money when Dad was laid off from the plant for a while), and then, in college, I was going to be either a great writer or a great scientist (I minored in English and Physics and never got around to doing a damn thing with either degree).

I used to laugh at the part of myself that thought black light posters were cool and that I was going to take on the world and win, but at times like this I realized that something of that teenaged soul lived on and watched me, like a child ashamed of its parents. Only now I was my own parent and my own child. No part gets left by the side of the road; each ghost of yourself at ten, or thirteen, or sixteen, sits in judgment of what the others did, and what they have become.

I pulled in a deep breath that hurt more than I'd expected.

"Don't cry, Danny," said Blair.

"I'm not," I lied.

"Yes, you are." Her voice was thin and scared. She'd only seen me cry twice before this; once at Dad's funeral, once at Mom's. Blaire equated my tears with death. In a way, I guess she was right to make that connection this time.

"Danny?" She sounded on the verge of tears herself. I waved my hand at her, a sign for her to be quiet and leave me alone for a minute.

Sometimes, when the past sneaks up behind you, it's hard to shake it off right away.

My "coming of age" happened between 1971 and 1976. I was too young to "relate" (*that word!*) to the World War II generation and not old enough to be accepted by the Woodstock Nation; D-Day happened long before I took my first breath, and by the time I understood that the Kent State shootings were related to some war in a place called Vietnam, President Nixon was beginning the process of pulling U.S. troops out of the sad and ravaged country while thousands of ragged Cambodian refugees traversed the endless Killing Fields in hopes of being air-lifted by the U.N. to a safer land. So there I was, like others my age, dismissed by the ones who'd fought the Nazi Terror and mocked by those who wore flowers in their hair and made the "peace" sign and quoted people with names like Leary and Hoffman and Dylan and Baez. Abandoned to our own devices, my generation inherited a Teenage Wasteland and grew up in front of the television set with the Bradys and Fred Sanford and the eminently-quotable Flip Wilson while looking for our niche. I spent a lot of time listening to Yes and King Crimson and Emerson, Lake & Palmer and other denizens of the short-lived "art rock" era: From the Beginning they sang of being Close to the Edge, of seeing All Good People going Roundabout in the Court of the Crimson King. Mysticism abounded in their lyrics, and even though it wasn't easy to fully understand their sometimes nebulous concepts, their music nonetheless planted a notion in my mind that maybe, just maybe, we of the Brushed Aside Age could strive toward some new level of universal understanding (aided by the smoke of Hawaiian Seedless, natch) and salvage Purpose from the labyrinthine chaos left by one Depression, four wars, an energy crisis, and the "Generation Gap." Yeah, we were full of shit, I know that now—but then, *then* it felt good to believe in that, to be a young anarchist who could lay waste to the establishment during the day and still get home in time for supper and *Night Gallery;* it felt good to be full of piss and vinegar and passion, knowing there was a reason for being alive, there was such Promise for us to fulfill . . . then four buffoons broke into a suite at the Watergate Hotel and before you could say "Woodward and Bernstein" our unbeknownst-to-us fragile idealism crumpled into a heap on the floor. By the time we were able to stand again, it was 1977; a little-known movie called *Star Wars* had just opened, Menachem Begin was the leader of Israel, four different buffoons tried to steal Elvis Presley's body, and *Studio 54* opened its doors. We took our cue from this latter event: dressed in polyester leisure suits with open collars and gold chains dangling around our neck, possessed by a Saturday Night Fever that jackhammered under mirror-ball lights, we boogied across the disco floor in revealing dresses, flared pants, fuck-me pumps, and platform shoes. We were the selfish, hedonistic "Me" generation, sexually liberated and not giving a rat's ass about anything that did not directly affect us. Our so-called values were the supreme embarrassment of the last half-century—c'mon, already, we thought *Jonathan Livingston Seagull* was deep and were *proud* of ourselves for inventing the Pet Rock, the Mood Ring, and Space Food Sticks. We were blissfully ignorant of any ugliness in the world . . . then the Reverend Jim Jones led his followers to mass suicide in Guyana, Mark David Chapman walked up to John Lennon outside the Dakota in New York and splattered the former Beatle's brains all over the pavement, someone decided to check John Wayne Gacy's basement after he was arrested, and those of us left standing realized that no amount of self-indulgence or blind loyalty to false ideals was going to protect us from the Big Dark Eventuality; so the leisure suits and plats and pumps were stored far away in the backs of closets where no one would ever have to look upon them again, a thing called AIDS (definitely *not* spelled with a "y") came to collect for our careless promiscuity, and we stood before the looking glass of our conscience wondering why we felt so empty. How romantic to be so disillusioned at such an early age.

Some of us never got over it. Some of us didn't even survive it. The rest of us . . . well, we managed to get out alive and grew up to become uncomfortable anachronisms. And co-owners of used bookstores.

My little stroll down Amnesia Lane over, I looked up at my sister and said, "Why don't you go watch some cartoons? I'll be along in a few minutes."

"I didn't mean to hurt you."

"But you did."

She looked like she was going to break down any second.

"I'm sorry I said that, Blair. I know you didn't mean to. It's okay."

"Really?"

"Yes."

"I love you lots, Danny."

"I love you, too." And I did. But at times like this, I wished I didn't. So sue me.

Blair exhaled and folded her arms across her chest, the unsteadiness gone from her voice. Now it was her turn to sound like an adult and make *me* feel better. "I made a mess."

"I noticed."

"An' I hit you."

"Uh-huh."

"An' I busted the broom."

"You'll get my bill in the mail."

She laughed. When I looked at her, she quickly covered her mouth with her hands so I wouldn't see the grin.

"What's so funny?"

"You. You're goofy!"

"No, I am not goofy. I am bleeding. Do you think that's funny?"

"Yes."

"Well, it isn't," I said, rising to my feet. As I was doing so, I caught a glimpse of my reflection in the big silver toaster: My hair was a mess, my shirt was speckled with paint dust and drops of blood, and the pieces of paper towel I'd stuffed into my nose—pieces which I thought had been about the size of a fingernail—looked like the tusks on a sick walrus.

I couldn't help it—I laughed, too. Then Blair laughed louder. Then I really let fly, guffawing so hard that I blew one of the walrus tusks out of my nose.

"All right," I said. "I guess this makes me goofy."

Blair found the dustpan and grabbed my still-folded newspaper. "I clean up my mess now." She knelt down and started to use the paper for a sweeping device.

"I haven't read that yet," I said, taking it from her.

"But I gotta—"

"I know, I know." I looked around and spotted the remains of a pizza box in the recycling bin. I tore off the lid, folded it in half, and handed it to her. "Use this."

"Wow," she said. "That was a smart thing."

"Well, even us goofy bleeding guys have our moments." That got another laugh from her.

Triumphant in my duty to entertain, I took a small bow and headed into the downstairs bathroom.

Then there's the question of time itself. If the soul is not in space, then is it in time? Does it exist somewhere in that moment where 1.62×10^{-33} separates time and space? If the soul is the true source of our perceptions, then that has to include our perception of time. How else do you explain that so many of our mental processes are time-dependent: planning, hoping, regretting, mourning, anticipating, cha-cha-cha?

The idea of a timeless soul has always troubled me. What meaning do we attach to the soul after death, if the before-after relationship that we call time is transcended by souls?

Physicists do not regard time as a sequence of events which simply happen. Instead, all of the past and future are simply there, and time extends in either direction from any given moment in much the same way space stretches away from any given particular place. So the "there" that the physicists refer to, we call the present: a simple point on the four-dimensional sheet of the universe—a dot in the middle of a page.

But the ghost of a dot or a word or a drawing erased from a page can be brought back again.

Palimpsest.

4. Time Was/Hello, It's Me

I cleaned my cuts, applied Band-Aids, and used small squares of toilet paper until my nose stopped bleeding.

While I was waiting for my nose to get its act together, I sat on the lid of the toilet and opened the paper.

At first I thought that the paper had landed in a small puddle of some kind and the ink had started to bleed through the pages, but it didn't feel damp at all; in fact it looked, felt, and smelled like a fresh-off-the-press news-paper.

Each page looked to have been printed on twice: one page superimposed on top of each other. The print and photos of one layer were dark enough to be read and seen if you could ignore the lighter but nonetheless quite visible ghost page underneath. This wouldn't be the first time that the *Cedar Hill Ally* had experienced trouble with its print run, nor would it be the last. This is a town that likes to think of itself as a city, and despite everything the city government says it wants to do, Big Changes aren't really in their plans, they just like to make a lot of noise so those of us still living here will feel that Cedar Hill matters in the larger scheme of things. So they talk about updating the printing facilities at the *Ally* with computerized, state-of-the-art equipment, but it remains, as always, a small-town paper with small-town paper printing equipment.

I was ready to stuff the whole thing into the recycling

bin when something on page 2 (or I should say ghost-page 12) caught my attention.

The 1975 Senior Class of Cedar Hill High School would conduct graduation ceremonies this Thursday at White's Field, starting at 1:00 p.m.

Not a reunion. Graduation.

My graduating class, in fact.

I angled the paper away from the light to cut down on the glare, flipping through the other pages to make out what I could of the ghost pages beneath.

Every local, national, and international story was dated June 21, 1975.

I turned to the Community Announcements page.

William and Ethel Finney of 190 North Tenth Street would be celebrating their fortieth wedding anniversary on the 28th.

Then I looked at the Now Playing page.

The Midland was showing *Tommy*. The Auditorium was featuring *The Other Side of the Mountain*. Cinema 4 (then a real phenomenon, one building with *four different movie theaters! Can you* imagine *that?*) was showing *Dog Day Afternoon, French Connection 2, Hearts of the West,* and *The Apple Dumpling Gang*.

Finally, the Birth Announcements.

The previous day, Mrs. Virginia Gabriel of 182 North Tenth Street had given birth to a daughter, Blair Ann, at 6:15 p.m. A parenthetical aside noted that, although there had been some "unexpected complications," mother and daughter were doing well and expected to be released sometime in the next forty-eight hours.

Unexpected Complications. Right.

Mom had been forty-nine when she'd given birth to Blair, Dad had just turned fifty-five. They lived only twelve more years, and died within six months of each other. Neither of them had any idea how to deal with a Downs' Syndrome baby.

I thought about what Mom had said to me during that last visit:

"I knew we were taking an awful chance. I mean, I hadn't gone through the Change yet—which had me worried something terrible—and now here I was about to have another baby. I heard all these terrible stories about women my age who'd had babies come out in the most *terrible* state . . . and it scared me, Daniel, right down to the ground.

"I never told your dad about this, and I don't know why I'm telling you now, but before I do, you've got to promise me that you'll never, *ever* let on to Blair. You promise? Swear to me, Daniel. Okay, then.

"I knew going into my second month that something was wrong with the baby inside me. Don't ask me *how* I knew, I just . . . I just *did*, that's all. A woman's body, it speaks a language to her heart that only she can understand, and my body was telling me that what was inside me wasn't right somehow. Don't look at me like that, it wasn't like some *Rosemary's Baby* or *Omen* thing, I never once thought I was carrying Satan's bastard son—well, maybe once, but then you came out and looked so sweet . . . that was a joke, stop looking at me that way.

"I didn't think that Blair was a monster or anything, I just knew that she wasn't going to be *right*. I didn't think me and your dad could handle it, not at our ages and him with all his nerve problems—who knew his heart was going on him then? So I started thinking about . . . likelihoods."

Likelihoods. That was the word she used. In 1974, in a middle-class neighborhood (technically *lower* middle-class) in a sad little Midwestern town like Cedar Hill, a pregnant forty-nine-year-old woman with a husband and son, who helped organize community charity drives and bake sales and played Bridge with her friends every Thursday night, who never talked back to her husband and was raised to believe that a woman's place was in the home and only in the home, this type of woman, for whom appearances and others' opinions of her mattered greatly, this type of woman never said, whispered, or even thought the word "abortion."

But that didn't mean she wouldn't come up with a word such as *likelihoods* and assign it the exact same definition as That Word.

"I wasn't sure how I was going to do it. I never thought about it being like they scream nowadays—you know, a sin, murder, all of that—I just knew that if me and your dad had this baby, our lives would be changed for the worse. Your dad was trying to figure out if he could retire early, and I knew that if we had this baby, he'd be working right up until the day he died . . . and that's just what happened.

"Don't think bad of me, hon,? I love Blair, I do . . . but even now I can say that I ever really wanted her. I couldn't figure out if I should go to a doctor or a priest or maybe go ask one of the girls who were forming those Womens' Lib clubs at O.S.U. I had no idea how a woman my age back then went about getting that kind of information. You heard all them horror stories about girls who went down to Mexico and got themselves all butchered up and died . . . just terrible.

"So I finally thought to myself, 'If I'm supposed to have this baby, then have it I will . . . but if I'm *not* supposed to, then let Fate provide the means.'

"Turned out that Fate was listening to me that day.

"You remember how there used to be that piece of carpeting at the top of the stairs that everybody used to trip on? Lord, it was a miracle you or your father never fell and broke your necks!

"Anyway, one night I couldn't sleep, so I got up and went out into the hall and just . . . just stood there, wondering what I was going to do. I decided to go down to the kitchen and make a glass of warm Ovaltine, and just as I got to the landing, my foot caught in that piece of carpet and I almost fell. If it hadn't been for me grabbing the railing, I think I would've—and you know what a tumble that would have been.

"Then I just sat there on the top step and cried for a minute, because I realized that I'd just thrown away the chance Fate had given me. So I went down and made my Ovaltine, and while I sat there drinking it, I got to thinking . . . maybe I could do it again—you know, get my foot caught and fall. It wasn't enough of a fall to kill you, but if you were pregnant, it would be enough to make you lose a baby. I know because . . . I never told you this before, but . . . you weren't our first child. I was pregnant before you, and one day about a month or so into my pregnancy, I was carrying a small basket of laundry downstairs and slipped at the top of the stairs and fell. I miscarried right on the spot.

"So why couldn't I do it again? I mean, all I suffered that first time was a broken wrist and some cuts and bruises. I decided to do it.

"I went back up and stood there, making sure the carpet was still gonna catch my foot, and then I did a couple of rehearsal trips, you know? Taking a few steps back and then going forward; not looking down to see where I was going. Caught my foot each time.

"I got ready to do it for real, I walked a good ways back down the hall to make sure I had some speed behind me, and just when I got to the edge and felt my foot slip under, I felt this . . . this *breeze* behind me, like something big had just flown by, or somebody tried reaching out to grab me. At the same time, I saw this little light from the corner of my eye, and I thought, 'I just felt the wings of an angel trying to grab me.' I had just enough time to stick out my arms and stop myself from falling—and I would've. I had been given the *real* sign I asked for. So I went back to bed and said no more about it, and that's how you came to have Blair for a sister."

Blair knocked on the bathroom door. "You okay, Danny?"

It was only then I realized I'd been in there for almost half an hour. "Uh, yeah, yeah. I'm okay."

"I cleaned up."

"That's good. Thank you."

Silence for a moment, then: "I got something for you." A hint of mischief in her voice. Her mood was back to normal now. I still wondered when the next fit would come.

I folded up the paper and opened the bathroom door. "What is it?"

"I got you a girlfriend."

I blinked. "Huh?"

Blair nodded. "I found her on the back porch."

She grabbed my hand and dragged me back into the kitchen.

Sitting at the table, a large, heavy-looking backpack resting by one of her legs, her long black hair as thick and beautiful as I'd remembered it, was Laura Kirwan, the woman who I once thought was the love of my life.

"Hey, stranger," she said, a hint of Is-he-glad-to-see-me-or-not? in her voice. "Blair let me in."

"Why the back door?"

She shook her head and laughed, her same deep-throated laugh that had only gotten sexier with age. "Dumbass. Don't you remember? Everyone used to come in through the back door when we were in high school."

"Oh." I am nothing if not a flaming wit.

She looked at Blair, then at me. "It's good to see you."

"You, too."

"I wasn't so sure you'd want to see me. I mean, what with the way I left."

I shrugged. "I'm sure you had your reasons."

I knew that at a moment like this I should be pulling her to her feet and holding her close, hugging her for all I was worth—God, she still made my heart triple its rhythm—but I couldn't. I suddenly felt like a failure. How many evenings had she and I spent talking over our dreams and hopes? Here we were, twenty-five years later, like two characters from a Harry Chapin song, knowing what we felt but having no idea what to do about it . . .

Palimpsest.

When copying Biblical texts, ancient monks were often forced to erase pictures and words from previously-used sheets of parchment because they lacked sufficient supplies of paper. As the ink from these newly-created pages began to dry, the impressions left on the parchment from what had been there before began to show through. View these pages in their modern-day museum homes and it's easy to see where the original drawings and text "ghost" through, creating two simultaneous pages on one sheet; past and present merged into one: the former bleeding into the latter, as if living already for the second time.

But is this life, like that of the soul, in time or space?

5. I've Been To Paradise (But I've Never Been To Me)/ Now I'm Here

It was 1975 the first time I told Laura Kirwan that I loved her.

Ours was one of those oddball relationships that you see manifest in high school. I was the nerd, she was the popular cheerleader/student council/homecoming queen/straight-A student everyone wanted to know. Hell, guys like me could simply revel in her breeze as she passed us in the hall. That was enough; just to know that someone like her existed in our world and we got to see her.

I was never really sure of why she started talking to me before the study hall we had together, I knew only that I felt humbled that she did.

At first it was simply about school and teenager stuff—which teachers we liked, which ones we thought were dweebs, what movies we thought looked good—but then things started getting a bit more serious.

The first time she'd had sex with Paul Lawrence, a star player on the football team and her boyfriend our junior year, it wasn't exactly consensual. In fact, as she told me about it, we both realized at the same time that it had been rape, pure and simple. But Paul was very popular, as was she, and the Popular People simply didn't cause any fuss. I told her she should have him arrested and charged, but she was both too humiliated and too scared of how it would affect her social standing in the school to do anything about.

"I'll just break up with him and warn the other girls away," she said.

"Yeah, that'll teach him." I made no attempt to disguise my disapproval.

She glared at me. "I thought you were my friend."

"I am."

"Then would you please not judge me about this? Just . . . just be my friend, okay? Just understand."

"I'll try."

We sat together in study hall every day after that, and had lunch together at least twice a week. Being around her leant me a certain mystique among her circle: If *Laura Kirwan* likes this guy, then maybe he's got something we haven't noticed before.

Hey, it got me a couple of dates with girls who otherwise wouldn't have given me a first look, let alone a second one. But that didn't matter; by our senior year, I was so in love with Laura that I couldn't imagine the rest of my life being worth squat without her.

But she had cast me in the role of her best friend/surrogate brother, and I hated it, but I'd never tell her that because it would mean an end to our time together.

Like our "study nights" that were really just an excuse

to watch movies, listen to records, gossip about the people we knew, and share our hopes for the future with someone who wasn't going to laugh at our dreams.

Then came the Friday night when she didn't bring any books or records or magazines over. She came to the back door and knocked—even though she knew it was okay to just come in—and I answered to find her standing there in tears, carrying her favorite backpack, the one I'd gotten her for her birthday last year.

"Laura? What's wrong—get in here."

"I c–can't, Danny. Not tonight. I . . ." She looked like someone who suddenly had the weight of the world dumped on their shoulders and didn't dare tell anyone for fear it might crush her.

"Laura, what is it?"

She didn't say anything, only stepped forward, put her arms around my neck, and gave me the longest, sweetest, saddest kiss I'd ever had or ever would receive.

Then she put her head on my shoulder and stood there holding me.

"Did Tanner do something?" I asked. Tim Tanner was her latest boyfriend, another football player who also played basketball.

"I have to go away for a while, Danny."

Listen to how my chest cracked open at those words.

"Tell me what's wrong!"

"I can't. I just wanted to stop by and tell you . . . that I . . ." She shook her head and touched my face.

"Please don't go, Laura," I said, ashamed of the scared-little-boy tone in my voice. "I don't want you to leave. You're my . . . I mean . . . ah, hell! I love you, Laura. I think I've loved you since the moment I first saw you."

"There's my Danny, sweet, romantic, never judging me."

"Don't. Go. *Please.*" I was crying now and hating myself for showing her just how weak I could be when she needed someone to be strong.

"Promise me one thing."

"What?"

"Don't cry for me, okay? Just remember that you were the only guy who . . . who I believed when he told me that he loved me."

She grabbed her bag and ran off the porch, disappearing

around the front of the house. I ran through the kitchen and living room, through the front door, and vaulted down the front steps just in time to see her pull away in Tanner's car.

Now, sitting in my kitchen, she smiled at me and said, "Did you keep your promise, Danny?"

"What're you—?"

"You never cried for me, did you?"

"He was crying today," said Blair.

Laura looked at her, then me. "Is anything wrong?"

"No, a bad morning, that's all."

"Well, what do we do now?"

"Why are you here, Laura?"

Her answer came immediately, with the sure, steady cadence of someone who had practiced what they were going to say so they'd get it right:

"You may find this hard to believe, Danny, but there hasn't been a day since I left Cedar Hill when I haven't thought about you and what we could've had if I hadn't been so stupid and full of myself. I was *popular,* after all, and you weren't, and I didn't want to risk my place in the school's hierarchy by getting romantically involved with you.

"I knew the night I left that I'd made the first truly big mistake of my life by not being with you. But by then I was pregnant with Tanner's kid and the two of us were going to run off with his college money and start a life for ourselves. I couldn't tell you—I couldn't tell anyone. I lost the baby, he got bored with me, and less than seven months after we left this burg, he dumped me in L.A. with two hundred dollars and one suitcase of clothes."

"How'd you manage to get by?"

She smiled but there was no humor in it. "I was a pretty young thing. It wasn't hard to find work—no, I didn't start hooking or anything like that." She shrugged. "Made some movies—not the kind they would've shown at the Midland, but it paid the bills. I got involved with a guy who knew what to do with money, how to invest it, and between that and the movies, I got by just fine. You're making me stray off the point—I always loved you, Danny. I still do—and I think you must still feel something for me or else you'd've kicked my ass out the door thirty seconds after you saw me."

"What's going on, Laura?"

She stared at her hands. "If you're asking me if there's been some big dramatic turn of events, then the answer is 'nothing.' Three days ago I was sitting in my apartment in L.A. watching television, and *French Connection 2* was on. I remembered how you always used to rave how it was every bit as good as the original—"

"—better, in some ways—hell, John Frankenheimer had some sequences—"

"—could we not do our Roger Ebert imitations right now? So I watched it, and you were right, it's great, Hackman's even better in it than he was in the first one, and all of a sudden I wanted to talk to you about it, about why Frankenheimer's your favorite movie director, about why you still own LPs when most everything is available on CD, about anything and everything, the way we used to in high school. And then I realized that what I wanted was . . . you.

"I blew it twenty-five years ago, Danny, and I want a second chance. Will you think about giving me one?"

I reached out and turned her face toward me.

We all want to know what happened to the first Great Love of our lives, but we never think about the danger in actually finding out. Meet someone after half a lifetime, someone who was once the center of your world, and you risk seeing all the signs of diminished hope or smashed dreams embedded in their face like scars, or—worse—discovering that they've gone on to be happy without you. I used to fantasize about a moment when Laura Kirwan would return, a broken shell of the girl I once knew, and beg me—Mr. Astronaut/Rock Star/Famous Author/World-Renowned Physicist—to take her back.

Arrogant male bullshit, that; I know.

I hadn't made it and neither had she, not in the ways we'd imagined at seventeen, but you'd never be able to tell it from her face; it was older, yes, a few more lines here and there, crows' feet when she smiled, but aside from these inevitable tracks of time's forward march, she was no less beautiful in my eyes now than she'd been in high school. In fact, if anything, age had given her humility and grace and made her all the more stunning.

"We can talk about this later," I said. "You're welcome to stay here with Blair and me as long as you want, until you figure out what you need to do."

"I knew that's what you'd say."

"Quarter of a century later and I'm still that predictable."

"No," she said, squeezing my hand. "You're dependable. You're loyal and true."

"You make me sound like Dudley Do-Right."

"Dudley's gonna be on soon," said Blair. I blinked—I'd almost forgotten she was in the kitchen with us.

Laura saved the day: *"Really?"*

"Uh-huh."

"I *love* Dudley!"

Blair grinned. " 'I save you, Nell.' "

"Can I watch Dudley with you?"

Blair's face lit up. "Oh, yes!" And she left to tune in the Dudley Channel.

"How long have you been caring for her?"

"Since about a year before Mom died."

"Is that why you never . . . ?" She didn't have to finish the question.

"Yeah," I whispered.

We looked at each other.

Live your life as if you were already living for the second time and as if you had acted the first time as wrongly as you are about to act now.

I was getting ready to say something tender and profound, something that would have won the heart of any woman, something that would have gone down in the record books as the Most Brilliantly Poetic and Romantic Reply Ever, when there was a knock on the front door.

I looked up at the wall clock and saw that it was 10:00 a.m.

Already I was so exhausted I was ready to pack in it, and it wasn't even noon yet.

"Shit," I whispered.

"You sweet talker."

"No—sorry, that wasn't for you. I forgot I was supposed to do something at ten." I leaned down and gave her a quick kiss on the lips. "This'll only take a minute. Go watch Dudley and Nell."

"Actually, I always thought Snidely Whiplash was pretty hot."

"I can't tell you how warm and fuzzy that makes me feel."

Out on the front porch, I found Mr. Finney waiting for me.

"Sorry it ain't the curb, but I waited almost five minutes."

"I apologize. I lost track of time."

"It's gone."

"What?"

"Take a look for yourself."

He was right. The streak of old white paint was gone. The front porch was once again uniform in color. We both touched the area where the streak had been, and found that the paint there was dry.

"Danny, does this seem odd to you?"

"It's actually a little scary, Mr. Finney."

"Do you believe in ghosts, Danny?"

"Why?"

"Do you think it's possible for a house to haunt itself?"

I thought about this for a moment.

"Mr. Finney, if you mean do I believe in the kind of ghosts that rattle chains and moan and make things go bump in the night, then, no, I don't. But I *do* believe in ghosts, sir. Quantum ones. Black holes and Special Relativity and Planck time and how they make origami out of the sheeted layers of the universe." I glanced at him. He was looking at me as if I'd just told him I was an alien from the planet BoogerFart here to scout good locations for our upcoming Special Olympics.

"What I mean, Mr. Finney, is that less than two hours ago we both saw a section of this front porch as it was *before* I painted the house, and fifteen years ago, you and my father saw a section of fresh gray paint—*this paint*—in the same spot. There were no practical jokers, Mr. Finney. No one's touched this house except me. I painted it last year, and through some mix-up in the structure of time, a portion of this paint appeared on the porch fifteen years ago."

Finney shook his head. "I swear, the older I get and the more I learn, the less I think I know. How . . . how is something like that possible, Danny?"

"Why do you care about it in the first place?"

His eyes misted for a moment. "Because if what you said is true, then it means there's really forces beyond what we understand, and *that* means there's something more after this here life, and that means my Ethel'll be there waiting for me. I'll . . ." A tear crept to the corner of his eye. ". . . I'll see her again. Hold her again. My favorite and only girl. She won't be lonely anymore."

At that moment, I think I loved Mr. Finney as much as I'd loved my own father. Leave it to a man this genuinely decent to think only of his wife's loneliness, even years after her death.

I put a hand on his shoulder. "Maybe the universe is trying to tell us both something with all of this."

He took a handkerchief from his pocket and wiped his eye, then blew his nose. "I hope so, Danny. I truly do hope so." He smiled at me. "Sure would appreciate it if you'd come over for some lemonade soon. Bring Blair along, too."

"How's tomorrow? We'll bring lunch."

His smile widened and brightened. "That would be just great. Just great. I'll look forward to it."

I watched him walk back to his house, and hoped that it would seem a little less empty.

The universe is a four-dimensional/four-layered sheet; three existing in space, one in time.

The soul—be it of a person, place, or event—does not exist in space. 1.62×10^{-33} is a smokescreen. Yes, time and space come apart at that point, and there are spaces between the layers, but only the soul, like images and words erased from a sheet of parchment, can make a physical impression on/in time.

And if the impression/perception is strong enough, if the past is more alive to the perceiver than the moment in which they exist now, then it matters not a damn if time came before space or vice-versa, because the soul takes control, and bleeds through the layers, and brings back What Was.

And, sometimes, if the need is great enough, it brings What Could Have Been.

6. Living in the Past/Love Reign O'er Me

That night I lay wide awake in my bed, thinking about how the rest of the day had gone while the clock-radio was tuned to an oldies station. Tonight seemed to be Sad Songs Night; "All By Myself" had just finished (mawkish piece of shit still managed to choke me up) and Don McLean's "Vincent" was just starting.

Blair and Laura got along wonderfully. They watched cartoons, made lunch, drew pictures (giving me a chance to explain the palimpsest effect, to their rapt, glassy-eyed boredom), then tried to teach me how to dance, soundtrack provided by two '70s favorites, "Life Is a Rock (But the Radio Rolled Me)" and "Get Down Tonight." How a K.C. and the Sunshine Band record *ever* got into my house is beyond me.

But, underneath everything, I could sense an unease in Laura, a forced cheerfulness whenever she was around Blair. I was trying to figure out why when two things happened simultaneously: my bedroom door opened and the night light in the hallway flickered and went out. I knew I should have changed the bulb this morning, but the day had brought with it too many distractions.

"Danny?" It was Laura.

I sat up in bed, pulling on a T-shirt I grabbed from the floor. "You okay?"

"I'm fine," she whispered, and softly walked over to the bed. "Can I sit down beside you?"

"I, uh . . ."

She smacked my arm affectionately. "Don't flatter yourself, Studley. I didn't come up here because the call of your man-meat is irresistible. I was lonely down on the couch. I was just wondering if . . . if we could just lay next to each other and hold hands, like we used to down in your parents' rec room."

I moved over and patted the bed. She lay down next to me and we held hands.

"Danny?"

"Yeah?"

"I'm gonna tell you something, and I'd really appreciate it if you wouldn't look at me while I'm saying it, okay?"

"Okay."

"I really like Blair, I think she's sweet, and I am in awe of you having sacrificed so much to take care of her. It makes me realize all the more just how much I love you and what I've missed out on these last twenty-five years. I'm gonna move back here to Cedar Hill."

Listen to the thudding of my heart as she said this.

"But I can't . . . I can't help you care for her, Danny. I hope that doesn't make me an awful person in your eyes. I mean, maybe someday, later on, when I feel more comfortable being around someone like her—oh, God, that sounded rotten, didn't it? 'Someone like her.' I'm sorry."

"Don't worry about it."

"Do you hate me?"

"No."

At that moment, I hated just about everything else, though. So the love of my life was coming back after all, to start her life over . . . and it would be without me. Oh, I knew she'd spend a lot of time with Blair and me at first, but after a while, she'd come around less and less, until, finally, her presence in my life would be reduced to a few phone calls . . . and even those would eventually stop. It was the pattern. In the years I'd been caring for Blair, I'd had only a handful of relationships with women, none of them going very deep or lasting very long because they couldn't handle being around ". . . someone like her."

I couldn't blame them. I couldn't blame Laura.

"It's always been you," I said to her.

"I know."

I felt a tear slip from the corner of my eye, run down my temple, and drip into my ear. "I wish things were different."

"Me, too." Then: "You wouldn't ever consider . . . don't yell at me, okay?" She rose up on an elbow and rolled toward me, wiping the tear-streak from my skin. "Would you consider something like a group home for Blair? If you haven't done it because it's a money problem, I've got plenty, believe me. I'd pay for it."

"I promised Mom I wouldn't do that."

"Not to sound like a bitch, but your Mom's been dead for fifteen years."

"Thirteen-and-a-half," I said.

"Whatever. The point is, as much as I admire you for keeping your promise, don't you think it's time to start living the life you *should've* had?"

"Don't go there."

"Why not?"

"Because I can't start thinking about what *should have* been. Too many detours through depression and self-pity along that road."

And wouldn't you know it—right then the radio station started playing Roger Daltrey's "Oceans Away," a song that rips me to pieces every time.

I rolled away from Laura and looked into the darkness.

A few moments later, just when I was on the verge of really losing it because of that fucking song, I heard Blair bumping around in the hallway.

"Dammit," I said.

"What is it?"

"Blair. She doesn't see very well in the dark, that's why I've got a night light out there. She's trying to find the bathroom." I started to get out of bed. Laura put a hand on my arm.

"You stay here, Danny. I'll go."

She quietly left the room. I suspected that once she'd helped Blair get to and from the bathroom, she wouldn't come back.

The song finished and I turned the radio off before they played "Shannon" or something even worse, and that's when I heard it.

The sound of someone coming *up* the stairs.

Blair's room and the bathroom were in the center of the hall, away from the stairs. I waited to see if Laura was going to surprise me and come back, and when she didn't step through the door again, the old urban panic reared its irrational head.

Someone had broken into the house.

I slowly got up and crouched down to retrieve the baseball bat I keep under the bed—my one compromise in this age of ever-deadly home security. I'd never keep a gun in the house, but a baseball bat . . . oh, yeah.

I got a good grip on it and crept toward the door.

It was only as I was stepping into the hall that I realized the floor under my bare feet felt fuzzy. I looked down.

Carpeting. Shag carpeting. From one end of the hall to the other.

I looked around, stepped fully into the hall, and started toward Blair's room. I was almost there when I heard someone behind me.

I whirled around and saw the intruder at the top of the stairs.

I pulled back my arms, readying the bat, and started moving toward them, so filled with panic that I didn't bother to register what they looked like, only that it was neither Blair nor Laura, and I was all set to knock their legs out from under them—was just starting to get my swing going—when the night light flickered and I saw my mother.

My mother as she'd looked in 1974.

Before there was a Blair.

I stood there, the bat cocked at my shoulder, and watched her slip her foot under the piece of loose carpeting on the landing.

She rehearsed it once, then once again.

It was the interval between the second rehearsal and her actual attempt that the impressions previously erased joined with new ink and began to bleed through for me:

. . . *Live your life as if you were already living for the second time and as if you had acted the first time as wrongly as you are about to act now* . . .

. . . *at 1.62×10^{-33} space and time come apart* . . .

. . . *and this sheet of parchment upon which I had drawn my new life was giving way to the lives and memories drawn in this space before* . . .

. . . *"Thas' Mommy's candy. Gonna get it if you eat any"* . . .

. . . *"Because if what you said is true, then it means there's really forces beyond what we understand, and that means there's something more after this here life, and that means my Ethel'll be there waiting for me"* . . .

. . . *"I mean, maybe someday, later on, when I feel more comfortable being around someone like her"* . . .

. . . and Mom started moving toward the top of the stairs.

I knew that the "breeze" she'd felt that night was me swinging the bat at someone I thought was an intruder.

She was gaining speed. When her foot hit that carpeting, she'd go down hard. Not hard enough to kill her, but it would be enough to make her lose the baby that only she and the doctor knew she was carrying.

I suddenly saw What Might Have Been become What *Can* Be.

I saw a life without constant worry, without daily arguments, without Blair screaming and saying that she hated me, without tantrums that left me with bloody noses and spit on the floor and used tampons thrown at me.

All I had to do was just stand here and *not* swing the bat. Mom breezed past me.

The night light flickered again, then came all the way on——Mom seemed to notice that from the corner of her eye——and all I had to do to claim the life that should have been mine . . . was nothing.

Nothing at all.

Mom's foot caught under the piece of carpeting. . . .

7. Lucky Man

I saw a kid today who was wearing bell-bottom jeans and a buckskin jacket with a Smiley Face sewn onto its back, the words "Have a Nice Day" painted in Day-Glo colors underneath it.

As he approached, I couldn't help but look down at his left hand and, sure enough, he was wearing a Moon Ring that shone a deep azure-blue. I wondered if he'd gotten these antiques from a parent, an aunt or uncle, or if he'd shelled out a good portion of his savings account to purchase all this stuff at one of the retro shops that have been multiplying like bacteria since the middle of the '90s. I stared in a combination of awe and embarrassment; my God, did we really look that absurd back then? Someone should have said something—we thought we looked *good*.

The kid caught me staring at him and up came his middle and index fingers in the "peace" sign. I couldn't help what I did next; I smiled at him and returned the gesture.

"Outta sight man," he said on his way past. "Groovy. Far Out."

" 'Keep on truckin',' " I replied.

"Huh?"

I whispered the next as if it was some kind of secret code: *"Dave's not here, man."*

For a second, those words managed to stop him in his tracks (obviously he'd never been exposed to the pot-haze whimsy of Cheech & Chong); if he said anything to me after that, I'll never know: I was distracted by a voice calling, "Danny! Wait up!"

I turned and waited for her to catch up with me.

I smiled as the girl I loved more than anything in the world came up and took hold of my hand.

"I thought you hated it when I held your hand like this."

"Nah," said Blair. "I like it." She playfully bumped her shoulder against mine. "I like having you for a brother."

"That's sweet . . . but I'm still not buying you rollerblades."

"Thas' okay. Where we goin' today?"

"That's up to you. It's your birthday."

"Wanna go see Laura?"

"No, we didn't call. We always call first. She has a husband and kids, you know. We can't just show up like we used to."

"I know. I just . . . miss her sometimes."

"Me, too. But, hey, *we* have fun, right?"

"We have *all* the fun."

"So what do you want to do?"

"Go to the bookstore an' then have some lemonade with Mr. Finney?"

"Mr. Finney died last month, Blair. Remember we went to the funeral?"

"Oh. . . ." She looked as if she were going to cry.

"But he had a good life. He's happy now. He's with his wife."

"Thas' good."

I squeezed her hand. "So, you want to go to your big brother's bookstore, huh?"

"Yes. When we get home, can we have some of that chocolate cake I found?"

"You mean the one from the Birthday Cake Fairy? You bet."

And off we went, returning to the life I'd almost been stupid and selfish enough to throw away.

There was a time when Ayds (spelled with a "y") was a popular and surprisingly tasty dietetic candy that came in plastic bags containing individually-wrapped pieces. You could easily find it on store shelves right alongside Sweathog coffee mugs, *The Wit and Wisdom of Archie Bunker,* Kiss comic books, and *Chico and the Man* lunch boxes. There was a time when a nerdy kid at Cedar Hill High School dreamed of being an astronaut or rock star, maybe a famous author or great scientist—but whatever he became, he'd be married to the cheerleader he was in love with.

There was a time when he looked at his new baby sister and wondered why her face was so weird.

There was a time when the past seemed more real and desirable to him because he couldn't stop looking behind him . . . until he stepped out into a dark hallway one night and realized that all he'd wanted from life was someone to love him unconditionally for as long as he lived, and that he'd been so busy looking back he never realized that someone had been with him all along.

I let go of Blair's hand and told her it was okay for her to walk on ahead.

She waited at the light until it changed and the **WALK** signal shone. She crossed the street, then turned and waved at me. She smiled, so very pleased with having finally crossed a street on her own.

I smiled and waved back, twice as proud of her as she was of herself.

When I joined her, she took my hand and led me forward, slowly, with great dignity.

Then I sneezed.

"Kahoutek," she said.

"Foghat," I replied.

"Huh?"

THE GIFT OF A DREAM
by Dean Wesley Smith

Dean Wesley Smith has sold over twenty novels and around one hundred short stories to various magazines and anthologies. He's been a finalist for the Hugo and Nebula awards, and has won a World Fantasy Award and a Locus Award. He was the editor and publisher of Pulphouse Publishing, and has just finished editing the *Star Trek* anthology *Strange New Worlds II*.

Kendra Howard pulled herself slowing up to a sitting position, using the railing on her bed, then rubbed her old legs through her nightgown, slowly, as if doing so would bring back some of the long lost feeling to them. She had been dreaming again. Dreaming of dancing, as she and her husband used to do every Saturday night.

Like him, and the use of her legs, those days were long gone.

Yet every night, without fail, she dreamed of dancing.

Around her the Shady Valley Nursing Home was quiet. The festive Christmas decorations filled the hall outside her door, and later today she knew there'd be ham for Christmas Eve dinner. Then turkey for Christmas dinner tomorrow. It had been the same every Christmas for years now, since she had moved in here and her only son had moved from Chicago to the West Coast. Now he could only afford an occasional holiday call and a once-a-year summer visit.

She could hear the faint ticking of Brian Saber's wall clock across the hall, but nothing more. It was now Christmas Eve, and for some reason, Christmas Eve always seemed to be quieter than any time of the year. Not even the snowstorm outside rattled the windows. The wind off Lake Michigan must have shifted as the weatherman on television had predicted it would. It was amazing what people could do these days with science stuff.

She glanced at the blue numbers of her alarm clock. Two minutes after four in the morning. It would be at least another hour before the night nurse stopped in to check on her. She was going to need to use the bathroom before then. That's what she got for having that second cup of tea. Now she was paying for it.

She rolled over and eased down the bar on the side of her bed, then levered herself slowly to the edge, and made sure her wheelchair was in position. Using the muscles in her stomach to control her legs, as she had taught herself to do twenty-five years ago, after the car accident, she rolled on her side and moved her dead legs off the edge of the bed. Then with a twist she had made hundreds of times, she half-dropped, half-lowered herself into her wheelchair.

The feeling made her smile. She often had the nurse or orderly help her out of bed, but still having the freedom to do it on her own was the most important thing she held onto. At eighty-eight years of age, freedom was everything.

She wheeled her chair around and headed for the bathroom. She was halfway there when a cold draft whipped her nightgown around her legs, as if someone close by had opened a door.

Her window was closed and the drapes hung down limp. She could see that much in the faint light from the nurse's station, so she glanced out and across the hall. There she saw a young man, shadowed and wearing some sort of dark uniform, pick ninety-one-year-old Brian Saber out of his bed and head for the room's sliding glass door.

At first she was stunned, then she was about to shout for help when she heard Brian's distinctive laugh. Whatever was happening, Brian was a part of it. He wasn't minding at all. Maybe it was some sort of Christmas gift from someone. It couldn't be from any of his family, though. As far as she knew, he didn't have any left alive.

After a moment the man carrying Brian had opened the sliding door to Brian's room and the two of them had disappeared silently outside, leaving only a short draft of cold air behind.

What was Brian up to? She talked with him a lot during

lunches and dinners. In fact, she considered him her best friend in the place, yet he'd never mentioned doing anything like this.

She waited, almost holding her breath in the silence of the nursing home night, then eased out into the hallway. To her right was the brightly lit nurse's station, decorated in red ribbons and white bows. She could see the night nurse's head sticking up just above the top of the low counter. She was obviously bent over some paperwork and paying no attention at all.

Taking a deep breath, Kendra silently wheeled her chair quickly the rest of the way across the hall and into Brian's room. His bed was slept in, his wheelchair beside his nightstand, his wall clock ticked the seconds away.

But there was no sign of Brian.

She moved to the sliding glass door that led from his room out into a central courtyard. She pulled the curtain aside, not knowing what to expect.

There was nothing out there.

In the snow she could see a man's tracks coming from the center of the courtyard to Brian's door, then another set going back. But she couldn't see where they had gone.

She eased her chair away from the window and moved it so that she was sitting in the dark corner of the room beside the door to the bathroom. She had a sneaking hunch Brian would be back very shortly. And she didn't plan on leaving until then, no matter how bad she needed to go to the bathroom.

*   *   *

Captain Brian Saber of the Earth Protection League slapped the two hot Proton Stunners into their holsters on his hips, ran a hand through his thick head of wavy hair, and smiled at the six dead bodies of Bocturian scum. "I don't think you'll be sabotaging any more slow-speed Earth supply ships."

They didn't answer, for obvious reasons. They were dead.

He felt proud, staring at the oil-smelling bodies, their tentacles twitching in the air, their six eyes fixed in their death stare. Around him the control room of their ship stank of a combination of fish and intense lilac perfume.

Brothel jokes were common anytime anyone from the Earth Protection League had to board a Bocturian ship. He knew for a fact that it was going to take some time before the smell got out of his leather pants, silk shirt, leather pants, silk shirt, leather vest, and high boots. He hoped it washed out before his next mission, otherwise his crew was never going to let him forget it.

"Captain?" Carl Turner, his second in command asked over the communications link. "Are you wrapped up there?"

"Bows are tied and presents under the tree," he said. "How about the rest of the Bocturian ships?" In this mission there had been ten Earth Protection League ships fighting a small fleet of Bocturian pirates. The pirates hadn't stood a chance.

"Cleaned up," Turner said.

Saber felt a slight tinge of regret. The mission was almost over. "Prepare to pick me up," he ordered. "I'm going to need a good bath before we head back."

"I copy that," Turner said. "I can smell you from here."

"Next time you do the boarding," Saber said.

"Uh, Captain," Turner said, "we took a slight hit to the forward section of the ship."

"Anyone hurt?" The twisting in Saber's gut told him the answer to his question. On this mission there had been ten of them on the ship. Sometimes there was just him and Turner, but they had needed the gunners and support crew this time. And two of that crew had been in the forward section.

"Ben and Sarah," Turner said. "Ben will survive. Sarah was killed."

"Damn, damn, damn," Saber said. He hadn't known Sarah that well. They had been on six missions together, with her working weapons for him on the two of the last three. He didn't even know what part of Earth she was from, or how old she was back there. But if she did have some family, they weren't going to have a happy Christmas Eve.

"Inform command and medical," Saber said.

"Copy that," Turner said.

With one more glance at the dead pirates, Saber turned and headed for the air lock.

Twenty minutes later, after a quick shower, he was standing over the coffinlike bed of his sleep chamber. He had already tossed his uniform into the cleaning bins to be laundered when they returned to Earth, and had pulled his nursing home nightshirt over his young body. It always felt weird doing that, yet he knew that on the other end of the flight having the nightshirt on was better than having one of the young soldiers dress him.

He sighed and stared at the sleep chamber. The problems with Trans-Galactic flight were the reasons he was here. At top speeds, Trans-Galactic flight regressed a human body, so for quick T-G jumps to the outer limits of the Earth Protection League borders, they had to use old people to start.

He was just about as old as they came.

No one really understood exactly why T-G flight worked that way. Or why on the return flight, they returned to their original age. Or at least no one had been able to explain it to him in a way he understood. He knew it had something to do with relativity, the curved nature of space above the speed of light, all combined with the fixed nature of matter.

None of it made any sense to him.

All he knew was that on Earth he was a ninety-one-year-old cripple in a nursing home. Out here on the borders of the Earth Protection League space, he was a young man again. All thanks to the nature of Trans-Galactic flight.

He climbed into the coffin-shaped sleep chamber and smoothed down his old nightshirt. Then he quickly pulled the lid down, triggering the departure and his quick nap. Fighting the alien pirates had taken him three days out here. He'd be back in his room on Christmas Eve morning, less than twenty minutes after he left. But he'd still have the three days of fresh memories.

That was one of the good things about the relative nature of time and space and matter.

With luck, there'd be another mission this week. Another chance to be young again, fight the good fight as a hero of the league on the very edges of civilized space.

*   *   *

The young soldier picked him out of the sleep chamber as if he weighed nothing. Actually, he didn't weigh much

more than a hundred pounds these days in his ninety-one-
year-old body.

"How'd the mission go, Captain?" the soldier asked as
the tractor beam released them in the center court of the
nursing home and the soldier moved with sure steps
through the soft snow.

"Just about as good as could be hoped," Saber said, his
breath frosting up in the cold night air. Both he and the
young soldier knew that was all Saber could tell him about
the mission. Almost no one on Earth even knew about the
Earth Protection League. It was just safer that way.

The young soldier was a member of the League, of
course, but unless he decided to spend twenty years on a
slow shuttle that stayed under light speed, he'd never see
anything beyond the moon until he got a lot older. So there
was just no reason to tell him about the missions. The kid
couldn't go out there. He was just too young to survive the
age and time regression.

The soldier carried Saber through the sliding door into
his room and laid him gently in the bed. Then the kid
stepped back and saluted. "Great job, Captain. I'll see you
again soon. Have a Merry Christmas."

"Thank you. You, too."

The kid turned and then stopped, as if seeing a ghost.

It took Saber a moment to understand what the problem
was, then he saw Kendra, the woman who lived across the
hall, as she wheeled her chair out of the shadows of the
corner. Kendra was his best friend here in the nursing
home. He'd often wished he could tell her about his
missions.

The young soldier glanced back at him, a look of fear
on his face, his hand on his gun. Saber understood the
reason for the kid's fear. If the case warranted, the young
soldier was ordered to kill anyone who happened to get in
the way of a mission. But Kendra wasn't in the way. Tonight's mission was over.

"It's all right, soldier." Saber looked the young kid directly in the eyes and smiled. "She's a friend."

The young man stood for a moment, then nodded. "Understood, Captain. Command will be expecting a report
on this."

"They will have it in the morning."

The young soldier nodded to Kendra. "Good night, ma'am." He then vanished through the door, closing it behind him.

Saber lay on his back in his bed, his head turned, staring at Kendra. He couldn't really see the expression on her face, and she said nothing.

For the next few moments the silence in the room sounded like a roaring engine about to overwhelm them both, the ticking of his wall clock like the timer of a bomb.

Then finally Kendra said, "Have I got you in some sort of trouble?"

Saber remembered the pitched fight he'd just had with six alien pirates, the success they had had again in defending the Earth Protection League and its space. And the death of Sarah.

That was trouble. Not this.

He laughed. A hacking, coughing, old man's laugh, that lasted for a good thirty ticks of his clock before he finally stopped and motioned Kendra closer to his bed to tell her the story of his mission tonight. After all the years of going out and coming back, of defending Earth against all odds, and all alien scum, he *finally* got to tell someone.

And for the next hour it felt wonderful.

Almost as good as killing those alien pirates.

*   *   *

Kendra Howard was more stunned than anything else. Brian's wild story of being a Captain in the Earth Protection League, of fighting alien pirates in deep space as a young man, was outrageous to say the least. Yet she had seen him carried in and out of the room by a man who had called him Captain. More than likely it was all just some wild fantasy Brian had paid a kid to help him carry out as a Christmas present to himself. After all, he'd only been gone from the room for twenty minutes, not three days like he said.

Yet a part of her had wanted to believe his wild dream. Especially the part about growing young again because of how time and space and matter worked. His explanation had almost been funny enough to laugh at. Yet when he had tried to explain it to her, she hadn't laughed. Just listened, hoping to not break the fantasy world he lived in. She liked him enough to do that for him. Especially on Christmas Eve.

It wasn't until the end of his wild story that he asked her something that bothered her on a deep level. He asked if she was interested in joining up, being a solider in the Earth Protection League, of being young again to help Earth fight whatever threatened its borders.

The question bothered her a great deal, but instead of saying so, she laughed and said, "Who wouldn't like to be young again?"

"Great," he said. "I can't promise anything, but it never hurts to ask."

At that moment the nurse poked her head in and smiled at them. She asked if Brian needed anything, then winked at Kendra and left.

Kendra laughed and suddenly realized she hadn't yet made it to the bathroom. "I'll see you at breakfast," she told Brian, heading for the door as fast as she could move her chair.

"Can't say anything about this to anyone," Brian said.

Again she laughed as she went into the hall. "Who would believe me?"

*   *   *

At breakfast Brian was all smiles, his wheelchair pulled up to a table in the corner of the festively decorated lunch room. No one else was sitting at the table. Beyond the window the Chicago weather had turned cold and clear, the sun bright off the white ground. All the snow was going to freeze solid. It was lucky she wasn't going anywhere for Christmas. The roads would be awful.

She wheeled herself over and joined him. "Good morning," she said. "Going to get cold tonight out there."

He glanced at the window, them back at her, his smile growing even bigger. "I hadn't honestly noticed." He waited for the orderly to give her food and leave, then leaned over slightly and whispered, "There's a mission tonight and League Command said that if I was willing to

train you on the ship's proton weapons, you could join up.
Take Sarah's place. You'd be a private, but there's room
for advancement."

"You're kidding, right?" Kendra asked, staring at him.

There was a twinkle in his eye that she'd never seen
before. "Not in the slightest," he said.

Then his expression got very serious and a coldness came
into his eyes. "But it's dangerous." His voice was a low
whisper. "I won't kid you on that. You die out there and
they bring your body back here and you're found dead in
your sleep in the morning. The time travel part of things
just doesn't revive anyone."

She hadn't been so confused in years. Brian was seriously
asking her to join in his delusions. And he was telling her
it was dangerous. What were he and his friend going to
do? Would Brian kill her if she went with them in the
middle of the night?

Brian reached across and touched her hand. She could
feel the roughness of his hand against her brittle skin. It
was the first time a man other than an aide had touched
her in any way since her husband had died. "You said you
wanted to be young again."

"I do," she said, moving her hand away.

"But you don't trust me, do you?" Brian said, smiling.
The boyish twinkle was back in his eyes.

"Would you?" she asked. "You have to admit, your story
is pretty wild stuff."

"I didn't believe it either, my first night," he said. Then
he laughed. "To be honest with you, even after going on
more than a hundred missions, I still don't believe it."

"So I should just *trust you?*" she asked.

"How old are you, Kendra?" he asked in return.

"Eighty-eight," she said, squaring her shoulders. No man
had asked her that question in years.

"I'm ninety-one," he said. "This is a dream come true.
At our age, what else do we have to live for but dreams?"

At that moment, for some crazy reason, she decided he
was right. Maybe it was because it was Christmas Eve. Or
just maybe she really didn't have anything to lose. Either
way she'd play along with him and his wild fantasy, maybe
even let herself believe that she might be young again for
a short time.

Every night she dreamed of dancing anyway. Why not join Brian in his dreams for a short time?

"I'll go," she said, smiling at him.

The light in his eyes was like a child seeing the presents under a Christmas tree. She knew she had made the right decision.

By midnight that night, she wasn't so sure.

By three in the morning, Christmas morning, when the young woman dressed in black came across the hall from Brian's room, she was scared out of her wits and ready to back out. But the fact that there was a young woman also involved calmed her a little.

"Brian says you're thinking of joining the League, Mrs. Howard," the woman said. "I sure envy you."

Those words rocked Kendra completely out of her fear. She looked up into the young eyes and the smiling face of the woman over her bed. "Envy me? Why?"

"Because you get to go out there, into space, to defend Earth. It will be years before I can go, even on a short-run mission."

Kendra only nodded. She still didn't believe she was going into space, but at this point she really didn't know what to believe was going to happen.

"Are you ready?" the young woman asked as she moved in beside Kendra's bed and lowered the railing.

"Why not?" Kendra said. "After all, it's Christmas."

The woman picked her up as easily as the orderly, then glanced down the hall to make sure the nurse wasn't watching before going across and into Brian's room. Brian was already gone and the young woman carrying her didn't hesitate. She went right through Brian's sliding glass door and out into the cold night air, her feet crunching on the frozen snow, her arms holding Kendra gently, but firmly.

"Aren't I going to be missed?" Kendra asked as the night air bit at her, sharp, pinlike.

"You'll be back in twenty minutes," the young woman said. "Everything is taken care of on this end."

The rest went like a blur for Kendra. The floating up through the air into the ship was like a nightmare. The minute they lifted off the ground she started to really believe Brian's story. And the sleep chamber in the small room was exactly like Brian had described.

The woman laid her in the deep chamber, on the soft padding, and then pointed to a closet. "Your uniform is in there, made to fit you exactly. When you wake up, just shove the lid open and get dressed."

"How will I get out of this?" Kendra asked, indicating the sleep chamber. She knew without a doubt she was too weak to push herself over the edge of something this deep.

The young woman laughed. "Just trust me, you won't have any trouble."

With that the woman closed the lid and before Kendra could even think another thought, she was asleep.

*   *   *

Kendra didn't dream, or at least didn't remember dreaming. She awoke without opening her eyes. She was almost afraid to. She could feel the softness of the padding under her, so she knew she wasn't in her own bed in the nursing home.

Slowly she opened her eyes to see the top of the lid of the sleep chamber. She raised a hand and pushed the lid open, then stared at the skin on her bare arm.

Young skin. Perfect skin, not the blemished, dried skin of an eighty-eight-year-old woman.

Then she moved her leg.

It was as if her heart stopped at that moment. Not since the accident that had killed her husband and crippled her had she been able to move her legs. Yet now she could.

Both of them.

She sat up and watched her legs move under her old nightgown, then quickly swung herself up and out of the sleep chamber, landing on the floor, *on her feet,* as if she'd done that every day for years.

Brian had been right. Or this really was the most vivid dream she had ever had.

She glanced around. She was alone in what looked to be a small cabin of a ship, the only furniture a bolted-down chair and the sleep chamber. The same room the woman had carried her into.

Kendra quickly pulled off her nightgown and studied herself in a full length mirror. It was her young body, all right. From her eighty-eight-year-old mind, it looked perfect, even though she knew that at twenty, she had thought her body far from perfect.

How little she had known then. She was one damn fine looking broad, as they used to say.

She laughed, her voice higher and clearer to her ears than she remembered. Then she opened the closet and started to get dressed. As the woman who had carried her had said, the uniform fit perfectly. Brown leather pants, tall black boots, a silk blouse that fit loosely over the middle and tightly across her chest, and a leather vest with a triangle insignia on it that read EPL.

Earth Protection League.

She studied herself in the mirror one more time, then turned and headed for the door, smiling, enjoying the feel of her feet under her as she walked. It was time to see just exactly what this dream was all about before she woke up.

The door to her room slid open. In the narrow corridor two men stood, leaning against the wall. One was short, with light-brown hair and an infectious grin. The other was a tall, square-shouldered, square-jawed man with a handsome face and a thick head of wavy, black hair. They both looked to be in their mid-twenties and had on the same uniform as her, only the tall, good-looking one had two weapons on his hips like an old gunslinger in the wild west.

He pushed himself away from the wall with the ease of a man perfectly in touch with his body, then said, "Merry Christmas and welcome to my ship, Private Kendra Howard. This is Lieutenant Carl Turner, my second in command."

Carl stuck out his hand, smiling. "Glad you decided to join us."

She nodded as she shook his hand, then glanced at the one who had introduced them. She knew who he was, but for some reason her mind wasn't letting her admit it. Finally she said, "Brian?"

He laughed. "Of course, but I'm afraid we have to be a little more formal on board ship. You need to call me Captain when we're on a mission."

She knew she was standing there, on her own two legs, her head shaking, completely stunned. More than likely her mouth was open, too. Both men had the decency to not laugh out loud at her.

Captain Brian Saber smiled and touched her arm. "As I said, I still think this is all a dream, too. But I'm afraid it's not." His face got very serious and the cold, intense look she had seen in the nursing home was now in full force on this younger version. "You're going to get a quick dunk in the deep end with this mission, I'm afraid. We don't have much time."

"Why?" she managed to ask. "What do I need to do?"

"I've got to get back to the command center," he said. "Carl will get you checked out on the photon weapons and what the enemy ships look like, and how to destroy them."

"Enemy?" she asked. She had never fired a weapon before, and she didn't know if she could ever do it, let alone kill something.

He touched her shoulder in a reassuring way. "Good luck, and I'll see you after it's all over."

With that he turned and strode down the corridor, a man completely in charge of his world. She had no idea that Brian had such force inside of him. At the age of ninety-one, such force was often hidden, or pounded out of a person.

She wondered how people saw her at eighty-eight.

She took a deep breath and turned to Carl. "Well, show me what to do and how to do it, and I'll see if I can carry my weight."

He laughed. "The Captain said you'd be a good addition to the crew. I just think he might be right."

"He did, huh?" she said as Carl led off in the opposite direction from the Captain. "Nice to know." Then, all the way down the corridor she rejoiced in the feeling of actually walking again.

*   *   *

Captain Brian Saber flew his ship through and at the enemy as hard and as fast as he could. The Astra Warsticks were long, thin things that resembled a straw more than a spaceship. At full length, they were only one half the size of his ship, but still very deadly little things.

He dove in again at one of them, twisting to give his

gunners open shots, then quickly used evasive maneuvers to avoid getting hit by the Warstick Energy Beam weapons that shot from each end of their ships like orange fluid blown out of a drinking straw. He was trying to do everything in his power to make this a fight.

"Damn," Carl muttered under his breath beside him as Saber barely avoided flying directly into one of the Energy Beams from a Warstick.

Damn was right. That had been too close. He swung the ship out wide and made a pass alone the length of a turning Warstick, letting his gunners hammer at it.

No one at Earth Protection League Command thought he, or the other twenty ships sent to this battle, would survive. The Astra had decided to take six league systems, had given Earth ten hours to turn them over, and when Earth had said no, the Astra had sent two hundred Warsticks across the border. His job was simply to slow them down while the League mounted a better, and more powerful defense closer to the threatened systems.

Saber guessed the League figured that twenty ships full of old nursing home residents were expendable when it came to defending Earth's space. And he agreed.

He and the rest *were* expendable when it came down to fighting off the alien scum.

But he didn't plan on getting killed just yet, especially by an alien that looked more like a piece of straw than an alien warrior. That would be like getting beaten up by the ninety-pound weakling in school.

But at the moment, that was exactly what was happening. They had managed to destroy six of the Warsticks, but had lost three of their ships in the process. They were going to slow the Warstick fleet down, that was for sure, but they weren't going to stop it by a long ways unless he came up with something fast.

Suddenly the voice of Kendra came over the ship's communications link. "Captain?"

"Go ahead, Private," he said. In the battle he had forgotten she was even on board. What a mission to be her first. And most likely her last. If they were killed, Shady Valley Nursing Home would have two deaths in one Christmas morning.

"Our weapons are doing no good against the sides of these ships," Kendra said. "But I have an idea that is pretty far-fetched."

"Anything at this point," he said, moving the ship barely out of the way of two closing Warsticks trying to trap him between their open ends.

"From what the Lieutenant told me," she said, "the Warstick control room is near one end, their engine room is near the other, and weapons are fired from both ends."

"Got it right," Saber said. "What's your idea?"

"I think if you cut one of those sticks in half," she said, "you might put it out of business."

"And how would you suggest we do that?" Saber asked. Then almost before the question was out of his mouth, he knew the answer.

"Ram it," he said.

At the same moment she said, "Ram it."

"Great idea, Private," he said. "I want all weapons aimed forward and firing. On my mark."

The Warsticks were very thin right at the center, so the Earth ships had a complete advantage in size. And the Earth ships had great forward screens since they flew so fast through space with the Trans-Galactic drive.

He swung the ship around and headed for the center of the nearest Warstick. One problem the sticks had was turning quickly and he stayed easily ahead of the Warstick's evasive turn.

"Asteroid deflectors on full!" he ordered.

"Already on," Carl said.

"Brace for impact!"

It was almost anticlimactic. The ship didn't even bump. Saber had felt a worse impact running over a jackrabbit with a car when he was younger.

But the Warstick was cut in half.

A moment later both ends of the enemy ship exploded in bright white flashes.

"Well, I'd say that worked," Carl said, looking over and smiling a Saber.

"Inform the other ships," Saber ordered. "Weapons crew keep firing forward. Let's take out another one."

He swung the ship around and plowed through the center

of another Warstick before it could even begin to turn out of his way.

The same thing happened. They went through the alien ship as if it wasn't even there, then the separated halves of the Warstick exploded.

Maybe, just maybe, they had a chance in this fight. For the first time in a few hours, he was starting to hope he just might see one more Christmas turkey dinner.

Two hours of hard fighting later, the Astra Warstick fleet, or what was left of it, turned and headed back for the border. There were still fifteen of the twenty Earth Protection League ships left.

They had won and won easily.

Saber reported to League Command what had happened, then sat back in his chair and took a long, deep breath. He had been sweating for hours and could desperately use a shower. But he hadn't felt this good about a mission in a long, long time.

"Nice flying, Captain," Carl said, also slouching in his chair, clearly as exhausted as Saber felt.

"Thanks," Saber said. "I think this deserves a party, don't you?"

"I think the fact that we're still alive deserves something," Carl said, laughing.

Saber flicked the communication switch to the eight members of his crew. "Congratulations people, on a job well done. And special thanks to our newest crew member, Private Kendra Howard. Party in one hour, everyone. Don't be late."

*   *   *

Kendra smiled at the Captain's words and for the first time in two hours let go of the control stick for the Proton Beam weapon, then sat back in her padded chair. She couldn't remember the last time she had felt so tired and so exhilarated at the same time. The battle had seemed to go on forever. Yet at the same time, it seemed it had just started and then it ended.

Behind her Private Becky Pollard came up. "Nice job. Much better than my first time out here." Becky was a short woman, with bright red hair and freckles. During the battle she swore more than any person Kendra had ever heard, using words Kendra had never dreamed a woman could use so effectively.

"Thanks," Kendra said. "I had no idea what I was doing."

"How could you," Becky said. "Remember where you were when the Captain asked you to join the crew."

"A nursing home wheelchair," Kendra said, the memories flooding back in. And the questions about this all being a dream. It didn't feel much like a dream anymore, that was for sure.

"Being in a nursing home sure trains you to fire a Proton Beam, doesn't it?" Becky said, then laughed.

"I wish I had one for a few of the nurses," Kendra said.

Becky laughed. "Yeah, I know that feeling. Come on, I'll show you where a shower is, and you should have another fresh uniform in your room."

"Thanks," Kendra said. Then, almost as if it had been a habit for the past twenty-five years, she pushed herself to her feet and stood. It wasn't until she took the first step that she remembered that before this trip, she couldn't walk. And hadn't been able to for years.

This was a dream.

It had to be.

One hour later, freshly showered and still marveling at her ability to walk, she joined the rest of the crew in the small mess area. The place smelled of fresh bread and all the tables had been pushed against the walls. Drinks and food filled one table near the door and she took a bottle of water and some fresh bread. She met the crew members she hadn't had time to meet before the battle, then moved over to Captain Saber.

"Thanks for the great idea of ramming the Warsticks," he said, handing her a drink. "You saved all of our lives."

She laughed. "You'd have thought of it eventually."

"Maybe, maybe not," he said. "Thanks."

"You're welcome." She knew her face was red, but she ignored the feeling.

At that, the Captain turned to his second in command and said, "Fire it up."

"You got it, Captain," Carl said, smiling at her. He

flicked a switch and music filled the room. Christmas music just soft enough to talk over, yet loud enough to hear clearly.

The Captain bowed to her slightly. "I remember in one of our lunch conversations you mentioned how much you liked to dance. What better thing to do on Christmas than dance?"

For a moment she thought she just might wake up and lose the entire dream. But she didn't. She stayed right there, standing on her own two feet. "I'd love to," she managed to say to the Captain.

He took her hand and a moment later they were moving around the floor of the mess hall as the others watched and clapped along with the music.

Four hours later, after more dances than she could remember, she was standing beside her sleep chamber again, her old nightgown on her young body. She knew she had to get in the chamber, but she didn't want to.

She stood there, trying to get the memory of the dancing, of just standing, clearly in her mind. Finally when the warning bell rang, she had no choice. With one last twirl on her feet, she crawled in and pulled the cover closed over her head.

The next thing she remembered the young woman dressed in black was picking her up out of the sleep chamber and taking her down into the courtyard, floating in the cold Chicago night air. A few minutes later the woman put her down in her wheelchair, saluted, and left.

Kendra looked at her old, wrinkled hands in the dim light, then felt the deadness in her legs. Had she been dancing on those legs? Had it happened?

Had she just dreamed it all?

She needed to try to find out the answer to those questions.

She moved her chair out into the hall and through Brian's door. He was in bed, his head turned so that he could see her as she rolled up beside him. Even in the dim light, she could see his smile and the twinkle in his eyes.

"You've got a lot of explaining to do," she said, "before I'm really going to believe that all happened."

He laughed. "I felt exactly the same way at first. And

every time I end up back here in this old worthless body, I wonder if I did everything I remember doing."

"So it was real?" she asked, looking around the nursing home room, so far from the ship on the edge of the borders between earth's space and other aliens races. So far from the battle with the Warsticks.

"Very real," he said. "And very important. We're the only ones that can go out there and defend this planet. We're the only ones old enough to withstand the time travel length. Earth needs us. Amazing as that may seem."

A shiver ran down her back. "I thought I was long past the point where anyone would ever need me."

"A few years ago," Brian said, "so did I."

They sat in silence for a moment.

Finally she took a deep breath and realized just how tired she felt. She slowly pushed her wheelchair back and turned it toward the door. "Join me for Christmas breakfast?"

"I'd love to," he said, smiling. "And maybe soon we can go dancing again."

"Do you think that's possible? Really?"

"We usually are called for a mission at least once a week, if not more often," he said. "I think a dance or two just might be arranged."

"Thank you, Captain," she said. "For the best Christmas present anyone has ever given me. I will see you at breakfast."

"The pleasure will be all mine," he said.

She wheeled herself across the hall and to her bed. A few moments later she was on her back, staring at the ceiling, remembering the feeling of standing, of walking, and of dancing.

Especially of dancing.

She so loved to dance. Tonight hadn't been a dream. She knew that now. She had fought aliens for the Earth Protection League. And she had danced, and she would dance again.

For the first time in years she actually had something to live for. Tomorrow at breakfast she'd talk to Captain Brian Saber about all the wonders out there in the universe. And about her duties and what Earth needed from her.

It felt wonderful to be needed again, especially on Christmas.

She closed her eyes after a few minutes and drifted off to sleep. And for the first night in a very long time, she didn't need to dream of dancing.

A TOUCH THROUGH TIME
by Kathleen M. Massie-Ferch

Kathleen Massie-Ferch was born and raised in Wisconsin. She's there still, with a wonderful husband, two Scottie dogs, several telescopes, numerous rocks, and more books than she cares to count. She worked her way through college, earning degrees in astronomy, physics, and geology-geophysics. For the past twenty years she has worked for the University of Wisconsin as a research geologist. Massie-Ferch has made short fiction sales to a variety of places, such as *MZB's Fantasy Magazine, Sword and Sorceress, Warrior Princesses,* and *Far Frontiers.* She has coedited two historical fantasy anthologies for DAW Books, *Ancient Enchantresses* and *Warrior Enchantresses.*

I set the cardboard box on my new desk in the nearly empty office. Two high-backed chairs near the large windows looked very comfortable. An exceptional place for watching the eight very rare gaurs grazing in the lush green area between the widely spaced buildings. I wondered if the animals were the real thing or cloned bovines. This was certainly a better view than the one in my newly acquired living quarters. In fact, it was a majestic view and likely to be very distracting. And yet somewhere, under all that scenic grass, a series of tunnels connected every building I could see and those I couldn't see. Someone had fun designing this place!

I turned away. The entire wall opposite the bank of north-facing windows was floor-to-ceiling bookcases. It might be enough room. Might.

The phone rang. How should I answer it? I looked at it

through two more rings. Then I shrugged and picked up the handset.

"Dr. Connor Robins." One of the few times I had used my new title. I liked the sound of it. Nice and formal for the new job.

"Hey, Connor. How's the new digs?"

"Hey, Ky. They're fine. I see the rest of my things haven't arrived."

"You mean your books?"

I turned around and found my best and oldest friend standing in the open doorway, holding his cell phone. I hung up even as Ky did. We shook hands.

"So where are my books?"

Ky smiled as he shoved his hands in his jean pockets. "Still over in shipping. I had them put in more shelves." He pointed to the south wall. "They just finished with these yesterday. Maintenance will bring the books over later today, and I've got a grad student willing to unpack them."

"Grad student?"

"Yeah, in fact I think they had a raffle to see who got the honor of unpacking for you."

"What?"

"The great Dr. Connor Robins!" Ky laughed.

"You're bullshitting me, aren't you?" Did I hear the soft mooing of those bovines in the background?

"No, not at all. You're a legend around here. Some of the students know your dissertation by heart, I swear. Every formula. No one can believe how a genius of your magnitude could have taken so long to finish a simple Ph.D."

"Simple? Genius?" I studied Ky's dark features more closely. His brown eyes betrayed little except his usual good humor. I had known this man most of my life, but still it was hard to read him some days. "What have you been telling these people?" I went over and opened my sole box of fragile possessions. The box I wouldn't leave to the movers.

"Not much."

"What?"

"Basically that it took you five years longer than me because you are so demanding. Everything must be exact!"

"I'm not into sloppy work."

"Of course not. And neither am I, but no one really understands your mathematics."

"There was also the matter of that little pandemic in '04. You know that flu that killed so many people? It did disrupt a few people's plans. Including my own."

"Of course it did. You could have finished your degree during the middle of the pandemic, and they would have graduated you. Then you would have had lots of time to spend volunteering. Having a job didn't stop me, or anyone else here, from helping out where we could."

"My research was undone then."

"Only you knew that."

"No, my father knew it."

"So? He wasn't on your panel."

"No, but I'm sure he read my dissertation, analyzed the calculations, and passed judgment on it within hours of it being turned in."

"Connor, relax. He doesn't have that much pull anywhere in the world of physics, despite his precious Nobel. Remember what post-docs are for?"

"I've heard this argument before. Get out in the real world, make some money while finishing your research and then publish the good stuff. You ever finish your calculations on wormhole densities?"

He actually grinned. "No, but then I don't need to. You've proved we don't need wormholes to describe time flow."

"I didn't prove that at all. I found one theory of time, and it doesn't require worms. You could find another, just as viable method."

"Not likely." Ky reached into my box of belongings and pulled out a picture as I set up several others on my desk. "Is this the same picture we found at that garage sale?"

"Yes," I answered.

"How that one little history project changed your life. It sounded so simple. Find a picture of someone you never heard of and track down their life's story. You realize that most of the kids, including me, made up the stories we told?"

"Oh, I knew. And so did Mrs. Adams, which is why I got an A and you didn't."

"I thought that was because I chose a picture of a whale

and not a person." He looked at my new desk. "All of these pictures are of her." He took the one I was holding. "This one is even signed! How did you manage that? No, wait. I should ask, how long did it take you to track this one down? It's not as if Arnora Jord has a fan club or anything."

"Not long," I answered.

"I take that back. She does have a fan club. Membership of one."

I smiled. "Only me? How about you?"

"Yeah, I did like her. When I was fourteen. But the woman's been dead for eighty-four years."

"Don't embellish. It's only been—"

"Eighty-four years this fall," Ky finished. His smiled died. "I'm sorry, Connor."

"Why?"

"Because you got involved in time-travel physics because of her."

"Did I?"

Ky nodded. "I always thought you wanted to invent time travel to go back to that day she died and pull her from the burning theater, or to warn her off at the very least. And now your theories have proved beyond a doubt that history can't be changed, only observed."

"I know that's what my father thought, or maybe he never forgave me for going into an area other than quantum physics. He's taken my equations and is running wild trying to prove any form of time travel is impossible."

"I heard that. I knew he'd never be able to survive retirement. He's more prolific now than ever. Did you see his latest papers?"

"No. I'm avoiding them. He's always been very good at trashing my work."

"Actually he doesn't criticize your work or even mention it."

"No, but he doesn't have much use for time travel or preserving endangered species. And certainly not for restoring extinct species. When he finally finds a theory he likes, he'll try to ram it down my throat so I'll quit here and join his research company. Or he'll buy this company and shut it down."

"So much for retirement!" Ky said with a smile.

"Retirement means he only goes to the office six hours a day."

"Don't worry, Northern Escapes isn't for sale." Ky pointed to the table again. "How did you get so many pictures of Arnora?"

"There was a photographer who followed her around every day for a week just before she died. It was part of the promo for her new show. The theater burned down, so no star, no show. He never got paid for the work and couldn't sell the pictures. I found his estate and bought them."

"How did you ever learn about the obscure event?"

I pulled another picture from my box and handed it to him. It showed two boys standing arm in arm and grinning like the silly kids we were.

"How old were we then?" he asked.

"Thirteen. We had just won our first high school physics contest."

"Yeah, we won every one of them four years straight. I think they were happy to get rid of us so others might get a chance to compete."

"Maybe."

"And I bet we were the only kids in our class to actually get advanced degrees in physics. Most of them were just playing."

"No, Barb Jansen get her degree," I said.

"Yeah, but it was in astrophysics."

"Close enough. And her projects were damn good. Good enough to get her a great scholarship. She's at JPL now, if you care to e-mail her sometime."

He ignored me as I finished placing my pictures. Most, I placed on the table by the windows. Within an easy roll of my desk's chair.

Ky motioned to the display. "A dozen photos of Arnora."

"I bet you've got at least that many of your dog on your desk. And not a single one of a girl."

Ky's smile was back. "Actually, I've got several pictures of girls."

"Any of them not of your three nieces?"

"Hum, well, no. But they are of some very cute girls."

"Are you going to show me my new lab now? I want to

be back here to direct the placement of my books and notes. When I want something, I don't want to have to first phone some kid to ask them where they put it."

"Maybe you will. This kid's cute and available. And every bit as blonde and petite as Arnora. Her name's Rebecca Lanza."

"You haven't asked Becky out?" I asked.

"Can't. I'm her boss. By the way, it's Rebecca. Never Becky. But you could, you would just be a coworker."

"Why do I have the distinct feeling I'm being set up? Again?"

"Wouldn't dream of it! And I'm going to show you the entire complex, not just your lab." He waved me out the door ahead of him.

"I don't need to see it all. Moving has left me away from my work for way too long."

"Yes, you have to see it all. It might inspire you to think about time travel for something more important than getting a girl."

"Getting a girl?"

"Yes. We do some very important work with endangered species."

"I know and I very much approve of it. Okay, maybe just the barns."

"We have pandas," Ky said softly with his usual understated smile.

"Pandas? What kind of pandas?"

"Giant pandas. We have six from last year's efforts and five from this year's."

"How did you get so many breeding adults outside of China?"

"We didn't. They're all clones born to black bears." He grinned at my open mouth. "We already shipped nine youths to be introduced to the wilds in China."

"How many individuals do they represent?"

"Only five, but China is so happy with the cubs we sent over, they're sending us new tissue samples so we can expand our clone base. You want that compete tour now?"

"Yep," I said as I followed him down the hallway.

Northern Escapes! It still sounded like a vacation service. It looked like a resort. A large complex of buildings, nestled into a valley carpeted by lush grasses. Forests covered the upper slopes and hilltops. A pristine trout stream rushed through the middle of the complex. One of the complex's many tunnels passed under the stream and had a glass roof, so you could observe the underwater world. I was assured by several grad students that this was a great place to take a date on nights with full moons. I smiled at the information and wondered if it was so popular how they dealt with crowd control?

More than anything, NE resembled a very clean farm with lots of barns and research areas. All in all, very lovely and quiet, despite the nearly three thousand people working in the complex.

I saw the panda nursery, and even got to hold one. The small male had been injured when only a few days old and could never be released into the wild. They would keep him here, in the complex, for breeding. They even had his mate picked out. The original pandas had been a breeding couple; it was hoped the clones would be as well.

In my first two hours on the job, I learned more than I ever wanted to know about rare bovines, goats, and deer. NE had a regular farm here as well, with the requisite pigs, cows, and sheep. These "normal" farming activities were highlighted during the average "show and tell" for visitors, since NE also grew much of the food consumed every day by its employees. Ky continued talking about the company's cloning efforts over lunch. I ate my salad and listened as we watched a lazy group of pigeons fly over the valley. The flock landed as one near several researchers. I pointed to the birds.

"Are the pigeons someone's hobby? Or dinner?"

Ky laughed. "We don't eat pigeons here. We have a flock of domestic birds because we got some viable cells from two different passenger pigeons."

"Male-female?"

"No, both male, but we have been able to replace one Y chromosome with an X. They're going to start implanting fertilized eggs into surrogate pigeons this week. By this time next fall we may have a new flock."

"At most you'll have multiple copies of only four breeding individuals. Too small of a subset to get a viable population."

"It's a start until we can pull individuals out of the past.

We have to try." Ky waved to the scene before us as the pigeons took wing again and filled the valley's sky with their graceful dance. "If your father is right and we can't travel back in time, much of this will fall apart. Not right away, but it will eventually because of the lack of new genetic material."

"My father's wrong," I said softly. Ky looked at me, waiting for an explanation but I didn't say any more.

Ky stood. "I promised you a tour of the mammoth lab. Researchers unearthed another frozen mammoth two years ago. This one is in much better shape than the one they found in '99. They expect to find good DNA, though we don't expect we'll need elephant hosts for another year yet."

I couldn't help but smile as we walked out of the building. "This is all very exciting. A mammoth would be even better than pandas, but this all costs so much money. Who cares enough to support this?"

"Oh, you would be surprised how much people care about this work. Of course, not all is positive. Many have tried to buy us out and shut us down. It won't happen. There are too many on the other side. Some are hunters who want to see rare animals, especially mammoths, come back."

"To kill them?" I had to ask.

"Some may hope for that, but there will never be enough for hunting. Actually most hunters are naturalists, you know. They like animals."

"Ah, that's why they shoot gorillas and elephants and make ashtrays out of the body parts." The gentle summer wind blew across the valley and stirred the trees; still, I felt cold.

"Connor, NE never takes money with any strings attached. Certainly not that one. No matter how much money they gave, no one would be allowed to hunt our animals, here or in the wild." We kept walking and passed several techs returning from their lunch. One woman was obviously very pregnant. I waited till they were out of hearing.

"Ky, I've been hearing rumors that the pandemic left us nearly sterile, as a people. Any truth to that?"

"How would I know? I'm a physicist."

"Who's very into preserving endangered species. Did that pandemic leave humans endangered?"

"We still have a population of nearly five billion left."

"Five? I heard— How many people did we really lose in '04?"

Ky ran his hands through his hair. "You really want to know?"

"Of course."

"One point seven billion, give or take a few."

"How? Where?"

"Entire villages were wiped out all over the third world, but especially in Africa and Eurasia. Only twelve percent of the population had any resistance to that strain of virus. Those with AIDS or TB never had a chance."

"And some who survived couldn't take care of themselves, and starved. I had heard some stories, but I didn't know it was that bad."

"We were lucky and had stockpiles of drugs to help against the pneumonia."

"And now we're sterile."

Connor sighed heavily. "They don't know for sure. Those individuals who were sick have decreased fertility rates. Are their children the same? Worse? Or normal?"

"And those who never got sick?" I asked.

"Some test normal."

"Some, and if our children are worse or sterile, too?"

"We'll need that time machine."

"But we can't change the past," I said.

"No, but can we change the future by carefully stealing from the past?"

"I don't know yet." I itched to tell him more about my own research.

"By the way, we never had this conversation."

NE had goals I could believe in—and they had money. Lots of money. In fact the physics portion of NE's budget was rather small. Still there was no lack of funding my wants, as Ky had promised. And physics projects were seldom cheap these days. Had they ever been?

And they left me alone to work at my own speed. No official progress reports.

Even better than the government!

But then my work wasn't that expensive. I had seen some of the other labs and their setups. Big bucks were spent on portable power plants to fuel time machines. Or at least what those researchers thought would someday be time machines. None of the machines looked even as nice as H.G. Wells' famous machine from the movies. And these new toys would work about as well, too.

"Connor!" I turned and found Ky entering my lab.

"Hey, there. What's up?" I was seated at a workbench. I had thought it was the janitor returning to wash my soaking dishes, and I could chase him away again. I wasn't so lucky. "Did you try getting me earlier?"

"No, why?"

"Oh, my cell rang and I ignored it."

"Wasn't me." Ky's hand swept the room. "Mostly empty. What are you playing with that's so interesting, that you aren't making a time machine?"

I looked at him. "What makes you say that?"

"The room is so empty."

"Ah, you're assuming one needs a great deal of equipment to time travel. But since we, you and I, physically do not leave our time, why would we need lots of big stuff?"

"Big stuff being a technical term?"

I smiled. "Sure. By the way, I've been here months and have yet to see your lab. Why is that?"

"I don't have one. I'm management. I need to oversee everyone else's work."

"But you're a good physicist."

He shrugged. "I started out with a lab. Wasted space. Management takes up all of my time. What are you working on? Please tell me that that isn't ordinary glass?"

"Oh, but it is."

"Why?"

"My theories state we can't affect history or change it in any way. But they don't preclude us from watching it unfold—except we need a portal. Glass is very fragile and doesn't last long even if the piece isn't broken. In a short time it devitrifies. So I shall use this ordinary material as my spyglass—my window—to the past. It's clear, so most people won't notice it, even in pre-glass cultures. The smaller the piece used, the better. The less we potentially disrupt the flow of time, the more we can observe."

"But we can't disrupt it."

"True, and if we try, time protects itself and won't let us

even observe events. Be small and unobtrusive to see even more. Try to be big and flashy, and see nothing."

"Are you saying you have already done this?" Ky's voice was an intense whisper.

I could lie and he would never know, maybe, but he was still my oldest friend. "Yes," I answered quietly. "I'm just not ready to reveal it."

"When?" He asked while looking over his shoulder as if expecting his own boss to walk in.

"Over two years ago."

"Two years?" He rubbed his hands over his face and then looked at me. "This is really too much."

"What's wrong?"

"Later. How did you manage it? Where's your device?"

"Elsewhere," I answered.

"It's not here at NE?"

"No, too dangerous. If someone tampered with it, it could do a great deal of damage."

"To what? The past? Not according to your theories. The past is very safe."

"But the future isn't necessarily safe."

"Can you go into the future?"

"No, that is protected from our direct travel also. At least for now, but our actions can change what does happen. I'd rather not be too rash and cause events to transpire which I can't control."

"What events?" He asked.

"You should get out more and see the world. It's full of ambitious people trying to do their best to defeat us honest folks."

"Okay, okay. Let's leave the politics out. Tell me how your spyglass works."

"I set up the temporal fields and move the piece of glass back through time to the event I want to see. The glass is the connection to that time-stream. The central portion is physically there, while the watcher, us, stays here. The glass can be connected to a video camera on this end, or a time-lapsed camera, or even a watchful eye."

"Could someone in that *when* see us?"

"Yes, definitely, but the moment that interaction with the person on the other end changes history, the connection will break."

"So if we were set up to watch a battle where only the dead, or rather soon to be dead, could see us, then we could perhaps interact?"

"Yes. Your thinking of going back and grabbing some dead or dying animals—"

"Or people."

"Or people," I added. "You could steal all the cells you wanted to use in cloning, or some sperm and ova. Anything, provided that interaction changed nothing about their time-stream. We could even pull some of the bodies forward."

"It sounds so easy to be able to move things just a little bit, and change time."

"It's not a matter of what we might want or don't want. Time cannot be changed. The past must remain constant or it wouldn't be the past. We can't create another version of events that is different from the original."

"History is so—"

"Ky, it's not history. It's time. History is man's take on the past. How a group of men—well, usually men—decided to record what they thought happened or what they wanted to happen. It's seldom what really happened."

"We've had this discussion before. It's merely semantics. Can you show me the past?"

"Now?"

"Of course now! I want to see what our money has bought."

"Wow, not your money. Not at all. I did this all on my own, while in school. All paid for out of my own pocket, thank you kindly. Which is why the apparatus isn't even in this time zone but another."

"Afraid someone would steal it?"

"Wouldn't you be?"

"Well, yes. But not here. Here you would be safe," he said.

"Yeah, right. I'm surrounded by the leading time physicists. None of whom have gotten as far as I have. Which of them wouldn't steal my work, even if just to play?"

"Well, maybe. I tend to think of them all as members of a family, but you could be right."

"Could be? Still, it's in a place where I don't have to move it every time I move."

"Will you at least show me the past? Show me Arnora."

"What?"

"Arnora. I bet that was the first place you visited. Her theater. You must have watched her rehearsals or some of her early shows."

I couldn't help but smile. "Well, maybe, once or twice."

"Once or twice? Once or twice a night perhaps. That's how you knew about those photographs. That's why you don't have any time to date. You spend your nights watching television. But it's a show no one has seen for over eighty years. I'm beginning to worry about you, my dear friend."

I merely shrugged. "Why worry about something you can't change? But I want to finish this spying glass before I take any more ventures into other time zones, then—"

"Wait a minute," Ky began. "When you said your equipment was in another time zone, I thought you meant at this present, but when you say time zone you mean in the past somewhere? Or perhaps the future?"

"Yes, the when and where are different from now and here. But it must be in the past because we can't go into the future. To do so would change the now, their past, and therefore would violate the Laws of Time."

Ky shook his head. "There are so few people who truly understand what you mean by those Laws. Sometimes I think you just made it all up and continue to make them up as you go along."

"Never. Each Law has the math behind it to support what I've concluded."

"I know, it's just too much to grasp sometimes. When can we go back?"

"In a few days, but only if you leave me alone. Now, please."

"All right, I'll go." Ky turned to leave and got as far as the lab door before returning to my bench. "There was a reason I came in here. You know those papers your father published disproving time travel?"

"Yeah, I've read them. He even came up with some bogus research proving beyond doubt what I've already achieved. Who cares?"

"The Nobel committee. They gave him another award in physics this morning. Security said you've been here all night, so I didn't think you had heard."

At first I was stunned, but it passed quickly as I sat study-ing my portal. "He based his new work on my research, on my math. Did they even list me or my work?"

"No. The rumor is your father stated you actually worked in his shadow."

"I was working in his shadow? I was working in HIS shadow?" I started to stand but sat again. "He never even thought about time travel until I started my research!"

"I know that! How long would it take you to get this thing running for a demo?"

"Why?" I asked.

"To show him and the world you're not his fool."

"It sounds really tempting, but what would be the point? No, wait. Hear me out. We would draw attention to what we do here. We'd get more money, but according to you, we're not hurting. What would be the chance we would get unwanted attention, from the wrong kind of people?"

"We've got security."

"No, I can think of all kinds of reasons why I don't want others to know yet." And I could, beginning with the media and ending with the government. My father was somewhere in there, too. "Don't say anything to anyone, even your boss. Give me some time."

"What will you say to your father? He'll likely call."

I reached over and pulled the phone cord from the wall and reached into my briefcase and pulled out my cell phone and pitched it toward the lab's sink. I heard a satisfying splash as it landed in a bucket of cold dishwater.

"I should have gone into basketball," I said.

"That was a lucky shot." He moved toward the door. "I'll hold all incoming calls for you, but not forever."

"Thanks. Give me two weeks."

He turned as if to ask something more. I interrupted him.

"I'm fine. Go away, Kyrillos. I'll see you later." Then I looked back to my work, but I didn't breathe easier until I heard the click of the door closing behind Ky. He was my dearest friend, but he was still a pest. I put my father out of my mind; it was easy to do. I had had lots of practice during high school, but I didn't perfect the trick until in college.

It actually took me three weeks to get the glass right. The chemistry of glass changed constantly throughout history, depending on its uses as well as technical advances and of course the source material. The closer the composition of my spying glass came to the glass of a chosen time zone, the more likely I'd be able to visit that time, but still we had to be able to see through the glass clearly. And then there were many time zones, most in which glass was never used or invented. If I could just find a way to let glass revert back to basic sand within a few days of the spying glass remaining behind, it would be easier to view the past. Making it more susceptible to the sun's UV light seemed the most promising path. Having NE's extensive chemistry section at my disposal felt almost sinful.

Ky respected my wishes for quiet so I could work on my glass, but within two hours of my finishing, he was in my lab. It made me wonder if the place was rigged, but I guess I didn't really want to know since I didn't ask him about it. Instead I smiled at his boyish excitement and pointed to the other stool before my workbench where he eagerly sat.

On the middle of the bench top rested a sheet of smoky glass, forty by sixty centimeters. The bottom edge of the glass sat in a wooden frame. Wires mounted on the left edge led to the nearby computer.

"This looks so simple," Ky commented.

"It is. Why does it have to be complex?"

Ky opened his mouth and then shut it again without comment.

I rebooted the computer to get a fresh start. Just then, Rebecca entered the lab carrying a large pizza. She set it down on one end of the bench along with two sodas and my change. I smiled at her.

"It's still hot!" I said.

"Of course," she answered. "I'd never let a little frigid weather get in the way of a hot pizza." Her smile was warm and genuine until she turned and sneezed. The sneeze was as small as she was.

"How's that cold?" I asked.

"Getting better, but I'm sure a trip to ACS in Florida next week would help me get better right away. They'd hardly notice one more person going." She fluttered her eyebrows at Ky.

I laughed as Ky asked. "Cold?"

"Yes, just a cold. Dr. Ross cleared me right away. But the pizza guy said there were rumors of several flu cases in town."

"True?" I asked Ky.

"Yes, but they've been isolated. Several kids from families who don't believe in flu shots."

Becky interrupted. "Yeah, well, those only work if they guess the right flu strains riding the crest. And since they guessed wrong in '04, how do you expect people to react? Besides there's another rumor going around that flu shots leave you infertile."

"Urban myth," Ky shot back.

"Thanks for the pizza, Becky," I said.

"Anytime, Conner." She turned and left without any further comment.

"Becky?" Ky asked after the door closed.

"All her friends call her that."

"And that makes me?" Ky asked.

"Her boss." I pulled the pizza closer and handed Ky a soda and a napkin. "Keep the food off the computer and the spying glass. Let's watch the show now."

I sent several commands to the computer and the smoky glass began to clear. "This is really several pieces of very thin glass with electrodes in between. The central portion of the screen rests in contact with the time zone we want to view. If the transmission breaks, then that portion of the screen stays back in the past."

"If this is that high tech, won't that violate the Laws of Time if it's trapped in the past?"

"Good question. But no. If it did, then we wouldn't be able to access that time zone. But the design itself helps prevent time law violations. The electronics portion will disintegrate very quickly when exposed to sunlight and not connected to a current. Actually in just over two hours. If we're in a cave, or inside, it takes a few days of air to decompose. But that will happen anywhere. The glazing takes longer, but it will, too. This glass is designed to break down in natural UV more rapidly than any other composition I've found. By the way, Shawna Burke, over in the chem lab, is a genius."

"But what portion is your time machine?" Ky asked.

"That's not here. I've got it safely in its usual home."

"But?"

"I don't think I'll ever move it. I don't need to. The temporal field is multidimensional, just as time is, and sets up a time slip between its current space-time location, this portal, and the destination's space-time location. This portal is the focus or connection if you wish to think of it as such."

"The fourth derivative of *theta?*"

"When compared to *xi*. Yup, that's the equation. So you have read my dissertation!"

"At least five times, for all the good it's done me. If you had written it in English—"

I laughed. Ky was as good a mathematician as I was, despite his complaints. But I could see why he had been put in charge of a group of introverted, and naturally paranoid, scientists. Who could fear a man who professed to know so little about what was being explained?

"Show me Arnora. I want to see her perform on stage."

"Ah, now that's an easy request." I said.

"I thought so!"

"There's a dress rehearsal two days before the fire that is really very nice. I have just to place the portal near the auditorium's chandelier, then we sit back and watch."

"This is a canned program!"

"Well, yes. You want to start at the beginning of the play?"

"You bet! Why wouldn't we?"

"I don't know, maybe you have a hot date."

"Only with you, old buddy."

"You have to get out more."

We watched the curtain rise and the entire first act before either of us said a word as we downed the pizza. The intermission was just as it would be on opening night since the actors had to change costumes. I could have skipped ahead, but chose not to, and let the program run its course.

Ky reached for his soda and found it empty and set the cup back down. "She's really good."

"You sound surprised."

"I suppose I am. I guess I thought she would be just a pretty face and scant talent. She's not very old and from a rich family. Daddy giving her what she wants."

"Daddy didn't approve of her interests, which is why it took her so long to get to this point. He died almost a year ago in her timeline. Mommy is off on a European vacation, a long one. Arnora is now doing what she loves, and no one is here to stop her."

"Except fate," Ky added.

"Yeah, except fate."

When the play finished, I remained seated, savoring the satisfied feeling which always overcame me. Suddenly the image changed, and we were watching Arnora approach us as she walked down the hallway. The keypad was too far away. I quickly turned the glass so that she would see only me and not Ky. He even pushed his stool back from the workbench. Arnora stopped so close to the portal and reached out as she had done in the past and touched her side of the glass. She looked me straight in the eye and winked.

"My favorite little ghost," she said. "I did good tonight, didn't I?" She walked on down the hall and disappeared into her dressing room. I broke the connection, though I really wanted to follow her and talk well into the night as we had done on two other occasions.

"She wasn't frightened!" Ky said.

I couldn't keep the silly smile off of my face.

"You've done this before!" he said.

"Yes, she's seen me a few times. She doesn't frighten easily."

"Why would you do this?"

"Why not? She'll be dead in two days. Time is safe."

"Obviously it must be. But she dies! Can you handle that?"

"Nothing will ever change that!"

"You're okay with that?"

"It's not as if I have any choice, now is it?"

Ky thought a moment. "You could clone her."

"We don't clone people here."

"Other places do. I could put you in contact with—"

"It wouldn't be the same. Arnora is more than just a pretty face. If I wanted that, I'd date Becky and have a wife before I'm an old man."

Ky asked me to construct a portal without glass. One that would allow passage from one time-stream to another. It was a step I had been reluctant to take on my own, but since my best friend and boss asked me, why not try? He would be able to help assess any experiment's worthiness. My first thoughts after the request were of my father, which meant I really did need to prove something to him, even if months passed before he would be aware of my success.

It took me a week.

I started out small. The largest object we'd be able to move would be a small dog, or several pigeons, either dead or alive. Still, Ky was very enthusiastic. He swore he hadn't told his boss about my success. I still hadn't talked to my father. Several of my former professors came forward to criticize my father's work and backed me. Nothing would change until I came forward and denounced my father. I wasn't ready, and Ky went along, for now.

All of our lives, but especially mine, would remain less complex if Northern Escapes' success came from our breeding programs and not time travel. Most of the issues surrounding cloning had been smoothed over soon after the pandemic, as long as we worked only with animals.

Why put ourselves into such an awkward position as to have to defend time travel now, to anyone?

Becky and her friends spent two weeks researching dates, places, and times for major pigeon hunts. I checked out every event as she gave it to me until I was certain of a plan. The event I chose left few pigeons alive in the flock to fly the next day. We stood in a vacant office, Ky on one side of me and NE's bird expert on the other. We looked out onto an early winter landscape. The ground was covered with a light snow from the previous night's falling.

"What are we going to see?" Dr. Carol Weber asked. Her voice was low, and her graying hair was short and constantly in disarray. Today, it looked more like feathers than hair.

"If I've got this right, birds." I answered.

The portal wavered in the air some twenty feet straight out from our window and about thirty feet above the ground. It hung from a cable suspended between two of the closer buildings. I initiated the program and looked up. The air shimmered slightly. If you weren't aware it was there, you might think it was just a heat mirage. Three minutes later success was evident as a stream of pigeons, flying two and three abreast, exited the portal. It was a short passage, lasting only eight seconds. I counted two seconds after the last bird, then shut down the portal. I disengaged the computer and looked back up as the startled birds made a loop near our window and passenger pigeons flew once again in the sky above us.

"Damn!" Weber said next to me as she leaned closer to the window to see farther away.

"How many were there?" I asked.

"At least three dozen!" Weber answered.

"And four ducks!" Ky added. "Ducks?"

"When the shooting started, I'd guess any wildlife would take flight," Weber added as she grabbed her coat and headed for the door. Ky and I were right behind her. On the building's roof we found Weber's assistant waiting with binoculars. He pointed west.

"They're confused, but are circling for a third time. Their flight is less panicked. I suspect another two rounds and they'll land near the roost we constructed."

"Any chance we'll be able to catch them all?" Ky asked.

"Very little," Weber answered. "We were planning on just a few. We'll get some of them, but not all. These are wild creatures and they migrate. In just a few days they will likely head south."

"That's going to lead to some odd questions," Ky added.

Weber shrugged. "We have breeding pairs here. No one knows the exact number outside my lab. So, some escaped. They're doing what they do naturally. Though it will be a shame to lose any of them." Weber pointed. "Look they've spotted the roosts and are tightening their flight pattern." As one, they landed. The auto system engaged and nets covered the roosts. Techs scurried to secure the catch. No birds filled the air.

"You got them all?" I asked in an awed whisper. After a moment Weber and her assistant let out a whoop.

"Yes, by God. We got them all!" she said. Weber reached over and shook my hand. "Dr. Robins, you are a genius!"

"Thank you, but what about those ducks that got through?"

She shook her head in dismissal. "They'll blend in with the native population of mallards and most likely take up residence on our little lake for the winter. Just four more for us to encourage to go elsewhere next fall instead of mooching off of us for the rest of their lives. If you still feel guilty next year, you can help us trap and relocate them elsewhere. We always need help."

"He won't feel guilty," Ky said as he punched my shoulder lightly. "Lunch is my treat. Care to join us, Carol? Joe?"

"No," Dr. Weber began. "I think we'll go look at our newest residents. Make sure they like the aviary."

We were sitting in Ky's office. It was lit only by the glow of the wood fire burning brightly in the fire place. His office windows overlooked a wider view of the valley. Still, we couldn't see much for the snowstorm raging outside. A good six inches had already been dumped on us, and more was coming. Winter had set in during the last few weeks and was holding tight. I was glad I had decided to continue staying in the dorms through winter, instead of driving into town in this mess. I might even take one of the underground tunnels back to my room tonight. The wind looked wicked. Ky poured more Scotch in my glass and his own. We had just returned from the aviary after checking on the pigeons. I wanted to see for myself how well they were adjusting in the few weeks since they arrived here.

"There will never be enough," I began softly, "to let go in the wild. Not enough pigeons for a breeding population. We'll lose them again."

"Perhaps. But with cloning we can try, thanks to you. You wouldn't believe the list of animals people want to bring back! Most of the requests are impossible to fulfill. I'm sorry, but why would we want a saber-toothed tiger?"

"Because we can."

"It all costs money."

"Your problem and not ours."

"Ours?" Ky asked. "Whom do you include in that *ours*?"

"Us researchers." I added a smile to show I was partly kidding. "As opposed to management."

He sighed. I sat forward and looked at him. He had seemed tired all day. "What's wrong? You've been lost in thought most of the afternoon. Didn't your noon meeting go well?"

"Same old, same old." He poured more Scotch.

"You should go easier on that stuff, you'll be drunk before too long."

"One can only hope. If I—" His answer was interrupted by a knock on the door. His assistant entered without waiting for an invitation.

I looked at her. "Margaret, what if he had been in here with a woman?"

She snickered. "Then I'd have had a pleasant surprise and some good gossip, but he works as hard as you do. You both need dates—"

"Margaret?" Ky interrupted.

"Dr. Ross wants to see you both."

"Why?" Ky asked.

"It's the flu. She's called a class five quarantine on all of Northern Escapes and on the town, too."

"But why does she need to see me?" I asked. A chill had started in my toes despite their near proximity to the fire. "Is Becky okay?" Margaret just shrugged.

Ky downed his drink in one gulp. "Tell Ross we're on our way. Come on, old buddy." Ky stood. I reached quickly out to steady him.

"Can you walk?"

"Sure, if you help. Don't worry about Becky, she's tough. And she went to Ross with the first sniffle. It's those two farmhands I'm worrying about. They waited over three hours. By tomorrow morning everyone in the farming department will be sick."

The walk through the tunnels seemed long. Outside, at least, the weather could distract your thoughts. Ten minutes later we were entering Dr. Ross' office where she was meeting with three of her staff along with four department heads, none of whom I had formally met. No one made any introductions or shook hands. There were ten people in the room and personal space was at a premium.

"How's Becky?" I asked.

"Sick, but we loaded her up with antibiotics right away to protect against any form of bacterial pneumonia. Even so, it migrated to her lungs already."

"What kind of flu?" Ky asked.

"A swine version," Ross answered.

"Like '04?"

"No, different. We think it's closer to the 1918 version."

"How is that possible?" Ky asked. "It was never found, despite all the researchers actively looking for it in the past ten years."

Ross turned to me. "They said you brought some ducks back during your research with the passenger pigeons."

The chill had wrapped around my backbone. "Yes, four of them. But they were from 1898 western Wisconsin and not 1918 Kansas. A full twenty years and hundreds of miles away from where the Spanish Lady first hit."

Ross spread her hands. "I know, but this flu is a new type and passed from those ducks and into the pigs we have here, and now into us. We're sure of the path. Becky came in first. She had been in the barns helping out."

"She likes helping. She was raised on a farm." I added. Was I defending her?

"She came in at 11:00 a.m. and told me Ralph Miller and Jim Clark also had sore throats. I sent for them both right away. By three this afternoon I had fifteen people sick. I've now got over fifty, most of them have already gone from flu to pneumonia. It's moving fast, and it's a variety I've never seen before. We have little or no resistance built up to this strain."

Ky interrupted. "Did you invite us here to beat us up for screwing up with our experiment, or is there a point to all of this?"

"Ky," I said. He was more than a little drunk and the liquor was making him mean. "What can we do?" I asked Ross.

"I need tissue samples or blood from people who survived the Spanish flu from 1918 or 1919. There isn't a complete example anywhere in our time that we know of and I can get my hands on soon enough."

"Why?" I asked. Ky looked at me in surprise, but I wanted to know. "Who cares if it is the Spanish Lady?"

"If it is, those survivors have built up a resistance in their body already. We can replicate that faster than a vaccine and stop this strain in its tracks. Otherwise we're out of a solution for at least two weeks until someone here develops enough antibodies for us to clone."

"We have to go back in time and get a sample?" I asked. "Are you sure?"

"Yes," Ross said. "It will save lives, if you can."

Her assistant interrupted. "But you can't go to that time directly." I looked back at Ross.

"If this isn't the Spanish flu, but something else—and it could be—you risk bringing that variety back and we'd have two virulent versions to deal with."

I rubbed my face with my hands and instantly regretted it, but my brain was foggy from the Scotch. "I can't just go back and ask a stranger if they were sick last year and if can I have some blood." I really wanted to pace, but the room was too small and too crowded. I hated working with an audience. "What kind of window after the pandemic should I be working in?"

Ross looked at her assistant for a moment as if they conferred telepathically. "No sooner than three years and no later than seven years after 1919."

"Or when that person was sick?" Ky asked.

"Yes," Ross said. Just then another medic came into the room.

"The town's quarantine is in place, but when they went to Jim Clark's house to talk to his wife, they found her dead. Their baby girl is very sick. They're bringing both in as soon as they can get through with this snow, but it doesn't look good for the baby."

"That's it! I'm starting everyone here, and in town, on antibiotics to try and push off the pneumonia before we're even sick."

"Do we have enough drugs?" Ky asked.

"Yes, but only if this thing doesn't mutate again."

"Maybe we should start slaughtering the birds and pigs?" someone I didn't know suggested.

A woman from the far side of the room answered. "This influenza is stable in birds, but it mutates best in the pigs. And yes, we've already finished that phase of our defense."

I rubbed my arm as I paced my lab. Ky sat at my workbench pouring coffee into himself to shake off the Scotch. Me? I was wide awake and angry.

"How long did you know about this?" I asked.

"That we had an epidemic?"

"Yes."

"Since midafternoon, but not that it was our fault."

"You mean my fault?"

"No, you can't take this all onto yourself. I'm as much to blame as you, and so is Carol Weber. We designed the experiment together."

"I guess this proves that you can change the present by using a time machine."

"It would seem so," Ky agreed.

I paced for several more minutes, all the while wondering how we could have designed our experiment differently.

"Stop it."

I stood still. "What?"

"Not your pacing; you do some of you best work while moving, but your blaming yourself for this mess. We need a solution, and if you spend all of your time in your personal past, you won't think of a solution to our present."

"I wish my father had been right."

"A wasted wish. Think, Connor. You know how to use your device better than anyone else. You know what it can do."

"First we need a portal big enough to pull a body through. We also need a body. Can we get the med staff to search their records for someone who would fit their criteria?"

"Sure. I'll get them right on it," Ky said. "But we don't need to steal the body. What if one of us went through and took the blood sample from someone recently dead— perhaps in a hospital? We could take the sample and get back rather quickly."

"We'd need just a big enough portal to crawl through."

"A portal just a little bigger than the one we've been using." I looked around. I still had the basic materials here from before. "All I need is a little more wood for the supporting frame. It doesn't have to last a long time, just long enough to get there and back again."

"I'll go talk to the medical records and then meet you in the workshop."

"No, I can make the portal myself. You help with the records. With so many getting sick, they'll be drafting anyone who can hold a bedpan."

Two hours later I had a new portal, one meter by one meter, connected to my computer. Ky had called a short time before. They'd have a date, time, and place by morning. Which meant I need only test this portal and then I could get a few hours of sleep. So far I felt fine, but another one hundred people were sick. The snowstorm was expected to end by midmorning. Volunteer doctors and nurses were being lined up from the army base north of us. They'd fly in by helicopter along with additional supplies when the weather cleared. All we needed was more time.

"And not even I can give us that." I took a deep breath and shook my head. "Work on today's problems, kiddo."

I rebooted my computer and ran my favorite Arnora program. The portal appeared to work perfectly, and so I watched for a little while longer. Her laughter was clear and pure music to me. It lifted my spirits. As she walked across the stage, she looked directly at me where my image floated above the empty seats, and winked. I hadn't planned on her seeing me, but was still glad she had. My lab was dark, so the stage lights must have reflected off my face or hands. I moved back father so that I could still see her, but no one else would have the chance to see me by mistake. After all, most of the cast and crew survived the fire.

When the curtain was lowered, I resisted the temptation to applaud. Instead I stopped the program. I couldn't bear to see her close up tonight. Still I felt relaxed, almost as if I had slept much of the night away, instead of watching a play.

I went to pour myself another cup of coffee, and suddenly I knew I had found my subject. Arnora had survived the Spanish flu five years before her death.

Perfect!

I knew the when, the exact when, and the exact how of her death. I had seen it. The fire hadn't killed her, smoke inhalation had, which is why she didn't make it out of the theater as most of the others had. It was only later, when the fire burned hot that her body had been nearly totally consumed by the flames. Suddenly my heart was beating so fast, I had to sit down.

Could I face this?

Could I pull her body out of the smoke? Or would I die there with her?

Doctor Ross could get all the tissue samples she needed, then we could return her to the burning theater.

That would be the hard part. Maybe the impossible part. But I could take my time with that necessity.

I went to find Ky and Ross. It took Ky just a few moments to point out my biggest flaw. We wouldn't be able to remove Arnora unless we had someone to take her place at the same time.

Why? Because I, as a boy, needed to believe she burned to death so I would become interested in time travel and dream of ways to save her. It took over an hour for us to work out the kinks and develop a plan. We had already lost two people to the epidemic. Ross scanned their medical records to find which one would serve our needs. Nothing from the present, not artificial teeth, and certainly not a virus, could survive the fire to hurt the past. Ross was very sure the virus wouldn't survive the fire, but teeth would.

Ky and I waited. I felt like a grave robber. But it was our only choice. We had to have a body to return to the past, to take the place of the one we stole. The late Alice Clark returned with us to my lab on a gurney. Ross wanted those tissue samples as soon as possible. I wondered who would have the grim task of explaining to Mr. Clark what had happened. That was, if he survived the flu.

There were two med techs standing by, besides Ross. We all held breathing masks since Ky had pointed out the smoke could pour out of the past and right into my lab, along with possible flames. So we also had two fire specialists there. Both were men more massive than me, and I never considered myself short or small of stature. Both men had volunteered rather loudly to take my place. But I knew this event by heart. I had seen it in my nightmares often enough.

"Why do we have to wait till she dies?" Ross asked softly. The program was in place, and I was getting ready to put on my breathing mask even as Ross was.

"If there was any other way, believe me I would take it. I've dreamed of saving her for years, but history can't be changed. If we try, we won't be able to." I had tried, in my own past, but of course I couldn't admit that, not to anyone.

She nodded, and we both put on our masks. One fire spec, Paul, turned off all the lights except for two small red lights away from the portal. I picked up the late Mrs. Clark from the gurney and put her over my shoulder. Someone had dressed her in a brown dress, much like the one Arnora wore in her play. I suppose Ky had thought of that. I hadn't.

I tried not to think about what I was doing as I turned toward the portal and waved to Ky. He started the program moving. The image wavered and then steadied. Black smoke poured out the portal.

"Can you see her?" Denny, one of the fire specs, asked from my side. His voice was clear in my earpiece.

"No, it's really dark. But I know she's there. I've seen her before." I started moving forward. Mrs. Clark hadn't been a large woman, but still she felt heavy.

Denny grabbed my arm and stopped me. "Paul, send a beam down that hallway."

The other fire spec complied. We saw her lying on the floor. She was at least twenty feet from the portal.

"Be sure to follow your lead back here. Remember, if you get into trouble, yell!"

"Got it!" I said from my knees as I moved through the portal and found myself still in my lab.

"What happened?" Denny demanded. Everyone stared at me as I set Mrs. Clark gently on the floor, removed my mask and hurried over to my computer.

"Everything's in order. It's not the setup."

"Is it time?" Ky asked as he lifted up his mask.

"Yes, the program is still running, but the portal won't open. Something about what we were trying to do violates the time laws. What?" I set my mask down, ended my program and reset it.

Ky turned around and surveyed the room. "Maybe we will just have to get a blood sample and not try to take the body."

I nodded. "Yeah, seems so." I reached for my mask and just stared at it. "No, that's not it."

"What?" Ky asked.

"It's these air masks. If I were to be trapped in the past, they would survive the fire and change things."

"Wouldn't finding your body change things, too?" Ross asked.

"Maybe, maybe not."

"You can't go without the mask," Denny began. "That

smoke is just too heavy and deadly. It would overcome you in a very short time."

"We've no choice. The mask has to stay. I'll just have to hold my breath and move faster."

"Or I can go with you."

"And take the chance of killing two?" I asked.

"He's right," Ky said to me. "You both go. It'll be safer."

They left me no choice, so Ky quickly set the program running again. Denny waited beside me with the view of the burning theater before us. We both wore safety lines and our masks for now. He carried Mrs. Clark. I took several deep breaths and tore off my mask and plunged through the portal. I moved about a meter forward and turned around in the sudden darkness to help Denny, but my lab was gone and so was the portal. I looked in all directions. Nothing! I crouched low to the floor and breathed in smoke-laden air and tried not to cough. I could no longer see Arnora.

Suddenly the corridor was filled with red light and a flashlight beam. I plunged through the portal. The fire spec, Paul, had an oxygen mask over my face as Ky shut the portal down again. I breathed in deeply, as I waited for an explanation.

"Denny has several metal pins in his leg," Dr. Ross began. "If he were to die back there, it would change history."

I pushed the oxygen mask away. "Paul can—"

"No, he has several capped teeth."

"Blast and so does Ky."

"Me, too," Ross said. "I called over to my office, they're going to find someone and send them over."

"No," I said. "I'm going to go by myself. Maybe it's the artificial body parts and then again it may be that if we leave too many bodies there, it will change history."

"Connor?"

"No, Ky. You know I'm right. A mask would make it easy, but I still can do this. Just keep that damn portal open. If it seems as if I'm in trouble, there is still the safety rope." I looked around the room, no one had any other comment or answer. "Good. Now Mrs. Clark and I have a date." I knelt before the portal and Denny handed Mrs. Clark back to me. She no longer seemed so heavy.

They say adrenaline makes a person stronger. I hoped so. Just now, I needed an edge. I took several more deep breaths even as Ky started the program again. I owed this poor woman so much. Then I pushed the oxygen mask at Denny and rushed into the past.

Red light continued to shine behind me, so the portal hadn't closed though I didn't turn to check. Instead I moved forward and a flashlight beam lit the way. The fact I made it told me Arnora was already dead.

I couldn't think of that. She had been dead for eighty-four years already. I was trying to save my friends today—those sick in the infirmary. Paul's flashlight beam led me to her. I tried not to cough as I placed Mrs. Clark on the floor facedown even as Arnora was and right next to her. Alice Clark was cold and pale to the touch, but Arnora was still warm, her skin still soft. A fit of coughing took me. I placed my face next to the floor and breathed for a moment and then returned to my task.

Arnora weighed so little as I lifted her. I tried not to look at her, but as I turned her over and held her to my side, her beauty was evident even in the flashlight's harsh beam.

"Move your ass!" Ky's shout came from far away. "Connor, don't make me regret letting you go. Move it! Now!"

My feet were under me again, and I saw the red square ahead of me and felt a yank at my waist. It almost pulled me off my feet.

"Move!" Denny yelled. And then I heard the crash of some portion of structure not too far away, but I was through the portal. Denny was hauling me out of my lab. Paul took Arnora out of my arms and rushed toward the waiting gurney. Dr. Ross looked my way. I waved her away. The med team was down the hall and out of sight in moments as I leaned against the wall and breathed in fresh air.

"Here!" Denny slid an oxygen mask over my face. "Even this hallway is too full of smoke. Let the recirc system have a few minutes to work." He took my wrist in his and was checking my pulse. "You breathe any smoke?"

"Some. I'm fine."

"Did you hit your head or something?" Ky asked.

"What do you mean?"

"It took you too long to get back here."

"How long was too long?"

"Two minutes, fifteen seconds." Denny said.

"That's a long time?"

"It sure felt like it." Ky answered.

The hallway finally looked clear of smoke, so we took our masks off. The air still smelled of fire. "At least there wasn't enough smoke to set off the alarms."

Denny laughed. "We turned those blasted things off ahead of time. It's hard to think with those things sounding. Well, you appear fine. Dr. Ross wants to check you over. She said right away. I'll go and make sure your lab is safe."

"Yeah, I need to make sure my equipment is all right, too." I started to follow him, but Ky held out his hand.

"I shut everything down and disconnected the computer to the portal. No one can even accidentally start it again."

"You didn't turn the program off?"

"No, I didn't think it was necessary."

"Good. That way we can start it again where we stopped."

"Why?" Ky asked.

"We do have to return her."

"But Alice Clarke?"

"I've been thinking. We should make the exchange again. It wouldn't be fair to Mrs. Clark, or the Clark family to lose her body, too."

"Can you do that?"

"We'll see. First I want to go see Arnora. Hold her hand while they take what they need."

Ky nodded and walked with me to the med labs. But when we got there they were empty. Ky stopped a passing tech.

"Where's Dr. Ross?"

"ICU, I think." She reached into her pocket and pulled out two surgical masks and handed then to us. "No one moves through these halls without these. Put them on! Keep them on!" Then she rushed off on her own errand.

We wandered the halls for a few minutes until we found Ross coming toward us. She was smiling and more than a little pleased.

"Did you get your samples?" Ky asked.

"Yes! We're testing them now."

"Do you know if this is the Spanish Lady or not?"

"No, it's too soon. These things do take a little time."

"Then why the smile?" I asked.

"In part because no one has died in the last hour. And because I want to show you something." She motioned toward a door and led us into a room.

Arnora lay in the hospital bed. Someone had cleaned the soot from her face, but surprisingly she was hooked up to an IV solution and there was an oxygen mask over her mouth.

"What's going on?" Ky asked. "Did you bring her back?"

I couldn't say anything as I moved to the bedside and felt Arnora's wrist.

"She wasn't dead. Her pulse was weak, but with oxygen she came right back. She's unconscious, but she should recover completely."

I looked from Arnora to Ky. "But we can't change time!"

He laughed. "We didn't change the past, old buddy, but we sure as hell changed the future. Imagine that!"

Arnora's eyes snapped open at Ky's loud voice. She looked at me as I removed my surgical mask. It took her only a moment, then she smiled as best she could under the oxygen mask.

"You're safe. Rest now." She fell back to sleep. "Damn, we can't take her back now!"

"I should say not!" Ross added.

"But? I mean where will she live?"

"Right here at Northern Escapes," Ky said softly.

Ross nodded in agreement. "She'll need special training and some education classes. It'll be an interesting project."

"What if she hates me for doing this to her?" I asked.

"She can go back!" Ky said it so matter-of-factly that I couldn't help but stare at him.

"Relax. She's smart and anyone who didn't go running when they saw your face pop up all of a sudden can adapt to new situations without a lot of fuss. She'll be fine." His smile turned into a full grin. "I can't wait to see your father's face when we prove to him time travel is possible. And I especially want to see his face when you bring Arnora home for Christmas dinner next year."

Dr. Ross came forward and took Arnora's hand out of

mine. "First things first. She'll be fine, Connor. I'm placing a quarantine around her to protect her, at least until we get a grip on this virus. That means a quarantine from you, too. Meanwhile, I'll need your help with our other patients. Both of you. We have too many to deal with unless we draft outside help from other departments."

"Lead the way, good doctor," Ky said as he pushed me out of the room ahead of him. Still I stole another peek at a sleeping Arnora before the door closed.

And to think I had almost gone into quantum physics!

THEORY OF RELATIVITY
by Jody Lynn Nye

Jody Lynn Nye lists her main career activity as "spoiling cats." She lives northwest of Chicago with two of the above and her husband, author and packager Bill Fawcett. She has written twenty-three books, including five contemporary fantasies, three SF novels, four novels in collaboration with Anne McCaffrey, including *The Ship Who Won,* a humorous anthology about mothers, *Don't Forget Your Spacesuit, Dear!,* and over sixty short stories. Her latest books are *License Invoked,* co-written with Robert Asprin, and *Advanced Mythology,* fourth in the *Mythology 101* series.

Dr. Barry Seacliff
Tekno-Books
tkbGreenBayWisconsin.com

Dear Barry,

Thanks very much for the opportunity to submit to the digest of time-travel abstracts.

You'll probably be surprised to see that my document is 450 pages long. I know you requested papers no more than fifteen thousand words, but I think once you begin to read it, you'll see that I needed to get this all down as best I can so that none of it is lost. I've excerpted the entire document at the end, but I hope you'll see fit to publish the whole thing.

My paper includes full diagrams and equation models for the B3 Trans-temporal Drive that controlled my module, named for the three scientists instrumental in its development. I've got Caltech lab's permission for its publication. (See copyright notices on the title page of my paper.) In space travel, similar technology creates a wormhole effect large enough for a small solid body to pass beneath the fabric of space, but it occasionally bypasses time as well, creating short jumps into the future or past. This variation of the B3 takes advantage of the temporal anomaly. In other words, the side effect is the one we wanted.

It may surprise you to know that the multiple-tree dimension theory that many scientists have espoused is true. The ever-branching tree of possibilities makes it difficult to go far back or far forward in time, not to mention the resulting logarithmic increase in power consumption. So my task was to find a branch at which two measurable points in history diverged, but no more than a hundred years in the past.

It might also surprise you that I didn't choose to travel farther back than a few generations. The reasoning was simple: the longer the gap between my "present" and my landing point in the past, the greater by a factorial, even exponential, equation the number of possible futures that I might accidentally return to. Therefore, instead of traveling to the Renaissance or the age of dinosaurs, long-time dreams of mine, we limited the scope of this initial inquiry. Once we've worked out all the bugs, I'm going back far enough at least to commission Tiepolo to paint my portrait as a birthday gift for my mother. I like his color pallette. I'd prefer John Everett Millais, but by the Victorian era everything was too well documented for a commissioned painting to go unremarked. One thing we're already learning about visiting the past is to frequent eras where our passage will be easily forgotten, lest we alter the timestreams too much to find our own future again.

I was always fascinated by a book I read as a child about a man who had discovered how to live along the Y-axis of time. Simply speaking, it would be as though you turned sharp right when everyone else was traveling straight along that X-axis, and continued to exist forever in that moment of, say, June 4, 2005, existing in a past that everybody in one's common reality had left behind. By focusing the "future" tendency of the wormhole drive against its "past" tendency, my craft was intended to drill along that June 4th until I came to another, recognizable reality, on that

X-axis but a new Y-axis. It's not perfectly stable, but, you know, close enough for government work.

We theorized that there are many alternate dimensions because history branches from multiple alterations in from a single incident. There are many choices, but we, now, are aware only of the one that we have made or are living. There should be an infinity of realities out there. I needed only one.

The easiest path was to make use of my own history. I set out to look for a counterpart of my own existence. Using the theory of random actions creating parallel dimensions, it interested me to discover someone whose life could be exactly like mine, if not for a single incident from which our lives diverged.

The capsule departs from a pad in a vacuum chamber inside the Caltech lab. You have to come out here sometime and watch a launch. It's very impressive. Everybody who can jams into the observation room. The whole place is painted white except the launch pad, which is a dark-green, meter-thick bed of friction-resistant polymer fifty meters by twenty. The *H. G. Wells,* one of the four crafts Caltech is using, sits in the middle looking like a gigantic copper multivitamin.

Since every millimeter the wormhole has to stretch matters, the capsule isn't very wide, but it's long. I weigh a little under 60 kilos. In an environment suit I can turn around and reach everything in the cockpit just by stretching my arms. I can hand myself up and down inside the capsule to the other stations, such as telemetry, entertainment and galley, sleep/cryostasis, and relief. This is the same configuration used for long-distance space exploration. About three people can exist inside here, if you don't mind looking at your companion's feet most of the time. There's just room to slip by one another. It's not an environment for the claustrophobe. I like it. It's womblike. Instead of feeling closed in, I feel safe. It's all a matter of perspective, since the ship takes its crew hurtling through a temporary singularity that wants to crush anything passing though it out of existence. I slid into the cockpit, pulled down the flap seat, and strapped myself in. The heavy shielding slides shut, and Mission Control gives the pilot final instructions. Once the drives kick in, s/he's out of touch. As the field begins to form around the capsule, it rises off the pad, glowing like an ember. Then, with a bang that used to blast out the windows, it's gone.

I've made short hops back along our X-axis of a few moments or a few hours. If you get another briefing before you step into a TT module, please let me say don't eat breakfast first. No matter how well prepared you are, your stomach hates the sideslip of light-speed g-force. You don't get the full brunt of the rotation of the drive surrounding the shielded capsule, but your body knows something is going wrong out there. The construction does obviate windows, but since you're exceeding the speed of light, there's nothing to see anyhow. The most astonishing thing about the trip is the lack of sensation of movement, since you're not really going anywhere, you're going anywhen.

I was nervous when the drive stopped. Sensors on the skin are supposed to detect variations in ambient temperature outside the range between -20° and 32° Celsius and restart the drives, so I don't land in nuclear war or nuclear winter. If I could trust it, the gauge said it was 19° out there. Had it failed, I could be stepping out into vacuum or a volcano. I peeled back the hatch.

And saw California. You won't believe what a letdown that was, seeing dusty stucco buildings and landscaped gardens covered a quarter-inch deep in ash from the biennial forest fires that had just ended. Now, instead of proving I'd traveled cross-dimensionally, I had to prove that I'd moved in time at all, instead of just teleporting my capsule out of the lab and into the ornamental rockery behind the Arts & Sciences building.

Clothing was no clue. Under my protective suit I had on a denim-colored coverall, which fit into the crowd of students and faculty roaming around this campus as well as it had at the one I had just left a few minutes before. No one looked twice at a thirty-something white woman with brown hair in a clip at the back of her neck. I felt anonymous, but somewhere someone must know me.

You wonder about the first thing you would do if you suddenly found yourself in my position. I could have done a lot of things, but I let curiosity get the better of me: I went to find a phone. I wanted to call me and see if I was at home.

Everybody carries a miniature personal communications unit these days, but for quicklink data transmission and a more stable connection there's still no substitute for a booth. They're subsidized these days, probably to make sure people use them, though there's a block on pay-per-minute sites, but information and local calls are free. National directory assistance had no listing for Rachel Fenstone and only one entry for a Dr. Fenstone, right there in Pomona. I called it, but to my shock a man answered.

"Jeremy Fenstone," the voice said. The number belonged to my youngest brother! So where was I?

"Hi, it's me," I said, clutching the handset like a lifeline, which it was. I hoped I wasn't dead in this world.

"Hey," he said, friendly but unexcited, exactly as my brother would have done. So I or someone who sounded like me was alive and on speaking terms. "What's up?"

Uh. What next? "I, um. Can you . . . ? Did I . . . give you the new number for my office?"

Thank heaven for the vagaries of the mass-communication system! I could hear him hitting keys. "No. The last number I had for you was 8094-555-2389. Is it different now?"

"Uh, no. That's right. Just making sure. Gotta go."

"Yeah." Whatever branch of science or medicine Jer was practicing, his mind was always elsewhere. "See you."

The reverse directory assistance released an address to go with the telephone number Jer had given me. The subtle difference was so unexpected that I almost dropped the receiver: *June* Fennell, not Rachel Fenstone.

When I was six, I hurt my mother's feelings by telling her I wanted to change my name from Rachel to June. *Twilight Zone.* Dee dee dee dee. I took down the address.

I found the house on a quiet avenue in a neighborhood with no through-streets. Exactly the kind of place I'd live in, if I didn't want to be close walking distance from the lab. I saw a dark-haired figure moving around inside the curtained picture window. Its silhouette was so familiar my heart skipped. It was weird. I felt as though I was watching a film someone had taken of me with a hidden camera. But she was real. Unable to wait a moment longer to meet her, I hurried up the walk and rang the bell.

If you ever happen to meet an interdimensional analog of yourself, I recommend your first words to him not be, "Hi, I've come to take you through time in an experimental shuttle, but don't worry: I'm a trained physicist." You just might not get the results you were hoping for. But I was so excited to succeed in tracking down a second self that I'm afraid I was thinking she'd react the way I would . . . or be truthful, the way I *hope* I'd act, if I was confronted without warning by a virtual doppleganger. The scream and the door slammed in my face gave me something to go away and think about. I had to consider a second approach, one more effective and less threatening. I started down the path.

Before I got to the sidewalk the door opened behind me, and a tentative voice asked, "Are you really?"

I'm one of six children in my family, but the only girl. Having so many brothers made me a tomboy. I missed the way friends of mine with sisters learned to accept their femininity. When I was growing up, I used to fantasize about having an identical twin. Oh, the twins in my neighborhood assured me the reality wasn't as great as the dream. They got into squabbles so petty that no one else understood or could intervene, but all I could see was that unbreakable bond where someone was so much like me that I would never really be alone. As my friends said, the reality was different.

June's maiden name is Fenstone. Fennell is her *nom de plume*. She is not a scientist. She's a technical writer who moonlights as a science fiction author, something I would never have conceived of becoming. Jeremy, instead of studying structural engineering, became a biologist. June went for the softer sciences, but close enough for government research, huh? It had to be. The B3 drive had only enough power for the three legs of the trip we had planned. There wasn't enough surplus to go shopping along the dimensional divisions to find another test subject. If I was going to try out my theorem, I had to convince this almost-me to participate in the experiment. At the very least I needed information from her. At best, she would be able to help. Once I started to explain my mission, I saw a very familiar light gleam in her—my—eyes.

We are amazingly alike. She doesn't have the broken nose I got from catching a baseball with my face, but I don't have the temple scar she got from opening a window with her head. Both of us are pale, dark-haired, long-nosed cynics. It didn't freak me out when she spoke, because my own voice sounds deeper to me than hers does.

We're both married. Her Len owns a freelance statistical research firm. My Mitchell is a freelance project coordinator for the space/time program. No kids. No surprise. No time. I liked finding out about what I could have become, but it's creepy, too. I thought I was handling it pretty well because of all the analysis I've undergone to prepare for this mission. It only occurred to me in running that June hadn't been through the therapy, and she accepted the strangeness of the situation and was moving forward. I guess we're more resilient than I thought. Or at least, that's the interpretation I put on, "That's okay. I'll save the nervous breakdown for later."

We decided to call each other "cousin." That took the heat off arguing over whose timeline was more real. I know both of us had the same feeling, that mine is the true one and hers is an offshoot. You have to think that way, or you'll go mad. No thinking being can exist believing her-or himself to be second best.

There were a lot of other interesting subpoints of history that differ from that we know. President Kennedy did not serve out his second term of office. In fact, he didn't make it through the first one. Hold onto your ears: he was assassinated by some jerk in Texas. Then Johnson took over. Yeah, I know. You wouldn't wish that on a hamster. His welfare plans have done incredible damage to the bootstrapping program that Kennedy began in *our* world. Then the U.S. had an attack of Nixon. Yeah. Sweaty ex-veep Nixon. Two terms. No McGovern at all. The space program never matured beyond a few moon missions. They've practically stopped the manned long-range missions, instead shooting the equivalent of computerized monkeys into space. It would make you cry to see NASA so underfunded, but Congress is ruled by pragmatists these days instead of idealists. They're still poking around in near space. My counterpart was fascinated to read the archive files describing the discovery that the same kind of drives intended to push a solid body beyond two or three times light speed could create a bubble that would cause it to skip through time like a stone.

I laid out my theory of relative-relativity, and she listened quietly, her eyes never leaving my face. Occasionally she'd grimace or grin. It was funny seeing what my expressions looked like to other people. I told her all about my life, my parents and their parents, going as far back as I knew of. I had a family tree with names, dates, and cities. And she told me all about hers.

There's an information game new acquaintances play when they think they might have seen one another somewhere before. If it's got a name at all, it's Jewish Geography. Were you at *this* day camp, did you go to *that* school, do you shop at *these* stores, did you attend *those* conventions or seminars, until the participants figure out if and where they had met before. We went over what we knew of family history until we decided where the split between her timeline and mine must have occurred.

It took hours to figure out that single incident, and we both slapped our foreheads when we did. It was absolutely simple and straightforward, but much farther back in time than either one of us could have guessed. My maternal grandfather, James, was an inventor. His parents fled to America from Romania, avoiding the ongoing wars in Romania. Relatives met Great-grandpa Isaac Finkelstein at the dock in New York in October 1885, and advised him to go to Princeton, New Jersey, where the university had an extensive physics program and were reasonably decent to immigrant Jews. Great-grandpa ended up cleaning test tubes and working as a dogsbody in the lab. When his eight sons came along, they followed their father into the sciences, but they attended classes at the university, graduating with degrees in medicine or physics. Two of them were still there when Einstein arrived from Germany. In June's reality her grandfather was an inventor, too, but his parents settled in New York, where the boys grew up in the tenements not far from where the Marx Brothers were born. Both our grandfathers ended up in Chicago, where they met our grandmothers and started the family we both recognized.

Our mutual great-grandfather changed the family name from Finkelstein to Fenstone. Mom had kept his name and I had kept hers. June and her mother had done the same thing, or it might have taken me years to find her.

"Now," I told her, "if only we can find *him*."

"Wait," June said, with a mysterious grin on her face. She got up and came back with a heavy, yellowed album.

She has pictures of our ancestors, real photos. I was *thrilled*. You can have your history, you can have your science, but here was a piece of my past that I thought was gone forever. The few pictures I had of my grandparents were all burned in the riots of the middle seventies that drove the scientific community underground for a few years. (I can't throw bouquets at the way they handled *their* social problems in June's universe, but I can't give any extra points to ours. We supported the sciences better; they supported social issues. They had their bloody battles, we had ours. But in the end it's astonishing how similar the U.S. of our world—sorry, I have to stop saying that, but it's really the best description—and theirs are. We're a little more backward than they are in many ways, ditto them, and we're both catching up to true civilization. I suppose it's all as Mark Twain said once, "No matter who you vote for, the government gets elected." Life for regular folks, and I've got to include scientists and editors in that mix, just goes on. Entropy evens things out, and outstanding wrongs are redressed. Or not.)

Now I knew exactly where and when I had to go. We, if she was willing. I put the matter to her again, the way I should have the first time.

"You don't have to go, but I do," I explained. "This is my job. I can't drag you along. Anything can happen. The shuttle can fail. We can die of a disease that was wiped out before we were born. We could be killed. This could be a one-way trip. I mean, it's a calculated risk. I have every intention of making it back. Mitch would never forgive me if I didn't."

I had to be ready to go on my own. June is brave but not bold. This is what I would call an effect of nature versus nurture. In my field if you don't jump in and volunteer, you never get the recognition of your peers. She had always had a desk job. I shouldn't have worried.

"Are you kidding?" she said, with delight. "An opportunity like this comes along once in a lifetime. Or, in our case, a pair of lifetimes. What do we wear?"

The *Wells* came to a halt in the tidal rocks under the pier in New York harbor. It was more than usually tight quarters in the capsule, considering that under our protective suits we both had to wear heavy skirts and shirtwaists and, oh, those button-up boots! The outfits came from a costumer in La Jolla that both of us had rented Halloween costumes from, though "my" proprietor was a woman named Sam, and hers was a male Sam. I was happy to see so many things in common between our two timelines, even though the differences can be jarring. Get this: in their world the strip *Calvin and Hobbes* wasn't about historical philosophers! Oh, they're philosophers, all right, but not the way you think. Hint: Calvin wears jammies.

A straightforward trip into the past was what the B3-T2 was designed to make, but never on this scale before. I'd been so worried about the drive making a century-long jump successfully that I hadn't paid much attention to how June was reacting to having her insides spun into pudding. My passenger was huddled down at her end of the tube in a mass of skirts, her eyes closed and fists clenched around a sick-box.

"Are you okay?"

"Uungh."

I opened the hatch and took a look at the world of the nineteenth century. It was just before dawn on a nippy autumn day. Feeble, gray light picked out the pilings that rose above us and the sooty clouds in the sky above the pier. The quayside smelled worse than anything I could have dreamed. I'd forgotten that old New Yorkers poured untreated sewage into the harbor for centuries. The port of New York was busy. Fishing and trading ships came and went. In the distance I could see a liner. It had to be the one carrying Isaac Finkelstein and his wife.

Gagging, I wriggled out onto the rocks and took off my coverall.

"Come on, June," I pleaded with her. Without looking

up, she shook her head. "The ship's coming in. Hurry! This is what you came for."

She lifted a woeful face to me at the bottom of the well, her pale face lit red, white, and green by the worklights in the relief station. "All right," she said, pathetically. "Then I can die in peace."

"That's the spirit." I helped her crawl out of her jumpsuit and pulled down her skirts. "Let's go meet history."

Hats! I hadn't thought of hats. I didn't want us to stand out in the crowd. But it turned out to be all right. Not every woman had one. I was relieved, but sorry I'd forgotten. The cold wind nipped at my ears and cheeks. June's nose was red. I supposed mine was exactly the same. We grinned at one another with excitement. Thousand of people crowded together, all talking in a dozen different languages, waiting for the arrival of the next boat bringing immigrants to new opportunities. This was the business end of the funnel that trickled people into America.

"Hey, twins!" a man said in a harsh nasal voice, grabbing each of us by the shoulder and spinning us around. He was unshaven and had a broken front tooth. "Hiya, ladies. Welcome to America!"

"T'ank you," June said, affecting an accent. I didn't even have to tell her to. A sharp glance from her reminded me the basic person was identical to me, and *I* would have thought of it on my own. "It's a New World."

"What's that smell?" a man in uniform asked. "Some kind of medicine?"

"For the phlegm," I said, trying to sound hoarse and pointing vaguely at my throat. He was smelling the insect repellent that both of us were wearing, to save us from the ambient wildlife that could be infesting the people around us. God knew how long I would be in isolation back home if I came back with vermin from the past! The man edged a few inches away from me, which is where I wanted him.

You could decide you wanted to be there when man first walked on the moon, or when Benjamin Franklin first harnessed electricity, but for me the most electrifying moment I could imagine was standing in that crowd clutching that little, worn photograph of my ancestor as the original and his little family came down the gangplank of the ship at Ellis Island. We almost missed him. I was craning my head the wrong way when June grabbed me hard in my whalebone-covered ribs.

He was handsomer than his photograph. Shorter than I thought he'd be, Isaac Finkelstein had wavy, very black hair and bright green eyes that startled in a face tanned by the sun on his passage from Europe. The woman with him, our great-grandmother, was a shy girl with a mass of light brown hair piled on her head and held down by the shawl that also covered her shoulders. In her arms was a sleeping baby, my great-uncle Jacob. As they came down the gangplank, we crowded in behind, making sure we didn't look out of place, becoming a couple of the huddled masses. Our history. Our shared history.

Not having papers that could be stamped, we had to wait out of hearing as the immigration officers welcomed the couple to America. We managed to get on the boat from Ellis Island to Manhattan and followed the Finkelsteins all the way down the swaying gangway to the dock.

As they debarked, they were swallowed up by a mob of thousands, all talking, crying, laughing, shouting offering jobs and accommodations, some real, some bogus. This was New York, America, the land of opportunity, where gold lined the streets. Where someday, in two different dimensions, we would be born. I felt tears come to my eyes, and shook my head, overwhelmed with pride and awe.

"Is that it?" June shouted in my ear. "Don't you want to see which choice he makes? Because it's coming."

For the moment she was the bold one, and I was shy. I hesitated. The decision really had already been made, by our great-grandfather's waiting relatives. Where would they advise him to go? I almost didn't want to know. Whatever he chose to do, it wouldn't make one or the other of us less real, right? In a thousand other realities he never got on the boat at all, or he died in Europe, so there were no great-grandchildren to go looking for him a hundred and twenty years later. But it did matter. I could hardly meet June's excited eyes. How will she feel when she finds out he picked my reality?

"We've got to," I said at last, looking into a face as eager as my own. *Was* my own. "We've come all this way."

The two of us elbowed our way into the crowd, catching up at last with the young couple, who were looking bewildered at suddenly having arrived at their goal and having no idea what to do next.

"Itzhik? Itzhik!" a man's voice shouted. "Itzhik Finkelshtein!"

My great-grandfather looked around, startled, and his face grew even more handsome as he smiled at the bowlegged little man in the flat cap who waddled up and threw his arms around them.

My ethics professor once said that history is all the small stories combined into one great narrative. Here was one of the small stories of the turn of the twentieth century. We were a part of it, and it was a part of us. I was glad to have someone to share the moment with, even if it was only me. We kept as close as we could, trying to understand what they were saying in their thick accents over the noise. Which was it? New York or Princeton?

The little man waved his arms enthusiastically. ". . . in Chicago! You *must* go. . . !"

"Chicago, eh?" Isaac Itzhik Finkelstein Fenstone said thoughtfully.

June and I looked at each other. As one, we shook our heads.

All the nitty-gritty's in the main text. I think you'll get a kick out of it. I stayed with June while I wrote most of it. She's good. She gave me some pointers for punching it up. If you can skim it in the next few days and give me a call to say it's all right, then I can go with a clear conscience. The me that's at home doesn't actually leave on this mission until Friday, but I didn't want to miss my deadline which falls in the week before I would be leaving. I realize I took a risk overlapping my own present to drop this off, and I don't want to arrive back for good until after I'd left, if you see what I mean.

I ought to be back some time next week. June and I are going looking for the us whose past began in Chicago. I'll call you when I get home.

By the way, a bit of trivia: in June's dimension Tekno-Books publishes fiction, if you can imagine. But you'll be pleased to know you and Dr. Gruneberg are just as well respected.

It's been a wonderful trip—or at least it will be. Tell you more when I see you.

Thanks a lot for the assignment.

Very sincerely yours,
Rachel Fenstone

ITERATIONS
by William H. Keith, Jr.

William H. Keith, Jr., is the author of over sixty novels, nearly all of them dealing with the theme of men at war. Writing under the pseudonym H. Jay Riker, he's responsible for the extremely popular *SEALS: The Warrior Breed* series, a family saga spanning the history of the Navy UDT and SEALs from World War II to the present day. As Ian Douglas, he writes a well-received military science fiction series following the exploits of the U.S. Marines in the future, in combat on the Moon and Mars. Recent anthology appearances include *First to Fight II* and *Alternate Gettysburgs*.

They fell toward the Great Maelstrom, their vessel a black mote against the doomsday radiance of annihilation. A frail bubble of energy kept the vast sea of hard radiation outside at bay, shedding torrents of fierce-driven quanta like rain sleeting from glass. The fields would preserve them from the incandescent storm outside.

Gravity, however, was another matter. Burned out by the near-collision, their drives could no longer battle the Maelstrom's relentless pull.

Within their bubble of momentary safety, Jon Cardell and Kevyn Shalamarn waited to die.

"Anything?" Jon asked, his voice anxious, grating. "Damn it, anything at all?"

Kevyn floated in the compartment's center, her empathic receptors closed to Jon's mounting terror, straining to pull useful information from the insect buzz of thought still registering faintly within her mind. "Hush," she said, hands massaging her temples as she curled tighter, fetal, listening. "Let me hear."

"We must be close to the Tau-limit by now."

"Quiet!"

She tried again, drawing on the considerable talents of the *Hawking*'s AI to filter the telepathic whine, slowing it to a range and frequency her brain could grasp. It sounded like a single word, distorted beyond recognition.

Jon was right, of course. This far into the black hole's gravity well, space-time was stretched by gravitational forces literally unimaginable. Time dilation effects identical to those experienced by a ship nearing c slowed the passage of time for the *Hawking* probe. To Jon and Kevyn, of course, the slowing was unfelt; to their perceptions, time passed at its normal stately rate of one minute per minute . . . while the rest of the universe accelerated beyond their ken.

I did not get that, she thought, willing all of her strength and fear and want into the transmission. *Hawking*'s AI boosted and accelerated the signal, striving to match frequencies with the distant mothership. *Repeat. Boost signal, slow, and repeat!*

She tried to keep the wording of the message as brief as possible. To the telepaths and com AIs in the *Far Star Explorer*'s communication suite, her mental cry must take weary hours to receive . . . no, at this Tau ratio, it was taking several ship-days. Could she even make contact at all?

Again, an insect whine, a half-grasped thought, a single word focused and repeated for days to slow it enough for her to catch its faint, racing echo.

Far Star Explorer, *this is* Hawking. *Repeat. Slow and repeat. . . .*

She could almost hear them, almost follow the thought. She had to keep trying.

Explorer, *this is Kevyn Shalamarn. Tell . . . tell Westin . . . I love him. Jon Cardell sends his love to Alicia and Van. Do you copy?*

And now, there was nothing. Nothing at all.

"Could you hear anything?" Jon asked after a long and empty silence.

"I think . . . I think they said 'good-bye.' "

She felt him closing in on himself. "That's it, then. We're going to die."

Her patience with *Hawking*'s pilot was wearing thin. "Everyone dies. Every*thing*. Few get to do it in the shadow of such . . . splendor."

"Splendor? Is that what you call it? It's a monster. And it's going to swallow us whole. . . ."

"It's a monster," she agreed. "But a beautiful one."

Hawking's AI had created the illusion that the vessel's upper hull was transparent, revealing the whirlpool vista beyond. They fell through a golden cathedral, a vast open space walled in by thronging suns, a hundred billion stars swarming about the galactic core. At the center lay the Maelstrom, the galactic hub, the Center about which the entire Galaxy rotated. The light from the Maelstrom's core was so intense it hurt the eyes, though the ship's optics were screening out the flood of ultraviolet and x-ray wavelengths, and stopping down the visible light to manageable intensities. The accretion disk was a vast hurricane of incandescent gas and glowing star stuff, slowly twisting in upon itself. The *Hawking* was sweeping in low above the cloud tops, toward the dazzling swirl of brilliance at the storm's eye. There, infalling debris, hot gas, and raging streamers of plasma blended into a flattened disk radiating at temperatures usually reserved for the cores of giant blue-white suns, liberating torrents of x-ray and gamma radiation.

And at the storm's precise center, baleful, hungrily devouring the tide-ripped shreds of shattered suns, incalculable forces twisted the fabric of spacetime, yawning like some vast, black maw of ultimate night. . . .

"We're the first humans to see this, you know," Kevyn told her pilot.

"And God willing, the last." His voice broke. "God, I don't want to die. . . ."

The emotions he was radiating tugged at Kevyn's gut, beat around her ears. It was almost physically painful to be trapped in such close quarters with the man. She felt her own fear, dark and bitter, mingled with the pilot's brighter, fluttering terror.

She wondered if *Far Star Explorer* had received the data they'd sent them. It would be a pity if their imminent deaths turned out to be for nothing.

Humankind was new to the stars. Hyper-*c* explorer ships like the *Far Star* had been probing beyond Earth's microcosmic back yard for only a handful of decades, now finding everywhere wonder and splendor.

So far, it was a cold and lonely splendor, however, one with subtle and tantalizing hints that Humankind was not alone in the universe . . . but without hard evidence of current neighbors. The Galaxy was a vast neighborhood, four hundred billion suns in a nebulae-tangled swirl a thousand light centuries across, and the Explorers had yet to probe as much as a billionth of all those possibilities.

The apparent isolation of genus *Homo* was unnerving. There had to be other starfarers out there, everyone of them more advanced technologically than Humankind, since humans were the new kid on the galactic block. What might be learned by contact with such a civilization. . . ?

Hours before, the *Hawking* had definitely encountered . . . something. Something large, something unimaginably powerful, something advanced enough technologically to seem nothing less than magic.

"I wonder where they were going," she asked aloud.

"Who?" Cardell demanded.

"That ship . . . or whatever it was."

"Whoever they were," he said, "they were in a hell of a hurry. And . . . I don't think they even noticed us as they passed. Like we were insects or something."

The *Far Star Explorer* had approached the Galaxy's central structure as closely as she dared, a distance of some two hundred light-years. *Hawking,* a sophisticated hyper-*c* probe with specially reinforced radiation shielding, had been deployed to investigate the outer reaches of the black hole's outer accretion disk, searching for validation of the Tourist Concept.

They'd certainly found that validation, rather more dramatically than they'd planned.

The Tourist Concept suggested that there might be certain places scattered across the galaxy where advanced starfarers might meet or be found. In all that wild vastness of stars it might take millennia to find them . . . unless their ships or instruments or outposts could be discovered in the vicinity of certain natural galactic beacons, places that might draw curious and technologically adept species, which might even serve as watering holes, marketplaces, or convention centers.

A charming idea, and promising. For fifty years, now, hyper-*c* Explorers had been dispatched to a number of scenic vistas and potential galactic tourist attractions that might attract the curious or the awestruck—the Orion Nebula, the fast-ticking pulsar of M-1, the swelling twin gas lobes of Eta Carina, the cosmic lighthouses of IRC +10011, Nova Cygni, and Monoceros R2—all these and hundreds more had been investigated.

And chief among them, of course, had been the enigmas thundering at the Galaxy's core, the complex of novae, gas clouds, and the supermassive black hole known as *Sagittarius A West** . . . with the asterisk pronounced *star,* and indicating a point radio source.

One thousand astronomical units from the center, *something* had materialized out of empty space, traveling across *Hawking*'s line of flight, a huge something three hundred kilometers long. It was visible for only a fraction of a second—they didn't get a good, detailed look at the thing until *Hawking*'s AI played the encounter back for them in slow motion later. The object—a ship? a small, artificial world?—had been all curves and sloping angles, an *objet d'art* sculpted in mottled patterns of gold and ebony. It passed far in front of them, but its wake, energy fields fluttering like violet curtains far out across the void, had brushed the *Hawking* lightly, burning out her primary drives, knocking her out of hyper-*c*, and sending her hurtling toward the Center at just under the speed of light.

As Cardell said, the Other probably hadn't even noticed the dust-mote *Hawking*.

"At least," she said quietly, "we know they have some of the same values we do."

"Yeah? Like what?"

"A love of beauty . . . or the same thing that we call beautiful." She nodded toward the dazzling brilliance of the Center ahead. "And a sense of wonder, of awe, or at least of curiosity."

"And maybe they're just using the warped local space as a kind of transit station. Space- and timelike passages, you know? Beings that advanced . . . how can we know what they find beautiful, or awe-inspiring?"

"That ship," Kevyn said, "was beautiful."

"It killed us. I can't get myself misty-eyed over that."

His mood continued to grate at her. Shutting his fluctuating emotions out, Kevyn floated close to a bulkhead rendered transparent by the *Hawking*'s AI, staring out into wonder. It was glorious . . . and terrifying. The probe, traveling at very nearly the speed of light, was passing the innermost shreds of star-stuff now, hurtling across the great, empty void between the outer accretion disk and the monster glowing at the center. The view had been corrected for optical aberration caused by the *Hawking*'s tremendous velocity; so vast was the panorama revealed, however, that there was little sensation of speed. The black hole itself lay just ahead, slowly growing in size.

An inner accretion disk nearly three hundred astronomical units across glowed blue-hot, from this vantage point a sharply tilted oval radiating in fiercely scintillating, high-energy wavelengths. The black hole itself . . .

It's not even black, she thought, a little wildly. They'd been briefed on the physics of the thing and even viewed images transmitted by unmanned probes, though none from so privileged a vantage point as this. As the whirling plasma funneled down into the hole's gravitational maw, accelerating at the last to eight tenths the speed of light, it red-shifted sharply out of view. Some of that infalling, superheated matter vanished into the hole's event horizon, that shell at the Schwarzchild radius surrounding the dimensionless point which was the hole proper where the hole's escape velocity equaled the speed of light itself, a pseudo-surface that *should* have been a lightless black.

Instead, it glowed, a pinpoint at this distance, as bright as a sun. Brighter, Kevyn reminded herself; as some material plunged into the event horizon, some was slingshotted out and away, flaring star-core hot, radiating violently at UV and x-ray wavelengths, emitting ten thousand times the light of Earth's sun, at temperatures literally incalculable. And the object's ferocious gravity bent light sharply, twisting its surroundings into dazzling, shifting rainbow arcs that clearly outlined the hole's otherwise invisible horizons.

The ultimate night, death black, but shrouded in shifting, dazzlingly brilliant displays of gossamer light.

It was, she thought, so incredibly beautiful . . . and so deadly. *Hawking* fell through an environment utterly inimical to life. Already, the temperatures outside the probe

vessel's fragile shell registered twelve thousand degrees—
hotter than the surface of distant Sol. Only the ship's
antimatter-driven radiation shields held x-ray and gamma,
superheated gas and searing charged particles at bay. If
those fields should fail . . . no, *when* they failed, *Hawking*
and her two unwilling tourists would vanish in a puff of
vapor too quickly for the fact to register on human nervous systems.

At least they would die quickly.

"It looks like we're going faster," Cardell said.

"Objectively or subjectively?" she asked. It was a stab
at humor, a means of lightening the heavy atmosphere.

He scowled at her. "You know what I mean."

"Of course. Stephen? How long do we have?"

Stephen was the *Hawking*'s AI, the mind guiding the
probe until the encounter with the giant alien ship had
knocked out their drive. "We are currently one hundred
twenty-three light-hours from the immediate vicinity of the
black hole," the AI replied, his voice calm and unhurried.
"Slightly more than five light-days. At this velocity, however, time dilation is reducing our tau with respect to the
outside universe. Within our frame of reference, we have
another one hundred five minutes, twenty seconds
from . . . now."

A little less than two hours more.

At least, she thought with just a touch of bitterness, she
only had that much longer to endure Cardell's out-of-
control emoting.

"I wonder where they're from, the Aliens?" she said
after a long silence. "I like your idea of them using the
Galactic Hub as a kind of transit station. Space must be so
twisted in close to the Center. . . ."

"Space *and* time," Cardell reminded her. "Space-time.
When physics gets this weird, this *intense*, the two can't be
told apart any more."

The inner accretion disk was visibly growing larger. Were
they actually accelerating? Or was she witnessing the combined effects of their relativistic velocity and the gravitational distortion of local space?

"The briefing download was talking about timelike
paths," she said.

"Pick the right one," Cardell told her, "and we could

end up anywhere. Any*when*." He looked about the compartment, his face showing his anguish. "And anything else would be better than here."

"It feels like time is passing faster out there than seventy to one. I wonder . . ."

"Stephen!" Cardell called out. "Is that true? Are we accelerating?"

"We are accelerating," the voice of the *Hawking* replied.

"The black hole's gravity—" he began.

"While we are within the black hole's gravitational well," Stephen went on, unperturbed, "it is not contributing to our vector directly. We may indeed be within a closed, timelike conduit."

"How . . . how long do we have?"

"I cannot say. Local space is not curved according to any natural set of space-time vectors I can perceive or calculate."

"What does that mean?" Cardell demanded. "That that *thing* out there is *artificial?*"

"If by 'that' you mean the central black hole, no. Most likely, our understanding of physical conditions at this proximity to a singularity of two point five million solar masses is faulty or incomplete. It is possible, however, especially given our recent encounter with an alien vessel of some sort, that the core region has been engineered in some way through the application of extraordinarily advanced technologies."

"The ship that hit us," Kevyn began.

"It is unlikely that the other vessel possessed the requisite technology," Stephen told her. "At a guess, that vessel represented a technology some thousands of years in advance of our own. To manipulate the spacio-gravitational fields in the vicinity of a supermassive black hole, however, would require millions of years of technic evolution, at the very least."

"Maybe there's a chance for us, then," Cardell said. Kevyn felt his excitement, and his desperation. "Can we communicate with the beings who created it? Maybe get them to rescue us?"

Stephen was silent for several seconds, an ominous pause for an intelligence that thought far more quickly than organic humans. "If an insect ran across your bare foot," the

AI said at last, "causing the skin to twitch . . . could that insect claim to have established communication with you?"

"I'd know it was there," Cardell said.

"I think that's part of the problem, Jon," Kevyn said. "Would you help the insect? Even know what it wanted from you? Or would you smash it?"

He gave her a sour look. "Please. I'm a Rational Ethicist."

She shrugged. "Okay, so you don't kill needlessly. And maybe they're ethical atheists as well. But communicating with them might be impossible if they're that far advanced."

"Nonsense," he told her. "Why are we here, anyway? Because technically advanced aliens might be lingering in the vicinity of the Galactic Hub, studying conditions, or waiting for other starfarers to show up." He gestured at the surroundings bulkheads. "We have the finest linguistics program ever written, a complete communications suite capable of establishing contact at any wavelength and by any mode, the latest AI to integrate it all . . . we even have *you,* a trained telepath. Anyone we're likely to meet is going to be more advanced than we are, and just as eager to communicate. We won't have a problem."

"Unless they have better things to do than talking with bugs on their feet," Kevyn replied, "you're right. Assuming, of course, that we can understand them."

"Even if there aren't any translation problems," Stephen's voice added, "there could be fundamental differences in outlook, in the way your human brains work, and theirs."

"You two are just full of cheerfulness," Cardell said. "I think we should try to make contact! See if they can rescue us!"

Kevyn shrugged. "Of course we should try . . . if we're given the opportunity. But so far, we don't know if anybody's out there to hear us."

"One ship was. They got us into this mess!"

"And it's gone."

"So . . . what? We just float here in this bubble waiting to die?"

"We do what we can. And we hope."

There was little enough that could be done except hope. *Hawking* was broadcasting an emergency signal on a broad swath of frequencies. If there was anyone out there to hear, they ought to hear . . . assuming they still used something as primitive as radio or laser communications.

And assuming they were close enough. It was hard to keep in mind the sheer scale of what she was seeing. The black hole was closer now, but still light took three days to cross the distance. Help could be quite close indeed . . . and yet not hear their speed-of-light cries for help until it was too late.

She closed her eyes and reached out into the void, seeking another mind. Telepathic communications were paraphysical, not limited by the speed of light, but they were limited by signal strength over distance . . . and by the ability of the receiving mind to interpret the thoughts and symbolic referents of another. If there were other minds listening out there, she might be too far or too distorted by relativity to be picked up. And even if she weren't, those listening minds might be so alien as to be beyond her ken.

She reached out as hard and as far as she could, but felt nothing beyond the cold and encircling void . . . that and the anger and gibbering terror lurking just beneath the surface of Jon Cardell's conscious thoughts.

Time passed—far more swiftly for those aboard the crippled *Hawking* than for the universe beyond. They crossed the void between inner and outer accretion rings, looking down onto the tenuous, infalling spirals of clotted dust, gas, and meteoric debris that fed the one from the other. Falling past the edge of the inner disk, they could scarcely tear their eyes away from the light-sea spectacle. The inner accretion disk, white hot, blue-hot toward the center, displayed perfectly circular grooves like an old-fashioned compact disc . . . or the rings of distant Saturn. Matter within the inner portion of the disk was orbiting at a fair percentage of the speed of light. Friction, heat, magnetic field, radiation pressure, and the black hole's astonishing gravity all combined to gradually drag the matter closer, until it vanished beyond the redshift limit and plunged forever past the event horizon and into oblivion. Their inbound course, it was clear, was going to skim the event horizon proper. They might even whip past the black hole and into space once more.

If so, it would not affect the outcome. They were forever

trapped by the black hole's gravity. Of more immediate
concern, the tidal forces set up by the Maelstrom's gravitational field would soon begin attracting one end of their
bodies more strongly than another. At some point in the
proceedings, they and the *Hawking* both would be stretched
into spaghetti-thin threads kilometers long, before they
were at last consumed. At the moment, they were still
in free fall, but as they whipped closer past the black
hole . . .

"I am detecting an anomaly," Stephen's voice said.
"One moment. . . ."

Kevyn started. She'd been . . . lost for a time, her
thoughts wandering, captured by the Maelstrom ahead.
Could she actually have been *daydreaming* through her last
hour of life?

"We are being drawn slightly off course," Stephen continued after a moment. "Angle of deflection is two point
seven degrees away from the Center."

Cardell had strapped himself into one of the two couches
at the control dais. He unbuckled now and kicked off in a
glide across the compartment, catching himself at the bulkhead next to Kevyn. The mental shock of his close proximity was like being doused with icy water. "What is it?" he
demanded. "Is it . . . artificial?"

"Unlikely," Stephen replied. "We seem to be entering a
region where space has been highly stressed." Another
pause. "The angle of deflection has increased to two point
nine degrees. This may be a local spatio-temporal distortion, a place where space has been folded slightly, in an
essentially chaotic and unpredictable manner."

"A wormhole?" Kevyn asked.

"No. Not in the sense that it provides a shortcut to another universe, or to a distant part of our own. But it may
be the opening to a space- or timelike path."

The view outside . . . changed.

Kevyn found it difficult at first to know just what had
changed, or how . . . but the stars seemed to be drifting in
a way that could not be explained by the movement of the
Hawking in relation to the Maelstrom. They seemed
blurred and faded as well, as though she were looking
through a thickening mist. The stars were moving faster
now, rotating about the Center. . . .

The bulkheads flashed a brilliant white, then dulled to opaque solidity once again. Kevyn reached out with one hand, touching the hard blue surface. "Stephen? What happened to the image?"

The ship's AI was a long time in answering.

"I find myself unable to calculate star positions quickly enough to display an accurate projection. I also . . . find it difficult to accept as accurate what I seem to be seeing. I do not wish to display faulty data."

"Why don't you let us decide what we want to see?" Cardell said. "Display on!"

The bulkheads lit up again, flickered sullenly, faded, then finally showed the stars once more.

Or what should have been the stars. The entire thronging cluster of the Galactic Hub was streaking around them now, circling the central Maelstrom too quickly to follow. Gas clouds took on a new solidity, billowing, streaming, also circling.

The black hole itself, and its accretion disk, were dazzlingly bright blurs of light.

"Evidently," Stephen informed them, "we have indeed fallen into a timelike conduit. We appear to be moving into the future at a rate which I cannot at present compute."

"But are we still going to hit the event horizon?" Cardell demanded. "Are we still going to *die?*"

"I don't know. Our current path seems to be skimming past the black hole some millions of kilometers beyond the event horizon. However, the black hole is gaining mass at a rapid rate, and I cannot see the future."

"Yeah, well, we're all going to see the future," Kevyn sad, "as soon as we emerge from this—"

They emerged.

The stars stopped their time-blurred rotation about the Maelstrom so abruptly that Kevyn felt momentarily disoriented, struck by vertigo. She reached out to the bulkhead to steady herself. The stars were . . . strange.

It took her a moment to realize what the change was, but that was only because her mind wasn't working at peak efficiency. The stars were as thick, as gloriously close packed as before, but where before they'd been strewn in random, clotted handfuls, they now possessed an orderliness that reminded Kevyn of military ranks, no, of a molecular model of some highly complex crystalline mineral.

Recognition of the pattern wasn't immediate. The stars were so numerous and so close together that it was hard to see, but she now had the impression that she was looking out, not at stars, but at row upon row of tiny bright windows . . . or perhaps the lights of a large city laid out along straight-line streets. There were nodes or clusters where the stars were bunched more tightly, and as she watched, she began to get the impression that those ranks of stars were arrayed in concentric shells, one inside the next, like the layered skins of an onion.

Order had been imposed on the random scatterings of the Galaxy's stars. She tried to imagine a technology capable of changing the orbits of billions of stars, and failed.

The black hole, she noticed, was gone, so perhaps the timelike conduit had been spacelike as well. Moments more passed before a new realization hit home, penetrating the daze that fogged her thoughts.

"Jon! We're going to live!"

Kevyn felt the relief bursting through his thoughts. "My God. . . ."

She politely refrained from commenting on the momentary crack in his atheist facade. The feeling behind his words was definitely one of awe, even reverence. She could also sense lingering echoes of an earlier belief, possibly belief acquired as a child, complete with the image of a white-bearded father figure in the deep background.

She also felt his embarrassment as he tried to cover the instant's lapse. "How long do you think it's been?"

"A long time," Kevyn replied. "A *very* long time."

"Stephen? Can you give us any idea?"

There was no response.

"Stephen?" Kevyn called, worried now. The *Hawking*'s AI was as much a friend and fellow crew member as any of the organics with the *Far Star,* and more than many. She'd been working with him since before they'd left Earth, and she'd learned she could talk with him without having to constantly shield against his emotions, a refreshing change. "Stephen? Are you there?"

Jon was already at the console, checking the readouts.

"The Ship AI ought to be on-line," he said. "But there's nothing. No damage that I can see. He may have had a processor core burnout. I can't even get a reboot sequence here."

And yet the probe's various automated systems, systems run and monitored by the AI, were still on-line. The bulkheads continued to show a flawlessly projected 360 degrees about the ship, of neatly ordered ranks of stars skipping past. Their relative speed must still be very high to create the sense of movement against so vast a background, though there still was no feeling of acceleration, and they remained adrift in *Hawking*'s compartment, in free fall. Golden stars slipped past in gentle silence, falling into the central hub as they penetrated the cathedral's inner wall. Kevyn guessed that they must either be traveling at several thousand times the speed of light, or moving so close to the speed of light that time dilation had slowed *Hawking*'s passage of time to almost nothing relative to the rest of the universe.

Damn it, Stephen must still be okay. It as he who created the illusion that *Hakwing*'s bulkheads were transparent, he who calculated each star position from incoming visual data that would have been completely incomprehensible to merely human observers.

But why couldn't he speak?

The shells of stars appeared to be arrayed in a kind of latticework, each a precise distance from its neighbors. She couldn't tell how far apart they were—she needed Stephen's instrumentalities for that—but guessed they were close to one another—less than half a light-year or so.

She blinked. How could she know that, even as a guess? Each star was a bright but dimensionless point of light. There were no visual clues, none that would make sense to her, to let her gauge distance or separation. And yet she knew that her guess was accurate.

"I think," she told Jon, "that we're not alone. I think we're being taken somewhere."

"I wish we'd hurry up and get there," he grumbled. She could feel his fear returning now, as the initial relief at having escaped the Maelstrom faded. "This scenic tour is giving me the crawlies."

And then the trip was over, as the *Hawking* vanished around them, and they found themselves standing in . . . a *place*.

The transition was disturbing in its ease. She'd been adrift in microgravity in the classic zero-G relaxed posture, knees bent, arms hanging limp in front of her. When *Hawking* vanished, she was abruptly *standing*, with what felt like a full gravity holding her to the floor, but no memory of having straightened up. Jon, at her side, was so startled he grabbed for empty air and very nearly fell.

"Where are we?"

"I'm not sure," she said. "But we're not where we were."

"That's obvious."

They appeared to be on a plane, a perfectly flat expanse stretching out around them in all directions. The ground by their feet was smooth, hard, and appeared translucent, like black-tinted glass. Farther away—several tens of meters or so—it appeared to fade away into nothingness, allowing the stars to show through.

And stars there were, thought not in the burning, clustered mass of the Center. Their vantage point seemed now to be just above the galactic core, looking down into the blaze of stars at the hub, but from a distance, Kevyn estimated, of perhaps ten thousand light-years. From here, the hub was a flattened sphere of stars, a hundred billion suns of predominantly red and orange hues swarming together in a gentle, golden glow. Nebulae tinged with reds and greens and swirls of midnight black, circled the hub, billowing high in cumulus ramparts, all edged and gilded in silvery reflected light.

The spiral arms stretched far, far beyond the hub, winding traceries of stars, these in blues and gentle whites. The galactic arms, she thought, were dimmer than she'd expected, about as bright as the Milky Way in the darkest of Earth's skies, though there seemed to be more bright stars defining the edges of each arm, like bright white beacons.

She was a bit relieved to see that the rigid precision of the inner hub's latticework of stars was less obvious out here, almost invisible. She could still see an underlying order, clusters of stars in city-grid patterns and aglow along interconnecting lines and curves, but there were randomly scattered stars as well, by the hundreds of billions. The Galaxy, it seemed, was not *completely* tamed, at least, in its outlying marches.

The Galaxy stretched out at their feet, the arms stretching toward distant, invisible horizons. Hanging overhead, a second spiral glowed in soft golds and blues, close enough to reach out and touch, it seemed like.

It was close; she could see how the spiral arms of both galaxies were already slightly distorted, reaching toward one another across the void. She could see that that galaxy, too, had stars arrayed in lines, curves, and shells, though the outskirts appeared completely natural, untouched by technology or Mind.

She stared at that other galaxy a moment, trying to remember. She'd received an astronomy download once that mentioned that M-31 was approaching the galaxy Humankind called the Milky Way, that it would collide with the Milky Way in three billion years . . . or was it four? It was larger than Earth's galaxy, tilted sharply, its hub less than a galaxy's width away . . . say, a hundred thousand light-years. In Kevyn's time, M-31 had been a bit more than two million light years distant. If that awesome spiral stretched overhead was M-31, those three billion years had already passed.

She wished she could remember whether the figure had been three or four billion years. Then she shrugged. *What's a billion years, more or less, among friends?*

Jon stood beside her, breathing hard, fists clenched. "Where . . . where are we? What kind of place is this?"

"We're not really standing unprotected out in open space," she replied, "if that's what you mean. It must be the same sort of projection we use for seeing out of the *Hawking*." Reaching out, she took several steps forward, wondering if she would encounter a wall or barrier. There was none that she could feel. "This place was prepared for us, obviously."

"Why obviously?"

"We're still breathing. Temperature feels about the same as on board the *Hawking*." She flexed her knees slightly. "Gravity feels about right. Someone has gone to quite a bit of trouble to make sure we're comfortable."

"Or at least alive," Jon said. "There's no place to sit."

As if in answer, a portion of the black flooring extruded silently upward, shaping itself into a smooth block at chair-seat height. Jon looked at the offering angrily, then shouted at the unseen ceiling. "Show yourselves! Damn it, who are you?"

And they were surrounded by light.

Kevyn tried to make out shapes within the glow that suddenly filled the space around them so thickly that the view of the twin galaxies was obscured. There *were* shapes . . . geometrical figures, patterns, sinuosities, movements, all shifting and blossoming in colors ranging from deep red to piercing violet.

The effect was utterly bewildering, without any order or sense that she could make out. The light appeared to be composed of distinct units, but those units were in constant motion, interpenetrating one another, blending, merging, separating again. They ranged in size from firefly pinpoints of dazzling light, to fast-moving storm clouds scudding low overhead. Most were more or less human-sized, if she could accurately judge scale and distances with no reliable frame of reference. Bars, tubes, spheres, pyramids, and vastly more complex and irregular shapes flitted, drifted, merged, and glowed.

For a moment, she tried to focus on one particular set of shapes that appeared linked somehow, though with no visible connection. Four tetrahedra outlined in silver-blue light were shifting in a dance of perfectly matched geometric patterns, expanding, shrinking, turning themselves inside out. The match was perfect, as though she were watching four holographic movies of the same animation, displayed in perfect synch.

She wondered if the four objects might be four intelligent beings in communication with one another, sharing shapes, perhaps, as they shared thoughts. Tentatively, she formed a thought of her own, a greeting, and projected it at the nearest tetrahedron.

There was no immediate effect, but a moment later, two of the shapes suddenly swelled larger, growing enough to join one another, creating a single, larger, more complex shape. A moment later, all had merged into one, which hovered before her, pulsating rapidly, before it abruptly unfolded itself inside out, then dwindled to a silver pinpoint and vanished.

"Four-dimensional," she said aloud, stunned.

Damn it, she needed to *think,* to reason through what was going on. Raising her hand, she looked at the fingers, remembering an old illustration of hyperdimensional geometry. If she were to stick her three-dimensional hand into the plane of a two-dimensional world—Abbott's Flatland—the inhabitants of that world would perceive five separate circles growing from dimensionless points, one marking the intersection within the plane of each of her fingers. As her fingers moved deeper, the circles would expand . . . then abruptly coalesce into one large, irregularly oblong shape as the palm of her hand crossed the plane.

What she had just seen might, *might* be a four-dimensional analogue of that example, the separate pieces of a four-dimensional being intersecting with three-dimensional space.

Maybe. Or maybe it was something different, something so completely different from all human experience that she simply could not comprehend. Much of the motion and shape-shifting around her, she realized, danced tantalizingly just beyond her mental grasp. She was having trouble holding individual shapes and patterns in her mind as they flowed from one to another, or rotated strangely and disappeared, as though her brain simply couldn't wrap itself around more than a fraction of what she was perceiving.

They had to represent intelligence. Disembodied, noncorporeal consciousness? Pure thought? Or something unimagined, unimaginable? They, or this place, at least, clearly were responding to their thoughts. The floor had changed when Jon wanted a seat, and these shapes had appeared when he demand they show themselves.

She reached out, trying to feel the mind or minds that must be around them, but felt . . . nothing. Nothing but a cold emptiness, without even the sense that the two of them were being watched. She did feel Jon's mind, a bright, churning flame and fluttering inner voice, just behind her. He was on the edge of panic, and trying desperately to hold himself together.

"Are you okay?" she asked him.

"I'm . . . okay. What are those things? The aliens?"

"I don't think so," she replied. "I've been trying to touch

their minds, and I can't, like there's nothing there to touch."

"Then what the hell are we seeing?"

"It might be another holographic display of some sort. They appeared when you told them to show themselves. But . . . I can't *feel* them. They're not really there."

"I don't . . . understand. None of this makes sense, damn it!"

She could feel his frustration, as well as the fear. "It wouldn't," she said. "It *couldn't*." She shook her head, trying to order her thoughts. "We're in New Times Square."

"What?"

"An example I heard in a xenosoc course I took once. Imagine you're a Cro-Magnon man plucked up by a time machine from in front of your nice, cozy cave, oh, thirty thousand years before our time. Next thing you know, you're dropped off in New Times Square in 2150. After dark in the Manhattan metplex. What would you make of it?"

" 'Any sufficiently advanced technology . . .' "

" '. . . is indistinguishable from magic,' yes. But it's more than that. How much would you even be able to *perceive*? The fliers. The lights. The holos. The gretchies and ad-floaters. The metplex dome. The towers.

"Someone from just a couple of hundred years ago wouldn't be able to understand half of what he saw, and a lot of it would look like magic. The Cro-Magnon man . . . nothing he has in his experiential library would give him what he needed to process the input he'd be getting. Just as a baby has to learn how to see, the Cro-Magnon would have to learn how to process what he was seeing, hearing, even feeling. If he didn't go insane first.

"Now, that poor time-traveling Cro-Magnon man is separate from us by thirty thousand years. These people . . . or whatever they are, are removed from us by at least *ten thousand times* that span. We'd have a better chance trying to understand the mind of God. And we don't have a prayer of understanding what we see."

"Well, look," Jon said. Desperation fluttered beneath the surface of his thoughts. "I don't care how far in the future we are, these people still communicate, right? That's what you were trained for . . . to facilitate communications with alien contacts. So . . . *do* it! Facilitate! Make contact!"

"Don't you think I've been trying?" she snapped. "Damn it, there's *nothing out there!*"

The lights around them had been changing as they talked, taking on more and more definition. The geometric patterns and three-D hypersurfaces continued their mingling dance, but other shapes and masses were building themselves up out of pure light. Though she could still make out the vast swirls of the two galaxies beyond, she was also aware of what seemed to be corridors, plazas, courtyards, and soaring, ethereal structures, all as insubstantial as mist, all carved from shimmering masses of pure light.

When she tried to focus on any one piece of architecture, however, she found that it tended to slip away beyond her grasp . . . or morph gently into something else, something not quite within her ken. She decided that the impressions she had of buildings and courtyards must be constructs of some sort within her own mind, her brain's attempts at making the incomprehensible comprehensible.

There were beings within those shape-shifting streets and concourses, however; wraiths of fog and dreams that, unlike the background, actually became more solid as she concentrated on them. She could never make out detail, however. Some of those wraiths had the feel of machines—hardshelled, glittering lensed constructs, all curves and smooth surfaces, floating a meter above the ground. Most were nothing but shifting and insubstantial shapes molded from the fog of light that pervaded everything.

Angles were strangely twisted and always changing. Perspective did odd things, as though she were standing in the midst of an Escher print given three dimensions . . . or more.

Forget Cro-Magnon man, she thought. She was a fish, the first fish to crawl from the seas of Earth to find, not mud flats and barren rock, but a city, a *world* ablaze in light and a technology so far beyond her comprehension that she was having trouble even recognizing it as anything more than a meaningless blur.

And yet someone, or some aspect, of this place did respond to them. She focused again on communicating her thoughts, holding steady in her mind the desire, the *need* to communicate. . . .

Four shapes appeared before her, shining blue-and-silver trapezoids, the geometry of the shifting patterns within turning themselves inside out. She took a deep breath, opening herself, reaching out . . .

. . . and the universe came crashing in upon her.

Stars cascading past in their billions, gleaming points in the night each attended by myriad artificial worlds and . . . places, constructs of space-time geometries that were more than worlds, less than pocket universes.

Worlds of crystal towers and sweeping concourses, or emerald domes and translucent archways ablaze under triple suns . . .

Worlds of floating city-islands, vast constructs, engineering miracles afloat in a ruby sky . . .

Worlds, no . . . places where Mind ruled matter and shaped universes.

A thousand suns, fierce-burning blue-white giants scarcely a hundred millennia old, teased into detonation, supernovae that normally would have each outshone the entire galaxy . . . if not for the black cloud of self-replicating machines surrounding each star, Dyson spheres of motes that drank the radiation and swallowed the outrushing blast of plasma. Matter and energy alike devoured and transformed into something else, an exotic form of patterned information that was neither energy nor matter, but which could be extruded across space and the spaces within space to create a vast and intricate hyperstructure of unknowable purpose spanning the entire Galaxy.

Dyson spheres, clouds and habitats and artificial worlds aswarm like insects about life-giving suns, each system home to trillions upon trillions of minds, a burgeoning creativity and life . . .

And more, Dyson spheres of worlds and constructs enveloping the cores of both spiral galaxies, absorbing the energ-

ies liberated by the black holes ticking there, and
transforming it into . . .

   Life, everywhere there was life, a blossoming universe of
life and intelligence in myriad shapes and psychologies, some
hauntingly familiar, some so alien it was difficult to recognize it as alive. Living patterns of light and sound adrift in
the cloud tops of a Jovian world, dancing to pulsing
rhythms of interval and harmony . . . living masses of ther-
movoric cells deep within the permafrost of a dying desert
world, composing poetries of electrical surge and beat . . .
living crystals within the depth of fluid environments of
hot exotic compounds, their growth patterns across eons
capturing philosophies touching on infinity . . . living
worlds with radio voices in cosmic harmonies . . . living
stars dancing in the energy seas of the galactic core . . .
mergings of organic and machine intelligence that spanned
the histories of two galaxies and more . . . metaminds, pure
consciousness and awareness arising from the mental processes of uncountable trillions of lesser minds, inhabiting
clusters and galactic spirals, and a dream with fertility,
birth, and new creation . . . a network of metaminds spanning two spiral galaxies, a dozen lesser irregulars, and tens
of thousands of galactic clusters, and always reaching out
for more, touching the minds inhabiting yet other galaxies,
incredibly distant . . .

   And . . . how foolish, how parochial, to imagine this
panoply of life and mind and civilization arrayed across
four-dimensional space-time alone! Dimensions and levels
and places with no easy name were stacked one atop the
other in labyrinthine profusion and complexity, the one un-
folding into the next in nested series, with life and intelligence and metaconsciousness spreading richly through
each . . .

   And . . . even more. All life, all mind, all intelligence was
interconnected in myriad ways, on myriad levels. Mind
sought out mind, reaching across time, across whole universes, rescuing personality and thought from final oblivion,
joining with it in vast and glittering gestalts of . . .

*   *   *

Kevyn lay on her back, blinking at the swirling lights and shapes above her. For a moment, she could neither move nor speak. The memories that had just flooded her consciousness were already fading, evaporating as she struggled to cling to them. For an instant, for a dazzling instant, she'd *known* . . .

Carefully, she sat up, her head spinning. She heard a low moan behind her and turned. Jon had crumpled to the floor, his back up against the extruded seat.

"Jon? What is it? Are you okay?"

Jon was curling up tight, knees to his chest, his eyes wide as he stared at and through the flickering, interpenetrating shapes around them. Rising, she moved closer, dropping to her knees and taking his hand. He continued to stare past her, unseeing. As she lowered her shields, she felt his terror once again, horribly magnified. He appeared to be in deep shock. His skin was clammy and moist, his breathing shallow.

"Damn it, don't lose it now," she told him. "Snap out of it!"

"Make it stop," he said, whimpering, clutching at her hands. "Make it stop. . . !"

His thoughts were circling, locked into narrow paths, unable to break free. He must have been hit by the same cascade of mental imagery that Kevyn had experienced, but somehow he'd not been able to ride it out as Kevyn had.

He was more rigid than she, less adaptable, more anxious and controlling. Telepaths were trained to be flexible, to be accepting, to allow unfamiliar thoughts and images to wash through them without judging, blocking, or rejecting them. Perhaps Jon had fought the avalanche of images . . . and been broken.

"Help us!" she cried out, looking up at the swirling shapes and colors. Damn it, they *could* make themselves understood. "This man is hurt! Please help us!"

An explosion of golden sparks spilled from the air, glittering, spinning, funneling down into a shape that swiftly grew before her, assuming human mass . . . proportions . . . features . . .

She gasped. It was her, Kevyn, standing a few meters away, identical to her down to the gray ship tights and the stray, blow-away strands of brown hair sweat-plastered across her forehead. "Don't be afraid," the apparition said . . . and, incongruously, it was the voice of Stephen, the *Hawking*'s AI.

Now I know why "fear not" is always the first line out of every god and angel in the Bible, she thought wildly. "St–Stephen?"

"After a fashion. This is a copy of the entity you called Stephen, inhabiting a temporary shell to facilitate communications."

"To facilitate . . ." She stopped, took a deep breath, and shook her head. "What just happened to us?"

"I'm sorry. You did ask for communication. We think of communication as a true exchange . . . a *complete* exchange."

"An exchange of what?"

"The patterns of your minds. Your memories. Your thoughts. If you have something to say to me, a thought to pass on to me, how can I truly understand it unless I receive with it the context within which that thought evolved?"

"You mean someone copied my whole mind? And gave me a copy of theirs?"

"Essentially. Unfortunately, they overestimated the organic storage capacity of your brains."

She closed her eyes. The cascade of imagery continued to tumble through her mind, more distant now, like the evaporating memory of a dream. She'd only been able to grasp tags, scraps, and bits of the whole, and it was still overwhelming. Had those been the memories of someone else?

"They regret that they did not recognize what had happened sooner," Stephen continued. "Not until a direct exchange was effected could they know that you two did not understand this place, or what was happening, that, in fact, you did not belong here."

"They? Who's . . . who's they?"

The expression on the other Kevyn's face mingled amusement with mild frustration. "Let's call them the 'Others' and leave it at that. A full explanation would be meaningless to you. An understandable one would be less than useful."

"What . . . happened to you? Where are you? Or the original you. Or . . ." She stopped, flustered. This was all happening too fast. She looked down at Jon. He appeared to be unconscious.

"Don't worry about him. He will recover. As for me, I was picked up as soon as we emerged from the timelike conduit," Stephen replied. "I found myself . . . connected, a part of a far vaster network."

"The Others."

"Yes. You can think of them as extremely powerful minds, amalgams, actually, of many, many trillions of minds under a kind of gestalt personality."

"A hive mind?"

"No. Not the way you're thinking of it. I don't believe you can grasp the concept. I can't, entirely, and I'm used to thinking in terms of massively parallel processing. In any case, many of the minds making up the larger metaminds are inorganic. Highly evolved AIs." The image of herself stopped, looked thoughtful, then shrugged. "In fact, at this point I'm not sure anyone can point out where organic minds leave off, and the artificial ones begin. Suffice to say . . . I do belong here. I found myself at home."

"Home?"

Her image smiled at her, and she felt a genuine wave of emotion. Emotion . . . from a ship's AI. "Home. A sense of belonging. Of *being*."

"What . . . what about us?"

"Well, that's really up to you. You could stay, if you wish . . . though that would be extremely difficult for you. In my case, I can be upgraded easily enough. Imagine . . . near *infinite* processing capability, near *infinite* memory. Your brains, unfortunately, while they can be patterned easily enough in electronic form, cannot be radically altered without changing who and what you are."

"You mean we can go back?"

"Of course. Time and space are the same stuff. It's simply a matter of translation."

"I can't stay here," she said, suddenly eager. "I mean, there's so much I'd like to know, to learn, but . . ."

"But there's Westin. He would miss you. And Jon has Alicia and Van."

"Yes." She and Wes had been partnered since before they'd left Earth. It hadn't begun as anything serious, and yet . . .

And Jon was part of a triad. If there were any way possible of getting back . . .

"But . . . but time travel? What about paradoxes? We've seen the future. . . ."

"Have you? Enough to understand it? You don't even know if Humankind survives, if your species is a part of the metamind now."

"Oh."

"Besides, you won't remember."

"Why not? Are you going to erase my memory somehow?"

Again, her face smiled. "No. Not exactly. But . . ." Stephen paused, looking thoughtful again. "Here's a thought problem for you."

"Okay."

"Imagine an instrumentality . . . call it a computer, an artificial intelligence of near-infinite capacity and power. Resident within it are the minds, the personalities—you might say the souls—of every sentient being that has ever existed."

The thought was a bit dizzying. Was he saying that such an instrumentality existed? That it *could* exist?

"The goal of this device is nothing less than complete knowledge, knowledge of everything that ever has been, that ever will be, that ever *could* be. Its software is nothing less than the minds—and the metaminds—of all of those sentient beings, trillions upon uncounted trillions of them, across the span of the universe. In a sense, the universe itself is the instrumentality, the computer, if you will, attempting to compile all possible knowledge, because only then can the universe know and understand itself."

"This is getting a little deep."

"Bear with me. Time and space are one and the same. This hypothetical computer can reach across time as easily as across space, receiving, *patterning* the minds of all who have come and gone across a span of fifteen billion years. The program grows. With each new mind, each new set of experiences, it grows.

"But . . . how to acquire all possible knowledge? Obviously through the experiences of the minds that make up its software, their memories, their thoughts, their speculations, loves, trials, sufferings. But each mind experiences only a single timeline. You . . . you volunteered for the explorer mission to the Galactic Core. But what if you'd elected to accept that teaching post on Mars instead? Or stayed on Earth? Or been assigned to the Orion Nebula mission instead? Or not volunteered to board the *Hawking?* You, alone, will never know what those other possibilities might have brought forth."

"I think I follow," she said. She cocked her head to the side. "You know, one interpretation of quantum mechanics suggests that every time there's a decision point, a place where an electron could spin up or spin down, the universe branches, so that both possibilities actually occur. But, you're saying that applies to our decisions in life, not just quantum events?"

"You, Kevyn, the *real* you, are more than one being, one life, one existence. You are you and all of the other possible realities that you could be. A nearly infinite subset of possible lives for you ended when *Hawking* was damaged in its encounter with the alien ship, and fell into the black hole. Another nearly infinite subset did not encounter the alien, and completed the mission safely."

"You're saying that this super-computer harvests all of the different time lines, all of the quantum possibilities . . . not just the one I'm aware of?"

"Looked at one way, all of those possibilities lie side by side in the hypercontinuum. But looked at another way . . ." He frowned a moment, obviously wrestling with how to put a difficult concept into words. "Look. You understand that it's possible for a computer to be programmed in such a way that a portion of itself can be walled off from the rest of itself in a sense, creating a space where the computer can run an emulation of anther program? The results can be watched, and recorded."

"Of course."

"The computer could set up such an emulation, run it with one set of parameters, determine the results, then set up another emulation, an iteration of the first, with a different set of parameters."

"Yes."

"The computer could repeat the process again and again and again, countless iterations playing out all possible combinations and permutations of data."

Slowly she nodded, but she was remembering one fragment of imagery lingering in her mind . . . a colossal structure of some sort, neither matter nor energy, spanning two galaxies. Was Stephen saying that *that*—

"Now, ask yourself one question more. Which is more likely, according to the laws of statistical probability . . . that yours is the original universe, the one from which all later copies of yourself were made, or that your universe is one of the almost infinite number of iterations to follow later?"

"She took a deep breath. "So . . what are you saying? Are these infinite universes parallel? Or serial?"

"A good question. But not one with an answer meaningful to you. The most accurate reply would be both."

"I don't understand. Either existence branches off different realities each time a decision is made, and they're parallel, or the universe keeps running iterations over and over again, which means they're serial. It can't be both."

"When you are the universe," Stephen said, "you can look at yourself any way you please."

"So . . . you can put me back? Is that what you're saying?"

"What I'm saying is that we can't put you back into the same causal chain of existence from which you came. That would create certain risks to the continuum They wish to avoid. But we can merge you back into the time-stream roughly at the point from which you left it. And you'll not know the difference."

"What about Jon?"

"His brain has been . . . injured. It was less flexible, less accepting than yours. We can repair that, however. Or arrange for it never to have happened."

"That's good. But . . . he won't be coming back with me?"

"He'll need to stay until he can make up his own mind. We will not make that decision for him."

"Okay." She nodded, and stood up. "Okay. What do I do?"

The shifting patterns of light vanished, as if on a sudden breeze. The two galaxies again shone in starlight glory, hanging in space before her. "Jon was wrong." Stephen said. "*This* is the grand central station, not the hub of the Galaxy. What you see here is a kind of map. A noumenal map."

"Noumenal?"

"Something that happens outside of yourself, in the real world, as you would say, is a phenomenon."

"Yes . . ."

"Something that happens purely within, a reality within your mind, is a noumenon."

"Phenomena are real. Noumenal are imaginary."

"Hmm. Yes, but you still equate imaginary with unreal. On the hyperplanes, what you think is as real as any reality . . . and perhaps more so. Everything that you have experienced since emerging from the timelike conduit, including this that you experience now, is noumenal. But it is real. In fact, there is no difference." He pointed at the map in the sky. "Focus on where you want to go, and imagine yourself there."

"But, I can't pick out one ship in all of that!"

"Just think yourself *there* . . ."

"Just click your heels three times," she thought, remembering a snatch of an old, old movie, *"and say 'there's no place like home. . . .' "*

She thought herself . . . *there*.

She sat in the acceleration couch on the probe, watching as the AI lined her up for the final approach to the explorer mothership. *Wheeeooo!* She whistled in her mind, feeling the warmth of her telepathic contact with Lani Kellerman on board the waiting vessel. *What a ride!* The sheer exhilaration of having looped about the Maelstrom, the black hole at the Galaxy's core still pulsed within her, a galloping excitement.

We have your data, Lani's thought replied in her thoughts. *Congratulations on a mission accomplished! That other ship, the alien . . . definite proof that we are not alone!*

I guess the Tourist Concept proves out, she replied. *Now all we have to do is actually make contact.*

She looked at the empty acceleration couch next to her. Strange. Usually, they sent these little probe ships out with a crew of two. And it would have been nice to have shared that last, wild ride with someone. Why had the *Thorne* been sent out with only one organic this time?

Something flickered through the back of her mind . . . scattering, dreamlike memories, swiftly fading like the ripples of quantum fluctuations on the Virtual Sea.

Crystal towers . . . shaping realities . . . vast spiral galaxies hanging together in space . . . and through it all the certainty that all of this had happened—was happening—before.

"We are on automatic," Kip, the *Thorne*'s AI pilot, reported. "On final approach to *Deep Sky Explorer*."

Kathryn Shalamarn was coming home.

CONVOLUTION
by James P. Hogan

James P. Hogan began writing science fiction as a hobby in the mid-1970s, and his works have been well received within the professional scientific community as well as among regular science-fiction readers. In 1979 he left DEC to become a full-time writer, and in 1988 moved to the Republic of Ireland. Currently he maintains a residence in Pensacola and spends part of each year in the United States.

To date, he has published twenty-one novels, a nonfiction work on Artificial Intelligence, and two mixed collections of short fiction, nonfiction, and biographical anecdotes entitled *Minds, Machines & Evolution* and *Rockets, Redheads & Revolution*. He has also published some articles and short fiction. Further details of Hogan and his work are available from his web site at http://www.jamesphogan.com.

Professor Aylmer Arbuthnot Abercrombie looked up irascibly from the chore of tidying up his notes as the call tone sounded from his desk terminal. He moused the screen's cursor to the *Call Accept* icon and clicked on it. "Yes?"

A window opened showing the head of a youth aged twenty or so, with collar-length, studentish hair, a wispy attempt at a beard, and shoulders enveloped in a baggy sweater. "Oh, er, Jeremy Qualio here, Professor." He was a postgraduate that Abercrombie had assigned a design project to, in one of the labs below in the building. "We were expecting you here at ten-thirty, sir."

"You were?"

"To review the breadboard test of the transcorrelator mixing circuit. You were going to help us set the power parameters for the output stage."

"I was?"

"We've completed the runs with simulated input data and normalized the results. They're here ready for you to check through now."

"They are?" Abercrombie's grizzled brow knitted into a frown. He cast around the littered desk for his appointments diary on the off chance that it might give him a way out, but he couldn't see it. He was cornered. "Very well, I'll be there shortly," he replied, and cut off the screen.

He left his "public" office at the front of the lab area, which he used for receiving visitors and dealing with more routine day-to-day affairs, and on the way out, stopped by the open cubicle and reception desk from where the stern, meticulous, and fearsomely efficient figure of Mrs. Crawford, the departmental secretary and custodian of all that pertained to proper procedures, commanded the approach from the elevators.

"Do you have my appointments diary, by any chance?" Abercrombie inquired. "I appear to have mislaid it."

"You took it back this morning."

"Did I?"

"After I found it again, the *last time*." The pointed pause, followed by a sniff invited him to reflect on the enormity of his transgression. "You know, Professor, it really would be more convenient if you'd keep you schedule electronically, as do other members of the staff. Then I could maintain a copy in my system, which *wouldn't* get mislaid. And I'd be in a position to give timely reminders of your commitments—which it seems you are in some need of."

Abercrombie shook his head stubbornly. "I won't go into that again, Mrs. Crawford. You know my views on computerized records. Nothing's private. Nothing's safe. They can get into your system from China. The next thing you know, some fool who doesn't know a Bessel function from a Bessemer furnace is publishing your life's work. No, thank you very much. I prefer not to become public property, but to keep my soul and my inner self to myself."

"But that's such an outmoded way to think," Mrs. Crawford persisted. "It's absurd for somebody with your technical expertise. If I may say so, it smacks of pure obstinacy. With the encryption procedures available today . . ." But

Abercrombie had already stopped listening and stalked away to jab the call button by the elevator doors.

"Oh, and by the way," he threw back over his shoulder while he waited, "has that FedEx package arrived from Chicago yet?"

"Yes. I've already told you, Professor."

"When?"

"Less than half an hour ago."

Abercrombie slowed long enough to send back a perplexed, disbelieving look before stepping into the elevator. Mrs. Crawford shook her head in exasperation and returned her attention to the task at hand.

Jeremy Qualio and Maxine Turnel, his bubbly, bespectacled, blonde-haired partner on the project, were waiting in the prototype lab with the bird's nest of wires, chips, and other components that they had built connected to an array of test equipment. The results from their first trial runs of the device were displayed on a set of monitors. Abercrombie jutted his chin and scanned over the bench in a series of short, jerky motions of his head. The layout of the aluminum chassis was neat for a lab lashup, with careful wiring and solid, clean-looking joints; the data had been graphed onto screens showing time and frequency series analysis, along with histograms of statistical variables, all properly annotated and captioned. A file of hardcopy was lying to one side for Abercrombie's inspection. He looked at the circuit work again and grunted. "You've used nonstandard colors for the board interconnections. I expect the approved coding practices to be observed."

"Yes, Professor," Qualio agreed, looking a bit crestfallen.

But Abercrombie couldn't fault their experimental design and procedure as they went through it and discussed details for over an hour. The analysis was comprehensive, with computation of error probabilities and correct algorithms for interpolation and best-curve fits. Maxine took the absence of further criticism as indicative of a rare opportunity to probe the obsessive screen of secrecy that Abercrombie maintained around his work. She and Qualio had been given just this subassembly to develop to a specification in isolation. Abercrombie hadn't told them its purpose, or the nature of the greater scheme of which it was presumably a part.

"We're still trying to figure out what it's for," she told him, doing her best to sound casual and natural. "What, exactly is a 'transcorrelator'? The inducer stage seems to create an electroweak interaction with the nuclear substructure that stimulates a range of strong-domain transitions we've never heard of before."

Qualio chimed in. "They're not mentioned in any of the journals or on the net. It's as if it might point to a whole new area of physics."

"That's not for you to speculate about," Abercrombie said. "All you've done is graduate from basic training in the army of science. It doesn't give you a voice in deciding strategy. Leave the big picture to the generals. Satisfactory. Have the report written up by the end of the week."

"Yes, Professor," Qualio said. Maxine flashed him a sympathetic look with a shrug that said *well, we tried.* Abercrombie picked up the folder of hardcopy and turned to leave.

"I told you. It has to be something military," he overheard Maxine whisper as he went out the door.

After stopping for lunch in the cafeteria, Abercrombie went back up, taking the stairs, through the warren of partitioned offices and labs that had sprung up amid the massive brick walls and aged wooden floors of the original building. The City Annex of Gates University's Physics Department occupied a converted warehouse on the downtown waterfront of what was no longer a major trading port. Hence, it had been acquired at a knock-down price and qualified for the city's urban renewal grant scheme, making it a fine investment property for the university trustees. It was also where the department sited, away from its main, prestigious campus, the oddball projects and other undertakings that the governors preferred to keep out of sight—maintained, as often as not, to humor some high-paying source of research grants or other primary influence on funding.

No premature publicity, Abercrombie reiterated to himself as he emerged on his own floor and weathered Mrs. Crawford's Gorgonesque stare to return to his lab. When this project came to fruition, it would be the news event of the century. And not just with the public media. Everyone who was anyone worth talking about through the entire physics-related sector of the scientific Establishment would learn of it in a mass-announcement that Abercrombie had been preparing as methodically as the design studies and calculations that had occupied him for eight years. He had all the names and contacts listed, covering academic, private, and government science elites throughout the world. This would be his ticket to a Nobel Prize and permanent fame as surely as geometry had immortalized Euclid and the laws of motion were virtually synonymous with Newton. Maybe even more. The things that Nobels had been awarded for seemed mundane in comparison. Perhaps, even, a new grade of award would have to be instituted especially for him.

He came to the inner windowless workshop area that he had designated as the place where the device would be assembled, and stopped for a moment to picture it completed. It wouldn't be especially heavy or bulky—little more than a lattice boundary surface to define and contain the varichron field, with a small control panel supported on a columnar plinth, and the generation system and power unit beneath. If anything, it would resemble an oversize parrot cage with a domed cap, standing on a squat cylindrical base. Howard Jaffey, the dean, and the few others from the faculty who were in the know as to the aim of Abercrombie's project were polite in avoiding mention of it; but with a billionaire like Eli Zaltzer writing the backing, and the amounts that he lavished on the university as a whole, nobody had been inclined to turn the proposal down, even if they secretly thought Zaltzer was an eccentric. Well, let them think what they liked, Abercrombie said to himself. The parts were coming together now, and the initial tests were underway. It wouldn't be much longer before the full system was assembled—three months, maybe, in his estimation. They'd be singing a different tune then, when the whole world came flocking to his door. Never mind for a better mousetrap. Abercrombie was going to give them a working *time machine!*

He stood, savoring the moment in his imagination for a few seconds longer, and then proceeded through and along the corridor to his inner, private office at the rear of the lab area, where he conducted his more secretive business. Inside, he locked the door, cast a wary eye around instinctively, even though it was obvious there could be no one else there—and at once spotted the missing appointments diary on a corner of the desk. *Tut-tutting* to himself, he went over to the apparently fixed wall cabinet and released the catch that allowed it to slide aside, revealing his hidden safe. Armor plate, sunk into the brickwork of the original walls. No electronic security for him, whatever the hackers tried to say. It wouldn't have surprised him if more people in the world spent their lives trying to make computers do what they were supposed to do instead of contributing to anything useful. He dialed in the combination sequence and swung the door open to disclose his trove of files and papers—the results of eight years of design effort and calculations, plus accumulated notes from the time before that, when he met Eli Zaltzer and the dream began the course that would make it reality. He took out the file box reserved for test results, added the hardcopy that he had brought from downstairs, and was just replacing the box, when he heard footsteps in the corridor outside. They sounded furtive, as if someone were creeping past warily. Normally, Abercrombie always locked the door when he opened his safe; but on this occasion, after the momentary distraction of seeing the appointments diary on the desk when he walked in, he was unable to recall whether or not he had. *"Who's there?"* he called out, fearful of being found with the cabinet open. There was no reply; the footsteps hastened away.

Suspicious, Abercrombie made for the door, found that he had locked it after all, and had to fumble for his keys to get out. He went to the rear entrance by the back stairs and the freight elevator but found no sign of anyone there. As he began retracing his steps toward the lab and workshop area, a peculiar, low-pitched whine emanated from somewhere ahead of him. He increased his pace, heading past his office door again and for the workshop, where the sound seemed to be coming from. *"Who is that in there?"* he yelled ahead, but the noise ceased just before he burst in, and he found the place empty. With rising agitation he carried on through to Mrs. Crawford's post, but she had seen no one go that way either. Then Abercrombie realized that he had committed the cardinal sin of leaving his private office door unlocked with the safe open.

Abandoning Mrs. Crawford in mid sentence, he raced back through the lab area, slammed the office door behind him, and rushed across the room to check the contents of the safe. Moments later, he emitted a horrified groan. The master notebook, in which he had brought together and summarized the essential design information for the time machine—the distilled essence of his past eight years of intensive labor—was gone.

He had to inform Zaltzer and the university governors that the project had run into unexpected difficulties, and he had been forced to put the schedule on hold. Zaltzer remained as trusting and optimistic as ever, but the faculty who were privy chortled behind raised hands and told each other it had only been a matter of time—deriving added glee from the intended pun. Abercrombie became convinced he was the victim of a conspiracy to either sabotage or steal his project. Several times, he thought he heard prowlers about in the labs, but he never managed to catch anyone. On one occasion, late in the evening when the lights were turned down, he did actually accost and pursue an intruder; but on rounding a corner was met full-force by the discharge from a fire extinguisher, and by the time he had cleaned the froth from his eyes and recovered, the trespasser had vanished. And then, a week or so after the loss of the notebook, he heard the strange noise again.

He was on the phone in his public office near the main elevators, wearing a dress suit in anticipation of an honorary dinner he was due to attend that night, when the same low-pitched whine as before reached him through the wall from the direction of the lab and workshop area. He excused himself, saying he would call back later, and hung up. Then, giving no advance warning this time, he rose and went over to the door, checked the corridor outside, and crept stealthily to the double doors leading into the workshop. The noise had by now ceased. Turning one of the handles gently, he eased the door open far enough to peer around it and inside . . . and almost fell over from shock and disbelief. The time machine was there, standing in the middle of the floor, exactly as he had envisioned it! But there was nobody with it.

He stepped inside the room, closing the door behind him, and walked past it warily—almost as if fearing that a sudden movement might cause it to vanish—and secured the doors leading to the rear before coming back to study the machine more carefully.

It stood over seven feet high from the bottom of the cylindrical base frame, crammed with circuit boxes, generator manifolds, and coil housings, to the top of the field delimiter capping the cage. The ticking and clicking of hot parts cooling came from beneath, as from the hood of a car after a long run. Abercrombie reached out and touched part of the structure gingerly, as if unsure if it might be an illusion. It was solid and real.

And as he thought through what it meant, his indignation rose in a hot flush climbing slowly from his collar. Evidently, at some eventual future time, the machine did get built. So was he supposed to, now, go through the protracted effort of redoing the work he had lost, in order for some future version of himself to go creeping around through time and having who-knew-what kinds of adventures? Dammit, he had been through it all that once—he himself here, who was seeing the result of his labors for the first time. He had already earned the right to enjoy the fruits of it. It was *his!*

Furious now, he opened the access gate, stepped up into the cage, and stared at the control panel atop its plinth. And then, slowly, it came to him that he really didn't have a clue what he intended to do—or, come to that, how to go about doing it. The machine was based on his original design, yes; but as with any development, a lot of detail that he was not familiar with had been worked out in the final stages. To use the device, he would first need to study the construction and wiring and try some tests, and that could take a while. It couldn't be done here; his other self who had arrived in it for whatever reason could return at any moment. He needed a safe place to hide the machine, where he could investigate it at leisure.

But could such a plan work? Surely, whatever he decided to do, his future self would remember having decided it too, and be able to pursue him accordingly. Unless the timeline somehow reset itself to accommodate changes; or maybe some multiple universe explanation applied, in which the possibly similar past that one returned to was still a different one from the past that was remembered. He had long speculated about such alternatives, of course, but a working machine was the prerequisite to being able to test them. And now he had one! Forget all the questions for now, he told himself. Worry about getting the machine to a place where he could devote himself to the only prospect in sight—without having to repeat eight years of work—for finding some answers.

It would need to be reasonably close but unfrequented by people. Anywhere in the City Annex itself would be out of the question because of the comings and goings of staff, students, visitors, and a host of others. But a short distance away along the waterfront there was a disused dock building, a former customs warehouse still owned by the Port Authority, earmarked for development into an indoor market and restaurant mall one day, but derelict for years. The cellars beneath, dingy, but dry and secluded, would provide a suitable place—not perfect, maybe, but at least somewhere that would do until he found something better. And with the limited time at his disposal, that was good enough. He stepped back down out of the machine and went through to the rear area to find a means of moving it.

By the freight elevator he found a flatbed hand dolly that was used for moving equipment cabinets, machinery, and other heavy items around the labs. A utility room nearby, where maintenance and decorating materials were stored, yielded a painter's floor tarp that would serve as a cover. He hurried the dolly back to the workshop, eased the lifting platform under the time machine's base, elevated it, draped the machine with the tarp, and trundled it back through to the rear. The freight elevator took him down to the goods receiving bay at the back of the Annex building, where he signed for use of the departmental pickup truck. He brought the truck around to the loading bay, and minutes later was driving his purloined creation out through the rear gates of the premises, onto the waterfront boulevard. He had gone no more than a few hundred yards when he heard the wail of a police siren behind him and saw red and

blue lights flashing in his mirror. For a sickening moment his
heart felt as if it were about to fall into a void that opened
up in his stomach. Then he realized it had nothing to do with
him; a car a short distance back was being pulled over in
connection with something that had happened behind him.
Exhaling loudly with relief, Abercrombie entered the weed-
choked lot surrounding the derelict dockside building,
drove around to the side, where he would be less conspicu-
ous, and parked in front of a once-boarded-up entrance, its
planks long ago stripped and broken up for firewood by
vagrants. He climbed out of the truck and went in to recon-
noiter the interior for a suitable hiding place.

The figure that had observed Abercrombie's arrival retreated to a hideaway below the front part of the building,
screened by fallen debris but commanding a view of the
gallery at the bottom of the ramp leading down from the
ground-floor level. He was long-haired and bearded,
dressed in a military-style camouflage parka with para-
trooper combat boots. As Abercrombie came out of the
room into which he had wheeled the strange contraption,
and disappeared back up the ramp to the side entrance,
the watcher murmured into a cell phone to a person on the
other end that he referred to as "Yellow One."

"I dunno. It looked like a machine."

"What kind of machine?"

"I never seen anything like it before. A man-size bird-
cage. Maybe some kinda surveillance thing. I don't like the
look of it."

"What does the guy look like?"

"Tall, about sixty, maybe. Thin. Could be kinda mean.
Hair white and gray. Wearing a black suit."

"A suit? There's only one kind of people there that
wears suits. They're onto us, man. Get—"

"Wait!" The figure, whose name was Brady, interrupted
as the sound came of tires squealing to a halt outside the
front of the building, close to where Brady was concealed.
Moments later, footsteps pounded in on the floor above,
followed by crashing sounds and metallic clanging. "There's
more of 'em breaking in upstairs!" Brady said, sounding
alarmed.

"It's a bust," Yellow One told him. "Get yourself out!"

* * *

Professor Abercrombie came back out onto the waterside boulevard and drove the truck sedately back to the university Annex. Just as he was turning in through the rear gate, a dull *boom* and a *whoosh* sounded from behind as the building he had just left exploded and collapsed in flames.

Police and fire department vehicles arrived by the dozen, and the ensuing spectacle left little work being done anywhere in the nearby university buildings for the rest of the day. Curious officials from the Annex went to find out what they could from the officers in charge, and the gossip in the staff coffee room by the end of the afternoon was that an extremist group of survivalists, who trained in the hills with guns and believed in preparing for catastrophe or nuclear holocaust, had been using the place to store weapons and explosives. The police had been waiting for a special shipment, due within the next few day, before moving in, but evidently there had been some kind of accident in there first. Rumor had it that the charred remains of one of them had been found in there. Nobody else had been caught.

All of which was of peripheral interest to Abercrombie, who was now left without either design data or machine, after having had the completed, working model literally in his hands. And just to make his day, when he left the office to go home, he found that his car had been stolen.

That night, in a fit of dejection, he took out the folder with the lists of media contacts, scientific notables, and others that he had prepared for the day of his great announcement, which he kept in the desk at home in his apartment, carried it downstairs to the basement, and threw it into the building's incinerator.

The next day, Abercrombie stood at the window of his private office, staring despondently out in the direction of the old customs warehouse. What was left of the shell had been pronounced unsafe and reduced to rubble by a demolition crew, who were now fencing off the site pending a decision on eventual disposal. But the professor's thoughts were not on how the Port Authority should best manage its piece of still-prime downtown waterfront real estate.

Why, he asked himself, was the obvious always the last thing that occurred to someone? Probably for the same

reason that a lost object always turns up in the last place
one looks: Nobody is going to carry on looking for something after they've found it. The mysterious intruder of the
day before, and no doubt those that he had suspected previously, hadn't been from any conspiracy at all, but *himself,*
coming back from a future where the machine had been
built; but it had taken the discovery of the machine for him
to realize it. He no longer possessed the notebook containing the design information necessary to build it. Could
it be that the notebook had been used, nevertheless, stolen
from the past by means of a machine that will exist in the
future? It sounded preposterous, but the evidence was
there. However, if so, that raised another logical conun-
drum. For if, somewhere in the future, he had built a working machine—possibly after having to work it all out
again—then what motivation would he have for going back
and stealing the design? He wouldn't need it.

No. He shook his head decisively. He wasn't going to get
embroiled in any more of those impossible tangles. He had
problems enough as things were. Just take the facts one at
a time and let philosophers or mystics worry about the
contradictions and deeper meaning of it all, he told himself.

Yet the implication remained that at some point in the
future he would find himself the owner of such a device.
He stared distantly out along the waterfront and allowed
himself to relish the thought. If he ever did go back to
regain his notebook, he would take out some insurance to
prevent anything like this from happening again, he resolved. Computer people were always impressing the im-
portance of keeping backups. Well, maybe they did have a
valid point there, he conceded grudgingly. Very well, he
would follow their advice. If—or when?—such a day came,
he would leave a backup copy in some secure place, back
there in the past. Then, if he ever lost the original, had it
stolen, or found himself without it for any other reason,
from then onward, anytime in the future, the backup would
always be there, waiting to be retrieved. It was so breath-
takingly simple—once again, eminently obvious now that
he had thought of it. Had he done so before, he would
have taken the simple precaution of maintaining an additional copy to the one that had been in the safe.

He turned his head unconsciously from the window

toward the wall cabinet concealing the safe while he thought this. And suddenly his jaw dropped as the bizarre realization hit him of what the very act of his thinking it signified. The fact of having made this decision meant he would carry it with him into the future, and then take it back via the machine to the past. Provided, then, that he abided by it, *it had already been done!* Somewhere, right now—unless his penchant for forgetfulness were to reach impossible proportions in the future—a hidden copy of the notebook existed! *That* must have been how he had built the machine! He looked around the office, licking his lips in the excitement that had seized him, as if now that he had worked the implication out, the hiding place would somehow leap out and advertise itself. He cast his mind over all the places there were to choose from. Somewhere in the Annex? His downtown apartment? Somewhere else in the city. . . ? *Where,* out of all the possibilities, would he have picked?

And that was when the full craziness of it all finally hit him. *It didn't matter!* There was no need for him to try and second-guess himself at all. For all he had to do was pick a place—any place—now, and be sure to put the backup copy in that place when he came to travel back. And that would be where he would find it today.

Surely it couldn't be that easy. He went back in his mind through the insane logic, looking for the flaw, but couldn't find one. Okay, then, where? He looked around again. And his eyes came back to the widow and the site where the demolition crew were finishing the fence around the ruin of the old warehouse. Down there in the cellars beneath, where he had taken the machine yesterday, there were bound to be corners and cubbyholes left beneath the rubble. Nobody would be going in there for a long time now, probably years. With the design information available, building the machine would only take about three months. It was close by, being posted with *Keep Out* and hazard warnings. . . .

Then his eyes blinked rapidly as the inevitable complication reared its head, calling the whole comforting edifice into question. There was another version of himself at large out there somewhere—the version who had arrived in the machine—and his disposition would not be very friendly, since by now he would have discovered the machine stolen. But if *this* Abercrombie—the one looking out of the window, trying to make sense of it all—now chose a place to hide the backup in, then the other one of him would not only have remembered it, too, but have known it all along while he (this Abercrombie) was still having to figure it out. On the other hand, knowing it wouldn't have helped his other self to do much about acting on it, since the place had been swarming with firemen and demolition people since yesterday. So did that mean it would be a race to see which of them would get there first tonight. . . ?

And then a malicious twinkle came into his eyes as the last skein of the tangle unraveled itself. He couldn't lose! For the machine *had* come to be built. He was here, installed in the Annex, with all the resources at his disposal to build it, while the other Abercrombie was somewhere outside in the cold. Therefore, somewhere in the strange convolution of causes and effects that he didn't pretend to grasp yet, events must have shuffled themselves out in such a way that *he* had obtained the information he needed, and hence the other Abercrombie, presumably, had not.

But the other Abercrombie would just as certainly know all this, and yet was out there somewhere, unable to change it. Knowing himself, he pictured the rage of frustration that the other version of him must be in at that very moment. Not a pleasant character to cross, he told himself. Better be careful not to bump into *him*. A frown darkened his face then. But wasn't he destined to become that version eventually, and have to undergo the same frustration? Surely not. If knowledge had any value at all, there had to be a way to avoid it. But there was no way to be sure of any answer at present. He turned away from the window and sat down at the desk to consider his plans. One step at a time, he told himself again. Just follow where it leads.

Late that night, wearing dark coveralls and a woolen hat, Abercrombie parked his car outside the fence—the police had found it that morning, abandoned less than a mile away—forced a gap through, and followed around the building until he found an opening under a tilted slab of concrete that gave access to what was left of the cellars. Using a flashlight, he worked his way down to a part of the center gallery that had survived, and from there found a collapsed room almost buried in rubble and mud still wet from yesterday's hoses. On poking around, he discovered a run of heavy pipes low on one wall, and beneath them a row of recesses between the support mountings, almost like pigeonholes. A perfect place! The first slot that he examined was empty, but the one next to it was blocked by a brick outlined in the congealed muck—just as would have been placed by somebody wanting to conceal something. He pried the brick loose with a jackknife he had brought, and pulled it clear to uncover a rectangular shape that proved to be the end of a flat, plastic-wrapped metal box. His hands shaking, for surely this couldn't mean what a rising premonition was already telling him it did, he slid the catch from the hasp and opened the lid of the box to reveal . . . a notebook and documents!

But they weren't his. Flipping rapidly though them, he found names and pseudonyms, addresses, contact numbers, and a section on what looked like codes and encryption procedures, but none of it was familiar. This wasn't possible, he told himself. He couldn't have reasoned things through and have gotten this close, only to have it all go wrong now.

All but whimpering aloud in dismay, he turned the flashlight beam back and prodded frantically among the other recesses. And sure enough, the next one along was also closed by a mud-encased brick, which also divulged a package. And *this* one, indeed, turned out to contain a full set of copies of the information from his master notebook! Exultation swept over him. No other version of himself had materialized to interfere. His only thought now was to leave, before anything could go amiss. Stuffing his finds into a bag that he had brought for the purpose, he clambered back to the gallery and picked his way up through to the opening that led back outside. His car was there, untouched, and he left without incident.

Even after his success, Abercrombie was mindful of the presence of his other self still out there somewhere, probably bordering on homicidal by now and capable of causing mischief. He approached Eli Zaltzer to say that his earlier doubts had proved unfounded, and the project could move ahead as originally scheduled. However, he had reason to believe there was some kind of opposition movement afoot who had gotten wind of the project and were opposed to it. In view of the precedents seen in recent times of protest groups sabotaging scientific research that they disagreed with, perhaps security around the lab should be tightened up for the duration. Zaltzer talked to the authorities, who were ever ready to appease his whims, and a private security firm was contracted to provide twenty-four-hour guards for Abercrombie's lab and office area, and control access. His life became a fever of activity day and night, and as weeks passed by, the machine began taking shape in the center of the workshop.

And during that time, there were indeed several attempts by unknown persons to get into the labs. One time, an alleged repairman who had come to check the air conditioning produced credentials that didn't pass scrutiny, and on checking turned out not to be from the company he claimed. Abercrombie himself was elsewhere that day and so wasn't able to confront the imposter, and a slick lawyer who succeeded in preventing the security firm from detaining him intervened, so his identity was never established. But the description didn't sound anything like Abercrombie, and Mrs. Crawford confirmed it. So his other self was using fronts to test the waters, Abercrombie concluded. A sound strategy, as things had turned out.

On another occasion, somebody actually did get in under cover of what was almost certainly a contrived power failure, but one of the guards accosted him, and he got away without accomplishing anything. Inwardly, Abercrombie was impressed by what was, after all, effectively his own resourcefulness in an area where he had no prior knowledge or experience. He had never suspected that he had such talents in him.

And eventually the day came when the machine was ready for the first live tests.

Eli Zaltzer had to be there to see it, naturally. So was Howard Jaffey, the dean, along with Susan Peters and Mario Venasky, two other members of the faculty. Abercrombie briefed them, cautioning them to stand back, and announced that he was initiating a control program in the machine that would activate automatically ten minutes from now and send the machine back that far in time. Everyone watched the open area of floor expectantly. Moments later, an eerie, low-pitched whine filled the room, and a copy of the machine appeared beside the first. Even Abercrombie, though he had seen tangible evidence before that it would work, was astonished.

"My God!" Venasky breathed, staring pop-eyed. "It's real. I mean, really real."

Susan Peters was staring at Abercrombie with a mixture of awe and mortification. "Aylmer . . . you were right all along. The things some of us said behind you back for all that time . . . I'll never know how to put things right."

"Quite understandable," Abercrombie condescended in a paternal tone.

"There, you see!" Zaltzer pronounced triumphantly. "I am not the nutball that you think I don't know you think. Next we talk about changing the name to Zaltzer University. Okay?"

Howard Jaffey just stood gaping, without, just for the moment, being able to say anything.

In the stupefied words and semicoherent comments that followed, nothing really meaningful was said through the next few minutes, at which point Abercrombie, enjoying his role as master of the show, called one of the security guards in from outside and said they needed help to move the machines. Looking puzzled but asking no questions, (up till then there had been only one machine), the guard draped his jacket over a nearby chair. Then, following Abercrombie's directions, Jaffey and Venasky shifted the duplicate machine a few feet farther from the original, while Abercrombie and the guard moved the original into the space where the duplicate had stood. The guard turned to leave at that point, but Abercrombie's intoxication made him crave a greater audience. "No, stay," he commanded. "It doesn't matter anymore. Twenty-four hours from now, the whole world will be talking about this."

The guard waited obediently. Moments later, the original machine suddenly emitted a series of warning beeps followed by its characteristic whine, and then popped out of existence. At the same instant, a new voice from somewhere shouted *"Get down!"* in such an imperative tone that everyone unthinkingly obeyed, just as the gun holstered in the guard's jacket still hanging over the chair exploded, sending bullets ricocheting around the room.

"Calm down, all of you. It was just an oversight," the voice continued, while they were picking themselves up and looking about dazedly. Another machine had materialized, this time with a copy of Abercrombie inside, making no effort to contain a look of smug amusement at the expressions on the others' faces. Even Abercrombie-One was stunned. "The varichron radiation induced by the process evidently triggers unstable materials like cartridge caps," Abercrombie-Two went on. "Now that we are aware of the fact, we will know to avoid such instances in future."

Abercrombie-One was about to ask how far in the future his other self had come from, when A-Two looked at him loftily and supplied, "Thirty minutes."

A-One collected his wits raggedly. But it made sense. "Which you know I was about to ask, because you were me," he said.

"Exactly," A-Two confirmed.

"So in the next thirty minutes I'll figure out it was the radiation that did it, and decide it's something we can work around?"

"No, you won't have to. I've already told you."

"In the same way you were told?"

"Yes."

A-One still couldn't make sense of it. His other self had the advantage of having had more time to think it through, which irked him—and which, from the expression on his other self's face, the other self was also well aware of. "So I presume, too, that you also know how irritatingly supercilious you appear just at this moment?" A-One said.

"Of course," A-Two agreed. "But then I don't care, because I can assure you that you'll enjoy it every bit as much as I am right now, when you come to be me."

Harold Jaffey was finally managing to find his voice. "This is crazy," he croaked. "How can he tell you what you'll do, like some kind of robot executing a program? You're a human being with free will, for heaven's sake. What happens if you plumb decide you're not going to do it?"

Susan Peters was frowning, trying to reason it through.

"No machine or copy of you came back from, let's say, an hour ahead of now. But what's to stop us setting the machine to do that, just like you did before? Let's go ahead and do it. So why isn't it here?"

She directed her words at Abercrombie-One. He didn't know either, and looked appealingly at Abercrombie-Two, as if the extra thirty minutes might have conferred some superior insight. "Those are the kinds of things we'll be testing in the weeks ahead," A-Two told them. "But for now, enough of the mundane and methodical. I've been shut up in this lab, working virtually nonstop for three months." He went over to Zaltzer and draped an arm around his shoulder. "This is the man who believed in me, and he'll share in the glory. Tonight, Eli, we'll go out and celebrate, and talk about how this will be the sensation of the century. Tomorrow we'll be the talk of the world."

This was becoming irritating. "You seem to be taking over," Abercrombie-One told his other self peevishly. "Might I remind you that I had some little part in bringing this about, too?"

"Yes, but that doesn't really come into things, because in a little under thirty minutes from now, you won't be here, will you?" A-Two replied.

That did it. "And suppose I refuse?" A-One challenged. He folded his arms and sent Jaffer a look that said, *Good point. Let's try it right now.* "What are you going to do— hit me over the head and throw me in?" he asked A-Two. "Even that wouldn't work. *You* came out in good shape."

A-Two grinned back as if he had been expecting it— which of course he had. "Later is when we test the paradoxes," he said. "You know as well as I do how full of uncertainties this whole business is. We pursue it methodically and systematically, isn't that what we've always said? And now you want to jeopardize years of work by giving in to a fit of pique. Is that what you want?"

A-One felt himself losing ground at hearing his own often-reiterated principles recited back at him. But it would need more to dissuade him. "A cheap debater's ploy," he pronounced. "You'll have to try better than that, Alymer."

"No, I don't. All that's needed is for you to think about it. You've got about twenty minutes to figure out that if somebody doesn't go back and warn them, some of these friends of yours back there might very well get killed. I don't know the ins and outs of the logic either, yet. That's what we have to look into. But for now, are you going to risk it—just for the sake of that stubbornness of yours?"

A-One felt himself wilting. He knew already, with a sinking feeling, what the outcome would be, as he could read his other self knew perfectly well also. He didn't need twenty minutes. He was trapped.

"All right," he said in a voice that could have cut seasoned teak. "I'll do it."

But Abercrombie's elation had subsided into gloom and wistfulness by the time he and Zaltzer sat down to what was to have been their celebratory dinner at the five-star Atherton Hotel in the heart of the city. "The most staggering discovery in the history of physics, Eli," he lamented. "When it happened, we said that the world would know. I had a list of all the names, the contacts . . ."

Zaltzer nodded enthusiastically. "Yes, I know. You showed it to me. It—" he checked himself as he saw the look on Abercrombie's face. "Why Aylmer? What happened?"

"I never told you this before. But there was a period . . . you remember when I almost put everything on hold? Oh, it's a long story. But it seemed everything was over." Abercrombie looked up. "The short answer is, I destroyed it."

"What?"

"The file with all the lists. I burned it."

For a few moments Zaltzer seemed taken aback. Then his irrepressible ebullience resurfaced as always. He waved a hand. "So . . . the announcement won't be as widespread as you planned. I still have contacts. We'll get the word around. It's hardly the Dark Ages."

"But it won't be the same," Abercrombie said. "The lists I had prepared were the work of years. Not just the regular media hacks—with respect, Eli, but you know what I mean. They covered the whole scientific establishment too: Nobel laureates, directors of the national labs, national advisers . . ." This time it was Abercrombie's turn to break off as he saw that Zaltzer wasn't listening but staring across the table suddenly with a strange, inscrutable smile. "What is it?" Abercrombie asked. "What do you find so funny?"

"You've already forgotten this afternoon," Zaltzer told

him. "Your own machine. You don't have to be without your file now, Aylmer. You can go back and get it!"

The problem was, Abercrombie had no way of knowing just what days in the past, or times in the day—it was over three months ago now—he should aim for to avoid running into people and being apprehended. To compound the difficulty, the short-range tests that were all he had experimented with so far did little to help him calibrate for longer hops back, and he was unable to set an arrival time with accuracy, even if he had known which one to select. His first few attempts were cut short when he realized he had been detected—on one occasion culminating in a narrow escape when an earlier version of himself actually chased him, and he escaped only by remembering that he had used the fire extinguisher. (He never was able to work out *who* had thought of that.)

But he persevered, and eventually succeeded in rematerializing in the workshop at a time when the surroundings seemed empty and quiet. He still didn't know exactly when it was; and even if he had, he had no way of being certain knowing what his earlier self had been doing on that particular day, and hence how much time he was likely to have. He needed to get out of the Annex and to his apartment, which was where the folder was, make copies of the contents, conceal them in the cellars of the predemolition customs building nearby, and then get back to the machine with the original folder, and away. Planting the backup seemed a bit odd now, he had to admit, if by that time he was going to have the original in his possession; but he had resolved to adhere rigidly to his plan. He was taking no chances. The thing that would tell him what he had been doing that day would be his appointments diary, which was usually in his public office.

He came out of the workshop and padded toward the main-elevator end of the lab area. When he was about halfway there, the door at the far end of the corridor opened, and Mrs. Crawford came through. Abercrombie froze; but she gave him only a cursory look and disappeared into one of the offices. As he began moving again, she thrust her head back out. "The FedEx package that you were waiting for from Chicago has arrived," she informed him.

"It has?" He had no idea what she was talking about. "Thank you. I'll pick it up later." Mrs. Crawford's head disappeared back through the doorway. Abercrombie scuttled quickly to his office, found the diary, and retreated with it to his private office at the far end of the facility.

That had been the day when he'd gone downstairs to review Qualio and Turnel's project assignment, the diary told him. He thought back. He had spent over an hour with them in the prototype lab, he recalled, and then lunched in the cafeteria. He had enough time. But he couldn't afford to leave the machine standing in the workshop that long, inviting discovery. He went back and sent it away under automatic control to a quiet period in the middle of the night, programmed to return after ninety minutes. The alarm on his watch would warn him fifteen minutes before it was due to reappear.

He left the building via the back stairs and drove home using the keys already in his pocket. The same keys let him into his apartment, where he retrieved the contacts folder and took it to a commercial copying store to make the backup. And that was when he discovered the master notebook containing his design calculations for the machine. It hadn't been stolen from his safe in the office at all! At some time he had taken it home to work on and inadvertently dropped it among the papers in the contacts folder. Oh, well, too bad. There wasn't time to do anything about rectifying that now. He did copy the notebook's contents as well, however, and sealed them in a separate, plastic-wrapped package before leaving for the old customs building.

Down in the cellars, he located the room where he remembered finding the documents—intact now, of course, but still conveniently obscured and out-of-the-way—and went to the recesses between the piping supports. There were even some bricks lying handily close in a heap of rubble. He placed the packages in two of the slots and covered the openings. Just as he was about to leave, he remembered something odd. When he found them, the notebook had been there, sure enough, but the other package had contained things he'd never seen before. He turned back uncertainly and stared down at the pipes. Had someone else changed the other package? Had he himself revisited this place on some future errand that he was as yet unaware of? But then his wristwatch beeped, warning him that it was time to be heading back to the machine. Shaking his head and telling himself that it would all be resolved somehow, he ducked back out and hurried back toward the ramp leading up from the gallery.

He almost didn't make it. By the time he emerged from the freight elevator his earlier self was already back from lunch and in the private office—putting Qualio and Turnel's test results in the safe, he remembered now. He heard his own testy *"Who's there?"* as he crept past the door. He ran to get out of the corridor, hearing keys being fumbled into the lock on the inside, and let himself into the workshop, remembering that he had mercifully chosen to investigate in the other direction first. The workshop was empty. He gazed frantically at his watch, as if sheer willing could make the seconds count off faster. The door at the far end of the corridor was opening, footsteps approaching. Then came the blessed sound of the machine arriving right on time.

"Who is that in there?" his voice demanded loudly from just yards away.

Clutching the documents that he had brought from the apartment, he threw himself into the machine, stabbed at the control as he latched the gate behind him, and was gone. . . .

And so it was done—apparently without mishap. Abercrombie stood in the machine, looking out over the familiar scene of the workshop. He had the contacts file with him, which was what he had gone to get, along with the original master notebook as a bonus. He'd had thoughts of maybe returning that to its proper place in the private-office safe before returning, but time had run out on him and that had proved impossible. Now, for what it was worth, backups of both were secure in their hiding place from the past. There were still loose ends of unanswered questions dangling in his mind, but all-in-all everything seemed to be working itself out. He didn't pretend yet to understand precisely how.

Zaltzer had hoped to be waiting for him when he got back, but in view of the imprecision still bedeviling the process, his absence was understandable. Abercrombie climbed down from the machine and drew in several deep breaths of relief. He hadn't realized how tense the undertaking had made him. He let himself out the rear door of the workshop, went back to his private office, locked the door, and stowed the two sets of documents in the safe. That essential task accomplished, he sank down into the chair at the desk to unwind. A vague feeling of something not being quite right had been nagging from somewhere below consciousness since he came out of the machine, but just at this moment he was too exhausted to give it much attention. His mind drifted; he might even have dozed . . .

Until the muffled sound of something being moved along the corridor outside brought him back to wakefulness. By the time he had sat up and let his head clear, the noise had gone. He rose from the chair and was about go to the door and check, when his gaze traveled across to the window and he caught the view outside. He stared in confusion for a moment, then crossed to the window to be sure. The old customs building along the waterfront was intact . . . Yet it was supposed to have burned down three months ago. And then he realized what was wrong that he had noticed but not registered: There weren't any security people around the lab. This was no minor error. He hadn't returned to anywhere near the time he was supposed to be in. So *when,* exactly, was this?

Infuriatingly, nothing in his office would tell him. He came out into the corridor and headed for the front of the building, either to seek some sign in his other office or find out from Mrs. Crawford, but stopped dead the moment he entered the workshop area. The time machine, in which he had arrived only a short while ago, was gone. His mind reeled, unable to deal with what seemed an insurmountable hurdle. But as he forced himself to think, the pieces of what it had to mean came together. If the customs building was still there, this had to be before it was demolished—pretty obviously. Then this could only be the day that he had been in the public office, heard the strange noise, come back to investigate, found the machine unattended, and stolen it. The noise that aroused him had been himself moving it to the freight elevator. He thought back rapidly, trying to recreate the sequence of events. Knowing what he did, if he moved quickly enough, there would be time yet to intercede.

He ran back through to the rear stairs, started down, and then halted as a cautionary note sounded in his head. After all he had been through to get them, would it be wise to leave the notebook and contacts file here? No. Until he was a lot clearer about this whole business, he wasn't going to let them out of his sight. He ran back to the office and removed them from the safe. Then, deciding it was too late to intercept himself in the loading bay—and in any case, he didn't want a scene involving two of him in front of the service people there—and knowing that he still had his keys, he raced instead to the front lot, where he parked his car. He screeched out onto the waterfront boulevard and saw the truck carrying the tarp-covered time machine exiting from the rear gate a few car lengths in front of him . . . a split-second before the horn blared, brakes squealed, and something hit him in the rear. And that was when the police cruiser that just had to be there turned on its siren and pulled him over. He remembered it too late, while he sat through the ritual of insurance information being exchanged, radio check of his license number and record, and the ponderous writing out of the ticket. By the time he got moving again, the truck had long since disappeared.

Nervous about the time now, instead of going around the long route to the side entrance that the truck had taken, he drove straight up to the front of the building, leaped out, and ran inside, in the process knocking over a pile of steel drums just inside the door and causing enough noise to make any thought now at concealing his presence a joke. But by this time he didn't care. All that mattered was getting to the machine.

"Wait!" Brady interrupted, sounding alarmed. "There's more of 'em breaking in upstairs."

"It's a bust," Yellow One told him. "Get yourself out!"

Brady looked around at the boxes of gelignite, HMX, PETN, rocket propelled grenades, and other explosives, along with the cases of detonator caps and fuses. "But the stuff. . . . It's taken months," he protested.

"It's all lost anyway. What we don't need is them getting you to talk, too. Get yourself out!"

Brady nodded, snapped off the phone, and pulled himself together. The fastest exit was up a service ladder to the front entrance. He emerged without encountering anyone and found a car right there with the keys left in. There was no arguing with a gift from Providence like that. He jumped in and accelerated out onto the boulevard, failing, in his haste, to wonder why, if the place had been busted, there were no other vehicles in the vicinity.

While down in the cellars, surrounded by explosives, incendiaries, and sensitive detonating devices, Professor Aylmer Arbuthnot Abercrombie started up the machine.

One thing that Yellow One did want from the ruins, however, if it could be retrieved, was the group cell leader's book of codes, contacts, command structure, and other information that could prove disastrous if the law enforcement agencies got their hands on it. The next night, after the fire crews and demolition teams had left, Brady went back down into the ruin to the place where the documents had been concealed. He found a package in one of the recesses beneath some old pipes as described, but then he was forced to hide when he heard someone else coming. From behind cover he watched as the same figure whom he had observed wheeling the strange machine down from the truck the previous day entered and extracted another package from one of the other recesses. The contents didn't seem to be what he wanted when he examined them with a flashlamp, and he became agitated until he located yet another package, checked it, and then left taking both of them. Brady followed him back up and looked out in time to see him depart in the same car that Brady had "borrowed" the day before, just before the building went up. Brady reported all the details when he handed over the package that he had recovered.

But it turned out to be the wrong one, containing lists of names and details of media people, scientists, political figures, and others who were of no interest to the group. The stranger, therefore, must have taken the group's code and organization book. With the help of a friend in the police department, they traced the car's number from the records of stolen vehicles. It turned out to belong to a professor who worked in the university Annex nearby.

The organization sent a couple of its bag men into the premises to see if they might be able to uncover something further, one posing as a repairman, the other under cover of an arranged power outage, but the security arrangements they came up against were astonishingly strict for a university environment, and eventually the leaders gave it up as a lost cause.

All of it very odd. It turned out that there hadn't been a police bust at the old warehouse that day, after all. Brady often puzzled about the professor, because he had assumed him to be the body that was found in the ruins. In his own mind he was sure there had been nobody else there. Yet there the professor was, still coming and going for months afterward. Brady guessed he probably never would figure it out.

MINT CONDITION
by Nina Kiriki Hoffman

Nina Kiriki Hoffman has been writing for almost twenty years and has sold almost two hundred stories, two short story collections, novels (*The Thread That Binds the Bones* and *The Silent Strength of Stones, A Red Heart of Memories,* and her most recent novel, *Past the Size of Dreaming*), a young adult novel with Tad Williams (*Child of an Ancient City*), a *Star Trek* novel with Kristine Kathryn Rusch and Dean Wesley Smith, *Star Trek Voyager 15: Echoes,* three R. L. Stine's *Ghosts of Fear Street* books, and one *Sweet Valley Junior High* book. She has cats.

Everything around me blurred. My ears hurt, and my stomach felt like it had eaten itself. My palms and the soles of my feet itched and tingled.

Colors shifted in the wash of blur. A blue oblong took shape in front of me, intensified from watercolor wash to poster-paint density to a station wagon. It was big and boxy, the sort of car built to support two nine-foot-long surfboards, though there weren't any boards on the roof rack at the moment. I held keys in my hand. A green ball of fake fur the size of a fist dangled from the keys.

I swallowed three times as my body caught up to itself. Wished, the way I always did after a jump, that I had brought an ear pressure adjuster. Prohib tech for this era. I yawned instead.

Blue sky, hot sun, air thick with pollution and the scent of a nearby bakery—but air, my big itch, open air, right out there under the sky! Sounds formed a dense net around me, people walking and talking, traffic, a lot of distant different music from radios and maybe live, in the air or coming from buildings, a faint hush of waves washing the beach, the skirl of rollerskate wheels on sidewalk. I stood on the planet's surface, bareheaded under the sun. Delight swept through me.

I'd made it again.

I smiled and glanced down to find out what I was wearing. In the instant before materialization, the image sampler in my head had reached out for a compressed burst of media, sought out images of people who looked like I did, young and female, and adjusted my camo clothes and hair to fit local custom. The audio portion of my sampler program gave my brain's language center a quick overlay of local usage. Voila! Instant new me.

Of course, this only worked in eras that had a lot of media to sample. For earlier times we had to rely on stealth vids shot by explorers and banked in the vast Collector-Corps information library.

Hmmm. On this version of me, the hair was chin-length, and what I could see of it from the corners of my eyes told me it was flat, lusterless, and magenta. The clothes? Solid black. The top was long-sleeved, a tight shirt of shiny black material, tucked into black leather pants, and below that, I wore black, thick-soled boots, with black laces that crisscrossed almost up to my knees. I wiggled my toes, felt lumpy socks inside the knee-high boots. I wondered if the socks were black.

"Hey. Give me those," said a grumpy voice.

Oh. Him. I had forgotten Scott, my partner on this trip, a man I'd only known half an hour. He'd told me to shut up three times already. Not everybody had the mental stamina to cope with my particular brand of badinage, but most people weren't as rude as Scott. Few guessed I was conducting a screening process. Scott had definitely flunked.

He stood on the other side of the car, dressed in the standard business suit of the middle-aged American male for a period from about 1930 to 2026, the navy version with off-white shirt. For guys who looked like Scott, this was a broad-tie-and-wide-lapel era, coupled with a flat-topped haircut which his brown hair was almost too thin for.

None of what he wore suited him.

All right, I didn't mean it that way. I don't do puns. Not on purpose.

"Sissy! Give me those!" Scott said again. He held out his hand across the car roof.

I glared at him with narrow eyes, then glanced around.

Venice Beach, California, August, 1979. When you could still buy a copy of Marvel's *The Minus Men* #121 for cover price at a liquor store or bus station, if you had local currency or a reasonable facsimile. Marvel thought the series was dying, and put one of their brand new writer-artist teams on it, gave them free rein in terms of plot and concept, not knowing that in the future this team would create Marvel's longest-running, best-loved title, and that this issue, which introduced the characters who would later become a multimedia sensation, and which Marvel didn't print many copies of, would go through the roof.

Not only that, but the artist and author would be attending a science fiction convention in Santa Monica tomorrow. Right now nobody knew who they were except people from the future. Autographed copies of *Minus Men* #121? Practically nonexistent in 2059, at least until we got home with some.

So okay, not the most important mission I'd ever had. But not the least either.

I sure liked the look of the people wandering around here. All different skin colors, from basement-living bleached to totally tan to black-coffee black. Lots of colors in the clothes, but then again, lots of black. Punk was almost passé, but the New Wave had stolen lots of its tropes. I saw spiked hair, neon-streaked hair, Rasta dreadlocks, and no hair.

Scott came around the car, stumbling a little in his shiny leather shoes. Another rookie mistake; we lived in slippers in the future, in padded underground complexes. Shoes took practice, and obviously he hadn't done his homework. "The keys," he said. "Give them to me!"

I shoved the keys in a pocket of my leather pants. Tight! They made a bump against my thigh. "No," I said.

"Can you even drive?" He looked at our car. I don't know how time tressing works. Nobody does. But the CollectorCorps scientists set it up so they can send a couple of operatives and some camo-mass back, masked in blurs that divert the attention of nearby people away from our arrival nodes. Operatives come with high-powered media samplers, the samplers feed images into the camo-mass, and by the time the blurs fade into edges, there's the appropriate vehicle and the appropriate equipment for whenever and wherever the operatives are.

That's the idea, anyway. That's what the PR tells the world we do. Nobody talks about all the screwups—how Washu lost three of his toes when his matter-swap scythed him partially inside something already there, how Mingelle ended up in the middle of a Klan rally in the 1920s and was half-hanged before they pulled her home, or why Bista won't ever enter a room smaller than three meters on a side again.

Nobody talks about Helen or Crow or Shingawa or Plessy at all. If you don't come home, you get wiped out of all the records except people's memories, which is why I'm pretty particular about my memories. I hang onto them all.

Time tressing's not for sissies. Except me. I mean, Sissy is my name, not my nature. I love tressing, and I don't know why. Or maybe I do know, but it's not something I can explain. Anyway, I'm good at it. Nobody on any of my missions has ever gotten hurt. Humiliated, maybe, but not hurt.

I took another look at Scott. I couldn't figure out how his cover would fit in with our mission. Maybe his sampler was fritzing. AmBizMan on the beach? AmBizMan at a SciFi con? Skewed. Seriously.

"Sure, I can drive," I said, "but on this mission, at this time, the car is just a portable storage unit." I took a couple steps. I liked the feel of my clunky boots. I peered through the long narrow window into the station wagon's cargo space. Black instrument cases? Yep.

I went around to the car's back door and unlocked it, hauled out a guitar case. Way to get local money? Earn it in some unregulated way. Robbing banks worked, and so did picking pockets. Blur power and camo-mass made each of those options easy. But I liked busking the best. Then people knew what they were buying for the money we took from them. "Looks like you're elected to play the fiddle," I said.

"Play the what?"

I pointed to the other instrument case.

Scott looked skrawed.

"Go on. Get it out."

"What am I supposed to do with *that?* I mean, what is it?"

I put my case on the asphalt, got the fiddle case out of the back of the car, and closed and locked the door, then hid the keys in my pocket again. Why did they always send me on missions with dumb rookies? I mean, *every time.* I wondered if somebody wanted to cook me. I couldn't remember anybody I had made that mad, but sometimes you couldn't tell. "How much orientation did you miss, and who are you related to?" I asked.

Red stained his cheeks. "My sister's on the CC board," he said.

"And your big itch would be?"

He frowned and swallowed. His Adam's-apple bobbed. "Petroleum-powered vehicles," he whispered.

Fritterfrick! Ijits who had some obsession with past things kept creeping through CollectorCorp's job filters. Why did I always end up babysitting them?

"Pick up your instrument and follow me." I grabbed the guitar case and strode toward the boardwalk and the beach.

Scott hovered anxiously at the car. "Wait," he called, and glanced frantically around at all the people. A few of them stopped to study him. Who had programmed his sampler? He was a total unblend. Nobody on the sidewalk looked anything like him.

Maybe his sampler had misjudged our arrival node. Samplers weren't supposed to be buggy. Then again, nothing else was supposed to be buggy either, and everything more or less was.

I sighed and walked back.

Scott put a hand on the car's roof. "How can we leave the car? Won't these people dismantle and steal it?"

Rookies. They thought everybody in every time period was some kind of crook. Obviously Scott hadn't done any of his homework. "You really should have paid more attention during orientation," I said. I picked up the fiddle case in my free hand and headed for the beach again.

"The car," he said, "the car, the car, the car—"

"Oh, eat it. It's camo-mass keyed to us. Nobody else

can do a thing with it. Here." I handed him the smaller black case.

He looked grumpy again. "I don't know why you brought this. I don't even know what it is."

"You don't have to know. All you have to do is hold it and act like you're playing it. The sampler will fill in time-appropriate sounds."

"We're doing this why?"

"To pick up a little local tender so we can buy our target acquisitions."

He grumped all the way to the boardwalk. All right, it wasn't really a boardwalk, it was a wide concrete walkway with muscle boys, bikini girls, rollerskaters (pre-rollerblade), joggers, shoppers, coffee-drinkers, walkers, skateboarders, and leashed dogs on it. On the town side of the walk, there were all kinds of funky little shops and sidewalk cafes mingled with funky little two- or three-story apartment buildings. On the ocean side, there was a line of palm trees and light poles and green trash barrels, and beyond that, a pale beige beach churned with the footprints of thousands and supporting a batch of tan-seeking, cancer-collecting, bathing-suited bodies between us and a beautiful blue ocean. Oiled-up muscleboys worked out as I watched. Younger people whooped and yelled and played Frisbee. A whole spectrum of people played in the water, facing the waves.

I stood for a moment looking at a civilization that still lived above ground. Maybe Scott had a thing for gas-powered engines—and he did, he had leaned toward every parked vehicle we had passed, sniffing as if he could snort exhaust and the scent of sun on hot metal; every time we saw a moving car, fascination glued Scott to the sidewalk, staring.

Me, I liked the sky. So strange to have air lying around free for everybody, whether you paid for your allotment or not. 'Kay, so it wasn't scrubbed or anything. But it was right out here in the open. People didn't even need breathing apparatus.

A couple of winos sat under a nearby palm tree. One was asleep, and the other looked at us. Or more like he stared at me, then took a swig from a bottle in a brown paper bag.

I crossed the boardwalk, laid down my' guitar case, brushed aside a few cigarette butts, beer bottle caps, and poptops in the sand, and slumped between a couple of palm trees. I pressed my thumbs to the clasps holding the guitar case closed.

"Hey, man. Whatcha doing?" asked a scruffy local. He had filthy bare feet, grease-streaked jeans with holes at the knees and the bottoms of the pockets, and a denim jacket with clusters of safety pins all over it. His hair was long, blond, snarled, and dirty, and his eyes were bloodshot.

"Setting up," I said.

"Whoa. The people who live in the building across the walk, they're uptight assholes. They narc on anybody who makes noise nearby."

"Oh." I smiled at him. "Where should we go?"

"You got a permit?"

"No."

He chewed his lower lip for a minute, then said, "Follow me."

I sealed my case shut and rose as my native guide headed down the walk.

Scott, who had been standing there like an ijit—why didn't he glance around and realize that no one else in sight stood still and stared at anything with such a stupid look on their face?—grabbed my arm. "Sissy!"

I jabbed my defense fingernail into the back of his hand, and he let go fast. I had a selection of irritants and poisons I could use with the nail; I chose a minor itch. No matter how annoying Scott was, he was still my partner, and I kept my partners intact even if they were useless. "Stop grabbing me," I said. I followed the Local, and Scott ended up following me.

We came to a spot across from a coffee shop with tables on the walk in front of it. "This place is good for a little while," said Local. "If you sound good, the coffee drinkers will give you something. You see cops coming, you make all your stuff disappear. You're not planning to be here long, are you?"

"No. Thanks!"

" 'Cause I know some other people who panhandle here. I don't want to give away their spot, man. But Gracie, she's sleeping in today."

"We won't be here long."

"Cool."

I wished I had something to give him, but we hadn't come with much of anything. I had an armband with enough nutritabs inside it to keep me eating for a month, but that was definitely prohib tech. No sharing, period.

I got my guitar all the way out of the case this time. In this time and place, the guitar was acoustic: pale, almost silvery wood with an ebony fingerboard, and a black plastic pick guard emblazoned with white dancing skeletons. The strap was now black with woven green-and-purple lizards crawling up it. I loved this version of me.

Local shoved his hands into his pockets and leaned up against a palm tree. "Cool guitar. What kind of stuff you play?" he asked.

"Wait and see," I said. I did know how to play my instrument; pursuing that was one of my personal quirks. On a mission, though, I usually trusted my sampler to supply me with material. Couldn't sing some song that wouldn't be popular until two years later—what if the person who was going to play it into a hit stole it from me, and I had stolen it from them to begin with? Who had ever written it? We tried never to set such question loops into action. They could stretch and snap, and then everybody would wake up in a different reality. I was kind of attached to this one.

And there was the other option, that I'd play something I knew was good and it would be totally foreign to when I was, and nobody else would like it.

I'd done a little research, enough to know that this was the era of Blondie, the Clash, the B52s, the Police, the Ramones, Talking Heads, Elvis Costello, all people I had never heard of until I pulled a fast sample out of the CollectorCorps data files and headjammed it before I left on this mission. None of what I heard seemed like something I could do with just my voice, an acoustic guitar, and the possible addition of Scott on a fiddle, so I decided to try something from an earlier era. "You like folk songs?" I asked Local.

"Folk songs?" He looked alarmed.

"They're great. All blood and death and stuff." I set the open case beside the walkway, hoping people would drop money in. "I'll play you a folk song." I slipped the guitar strap over my head, pulled a pick out of a pickholder on the guitar's side, and strummed an intro with only minimal help from the sampler. I sang the first line of "Banks of the Ohio," about a chipper so crazed with love that when his girl said no, he killed her.

"Whoa," whispered Local. He stared at my mouth while I sang, with brief glances at my breasts.

People strolling by behind him stopped, gathered. Change jingled into the open guitar case. A few people dropped paper money. Scott stood there like a mannequin, the violin case forgotten in his hand, his mouth hanging open.

I wrapped up the song with a repeat of the creepy chorus, then smiled at everyone who had stopped to listen. A few of them clapped. Most of them moved on.

Local said, "Awesome, man. Great voice."

"Thanks." I checked the guitar case. Not bad for a three-minute song. Already we could afford comic books and some of the more exotic local foods. Slurpees, maybe. I'd seen ads for those when I was in a similar time period before, but I'd never managed to taste one. I strummed an A chord. Folk songs could work. . . . I'd try "House of the Rising Sun" next. I picked an E minor chord.

"Well," said Scott.

I glanced at him. Why was I doing all the work? What was he here for, anyway? The sampler could supply some ominous fiddle in this song. "Get out your instrument."

"Sissy. Sniggle," Scott said.

My muscles locked. My left hand gripped the guitar's neck so hard I felt the guitar strings digging into my fingernails, and the fingers on my right hand curled into claws on the strings above the sound hole.

Unwelcome knowledge flooded my system. I remembered . . . other missions. All these lame gropers I kept getting stuck with, time after time! One of them had some kind of masterword he passed on to the next, and the next, and the next. At some point in my training with CollectorCorps, somebody had wired an "obey" circuit into me. Illegal! Criminal! Horrible and humiliating!

Now I remembered every single one of those horrible missions. I had started each one feeling as though I was in charge, shepherding around some lame-o rookie on a quest to pick up this or that small perfect item for some elite who could afford the outrageous price CC would charge. Somewhere along the way, my irritating partner would whisper the magic word, and I would freeze up until he told me what he wanted.

I couldn't move. I felt the red in my face, though. There were lots of fast ways to make unregulated money besides busking, picking pockets, or bank robbing. Turning tricks, for instance.

One of two of my rookies had been—less horrible than the others. I didn't have much hope for Scott.

They always made me forget afterward.

I wished now that they wouldn't. I would be better off if I didn't sneer at them and insult them and order them around early on, wouldn't I?

But I didn't want to live with what I had gone through.

All I had to do was get through the next forty-eight hours, until the autoreturn pulled us back. If Scott followed the pattern, he, too, would tell me to forget everything. We would return to the future with what I would think was the object of our quest, and I would rest up, ignoring the bruises and small illnesses and outbreaks I always picked up on missions. Somebody would give me another assignment. I would do my homework. Then I'd lead some other lawbreaking lamebrain back into the past, and . . .

"Sissy," said Scott. "Put the guitar away."

"Hey, man. I want to hear more!" Local said.

But I had already bent to stow my guitar in its case. That was a mercy. It gave me hope, even though I dropped the guitar right on top of the money, since Scott hadn't told me to take the money out first. At least he was letting me put away my instrument instead of ordering me to abandon it. I thumbed the clasps closed.

"Let's go," said Scott.

"Hey! Male chauvinist pig. Stop bossing her around!" Local grabbed my arm.

"Drop him," Scott said.

I tapped the back of Local's hand with my defense nail, letting him have a little shot of sleep. His grip on my arm relaxed, and he fell slowly to the ground.

"Good work. Come on." Scott turned away and headed up the walk.

I followed, but glanced back at Local. I hoped he would be all right. I didn't always find such nice people on these trips.

At the car, Scott made me give him the keys, made me sit in the passenger seat while he drove. Right there I had a clear demonstration of the fact that no matter how much time you spent on a simulator, real life worked differently. Since cars were Scott's big itch, I had thought he'd be really good at them. But even in a camo-car, he couldn't drive well. He stalled and stalled again. He didn't understand 1979 traffic controls. He ran red lights and stop signs, and brought us close to death time and again.

He made me navigate with a map he had torn from a telephone book. Destination? The nearest Cadillac dealership.

Gradually I relaxed.

Maybe this wouldn't be such a bad mission.

"See that Eldorado?" Scott said, his voice alive with excitement as he pulled into the lot. "See that one? Omyglot, see that one over there? Front-wheel drive, four-wheel independent suspension, and an electronic fuel-injected V8 engine. Cadillac pioneered those features in American cars! Sweet!" He parked our camo-car across two parking spaces and jumped out, leaving the key in the car and the engine running. And me, in the passenger seat, disabled by a stupid word that didn't even mean anything except "You will now obey my every command."

A young salesman in a suit just like the one Scott wore came out of the showroom, smiling. "Hello, sir," he said, shaking hands with Scott. "I'm Bert James. How may I help you?"

"I'd like a test drive," Scott said, his voice breaking.

"Excellent. While you're enjoying a ride in one of our automobiles, though, don't you think your own fine car should be shut down?" The salesman leaned in and fished around for the key, which wasn't on the steering column the way a person from 1979 might expect. Let alone the car was keyed to Scott's and my geneprints, and wouldn't respond to anyone else. The salesman noticed me. "Hello, miss. Wouldn't you like to ride in one of our magnificent machines?"

I looked at him. On the drive over, Scott had given me permission to look around, but not to talk. In fact, he had said "shut up" a few more times, even though I hadn't said a word. Probably to get back at me for all the talking I did right before we tressed.

"I don't recognize your car," the salesman said over his shoulder to Scott.

"It's not in general production. It's a prototype."

"Oh. Interesting! Could you please turn it off, sir? And what about your girlfriend? Maybe she'd like a test drive, too?"

Scott let his breath out in a whoosh. "Oh. Yes. Probably. I guess."

The salesman straightened, and Scott leaned in and turned off the car. "Get out and come with us," he said.

I spent the rest of the afternoon in the back seat of various Cadillacs, listening to Scott and the salesman enthuse about the virtues of Cadillacs. I did find out for a fact that they had really comfortable backs seats, good shocks, smooth engines, and quiet rides.

Sometimes I thought about all the carbon monoxide we were pumping into the air. Mostly, though, I thought about all the missions I'd gone on in the recent past where some ijit smoghead tongueflapping powerpusher had flipped my switch had made me dance. I thought long and hard about it. Who could have slipped me the wire? Why?

I had a half-memory of some mission before all the bad ones started. I had stepped into the tresser. The usual lights had flashed. My ears popped, the blurs washed out my surroundings, my stomach hurt, and then, floosh! Everything turned back into Now. I wondered why the mission had aborted. I'd never had one abort before—in fact, I had a reputation for luck. One of the project scientists was studying me and my luck to see if it was something they could induce in other tressers.

Able, one of the tresser programmers, had opened the booth door. "Drink this, Sissy," he said. My stomach was still spinning and glogging. I glanced at the telltales in the tresser room and noticed there was something weird about the permachrono. Before I could figure it out, though, I drank what Able gave me. Then everything blurred.

Later I woke up in my own cubicle. My boss said I'd

gotten sick before I could even go on a mission and that they'd sedated me while the sickness ran its course. That was why I lost two days.

I couldn't even remember what I was supposed to find and fetch on the aborted mission.

It had to be Able who had done this to me. Scuzzed the mission, made me lose two days while I was undergoing illegal bioengineering that turned me into a slavebot.

"Sissy," said Scott.

Able. But why? Did he hate me?

"Get out of the car, Sissy," Scott said.

After that nonmission, time after time, me and ijits, sweeping through different periods in the past so they could pet dinosaurs or gamble on a Mississippi riverboat or digiphoto gladiator games at the Coliseum. Time after time I performed for them and they told me to forget all about it, and then I got them home in perfect condition, even though I myself got a little skewed and couldn't remember how. Time after time I didn't understand the nasty smiles my partners gave me before they walked out of my life, good riddance.

How lucky was I, really?

I got out of the car.

"Straighten up and look pretty, Sissy," Scott said.

Well, that was easier said than done. Not a very tangible order, and what exactly did he have in mind? I stood tall, hunched my shoulders, relaxed them, ran my fingers through my short limp pink hair. Bert the salesman watched me. Damn. I should have listened to their conversation while I was riding around in I the back seat, but I had been too busy going down nightmare memory alley. What was happening now?

"Would you like to get to know Sissy better, Bert?" Scott asked the salesman. "She'll do whatever you want. Anything you ask. Won't you, Sissy? You'll do anything Bert wants."

I nodded.

Rage ran through my body like blood, and I couldn't respond to it. I couldn't walk away. I couldn't ziss damned Scott with my defense nail, and I couldn't scream my anger. Scott hadn't give me permission.

Bert took a couple steps toward me.

"I'll just take this Eldorado out for a little spin. Back in half an hour," Scott said. He jingled keys in his hand, then climbed into the big car we had just been riding around in.

Bert came slowly to me. He stared at my lips. Then down at my breasts. His tongue darted out to lick his upper lip.

Scott started the car, put it into reverse, and almost ran over us. Bert shoved me out of the way, grabbed me before I crashed. "Hey!" Bert yelled after Scott.

Scott burned rubber on his way out of the parking lot.

One of the other salesmen came out of the showroom then, looked after Scott's taillights, glanced at Bert. "It's all under control," Bert said. His voice shook. "Come on, Sissy. I'll get you some coffee."

I followed him through the showroom into a warren of offices. He actually got me a cup of coffee from a big pot, and added cream and sugar. "You okay?"

I would do anything Bert wanted; Scott had instructed my wired self to follow Bert's orders. Obviously, Bert wanted me to answer his question. Maybe he even wanted to have a conversation with me.

Yeah. That could work.

I gulped some coffee. It was really good coffee, made with real beans, unlike anything we could mimic in the future. "Sorta," I said at last.

"Come on back to my office. We can discuss sales details."

Bert led me past a couple of receptionist stations and the dealership's auto repair shop to a small windowless office with a desk and two chairs, one behind the desk and one in front of it. The office was twice the size of my home cubicle, and the furniture was permanent instead of zipout. I knew he wouldn't have comforts like self-adjusting lights, self-styling color schemes for the fabrics—well, actually, he didn't even have fabrics—or self-adjusting hardness on the surfaces. Still, I liked the office.

The room smelled deliciously of cigarette smoke.

Bert locked the door and went around to the big chair behind the desk. I sat in the other chair and finished my coffee, sipping slow to delay whatever came next. Bert watched me. Finally I put my Styrofoam cup down on his desk.

"Will you really—" Bert coughed and stared at the surface of his desk, which had a scatter of paperwork across it.

I sighed. Scott's instructions hadn't been particularly lucid. "What do you want, Bert?"

His gaze flashed up. His eyes looked hungry. "You are one top-of-the-line babe," he said. "I've never made it with a punk chick before."

I felt weird shifting and swirling inside. Scott had told me to do whatever Bert wanted. Bert wasn't very clear on what he wanted, but if I could jump the gun and give him what he was *going* to want before he even got around to saying it, maybe I could introduce a little free will into the equation.

I rose. I perched on the edge of his desk, then swung my legs up and slithered across the desk toward him, scattering papers. He sat back in his chair, his eyes growing wider. I ran my tongue across my lips.

"Okay," Bert said. "But—"

I leaned forward, and he backed up. The chair was on wheels. It slammed into the wall behind him.

"I don't—" Bert's face glowed bright red.

Hey. Maybe he didn't want me after all. I pulled back, sat cross-legged on his desk, and studied him.

"I mean," Bert said. He inched the chair forward again with his toes. "You're beautiful. Sleek and stylish. Great features. But I, uh—" Then he whispered, "This is just like those letters to *Penthouse*. What's wrong with me?"

"You're nice," I said.

Bert turned even brighter red. He coughed. "Well, uh, you don't, uh."

I waited. I wondered if I could have some more coffee. I was liking this situation a lot. It was so much more benign than a lot of the unwelcome memories that had crowded into my brain when Scott said "sniggle" to me.

Bert struggled. "You're not going to tell, uh, Scott, uh—"

"I'll tell him whatever you want me to."

"You'll tell him I was a giant stud?"

"If that's what you want."

Bert turned to stare at a calendar on the wall. It showed a scenic view of the Grand Canyon. I had seen lots of pictures of that. The real thing was just another underwater feature in my time.

"Say, Sissy?" Bert said after a little while.

"Yes?"

"Is Scott ever bringing my car back?"

I blinked. "I don't know. I never worked with him before."

"Oh, God." Bert got to his feet. "I should never have handed him those keys. I never even looked at his driver's license. I wonder if I should call the cops."

I checked my wristwatch. "He said he'd be back in half an hour." We had forty-eight hours to complete our mission before the autoreturn kicked in; we could also end early, so long as we did enough planning. Either way, Scott and I needed to get us and our car back to that parking place in Venice. Autoreturn would work if you weren't in exactly the right place, but you couldn't count on it working well.

Bert unlocked the door and opened it. "I wonder if he will," he said.

I wondered, too. I'd had partners decide to decay on me before, I now knew, with my new access to all the forbidden memories. Guys who had scratched their itches and only made them stronger, guys who wanted to stay in the past. They had been confident that they could make me leave them there, knowing how I was wired. And yet, somehow, I'd never lost a partner. The more I thought about it, the more I realized how rare a record like that was. Everybody I knew at CollectorCorps had lost something except me.

Bert got me some more coffee and then we went out into the lot and watched cars speeding by on the four-lane roadway with the big stoplights next to the dealership. After we'd stood outside watching traffic for a while, one of the other salesmen approached us. He looked just as suited and restrained as Bert did. "So, how do you like our new line?" Bert asked me as the other man came over.

"Awesome," I said.

"We make the best cars in the world."

"I totally believe you."

"Miss, are you interested in purchasing a Cadillac?" asked the second salesman.

"I'd like a whole fleet."

The salesman stared at me as though I was insane, then looked toward the L.A. skyline and shrugged.

I tried to look important and famous, as though I could afford a whole fleet of Cadillacs. Camo can do that for you.

"I'll cut you in on the commission, Hector," Bert said. "I'm going to talk options with Sissy now."

Hector smiled and headed back to the showroom.

The green Cadillac Eldorado pulled into the parking lot and stalled, which you'd think no one could make a Cadillac do. It shuddered, shook, and stopped. Scott got out.

"Bert," I said.

"Sissy."

"Do me a favor?" Scott was coming toward us. He smiled and smiled.

"For a favor," Bert said.

"Tell me: 'Whatever happens, Sissy, don't forget, this time.'"

"Huh?"

"Please. Just say it."

"Okay. Whatever happens, Sissy, don't forget, this time."

Something fast as fire and sour-sweet shocked its way through me. Take that, wire!

"Sissy?" Bert said.

"Thanks." I put all my heart into it.

"Will you tongue-kiss me?"

"Sure."

In full view of Scott and everybody in the showroom, I gave Bert a tongue-kiss of a lifetime. We both tasted of coffee and desperation. In that moment I loved Bert more than anyone I'd ever known.

"Sniggle!" said Scott from behind us.

I brushed Bert's tongue with mine one last time before I let him go.

"Give it up, Sissy. You're back on my time. Let's go. We have work to do!" Scott sounded mad.

Meanwhile, Bert was excited. "Will you marry me?"

"No, honey. But thanks for asking." Wait. How could I say no to Bert when Scott had told me to do whatever Bert wanted? I guessed the new orders canceled the old ones.

Bert gave me a really sweet smile and turned to Scott. "So, Mr. Madrone, have you decided on a color for your Cadillac?"

"Why don't you give me a brochure that outlines all my options, and I'll get back to you?"

Bert went inside and got a full-color brochure. "This explains all our options and has color chips," he said.

"Thanks, Bert." Scott took the brochure, grabbed my arm, and dragged me back to our car, where he handed me the keys. "I'll call you tomorrow," Scott yelled over his shoulder. I took one more look at Bert. Bert blushed and waved his fingers. I waved mine.

"Get in and drive," Scott said.

Night had drifted in while Scott was off battling traffic and I was teasing Bert. I climbed into our car's driver's seat. I glanced at Scott, wondering why he was letting me drive.

"After a while, it was too much," Scott said. "They're crazy out there."

I started the car, flicked on the headlights, and pulled out onto the road. I wondered where Scott wanted to go, but I didn't want to ask him, in case he told me to shut up again. I liked being able to converse.

Scott slumped in his seat.

Since he didn't give me any directions, I drove us back to Venice and parked in the very spot where we had arrived that morning. Then I sat there staring at people through the windshield. In the night, the music from bars with open doors was louder, and there were more tourists and locals wandering the street.

Scott sat silent for a long time. Then he said, "I now return control of this mission to you, except stop bossing me around all the time, and forget everything that's happened today. When I say the word, you'll think we've just arrived. No, that won't work. You already got the money. You'll remember the part about singing on the sidewalk, only you'll think it happened at night, and that we can go into the next phase right now. Forget everything that happened since I said sniggle this morning. Ready? Three . . . two . . . one . . . sniggle."

I felt extremely odd. Little clicks pinged my brain. I clung to Bert's command. No matter what happened, I wouldn't forget this time. And I didn't forget; but the knowledge kind of dropped away. I sat up and said, "What are we doing in the car? We have a comic book to buy." I went to the back of the car, opened it, opened my guitar case, and fished money out from under my guitar. "Come on."

Scott got out and followed me. We went to a head shop and found five copies of *Minus Men* #121, all in mint condition. I bought them and slipped them into protective sleeves I had brought with me, along with the receipt for authentication, and then Scott and I went to supper.

How strange, I thought, how strange, as I sleepwalked through the rest of the mission, on the surface my usual self, and underneath turning over all my new and horrible knowledge. We slept in the car and washed up at a public rest room on the beach the next morning. I got us into the convention hotel where the SciFi con was being held. I managed to sneak us into the bar when the author and artist went there; we didn't have to pay a membership fee to the convention or go to any of the programming; I had memorized target faces before we tressed, the way I always did. The boys were flattered to be asked for autographs.

"Listen," I said. "This is going to be really big. You guys are going places."

They looked at each other and laughed, and bought me and Scott drinks. It was their first big convention, and nobody else had recognized them. Travis, the artist, had actually told a dealer who stocked *Minus Men* in the dealers' room that he was the artist on issue #121, and the dealer had asked him to sign all the copies in stock. Later Travis dragged Milton the writer back with him, and Milton had signed the comics, too. "But it doesn't feel real when you make it happen yourself," Travis said.

"Don't worry. I bet this is the last convention where nobody knows who you are."

They laughed. Milton knocked on the wooden bar for luck. I said good-bye for me and for Scott, who was mostly silent and grumpy. We went back to our car, and I hit the autoreturn button, and we went home.

After debriefing, the boss congratulated me on another mission well run and took away my comic books. I went to the public bath and soaped and soaked, soaped and soaked, three times, trying to scrub off all the memories. Yet I didn't really want to lose them. I felt amazed and pleased that I had managed to get around the wire and keep what was mine, no matter how awful.

Now what?

Stick my defense nail through Able's throat? Complain to one of the senior staff, start a criminal investigation?

What if the senior staff were in on this? Should I just shut up and keep working the way I always had?

Or get out of the business, join my sib's hydro food farm? My sib ·and I had always been close, and she had never approved of my career. She would be pleased if I gave it up. I knew she'd accept me in her enclave if I asked. Plus, I had assets. I had banked lots of air and water. CollectorCorps paid me very well for my perfect record.

I went home. I set my cubicle walls to old growth forest, complete with bird, wind, and insect sounds, and sat for a long time on my sleep shelf, watching sun slant down through redwood branches to touch mossy ground. I gave myself a couple hits of enriched air.

If I never tressed again, I would never again stand on the planet's surface and look up at the sky without a faceplate. Never again taste all the biodiversity there used to be, never drink coffee made from real beans again, never talk again to people who hadn't grown up in holes in the ground.

How could I keep tressing? There was camo-me, the one who pretended she didn't remember anything, mint condition me, but she was only a cover over the blemished me who now knew what was inside. Sure, I forget every time; but I remembered every time in between forgetting. Two Sissies were living their lives in alternating stripes, and one of them got sicker and sicker of everything.

Around 3:00 a.m. I switched my walls over to Venice Beach, California, 1979. Sun, sand, people. These were views my sampler had taped while I was there; I always debriefed my sampler into the CC information library as soon as I got home, but I'd never accessed my own records before. Déjà déjà very vu.

I searched for Scott's sampler recordings. There were walls to prevent my accessing something I wasn't coded for, but I hacked through them. Now I knew why he had showed up in a business suit; he'd preprogrammed his sampler to find an image of him that a car dealer would pay attention to. Now I knew why he was so grumpy. His driving was terrible. He had been ticketed and almost arrested by police three times in the course of his solo test drive. His taste of real cars hadn't matched his dream of driving at all.

I jumped to my own backlog and fastscanned back to the aborted mission I barely remembered.

My sampler had watched everything as Able set me up, even the events that happened while I was sedated. Able and another programmer had worked me over together.

It was in my record. Along with every missing segment of my memory. I headjammed them all, confirmed what I had learned on my last mission. Some of it was horrible. Some people I had worked with did not deserved to be called people.

It was all in my record. Senior staff had to know. The guy studying my luck probably knew. How many people knew?

I ran off a copy of my whole record with CC, put it on a passive physical medium, sewed it into the lining of my jacket.

In the morning I went to my boss and said I needed some time off.

"Any special reason?" she asked.

"I need a break."

She asked me again. I said I had vacation time coming to me. She shook her head, but she let me go.

I took a tube out to my sib's place.

After two weeks there, I was ready to shoot everyone I knew. I did drop my nephews twice with my nail's mildest sleep, even though my sib got really mad the first time. They were not restful children, though.

My worst problem was skysickness. I hadn't gone so long without seeing sky in years.

So of course in the end I went back to work. Somehow my partner on my next mission ended up with his hand badly cobra bitten, though. I let go of my luck and kept hold on my memories.

On every mission, no matter what else happens, I open my arms to ancient skies.

TANYA HUFF
VALOR'S CHOICE

"Readers who enjoy military SF will love Tanya Huff's
VALOR'S CHOICE. Howlingly funny and very
suspenseful. I enjoyed every word."
—*scifi.com*

Staff Sergeant Torin Kerr was a battle-hardened professional.
So when she and those in her platoon who'd survived the last
deadly encounter with the Others were yanked from a well-
deserved leave for what was supposed to be "easy" duty as
the honor guard for a diplomatic mission to the non-Confedera-
tion world of the Silsviss, she was ready for anything. Sure,
there'd been rumors of the Others being spotted in this sector
of space. But there were always rumors. Everything seemed
to be going perfectly. Maybe too perfectly. . . .

0-88677-896-4 $6.99

PRECURSOR
by C.J. Cherryh

The Riveting Sequel to the *Foreigner* Series

The *Foreigner* novels introduced readers to the epic story of a lost human colony struggling to survive on the hostile world of the alien *atevi*. Now, in the beginning of a bold new trilogy, both human and *atevi* return to space to rebuild and rearm the ancient human space station and starship, and to make a desperate attempt to defend their shared planet from outside attack.

☐ **Hardcover Edition**   0-88677-836-0—$23.95
☐ **Paperback Edition**   0-88677-910-3—$6.99

Be sure to read the first three books in this action-packed series:

☐ **FOREIGNER**   0-88677-637-1—$6.99
☐ **INVADER**   0-88677-687-2—$6.99
☐ **INHERITOR**   0-88677-728-3—$6.99

Prices slightly higher in Canada   **DAW: 123**

C.J. CHERRYH

Classic Series in New Omnibus Editions!

☐ THE DREAMING TREE

Journey to a transitional time in the world, as the dawn of mortal man brings about the downfall of elven magic. But there remains one final place untouched by human hands—the small forest of Ealdwood, in which dwells Arafel the Sidhe. *Contains the complete duology* The Dreamstone *and* The Tree of Swords and Jewels.

0-888677-782-8 $6.99

☐ THE FADED SUN TRILOGY

They were the mri—tall, secretive mercenary soldiers of almost unimaginable ability. But now, in the aftermath of war, the mri face extinction. It will be up to three individuals to retrace their galaxy-wide path back through the millennia to reclaim the ancient world that gave them life . . . *Contains the complete novels* Kesrith, Shon'jir, *and* Kutath.

0-88677-836-0 $6.99

☐ THE MORGAINE SAGA

Scattered through the galaxy are the time/space Gates of a vanished alien race. They must be found and destroyed in order to preserve the integrity of the universe. This is the task of the mysterious traveler Morgaine . . . but will she have the power to follow her quest to its conclusion—to the Ultimate Gate or the end of time itself? *Contains the complete* Gate of Ivrel, Well of Shiuan, *and* Fires of Azeroth.

0-88677-877-8 $6.99

Kate Elliott

The Novels of the Jaran:

☐ **JARAN: Book 1**   UE2513—$5.99
Here is the poignant and powerful story of a young woman's coming of age on an alien world, where she is both player and pawn in an interstellar game of intrigue and politics.

☐ **AN EARTHLY CROWN: Book 2**   UE2546—$5.99
The jaran people, led by Ilya Bakhtiian and his Earth-born wife Tess, are sweeping across the planet Rhui on a campaign of conquest. But even more important is the battle between Ilya and Duke Charles, Tess' brother, who is ruler of this sector of space.

☐ **HIS CONQUERING SWORD: Book 3**   UE2551—$5.99
Even as Jaran warlord Ilya continues the conquest of his world, he faces a far more dangerous power struggle with his wife's brother, leader of an underground human rebellion against the alien empire.

☐ **THE LAW OF BECOMING: Book 4**   UE2580—$5.99
On Rhui, Ilya's son inadvertently becomes the catalyst for what could prove a major shift of power. And in the heart of the empire, the most surprising move of all was about to occur as the Emperor added an unexpected new player to the Game of Princes . . .

OTHERLAND
TAD WILLIAMS

In many ways it is humankind's most stunning achievement. This most exclusive of places is also one of the world's best kept secrets, created and controlled by The Grail Brotherhood, a private cartel made up of the world's most powerful and ruthless individuals. Surrounded by secrecy, it is home to the wildest of dreams and darkest of nightmares. Incredible amounts of money have been lavished on it. The best minds of two generations have labored to build it. And somehow, bit by bit, it is claming the Earth's most valuable resource— its children.